PENGUIN BOOKS

PLAYING AWAY

Adele Parks was born in the North-East of England. She read English Language and Literature at Leicester University. Since graduating she has lived in Italy and Africa. She now lives in London with her son. Her novels *Playing Away*, *Game Over* and *Larger Than Life* were all bestsellers. Her most recent novel is *The Other Woman's Shoes*, also published by Penguin.

Playing Away

Adele Parks

PENGUIN BOOKS

PENGUIN BOOKS

Published by the Penguin Group
Penguin Books Ltd, 80 Strand, London WC2R 0RL, England
Penguin Putnam Inc., 375 Hudson Street, New York, New York 10014, USA
Penguin Books Australia Ltd, 250 Camberwell Road,
Camberwell, Victoria 3124, Australia
Penguin Books Canada Ltd, 10 Alcorn Avenue, Toronto, Ontario, Canada M4V 3B2
Penguin Books India (P) Ltd, 11 Community Centre,
Panchsheel Park, New Delhi – 110 017, India
Penguin Books (NZ) Ltd, Cnr Rosedale and Airborne Roads,
Albany, Auckland, New Zealand
Penguin Books (South Africa) (Pty) Ltd, 24 Sturdee Avenue,
Rosebank 2196, South Africa

Penguin Books Ltd, Registered Offices: 80 Strand, London WC2R 0RL, England

www.penguin.com

Published in Penguin Books 2000
This special sales edition published 2003
1

The acknowledgements on page 369 constitute an extension of this copyright page

Printed in England by Clays Ltd, St Ives plc

Prologue

Before the invention of networking, people simply met, social-climbed or licked arse. Now it's more hygienic. Now we have networking conferences in Blackpool. I don't know which is more depressing.

I walk into the hotel lobby, late, to demonstrate my mind-set. I shake the April showers from my umbrella and I'm immediately splattered with boisterous laughter from the hotel bar. The evening's entertainment is already under way. My esteemed colleagues are tipping sand buckets down the stairs and racing shots, badly, so that pink, sticky liquid comes out of their noses. My heart sinks; I don't want to be here. I want to be at home with my husband, curled up in bed, reading or making love. Husband! I love that word. It's my favourite word and I've used it excessively over the last nine months since I netted him.

I know the whole conference will be a fearful bore: too much testosterone and not enough intelligence. I work for a large management consultancy (Looper Jackson) and in six months' time we are merging with a mammoth management consultancy (Peterson Wind) to form a huge, dick-swinging one (Peterson Windlooper – I'm unsure what is to become of Jackson). The purpose of this conference is for the management to identify natural leaders, team players and losers in a bid to reconstruct departments. I imagine preferred scenarios. I want to be on a beach in Barbados, I want to be in All Bar One with the girls, the King's Road; I want to be just about anywhere other than here. I pause. Except the office. That was a very miserable thought. Best to check in, clean up and face it.

I drop my bag, sigh, cast a glance around the chintzy bedroom, then call my husband. Disappointingly but somewhat predictably, he isn't in. The bathroom is large and white, with hideous gold-swan taps; I turn the taps, breaking their necks, a butcher's window at Christmas time. I run a bath, emptying the Crabtree & Evelyn salts into the plunging water. After bathing I dress. It's a black-tie evening and every woman will opt for a conventional flouncy dress. To provide contrast I dress with a nurtured, rebellious streak, choosing a sheer black trouser suit. The top parts to show a tantalizing flash of my stomach – currently flat, brown and sexy. My hair is just long enough to wear up, so I pile it on top; it looks too serious, so roughly, hurriedly, I pull down random strands and twist them into dreadlocks. I check the result in the mirror and I'm pleased. I'm even more pleased when later I thread my way through the white tablecloths, black suits and predictable, unflattering ball dresses.

It's the usual corporate dinner thing: vast, unseemly and profligate. Everyone is really going for it, a scene from Sodom and Gomorrah. Beery, bleary men stand in pulsing packs leering at the women. Red, drunken faces lurch forward, slurring their words and thoughts. The women wear their make-up smudged around their eyes and their noses; their foreheads are shining, hardly vogue. Tomorrow will be the day for embarrassed nods and painful headaches, but fuck it, tonight is the time to go for it. Sod them and tomorrow. By contrast my plan is: dinner, excuse, retreat, retire and ring husband. I find my table and name-plate, sit down and pull my face into a practised, polished, social smile.

His eyes are unfair.

Too big, too blue, too overwhelming to allow any female a reasonable attempt at indifference. He has fine, transparent skin with a sprinkling of freckles. He is lean, taut, well defined, athletic. Not an ounce of unnecessary about him. He smells clean but not perfumed. He looks at me and his eyes level me, slice me. He's exploded a kaleidoscope of emotion. Fizzy splinters of rich colours blast internally, lodging in my head and breasts. My knickers and heart pull together. I'm shivering. The predictable masses surrounding us merge into one pointless, homogeneous blur; we're left in an appalling clarity. I'm shocked and disturbed by my jumping M&S briefs. I immediately dismiss any semblance of disguising, polite, small talk.

'I'm married.'

'I'm a tart,' he smiles.

Both the defence and challenge.

'That's the introductions over with. Want a drink?' He is already pouring me one.

We are outrageously overt. We flirt to an awe-inspiring level. Within minutes I slip back into my flirtatious ways that were second nature before I married, but have been unnecessary and unseemly for some time. I am direct, evasive, sophisticated, straightforward, coy, seductive. Much more seductive than I've ever been before. He is also full of contradictions. He talks about his job, which is dull, but he appears brilliant. He's jumped through burning hoops and balanced balls on his nose to secure his position at Peterson Wind. Now he can smell his own success, it reeks. He tells me he deserves the conference gig, the whole jolly. It's obvious he has no intention of doing any work, beyond scoring women and drugs. He stands up and is disappointingly short but seems majestic. It is devastatingly ambiguous. It is irreparably clear-cut.

We talk about sex and not much else, establishing the things we have in common. He confesses that he has an unsquashable habit of immediately identifying the most desirable woman in the vicinity. Wherever he is – a bar, at work, the pub, the tube, in a shop. I remember that skill and tell him so. He nods and simply affirms, 'It's compulsive. I don't think this talent is a unique one. Many a time a mate and I have settled on the same sleek bob of hair or slim set of hips. The odd thing is finding a woman who tells me she does the same.' He shakes his head in disbelief. 'Sometimes if I am on the pull I don't bother with chasing the most attractive. I mean it's a waste of fucking time if you just want to get your end away. So I identify the most readily available. Quite distinct and apart.'

'What am I?' I ask shamelessly. I know he is unlikely to admit he is keen for a quick shag and I'm giving off available signals. But I *so* want him to flatter me.

'You, Gorgeous, with your crazy, curly, blonde hair, beautiful face, cracking figure, full round tits and tiny waist – '

He touches my knee with the edge of his whisky glass. I shiver but drag it away.

4

' – you with your intelligent eyes, eyes which you turn on me with cold indifference, are undoubtedly the most attractive woman here.'

He touches my knee again and I don't move it.

'But you are different. Because, while being undoubtedly the most attractive woman here, you are also the most unobtainable. You see, I never dip my pen in the company ink, and besides which you're married.' Yet habit compels him to add, 'I've slept with ninety-nine women – how do you fancy being the hundredth?'

'Does that line ever work?' I ask, laughing at his audacity despite myself.

'Ninety-nine times, to my certain knowledge.'

'You're pathetic.'

'But it doesn't worry you.'

He is right. I fancy him so much I think I'm going to be sick. I fancy him so much I think I *must be* sick. He leans toward me. I'm so very close to his mouth I can taste, on the air that he expounds, beer and cigarettes, an intoxicating perfume.

'You fascinate me, Sweetie, you are fucking fascinating.'

I bristle with the excitement, have I ever fascinated my husband?

'You are so bloody cocky, full of your self. I like that in a girl.'

He adjusts his trousers, fighting his erection.

'I like your calmness of manner. It disarms me slightly that you are so confident. But, fair play to you, I admit, your assessment of your attractiveness is in no way over-ambitious. You are a very beautiful woman. You're also very clever, more intuitive than intellectual, and to tell the truth I rate the latter higher than the former, but neither should be ignored.' Without giving me time to be offended, he continues, 'You are dead amusing. You really must be, because I've laughed all night and I can't imagine that it is all motivated by my desire to flatter you.'

I nod, momentarily too hoarse with desire to answer. I sip some water.

'But we agreed I am unavailable.'

He smiles. 'Yes. Having said that, it seems odd to me that earlier, when I smiled and nodded to you, you returned with a smashing smile. It seemed to me that your eyes, well' – he shrugs – 'I'm experienced enough to know that your indifference is feigned. I think you are quite capable of myopic and hedonistic fucking; your brazen frivolity is obvious.'

'I'm married,' I insist.

'You mentioned that.'

'Blissfully so.'

He grins. 'How long?'

'Nine months.'

'Nine months and you are behaving like this?'

For a second I despise his smugness.

'We've been together for four years.'

He raises his eyebrows as if he's heard it all before. I'm furious with myself for trying to justify my actions.

'I've never looked at another man in all that time – '

'Until now.' He finishes my sentence with appalling accuracy. 'Can I get you another drink?'

I hesitate.

'Go on, a quick one,' he coaxes. He stands up and makes

towards the bar. I look at the gold and diamonds on my left hand and throw out a final, desperate clasp at respectability.

'It's OK our flirting like this, as I really *am* happily married and it can't go anywhere. I will never, ever have an affair. I will *never, ever* have sex with anyone other than my husband.'

I spell it out plainly before he gets the wrong idea, before I get the wrong idea! But just as I settle into smug self-righteousness, I hear myself add, 'But if I'm wrong and if ever I were to have an affair, it would be with you.'

'Yessssssssss.' He punches the air and practically skips to the bar.

Noooooooooooooo. I sit alone in the crowd, horrified with myself. As soon as his back is turned, I run to my room. I close the bedroom door behind me and lean heavily on it, shaking. I kick off my Gucci steel-heeled shoes, slowly undress and climb into bed.

'Shit. That was close, too close.' Angrily I punch the pillows and make a feather husband. Curling tight into the effigy I vow to spend the rest of the conference arduously avoiding him.

1

'Happy anniversary, darling.'

I struggle to open my eyes and sit up, as Luke carefully lays the breakfast tray on the bed. *Pain au chocolat*, fresh orange juice, coffee, cards and lilies. Anniversary fare.

'Oh, thank you,' I smile. My lazy, sexy, contented smile which I keep especially for wedding nights, anniversaries, birthdays, nights of seduction and other distinguished occasions. Since I married I've extended the usage to weekends, weekdays, sunny days, wet days, days with an *r* in the month and days without. I can't help it. I'm so happy. Delirious. I know it's a cliché, I know it's sick-making and I know single people or people in crappy marriages take an instant dislike to me. But it's just like that.

He puts the tray on our bed and I clap my hands and shout, 'How wonderful.' We kiss, slowly, gently. 'Thank you.'

'No, thank you for the best year of my life,' smiles Luke.

'No, thank *you*,' I insist. I love this conversation, which can carry on indefinitely, both of us arguing over who's the most lucky to have married the other. I am. But this time, before we get too carried away, Luke jumps up.

'Don't move,' he instructs. As if. He dashes downstairs and returns with a bottle of Bollie and two champagne flutes. '*De rigueur*,' he laughs.

We open our cards, drink champagne and make love; the usual kind of things that couples celebrating their first wedding anniversary do. We keep asking each other, 'Are you happy?'

'Delirious. Are you happy?'

'Never more so.'

This is another one of our favourite sketches. These words are so often repeated I answer without thinking. The truth of them is indisputable. We are wild about each other.

I've never been happier, more content or more confident in my life. I had been fairly disdainful when my three younger sisters all rushed down the aisle before me. Although my mother and father had the opposite reaction. They were delighted and mollified; more so when my siblings settled in Sheffield, within a three-mile radius of our parental home. I had confounded my mother by insisting on 'gallivanting off' to London, where, she advised me, 'I could expect nothing but trouble.' Therefore I laboured under the knowledge that every year that ticked by, I further disappointed her. I wore the cloud of shame quite stylishly, mostly in cocktail bars and nightclubs. Although my mother thought I had terminal china stamped on my arse, top shelf city, it surprised my friends that I got engaged so young. That I got engaged at all. I was not blushing bride material. Before I met Luke I'd positioned myself as the absolute *Cosmopolitan* woman. I had always been an outrageous flirt and when flirting became frustrating I had hurried to be a good soldier of the sexual revolution. Like many women I was desperate to shake off the embarrassment of not knowing, and desperate to be known. I rushed and jostled and queue-jumped, then carelessly shrugged off my innocence. I left the image of one Madonna behind and took on the pop star version as a role model. No reserve. No trepidation. There wasn't a position in the Kama Sutra I didn't try (except the unappealing up-the-bum). On scores of occasions I indulged in a number of extraordinarily romantic and sexual liaisons.

I thrived on the challenge.

I lived for the hunt.

I died for the kill.

I was grateful that women had chained themselves to railings for me. I enjoyed being a 'more than five less than ten girl'. After all, they were all nice blokes, or gorgeous-looking, or I thought I loved them, or at least one of the three. I quickly became a 'more than ten less than twenty girl'. I was more often the ditcher than the ditchee. I'd done it all: one-night stands, long-term commitment, sleeping with men because everyone else wanted to, sleeping with a man because no one else wanted to, because they were fit, or cool, or captain of a sports team, because they were older than me, because they were younger, to help me get over a disastrous affair, to help them get over their last lay, because they wore their hair longer than anyone else, because they wore it shorter, because I was too tired to get a cab home and, on one occasion because he did a clever trick with the wrapper of an amaretti biscuit. It was then that I stopped counting and began to wonder if shagging around was really what the suffragettes had had in mind. Even variety became boring.

Then I met Luke. At a wedding. He was an usher and took the opportunity to flirt with me as he led me to my pew. He is over 6 feet with straight, floppy blond hair that simply demands fingers are run through it; he has this huge enveloping smile, and, naturally, he was wearing tails. I instantly fell in lust. I couldn't take my eyes off him. I watched as he handed out song sheets, chatted to aunts and grannies, making them feel important and interesting. By the time Rose had cut the cake I was deeply in like. As she threw the bouquet I was in love.

Luke.

Luke had an altogether distinct seduction technique. A walking *Time Out* guide, Luke's fun to be with. Eternally unfazed and with an inability to do anything half-heartedly, he's one of those guys who will give everything a go: ceroc, body painting, mountain climbing, radio debates, canoeing, roller skating, greyhound racing.

'Fancy a game of squash?'

'I can't play squash,' I'd replied, cursing my hand to eye to ball coordination, or rather, the magnificent lack of it.

'I'll teach you.' And he did. Because suddenly, when I was with him, I could do things that had previously seemed impossible. He approached everything with steady confidence and patience and although my approach was more haphazard and impatient, the confidence was infectious. We never went to pubs or sat in front of the TV, instead we did exciting, extraordinary, wondrous things on our dates. He always 'just happened' to have tickets for the Comedy Club or opening nights for some obscure fringe performance, played out at venues with funny names like Onion Shed or Man in the Moon. We were always busy: swimming, wind-surfing, visiting galleries or throwing dinner parties. We did everything together; he became my new best friend. My best,

best friend. Pretty sharpish, I realized that he was the man I looked forward to looking back with.

I felt a distinct release and relief. I was delighted to rediscover sex really could be game free, pain free, shame free. Within months of our meeting Luke offered me a beautiful diamond ring, which I confidently accepted. It was love. Loving Luke just made sense. I thought the speed was romantic; perversely, my mother thought it suspect and insisted on a three-year engagement to quell rumours of visits to Baby Gap.

With Luke I feel shrouded and protected and decent. I've never been able to explain this to any of my friends, married or otherwise, drunken or sober. We discuss calorie intake, childhood experiences of shoplifting, the number of tampons you need for a heavy period and just about everything you can imagine. But *I* find buying into this renewal thing embarrassing and contrary; *they'd* have me committed.

We loll around in bed for ages. I'm thrilled to be spending time with him. Recently, Luke has been working a regular fourteen-hour day because, despite being an ostensibly normal bloke, he likes his job. When he's not working we 'do things around the house'. The eternal battle with cracked walls, and a garden that insists on growing. Fringe theatres and windsurfing are luxuries we can no longer afford. Today's a holiday, so we talk. We talk about our past, remembering films we've watched together, places we've visited, rows we've roared through and reconciliations we've run to. We plan our future, which is unquestionably coruscating. I moan about my job at Looper Jackson, saying that I am bored. Luke reminds me that it pays well and that perhaps the upcoming merger will offer me new challenges. It is sweet of him to try to make me feel valued and worthwhile but I remain unconvinced. Loving his work as he does means that he has no comprehension. It's not his fault. Talking about my work depresses us both, so I change the subject. I tell him the washing machine is leaking and he responds with a funny story about the neighbours' cat peeing on our herb garden. Unreasonably, this story makes us laugh so much (it must be the champagne) that he can hardly finish it and I have to run to the loo. He won't let me, but holds me down until I'm forced to shout playful threats. We drift in and out of intensity as we are firmly embedded in intimacy. It's sunny. He covers my body with little butterfly kisses and I give him the king of all blow jobs, then we fall asleep.

At 11 a.m. we wake up suddenly and act out that scene in *Four Weddings and a Funeral*. The one where Hugh Grant and his flatmate oversleep, then wake up and rush around shouting 'Fuck!' Everyone in the cinema laughs at that. Not because the script is so witty but because it is so familiar. We've all done it. It's usually on the day that you have a job interview for the job of a lifetime, or when you've got a really hot date, or on the first day of the sale at Harvey Nichols, or when you are expecting fifty friends for a buffet lunch and champagne, in less than two hours. We dash in and out of the shower, up and down the stairs, in and out of the freezer, up and down the garden. We clean, dress, sauté, spice and set up deck-chairs and umbrellas. We tidy magazines and strategically place nibbles. We arrange a hundred silver helium-filled balloons, we stack up film for the camera, polish flutes and dress in our Armani. We shout 'Fuck' a lot, too.

Caterers have prepared and delivered the food; all we have to do is take off the cling-film. I like to feel I've made an effort. It looks fantastic, set out on our big wooden table (an investment – both coming from large families we plan to have at least four kids). I look at the food with a mix of pride and amazement. *Zucca gialla intere al forno con pomodori secchi* (roasted peppers stuffed with sun-dried tomatoes), *zucchini carpaccio* (skinny bits of courgettes), *insalata prosciutto e fichi* (ham and figs – you wouldn't have eaten it if your mum had put it in your sandwiches at school), then a whole load of pasta and polenta salads, a stack of vegetables that no one ever knows the name of, and piles of fresh summer berries (colour coordinated). It looks just like something out of the BlueBird hyper-trendy supermarket on the King's Road, but that isn't so surprising because the caterers are from the BlueBird hyper-trendy supermarket on the King's Road. Frenzied activity is such fun, and I run around with my camera taking arty photos of food through champagne flutes, and food reflected on helium-filled balloons, and champagne flutes reflected on helium-filled balloons, and helium-filled balloons reflected on champagne flutes. Luke, rather more practically, remembers that we have four crates of champagne to chill and so while I am doing a good impression of Lichfield, he fills the bath with ice and about twenty bottles of fizz. As the food comes out of our huge, canyon-sized fridge the rest of the champagne goes in. Finally at five to one we congratulate ourselves on our indisputable hospitality, style and general success.

At five past one I check that the invite definitely says 26 July. No one has arrived. At seven minutes past one I check and re-check the doorbell. By ten past, I snap, 'Nobody is going to turn up.' Luke pours me a drink. 'People don't enjoy our parties,' I add. He hands me the drink and rubs my shoulders as I ask, 'Do you think that we have a reputation for meanness?' He kisses the top of my head as I bitterly mutter, 'It was stupid to think that anyone would give up a Sunday to celebrate our anniversary.' At eleven minutes past one I start to rewrap the *zucca gialla intere al forno con pomodori secchi* and I console myself that we won't have to visit Sainsbury's for a month.

The bell rings. Luke stands up to answer the door. He smiles at me and resists saying anything stupid like 'I told you so', or 'Patience is a virtue', as I am forever being reminded. He knows that my retort would be: that above all virtues, patience is the most overrated. Our friends begin to arrive, literally pouring through the door. All of them say nice things about the house, the food, me. All of them look marvellous and are carrying even more booze.

Luke and I have great friends. Really brilliant. They are all successful, healthy, intelligent, fun, good-looking and nice-natured. Sure, why wouldn't you be nice-natured if you are successful, healthy, intelligent, fun and good-looking? However, none of them are all of these things, all of the time. Without exception, at one point or another, our friends have had their moments. They have failed at things: relationships, exams, jobs. They have been ill but (touch wood) nothing too awful: flu, and dodgy knees brought on by overtraining for the London marathon, are about the sum of it. There are times when each of them can be really dense, dull, irritating or spotty, just like Luke and me. But generally they are extremely fit, bright and beautiful. But then I'm biased, because they are my friends.

So when they all arrive with their young, tanned, hopeful faces, absolutely gunning for an afternoon of hilarity and frivolity, I can't help but feel very proud. Proud of Luke, proud of our life, proud of our friends, and proud of myself.

Names to love and hate. Because life's like that – try as we might, and we all try to varying degrees, we can't like everyone. Wouldn't life be simple if we could? And a bit dull.

Luke; lovely, wonderful, kind, generous, clever Luke. Lucy and Daisy have been my friends since university. Rose, Daisy's sister, has come, too, with her husband, Peter. It was at Rose and Peter's wedding that Luke and I first met. And Sam, my closest friend at work.

Lucy is skinny (British size 8), tall, with clear skin, huge green eyes and long, straight, natural (ish) blonde hair that swings down her back. She is by anyone's estimation a great beauty, a stunning-looking woman; small ass, large breasts, tiny waist and ribcage. It is not possible to say she is unaware of her looks. She would have to be deaf, dumb and blind, living in solitary confinement, not to have noticed that she is absolutely modelesque. To her credit, she doesn't rely on her stunning looks to get along in life and yet she does get along in life. She trades derivatives (whatever that is – it's long past the time when I can politely ask), earning a ridiculously large amount of money and respect in the City. Not easy with her attributes. Both men and women assume that stunning women must be stupid. Both sexes want to believe this for different reasons. Men, because such affirmations of stereotypes save them from uncomfortable thoughts. Women because really, there has to be a God.

Lucy finds it hard to make friends. Men always say they want to know her more when what they mean is that they want to know more of her. Women find her too much competition. Lucy doesn't worry about this. It would be churlish to worry about being beautiful, clever, successful and rich. Instead she has adjusted to being alone.

She likes it.

To an extent.

Lucy comforts herself with the thought that few people are as interesting as her anyway. It isn't as if she is ever without company. There is always someone who wants to be her best friend, even if it's only long enough to find out if she diets or works out (moderately and moderately). There's always some man who wants to take her for dinner and invariably he is obscenely wealthy, with film-star looks and a lifetime membership of MENSA. The only thing is, it is never the same friend wanting to talk about her diets or the same man wanting to fatten her up. As a result Lucy has developed a brittle, impenetrable aloofness. This is her defence but the appearance is all attack. Most people find her impossibly intimidating. I guess they're right. I guess they are jealous. I guess they are a bit right and a bit jealous. She says I am her first, best, possibly only real friend. And I don't think she says that to *absolutely* everyone.

We met a lifetime ago, on our first day at university. Lucy's father parked their Daimler at exactly the same moment as my dad parked our Citroën in the hall of residence car park. I was a nauseating mass of energy, exuberance and optimism. I saw Lucy straight away and I also saw her give me a quick once-over. It was with a swift and practised eye that Lucy mentally noted: Connie (that's me), size 10, small boobs, 5 feet 4, good figure but not a sensation; then I had long hair. It's bobbed now, but (unlike Lucy's) mine is a mass of mad ringlets and curls, not silver blonde but natural streaks of numerous golden hues (magazine ad-land bollocks), odd-looking streaks of yellow (accurate summation by the jury). I hate it, everyone else loves it. Later Lucy told me that she thought my face was stunning and that was what had caught her eye. She describes it as the face of a cherub, but a cherub with a filthy, wicked, exciting secret. I find this description a bit embarrassing but definitely flattering.

Moving on. Daisy and I also met at university. We were both waiting to register for our supplementary subjects. I watched Daisy patiently and nervously queuing, carefully avoiding the eyes of the other students. I, on the other hand, chatted and smiled at absolutely everyone, desperate to ingratiate myself with anyone who'd give me a chance. I thought she was cool, calm and aloof. As Daisy turned the final corner of the queue and was about to pass through the door that signified the possibility of registering and being released to the Uni Bar, I rather too loudly called out to her. My voice cut through several other conversations, leading to an excruciating silence. Everyone seemed to be waiting for me to talk.

'What sup subject are you signing for?' It was very 'university' to develop an 'in' language. *Sup* for supplementary, *Uni* for university. Junior Common Room became JC. I was fluent by day two. I'm not good at languages but I do understand the importance of assimilating with the natives. Never carry a map, never ask for directions and never trust a driver wearing a hat.

I thought that Daisy looked really interesting and intelligent. She looked just like the kind of person I'd hoped I'd meet at university – all serious and worthy and challenging. She also looked astounded that I had called out to her in such an abrupt way. She later told me that her astonishment came, not from my calling out, but from me calling to *her*. She hadn't wanted to answer me, in case I was talking to someone else. We were all so lacking. Lacking in confidence, lacking in trust and lacking in reality. Youth really is wasted on the young. They are too poor, emotionally and financially, to enjoy it. I can say that now because I'm thirty, an age of confidence. Except when it comes to throwing parties. I'm assured, but not invincible.

Daisy had fumbled for an engaging or witty reply. Stumped, she settled for factual and told me she had chosen Classics, then she disappeared around the corner. Later, sitting in the student bar, on orange Formica chairs, I discovered that Daisy had loads of worthy reasons for her choice. She had some knowledge of Greek and Roman mythology and found it fascinating. She hoped that the classical references in English Literature (her main subject) would become clearer if she had a deeper understanding of the divas and Diomedeses.

I chose it because she did.

We subsequently shared lecture notes, secrets, tensions, successes, the usual thrills and spills of university life. We grew closer day by day. While I widened my circle of friends to an extraordinary array (some spectacular and difficult, some shallow but easygoing), Daisy limited herself to a few soulmates. Out of all my friends, Daisy considers herself my most true and dull. Lucy considers herself my most true and sensational. I guess they are both half right.

Daisy is 5 feet 10 and back then believed herself to be oversized and ungainly. She battled simultaneously with her weight and her self-esteem, one rose proportionally as the other decreased. She was ashamed of her glasses, her red hair, her M&S clothes and her spots. She perceived herself to be a fairly bright, but very plain girl. It amazed Daisy that everyone else seemed so very unaware of these shortcomings. She has beautiful eyes, quick wit, fair nature, unparalleled honesty and sensitivity. Try as I might, I could not see the drawbacks that Daisy insisted on periodically presenting.

'My hair is so wiry and unmanageable.'

'It's just like mine but red.' We stared at one another, aware of the enormous implication of the disparity. I ventured as comfort: 'Pre-Raphaelite muses all had hair like yours.'

Over the years Daisy has eventually been reassured that if I can see these good bits and Lucy can too, then perhaps, just perhaps, they really are there. Just before we all gave up and went home, convinced that Daisy would never like herself, she seemed to get the hang of it. She's swapped her glasses for contacts and as she relaxed her skin was less prone to stress-induced break-outs. Her hair remained curly and red.

Rose, Daisy's sister, is three years older than Daisy which makes her thirty-two, nearly thirty-three. I first met Rose when she visited Daisy at Uni. She was twenty-one but seemed about thirty-two even then, when thirty-two was ancient;

Rose now seems about fifty-two. It's not that she looks especially old. She looks perfectly fine. She looks perfectly thirty-two, or perhaps what you imagine thirty-two is when you are eighteen. She is a comfortable size 16. She also has red hair but it's darker than Daisy's. She has the same lovely eyes and smile. She wears leggings and comfy jumpers, the same ones that she wore in the 80s when she visited Daisy. She gardens. She sews, too. She makes her own jam. Not only does she have time but more peculiarly she has the inclination. Rose is married to Peter. When Rose first brought Peter to meet Daisy, Lucy and I hung out of the hall of residence bedroom window, ruthlessly elbowing one another aside to get the best view. It was worth it. Peter is tall, athletic and handsome. Later we discovered he is also clever and charming. Lucy would not admit Rose had secured a catch, instead she mumbled that he 'wasn't ugly', which Daisy and I knew to be high praise from Lucy. They have twin baby boys, Sebastian and Henry, who are just adorable. They seem happy and sorted and it's nice having them to our parties, because Luke likes Peter, everyone likes the boys and Rose helps with the washing-up.

Finally there is Sam. Not finally in the sense that I have no more friends. This is not a finite list of people I know and love. Although, thinking about it, I guess four really close friends is quite a lot. *Really* close. Bridesmaid material. Although, hell, what a combination – every shape and size in baby blue imaginable. I didn't consider this, even when I was linking my first name with his surname, but now I always advise the newly affianced to take a long hard look at their best friends and try to imagine what can possibly be bought in rose-petal pink that will make Sue look a foot taller, Jane look leggy and reduce Karen's waistline.

I've known Sam for just over two years. We work together. She is hilarious. She looks like butter wouldn't melt in her mouth, but it's been melted on every part of her anatomy, once when she'd had a few. Sam is simply lovely. She is kind and forgiving and sympathetic and generous and she mixes it all up with being fun. Sam is the type of person who likes spring mornings and autumn evenings. But, for that matter, she likes autumn mornings and spring evenings, too, and all the bits in between. She is thirty-three, which surprises everyone, including herself. If Sam had to describe herself she would forget to tell you that she has literally dozens of really cool, committed friends that she's earned through her unflinching loyalty. She would omit to tell you that she has the most stunning brown eyes, big velvet splashes (that's not very poetic, but believe me, they are fantastic). She would also omit to tell you that she can reduce people to tears and incontinence pads with her funny antics. She would say, 'Hello, I'm Sam Martin, I'm thirty-three and I'm single.' Because she is ridiculously honest, she might add 'and it bothers me'. Because she's a little bit obsessed about the situation, she might go further and add 'a lot'. Or she might just ask you to draw up a chair while she, in detail, documents love affairs and disasters from A to Z, or from age fifteen to thirty-three.

Sam has been trying for over half her life to get married. It amazes me that women like her still exist. Women that are beautiful, popular, ambitious, stylish and still alone. But there are lots of them, hundreds of them, offices are full of them, armies of them, here in the metropolis of London. They walk around with everyone else; with people who are married, people who are single and like it, people who never give their marital/romantic status a thought (I'm not convinced that there are an awful lot of these, but I have heard that there have been reported sightings). Women like Sam are identifiable because they wear that distinguishing look that is so late 90s, the look that asks, 'So where did I go wrong? Why was it so easy for my mother and so bloody hard for me?' They are always sniffing under their own armpits and breathing on to the backs of their hands, but they can't attribute their loneliness to stray body odour because these women don't smell. These women are gorgeous. I mean, I'd marry Sam and be proud. I'm not a lesbian. But if I was, and Sam was, and marriage between two consenting adults of the same sex were possible, then I would marry Sam.

It beats the hell out of me.

The party is going off brilliantly. There's loads to drink and eat, all our beautiful friends are having a fabulous time. People are dancing, or at least bouncing up and down doing star jumps, gesticulating madly. My female friends are lusting after chocolate profiteroles and my male friends are leering down the tops of my female friends. Due to the abundance of champagne we start doing the Macarena, but not the Birdie Song, which is only performed if we have whisky chasers. It's an outstanding party, people are drinking from the bottle, others are feeding each other *zucchini carpaccio*, although invariably the people feeding each other are not the people who ought to be feeding each other. There are people inhaling helium from the balloons, bent double with hilarity at, 'Hello, I'm Minnie Mouse.' It's all here, at our party: the surprised, the delighted, the riotous, the earnest, the cheeky, the flirtatious, the sceptical, the elated, the ludicrous. I measure the success by the number of people who are drunk and trying to look sober. The only people that actually look drunk are the unlucky ones that are driving and who are, in fact, stone-cold sober. It's a tribal thing. I can't explain it but I catch it all on film.

I watch Luke as he threads among the guests; filling their glasses, laughing at their jokes and listening to stories about their disappointments in love. People tell Luke things, they trust him. Everybody likes him and he likes everybody. Which is largely wonderful but does have two small drawbacks. One, he will *not* gossip. My telephone bills to Lucy are enormous. She is on my BT friends and family list, we often qualify for 20 per cent volume discounts. Two, I sometimes wonder if only really nice people would like me and only extremely exceptional men could fall in love with me. But these lapses in confidence are immediately repaired when again I think of Lucy.

'Are you dancing?' I grin, hopefully, at Luke.

'Are you asking?' He laughs.

I'm always asking, I love dancing. I'm good at it. I adore the sheer indulgence of it. Flailing my arms and legs, shaking my head, letting it out, letting go. Mostly I ignore the actual melody and beat but happily this doesn't seem to matter. My enthusiasm more than compensates. Luke is also a good dancer. We used to club together a lot when we first met. His style is quite different. He carefully learns steps and routines.

He's cautious and measured. I always leave the dance floor with a clammy stomach, hair sticking to the back of my neck, blistered feet, smudged make-up and exhausted, aching limbs. Luke rarely sweats.

'So?' I ask again as I begin to move towards the rug, the area naturally carved out to act as a dance floor. But Luke doesn't follow me. He's probably spotted an empty glass that needs refilling or noticed that the chargrilled peppers with anchovy and capers are being neglected. Luke is a far better host than I'll ever be. I don't look after people at my parties. More often than not, it's all I can do to look after myself. My idea of being the perfect hostess is to supply an array of good food, copious amounts of champagne and attractive and absorbing people. I put these ingredients in a room and see what happens. I enjoy the chaos of watching people mix with one another. I would never dream of introducing Bill to Jo because they both have an interest in Alfred Hitchcock. I expect my friends to have the nous to introduce them-selves to one another, to find the loo, and I'd be positively concerned if they didn't fill their own glasses. Luckily my *laisser-faire* attitude is in contrast to Luke's more traditional approach. He always makes sure that there are clean towels and plenty of loo roll in the downstairs bathroom, he is skilled at guaranteeing that everyone leaves with the correct coat and partner. It's really Luke that ensures our parties are successful. So it is understandable that Luke can't take time out to dance with me. And mildly frustrating. I look around for some other poor victim and drag Peter to his feet. After Peter I dance with Daisy, Sam, Bob, Phil and Claire. I'm indiscriminate in my choice of partner, the important factor is that I get to spin and twirl so madly I have a head-rush.

I sigh with relief as Luke and I wave goodbye to the last guests. Well, not quite the last, as Sam, Daisy, Lucy, Rose and Peter stay behind. But to us these friends are more like family than guests. I smile at Luke as he pours large brandies. He nods towards the garden, indicating that he and Peter are heading that way to smoke cigars and enjoy the balmy July night. I want him to stay and debrief the party, but he points out that we don't like people to smoke inside. We do have nice things and it would be awful to burn a hole in the antique French lace cushion covers or drop ash on the hand-tufted Moroccan rug. Anal retention, a thing that develops with age. Lucy joins the boys to smoke a cigarette. Not that it's unknown for her to smoke a cigar, we both did at university but only for effect. Absolutely no pleasure involved at all. It was simply a pulling technique. A successful one.

We've had in excess of a bottle and a half of champagne each, so it seems ludicrous to stop now. We start the post-party hunt for dregs. We find three half bottles. Champagne bottles are heavy and as there was so much to drink no one had to suffer the indignity of draining bottles, except us, now. Together this isn't tacky, it's sensible. Once our glasses are full we turn, with varying amounts of enthusiasm, to the issue of clearing up.

'No leave it, really,' I assure generously. 'I'll do it in the morning.' I only believe this because of the large quantities of alcohol I've drunk. 'Let's sit down and gossip.' The advantage of Luke being out of earshot is that I can indulge in a post mortem. Who said what? Who looked fab? Who'd been a victim? Who fancied who? Who ate too much? And, importantly, who threw up in my Tibetan hand-carved umbrella stand? Predictably, Sam and Daisy don't need to be persuaded, they literally drop what they are doing (mental note: two side plates to be replaced) and flop into our big leather armchairs. Rose, bless her, continues to carefully scrape discarded food and napkins into a huge black bin-liner. I pour everyone another large glass of champagne and then revert to loading the dishwasher. Haphazard as the execution of this operation proves to be, I know that I won't relax until at least one dishwasher load is whirling away. I blame my mother for that.

Woozy, full up, a bit icky, we all feel great.

'Put the wedding video on,' says Sam.

'No, you've all seen it.' I venture a polite, unconvincing refusal.

'But it's lovely.' Sam knows the formula.

'Go on, you're dying to,' Lucy says as she comes in from the garden. She really isn't as good at playing my game.

I don't need much persuading.

Luke wanders through to refill the brandy glasses. He raises his eyebrows and shakes his head. He does this uninterested, tutting thing because it is demanded of men whenever their wedding video, or similar, is being shown ('or similar' equals looking at pictures of babies, even themselves as babies, recounting of first date or proposal, choosing underwear or valentine's cards). No one really believes that they are hard-hearted or uninterested. It's a big global conspiracy so that we can pretend that they are all tough with the monopoly on being cool and we can maintain exclusive film rights on slushy stuff. On the whole it works. So Luke wanders past the TV, eyes rolling, and I don't let on that I caught him watching it at 3 o'clock yesterday morning.

'Ohhhh,' the girls let out in a Greek chorus and edge towards the TV cuddling cushions. Even Lucy softens. Sort of.

'My hair looked really good like that.'

The video, indeed all wedding videos, have a peculiar effect on women. We have loads of basics in common: love of chocolate, love of alcohol, an encyclopaedic knowledge of all high street clothes shops. We've all read everything Jane Austen ever wrote, and we all harbour unfeasibly high hopes for the world of romance.

Sam and Daisy, who are both single, become different animals as soon as the video starts to play. Sam starts to cry. She cried when we were buying my dress, throughout the actual ceremony, when we sung hymns, when we cut the cake, when I threw my bouquet and when we left for our honeymoon. She cried so much throughout the whole process that my Gran thought she was one of Luke's exes. Gran thought it very peculiar (but typical of her lovely Connie) that I'd let one of his ex-girlfriends ('who was no better than she ought to be') participate in the ceremony. She'd have given Sam a thrashing for having the cheek to turn up. Poor Sam. Sam has seen my wedding video more often than *The Wizard of Oz* but she still starts crying as soon as the organ cranks up and I'm sure that isn't entirely to do with the awful playing. She cries quietly. Not a sad booing but through a big 'it-will-happen-to-me-one-day' smile. She can smile too as I reckon she is also thinking *And I won't make the mistake of carrying my bouquet so high it obscures my neckline*. Sam has *really* studied this video.

Daisy's reaction is a lot more pensive and controlled. She's had a few boyfriends of course but she's never really lost her head and heart. She's really into 'The One' syndrome. Daisy becomes pensive and says things like, 'you know when you know', 'you can't hurry love', 'every teapot has a lid'. As fond as we are of Daisy, this pseudo-soothing mumbo jumbo irritates us all. Rose and I are fully paid-up members of the camp which runs along the lines, 'I knew, but he took some convincing', 'you can hurry love, you can race at Schumacher speed if necessary', 'but who the hell wants to marry a teapot?'

Lucy's viewing pleasure is derived from a cynical knowledge that every wedding she attends is a lucky escape. She thanks God that she isn't the one trussed up like a Christmas panto-mime fairy. Actually, she enjoyed my wedding and commented, 'So few are really stylish. Convention and tradition actively work against common sense and good taste, but yours Connie (pause, for effect) was not an embarrassment.' Luke and I had been pleased with this compliment. She likes watching our wedding video because she was my chief bridesmaid and therefore had quite a major role. Her comments are limited to how well she looks and the occasional beauty tip for the rest of us – 'In retrospect, would you have chosen those shoes?' However, she was great fun on the day. She tipped up at my house at the crack of dawn and bossed and directed the hairdressers, the make-up artists, the florist, the chauffeur and the other bridesmaids, with such equa-nimity that my day was entirely hassle free, a real delight. She did all this directing and bossing and stuff while dripping champagne intravenously into myself and my mother. She said this was to ensure I was drunk enough to go through with it, but I know she was kidding. So although Lucy sits playing super bitch, we all know that really this is only an act. She's not a *super* bitch.

Rose watches the video with a more gentle, wise attitude. She's done it herself so has no reason to feel competitive or resentful, or pitying, or hopeful. She just comments on how happy we both look and she laughs a lot at Peter's Best Man speech.

I watch the video feeling immensely proud. It's like I'm watching someone else's life. It's just so perfect.

Yet it is a fact that five minutes after you're married your dress is old news, your haircut an embarrassment and your make-up like a poor set-design on *Top of the Pops*. They don't tell you that in the wedding magazines. They give you endless tips on October flowers, or when you should remove your veil, or exactly what a *croque en bouche* is! Which is hardly life and death. I have a certain amount of sympathy with the 'How do I arrange the top table for my wedding, as both my father and stepfather will be attending?', less for 'I'd like to have Irish folk dancers/bagpipes/Morris dancers – do you know where I can find such people?' (surely the advice here should be 'don't bother'). 'Do you know where I can buy wedding shoes for size 8 feet?' is also a call with which I can sympathize, but really, let's cut the crap and get to the Aristotelean problems of wedding-day debate. 'How can I prevent my dress dating, so that I don't have to hide behind the settee on our fifth wedding anniversary when my husband gets the album out?' Another thought, 'Do you have any salient tips on how to avoid my make-up causing the same embarrassment to me, as legwarmers surely must cause Olivia Newton John?' But the magazines don't have the answers to this kind of thing, so don't even waste time looking for them.

The video is, by anyone's standards, the naffest thing about my wedding. I love it. I thought I wouldn't. I thought it would be intrusive (it was). I thought my friends would laugh (they did). I thought it would just be another thing to worry about (it was), but my mum argued that it was an essential part of the day and that I'd treasure it more than my dress (she probably said that I'd treasure it more than my husband, but I'm sanitizing her character for commercial gain). Anyway she was right. I love it.

I'd always said I didn't want a big day. I wanted a few very close friends, and something simple, cream and straight (to wear, rather than eat or marry). My nearest and dearest resisted an open belly-laugh. No one actually catcalled, 'But you love being the centre of attention. I can't imagine you letting this opportunity pass you by.' No one actually hooted, 'But you throw parties as frequently as the rest of us throw the duvet over the unmade bed.' Instead, my mother brought home that month's copy of *Brides and Setting up Home*. Artful soul, my mum.

I was fascinated. I was absorbed. I was hooked. I was a bride-to-be.

There is absolutely nothing amazing about these magazines beyond the fact that normally sensible women, of roughly sound mind and body, not only buy them but frequently repeat the purchase. Moreover we take them seriously. They become important to us, they become our trusted guides, our loyal friends, our Bible. I clearly remember my mum handing the magazine over and it was a moment of pure distinct revelation. From that moment on there was no heroic talk of simple, cream and straight and a few close friends. Road to Damascus. I understood that more was more. The cover was so . . . hopeful, pink, smiley, pink, informative, pink. Even if it is not actually pink, even if the cover is actively blue, it feels pink. Dreamy, girly, promising, innocent. Suddenly it mattered to me that I knew my, 'Step by step to perfect hair and make-up', 'How much a wedding really costs?' and 'How to cope with divorced parents' (and mine are married). I wanted it! This magazine was my secret arsenal in the lifetime battle of the 'Happily Ever After' because here it was in black and white, 'BE A PRINCESS FOR A DAY'. All for £2.95. Sold to the lady on the left. To the lady on the right. And the one standing at the back.

I devoted man hours that amounted to weeks choosing a dress, flowers, cars, menus, shoes, head-dresses. The groom had been the easy bit. More frightening yet I devoted man hours that amounted to months practising my wedding-day smile, my wedding-day walk, my wedding-day first dance, my wedding-day blush (I have never blushed in my life), my wedding-day thank you. I was well and truly ensconced in Fantasyland and I liked it there!

The video brings me back down to earth. My star appearance in the video does not reveal a demure, mysterious princess in sepia tones. It showcases a noisy, bossy, funny, happy, Technicolor twenty-something bride, who is having a huge laugh with her noisy, bossy, funny, happy, Technicolor twenty-something friends. The video shows Peter pretending to Luke that he's lost the rings, it shows Daisy stop me just before I enter the church to straighten my veil. It catches our friend Rob with his fly open, Sam and Lucy squabbling over catching the bouquet (both failed, Daisy caught it). It shows Luke's younger brother boasting that he held 'some bird's' hair back as she puked, my father tripping up as he staggers into the cab at the end of the night, and it catches my mum sighing fondly under her breath, 'You've never come home sober from a wedding in the thirty-five years I've known you.' Fondlyish.

The romantic bits are nothing like the magazines, they are much more real. They are much more simple. Luke smiling at me. Me smiling at Luke. Luke and me holding hands.

We watch the video, right the way through without hitting the fast-forward button. When it is over there isn't a dry eye in the house. Lucy's tears are tears of boredom.

The next day is a long one. There's always more paperwork the Monday after a great weekend. My head hurts with a combination of lack of sleep, excess alcohol and the low after a weekend high. Five more days before the weekend, I sigh, bored. My work is not that bad. I don't always actively dislike it. But it is work. By definition. I'm here because they pay me. Winning the lottery would definitely change my life.

Everyone is always impressed with the fact that I am a management consultant, but in reality my role is limited to plugging data into a computer system. As I become more senior I can look forward to deciding which data and how it should be plugged in. Ultimately, I will get to decide which computer system and whose it should be plugged into. It isn't challenging. It isn't creative. I feel terminally ungrateful and dull when I meet people at parties, who on finding out what I do for a living, shout excitably 'Well that sounds fascinating' or 'Marvellous firm to work for, how did you get into that then?' It seems so churlish to say, 'No, really, it isn't fascinating at all, anyone could do it. I've had more fun watching washing dry.'

However, there are good things about my job. Sam, always on hand for a chat and a lunchtime sandwich, sits three desks along from me. We work in one of those open-plan hot-desk environments, which are as intrusive as they are ineffective. No one ever really 'hot-desks'. If a new girl arrives having read the hype and sits down at any old desk, she'll soon discover the error of her ways. The good thing about the open-plan office is that as a married woman I only have clean linen to launder and therefore don't mind a public dissection of my relationship. *If* Luke and I have sex at the weekend, the general opinion on the floor is that it's really great that he still fancies me after one year of marriage. Alternatively, if we haven't had sex no one is surprised or suspicious, we have after all been together years, so we're past that stage where you overdepend on the physical. I am the only married person in my department, so the open-plan arrangement allows me the chance to gratuitously enjoy other people's liaisons, successful or otherwise. My department called 'Accommodation Management' is a new-fangled idea. The firm's heritage is in technology. 'Accommodation management' is all to do with helping the little people adapt to change when the big people thrust it upon them. As it's a 'people job' it is predictably, predominantly a female department. The firm is predominantly male, which means that someone on my team is always snogging someone in another team, which is strictly prohibited and therefore utterly compelling. Besides this in-house entertainment, the other advantages of my job are that we are based in the centre of Soho, which is brilliant for drunken nights on the town and handy for the gym (ha) and there is a really nice Pret a Manger next door but one.

It is a slow morning. I've played three unsuccessful rounds of electronic solitaire, taken two personal calls and sent six personal e-mails. To avoid the charge of complete abuse of my employer's trust, I do a bit of filing, take one business call, make one business call and I send three business e-mails. I also catch someone in my team pretending to take dictation but really listening to the Now 310 album on her headset. I quickly find her something equally pointless and numbing to do, by way of teaching her a lesson. Even with this amount of activity I am fed up and watch the clock drag its hands around to 12.30. On the dot, Sue pops her head around my cube.

'Fancy a quick one?'

Debate ensues. Monday choices are: visit the gym for a quick thirty-minute bums and tums punishment class or go for a cool glass of Chardonnay in the bar next door. Calories on or off. Fat on or off. Not so tough a decision. I grab my purse and kick my gym bag just a little bit further under my desk. I am a big advocate of 'out of sight out of mind'. Wine it is. Then the phone rings. It's Daisy. I gesture wildly to Sue and my other workmates, who have congregated around my desk, mouthing at them to *Get a round in, I'll pay*. They trudge off sulkily, sure that I've somehow tricked them.

That I'd planned the phone call and that I'll now slip off to the gym, having persuaded them to consume more calories. God if I was as bright as that I'd be working for MI5, not this shower. They leave with resentful looks.

'It's me,' says Daisy.

'Hi, me, what's up?'

'Just rang to say thank you for the party, it was brilliant fun.'

'Yup, quite successful I thought. However, I'm paying for it.'

'Oh, was it expensive? I suppose it was, all that champagne and caterers and everything. Would you like a contribution?'

'I don't mean that type of paying, I mean with my hangover.'

'Oh, of course. I can't very well contribute to that can I?'

'Are you all right Daisy?' Is she still drunk? If so I'm a really irresponsible friend. Daisy is a schoolteacher and I shouldn't be encouraging her in this excessive debauchery. I'm perturbed because Daisy is normally so bright and this conversation is laboured. Also there is only one telephone that she has access to, which is in the staff room and is treated with the height of respect, a mix between the Tardis and the Bat Phone. For emergency use only. There are no calls to Daisy asking her what colour nail varnish she is planning to wear with her open-toed shoes that night. I often indulge in these calls with our other friends. Come to think of it Daisy was acting a bit weird yesterday, too, all sort of spaced out.

'You're not ill are you?' I ask, concerned.

'Hmmm?' Vague.

'Ill, you know.' Anxious.

'I need help.' Unspecific.

'What is it? Are you in trouble?' (deeply worried).

There is no real reason for me to assume that Daisy is in trouble. She doesn't have a dark side, no criminal record. She was once late paying her television licence because she was on holiday. She was a wreck, I thought we'd have to fly home. No drug abuse. No bigamy. No husband at all. Is she going to announce that she's a lesbian?

'You know Luke's friend Simon – '

Oh, so it's the usual, some bloke. Momentarily I'm disappointed. I mean there's not much kudos in a friend having a fling with your husband's friend, is there? It's commonplace. I settle down and try to concentrate on what Daisy is saying to me.

'Yep?'

'What's he like?'

'What do you mean what's he like? You met him yesterday. He's about five feet eleven, brown hair, brown eyes, trendy.'

'Noooo,' she interrupts, now she's thinking I'm sick. 'I mean what's he *like*!'

I have, of course, immediately caught on to exactly what she is asking but think it's funny to wind her up – what are friends for?

'Oh, I understand. What does he like? Well I don't know him that well, not all his tastes and everything but I understand that he's partial to the odd Budvar and more strangely, scotch eggs.'

'Connie!' Sense of humour failure from Daisy.

I cave in. 'OK. He's great. Really good bloke. Luke has worked on a couple of projects with him and speaks really

37

highly of him. He is single, as far as I know. He's honest, a laugh, reliable, clever.'

'Oh, he's gay.' Resigned.

'No, no he's not.' Reassuring.

'So what's the catch?' Suspicious.

'You know what? I don't think there is one. Surprising as it may sound. He's been working abroad and so hasn't wanted to get tied – settled – ' (quick change of word choice) ' – but I understand he's back in London permanently now, and up for it.'

'Up for it?' Daisy's old insecurities are never far from the surface. 'What does that mean, is he shagging around?'

'Daisy,' I say becoming exasperated, 'I don't know. I don't usually get my guests to complete a questionnaire on moral criteria and recent sexual behaviour before they attend our parties. If I did that, who would I see?'

Daisy giggles at this and relaxes for the first time in the call.

'I'm sorry, Connie. It's just that he asked me out.'

'That's good, isn't it?' Nothing I like more than being responsible for the pairing of a couple of friends. Even though, strictly speaking, I hadn't specifically brought them together and I hadn't actually noticed that they were getting along. But thinking about it now, it's obvious. It's great, they are a perfect couple.

'Yes, it is good. It's marvellous. It's bloody marvellous. I think he's wonderful. He's so clever and funny and interested and interesting. Oh, Connie, thanks for saying that he is single. Thanks for saying that he's honest, a laugh, reliable, clever. Thanks for having the party.'

She's gushing. I wait for her to thank me for getting married so that I could have an anniversary or thank someone for inventing scotch eggs so that Simon was able to grow into such a wonderful specimen. She swings back to her world-weary self.

'Up for it? Is he a tart?'

Oh, what an age we live in.

'No, really, I think he is genuinely a decent person. When I said "up for it" I meant that he was keen to find someone special. Up for commitment.'

Understandably, Daisy doesn't buy this immediately. I mean she is a single girl living in London at the close of the twentieth century.

'I hope you're right.' Tentative.

'So how can I help?' I try to move her on.

'I was ringing to ask what I should wear.'

Good solid ground this. The battle-cry for centuries of women all over the earth – 'But what should I wear?' We like this one – Sam, Daisy, Lucy, Rose and I. We've grown up with this one. And although we can rarely answer the question for ourselves we can always advise each other. Telephone companies are very grateful. A small fortune has been invested on a regular and frequent basis as we solicit advice.

'When are you seeing him?'

'Tonight.'

'Keen. Where are you meeting?'

'I'm coming into town as soon as he has finished work. Meeting him at a bar near his office.'

'Well, won't you have to wear what you've got on?'

'Err, yes, I suppose.' The hesitation in her voice fills in the background for me. I imagine her scanning the wardrobe that she has hauled into work. She'll have carried everything she owns, except her Laura Ashley dress which she bought for the twins' christening. Now she is gazing at the enormous array of clothes, thinking that nothing is suitable except the Laura Ashley.

'Where are you ringing from?'

'The staff room,' says an urgent whisper.

'Not from *the phone*?'

'Yes.'

'But it's against the rules?'

'Yes.'

'And you've brought spare clothes with you?'

'Yes.'

It is the staff break. I imagine the other teachers weaving in and out of Kookaï and French Connection, as they make their instant coffee, open their tinfoil-wrapped sandwiches and squabble over custard creams and the best seat. The older men on the staff will be tutting dismissively at Daisy, who by introducing her wardrobe to the staff room, is fulfilling every deep-seated stereotype they have of the young girls on the staff. The women will be divided; casting grim, jealous scowls or excited, conspiratorial grins. They have the sum of her. I know this is occurring as Daisy often amuses us with stories of the staff-room Parliament.

'They'll know you are hoping for a lay. Where are the clothes now? Are they hung up? If they get creased they'll be no good to anyone.'

'I've hung them all round the staff room.'

I giggle. Pleased that I've got the scene so spot on. Misjudgement. Daisy snaps.

'Stop laughing and stop being motherly, *Help me*, what should I wear?'

She's got this bad.

'Sorry, really sorry.' Even I know I didn't sound it. I try to concentrate. I know this is important to her. It's just been a while for me. I guess I've forgotten just how important.

'Well, not your Little Black Dress, you don't want to look vampy.'

'Agreed.'

We all have one. It may not be little, it may not be black, it doesn't necessarily even have to be a dress but we all have one. That cert. garment. That hundred per cent seduction approved, come-fuck-me outfit. Mine is a sheer black trouser suit, Daisy's is a classic LBD, Sam's is a long black dress with thigh-high split. Lucy's is just about every garment she owns. Come to think of it, I'm not sure if Rose does have a LBD equivalent. I make a mental note to ask her next time I see her. The seduction cert. is as easily identifiable as a teetotaller on St Patrick's day, and for this reason Daisy and I agree that it is unsuitable for a first date. OBVIOUSLY.

'What are you doing?'

'Supper.'

'Supper . . . very clever, not quite as formal as dinner but more investment than a drink. Sounds promising. You don't want to look as though you've tried too hard but you do want to look as though you are always immaculately turned out and bang up to vogue.'

'Exactly,' says Daisy who no doubt is looking at her paint-stained jeans and Sloppy Jo T-shirt, painfully aware of how far away that description is to her current sartorial state.

'Blue Jigsaw trousers, cotton V neck from Next?'

'Too school uniform, I've tried it.'

'Silky black French Connection trousers, cream, slash-neck jumper?'

'Which trousers? Silky?'

'You know the ones Lucy persuaded you to buy. Not so much silky as with a sheen . . . they make you look very leggy.'

'Do they?'

And so it goes on, until the girls from my office return from their quick one (two or three, by the look of it). They look relieved to see that I am still attached to the telephone and haven't had the opportunity to sneak to the gym. We are debating *round* versus *V* neck when Sam swings by my desk and drops off a cheese sandwich. The love.

'What is wrong with you?' I ask Daisy, exasperated because my idea of white, linen trousers and black crop-top had been rejected as 'too juvenile'. 'It's not juvenile, it's very "All Saints".'

'Exactly, and I'm closer to the age of the Archangel Gabriel. I don't know. I like him. I've got a good feeling about him. Shit, that's the bell. I've got to go to class. Give it some more thought and call me if you come up with the answer.'

'On the emergency phone?'

'Yes, it is an emergency. See ya.'

'Bye.'

I put the phone down.

'Who was it?' asks Sam.

'Daisy. She's in love.'

'Nooooooo.' Sam's eyes widen. 'Who, who, who? Tell.'

'Simon, from my party yesterday.'

'He was cute.'

'Was he? I never notice now I have Luke.'

'I am so pleased for her,' says Sam. Then her smile crumbles. 'When will I meet someone?'

Christ.

Obligatory debriefing takes place on Wednesday evening in All Bar One Covent Garden. Sam and I arrive first, after another hectic day sending rude e-mails. Rose is next, excited to be out for the night, then Daisy (tonight's special guest) and finally, Lucy, who is, as ever, fashionably late.

'Did you shag?' greets Lucy.

Fair, I think. Succinct, to the point. The others scowl at her. Unperturbed, Lucy pushes her way on to the wooden bench which is like glass it has been so worn by denim-clad bums. She lights a cigarette and shrugs.

'Oh, spare me the prudery, gals, you are all dying to know. Why else would Rose have got a babysitter? I rush away from work and you two' – she casually waves her hand in the direction of Sam and me – 'cancelled your chummy client dinners, or whatever it is you get up to?' She has a point. This is exciting stuff. Daisy has met someone ELIGIBLE.

'I didn't shag.'

'But you wanted to, didn't you?' Sam sounds alarmed. Perhaps she thinks Daisy is gay, too. Or more likely she is obsessively comparing her reactions and actions to other people's. Her incessant search for the right response.

'Well, yes, obviously. But I stopped myself.'

'Very wise,' Rose and I chorus. Neither of us believe her.

'It was a lovely evening though.'

'Go on,' we urge, pouring generous glasses of Chablis to loosen her tongue.

'We out-sat, out-talked and out-drank everyone else at the restaurant. The waiters had long since stacked the chairs on to the tables and swept the floor around us before we even thought of leaving. They were huddled in a tired, hostile group near the bar intermittently tutting at us, continually glancing at their watches. It took us ages to realize that they wanted to be rid of us. We were just chatting and laughing and time flew by. Realizing how unwelcome we were we apologetically left an over-generous tip and hurried out of the door.'

'You are so soft,' Lucy leaps in with her dollop of disapproval. She never over- or under-tips. She is never embarrassed or bullied by the waiter who hovers inappropriately after appalling service. She never stumbles out of a hotel rummaging in her purse for coins for the bell boy. She seems to have an endless supply of 'just the correct amount'. The rest of us always wildly over-tip or stubbornly refuse to leave anything at all. Both systems leave an overwhelming sense of social failure.

'Shush, Lucy,' we silence her. 'A few quid here or there isn't the point now, is it? We want her to get to the tongues bit.'

Lucy huffily sits back, but at least she stops going on about fifteen and seventeen and a half per cent and stuff.

'He was so sweet. He held my hand in public.'

We nod our approval. This usually means that they are officially single.

'We had a sort of half-plan to catch a cab so we started heading up Piccadilly. The streets were heaving with tourists

44

and locals spilling out of pubs and bars. We both kept commenting to each other how happy and fit everyone looked.'

Rose asks, 'So you thought everyone looked tanned and well-dressed and content?'

'Yes.' Daisy pounces on the idea enthusiastically. The rest of us exchange glances.

'Tell me,' asks Sam, 'would it be fair to say that although you and Simon both agreed that everyone looked happy, fit, tanned, well dressed and content etcetera none of them were glowing quite as much as the two of you?'

'Yes. That's just it!' laughs Daisy. 'Do you think it is strange?'

'No. I think it is the alcohol,' says Lucy.

'Soon we were at Regent's Park. He suggested taking a short cut.'

'That sounds a bit dodgy,' comments Rose, looking perturbed.

'Thank God. I was beginning to think we'd never get to the action,' I add.

'Well, he must have been worried that I'd think he was dodgy 'cos he started going on about how safe it was and assuring me that he often takes this short cut in summer. He said that at this time of night they would have just wrapped up *A Midsummer Night's Dream*.'

We look at her quizzically.

'You know Shakespeare.'

We look at her insulted. She rushes on justifying her lust.

'Anyway, I decided that as Simon is a friend of yours, Connie, it was unlikely that he was trying anything really odd and that, as we couldn't see an available cab anywhere, the short cut did make sense. It could have been the two bottles of white wine that we'd drunk, or the surreal situation of walking through a London park, inhabited by imps and fairies, but it was so romantic.'

We're impressed. Impressed and pleased. For all our piss-taking we adore each other. A romantic story is always good, but one with our best friends in the starring role is brill. We each relate this to our own 'romantic' experiences.

'Let's get this very clear,' I say, 'romantic with a capital R, I take it? Not the romantic felt in countless hot and sticky bars, with countless drop-dead-gorgeous men, feeding predictable but indistinguishable lines slash lies?'

'No, better than that.' Daisy shakes her head shyly.

'Not the romantic where you close your eyes willing them to get your name right so you can believe that you are different and important?' asks Sam.

'Not that,' smiles Daisy, self-satisfied.

'Not the romantic of a summer holiday fling? Deeply intense by its very brevity,' Lucy throws in.

'No.' She confidently shakes her head.

'Was it the romantic that is sort of breathtaking, rather peculiar, real romantic?' asks Rose fondly.

Daisy nods. We're mesmerized and silently down our wine.

Lucy goes to the bar for another bottle. When she comes back we are all still sitting quietly respecting Daisy's really romantic story.

'Go on,' says Lucy, grudgingly.

'Well, we'd been getting on so well in the restaurant but I seemed to have used up all my quota of witty and entertaining things. He squeezed my hand. It was sticky and I was embarrassed so I said, "It's a really hot night."'

We stare at her, amazed and disappointed, how could she have resorted to something so perfunctory? The *weather*, for God's sake. We don't say this, we don't have to.

'I don't know why I said something so inane. I was disgusted with myself, disbelieving that I could be so dull.'

'Oh, I don't know,' says Lucy. I'm not sure she's being kind. I also hope Daisy's story is going to get a little bit more exciting, I have a pension to draw when I'm sixty.

'To compensate for my unimaginative conversation starter . . .' Daisy hesitates and waits for one of us to correct her.

Sam does. 'Non-starter, more like.'

I don't think that this is what Daisy was looking for. She hurries on, aware she is losing her audience.

'I blurted out that as we were so hot we could paddle in the pond.' Daisy looks aghast just recounting the story. We all sympathize. He'll now think that she is some sort of hippie, at-one-with-the-earth type. She's lost him.

'He said that was amazing as he was going to suggest the same thing but thought that I'd think he was mad or that I'd be scared of getting arrested. Isn't that staggering?'

Yes, we're astounded.

'Well, weren't you scared of getting arrested?' asks Rose.

'Or that he was a new age traveller in disguise?' asks Sam.

Daisy smiles benignly.

'No. I just tugged at the laces of my shoes and we both waded in, bare-footed with trousers rolled up to our knees. We had sex in the fountain.'

We each take another gulp of wine.

It appears that Daisy has found her teapot.

2

The summer is unusually hot and everyone's enjoying it. It is great to see babies in prams, old people in deck-chairs in their gardens, and young people sitting in boisterous groups drinking lager, imitating our more stylish friends on the Continent. Yet it is still fair to say that we haven't quite got that *je ne sais quoi*. Two weeks of homespun sunshine a year and fifty weeks of dull, depressing British weather culminates in SED (Sun Exposure Dementia). The symptoms of SED are widespread and easily recognizable but nonetheless very disturbing. Women suffer severe colour blindness and an inability to estimate dress size, manifesting in garish ill-fitting, unsuitable clothes such as boob tubes, floral ra-ra skirts, inflatable mules, pedal pushers (only acceptable if you haven't yet had your eighth birthday party). Men also suffer from SED, they confuse where items of clothing should be worn: handkerchiefs on heads, socks under sandals and the entire removal of T-shirts (not recommended, unless you've ever appeared on *Gladiators*). It isn't as though we cultivate acres of toned, bronzed, cellulite-free limbs, like those widely available in Europe. We Brits are a mass of barber-pole appendages.

Even accepting these sartorial *faux pas* as an integral part of the British summer and balancing the fact that we are really rather stylish in the winter, I still prefer the summer. Exceptionally, this year, we've had good weather since June and so we are beginning to adapt. Most of us have got past the barber-pole stage and although not exactly sporting an deep, even tan, exposed flesh has moved from white to beige, or at least from blue to white. Sandal-blistered feet have progressed from plaster-bearing softies to hard-skinned pros. The majority of us have forced ourselves through the doors of a gym, and although not quite Greek gods and goddesses, we are generally less flabby. By August we've exiled fuchsia pink, got the hang of white and beige, and reintroduced the temporarily banned black. All in all, a walk in Covent Garden is less of an assault on the senses than it was in June.

The consistently good weather has encouraged us to chance our luck, and we plan a Sunday lunch picnic. Promptly at 12.30, Luke, Sam and I stand at the gates of Hyde Park, waiting for the others. We watch little girls eating ice-creams playing shop and mummies and partners while little boys spit Coke from between the gap in their teeth, showering others with killing accuracy. Fat old ladies gather on park benches. Too fat to close their sweaty legs, they sit akimbo and unashamed, chuckling at dogs chasing their tails. Students, free from the horrors of revision and exams, play with Frisbees on the burnt grass or learn to roller-blade. Daisy and Simon arrive, holding hands and gazing at each other. Sam makes a face and pretends to throw up. I just grin. I'm with Luke so I can't be too childish. Their goo-goo eyes make me feel sloppy so I reach up to ruffle Luke's hair. He looks a bit surprised but grins and kisses the top of my head affectionately. At 1.20 Sam points over the road, at Peter, Rose, Lucy and the boys.

'There they are, at last.' From the moment we spot them we understand why they are late. Sam, Luke and I have one bag between us. It contains the things that we picked up from the deli on the way here. Crusty loaf, couscous with Mediterranean vegetables, an assortment of cheeses, black and green olives dripping in oil, a two-litre bottle of mineral water and a couple of bottles of chilled wine. We've also brought a travel rug and at Luke's insistence, his Frisbee. Daisy and Simon have brought a similar-sized bag, which will be full of similar goodies. Lucy is carrying a brown-paper bag, which by the look of it contains four bottles of champagne. She doesn't bother with food in summer. By contrast, Rose and Peter are carrying the volume of luggage expected for a two-week holiday. Admittedly they are carrying a baby apiece but they also have at least three other large bags each. It's obvious to us, their friends, that they are rowing. Lucy walks in front of them both, grinning and rolling her eyes. We all use this gesture to signal a domestic alert. Peter, red in the face and perspiring, strides ahead of Rose, trying to keep pace with Lucy.

The sun's almost directly overhead, it pours on to our eyelids and pricks our skin, making us uncomfortably hot; I can't wait to stretch out and sunbathe. Peter's red face is partly to do with the heat and the weight of his bags but I also recognize the sweating of pure fury. He is carrying Henry and inadvertently bouncing him up and down, rather too energetically. Henry looks a bit travel sick; although only eight months old, he has a built-in device that tells him that there is little point in drawing attention to his discomfort. Rose isn't looking angry and heated, she's tearful and heated.

She's carrying a wailing Sebastian, who obviously isn't quite as sensitive as Henry to the social acceptability of bawling his head off. She struggles along the path trying to avoid kids on roller-blades and people walking dogs. The gap between Rose and Peter widens as he allows her to struggle with the baby-equipment bags, picnic bags and the crying child.

I have *this* to look forward to?

Luke hands me our picnic bag and runs to meet Rose. He says hi to Lucy and nods curtly to Peter; he is obviously displeased that Peter is allowing his wife to struggle alone. Rose doesn't know what she's done wrong. She remembers that when they first met Peter was attracted to her motherly ways. He was always going on and on about her huge bosom and medicine cabinet. The reality has proven to be light years from the fantasy, Peter only just hides his disgust at Rose's leaking breasts and irritation that he's sharing her attention with the twins. I proudly watch Luke. His face breaks into an extraordinary smile for Sebastian and Rose. He soothes and smoothes the situation. He relieves Rose of her encumbrances and chats animatedly to her, telling her that her dress looks nice, that we've only been waiting two or three minutes ourselves. By the time they are at the gate Rose is laughing and looking a lot more relaxed. Even Peter looks calmer, more at ease. There are greeting kisses and hugs all round.

'There's so much to think about when we bring the boys,' offers Rose. We all nod and say it doesn't matter. Secretly, we girls are all in awe of Rose for producing not just one child but two, the way they do in films. Not only producing them but continuing to nurture them and even to bring them out, instead of making them stay at home for the first twenty years of their lives, which must be tempting.

'Especially when you change their clothes three times before leaving home,' snaps Peter. We hurriedly talk about other things – where we should sit and whether or not everyone is ready to eat.

'I'm afraid they'll burn. It's hard to find something for them to wear that is at once cool and protective,' comments Rose sensibly, not prepared to let Peter get away with criticizing her. Peter scowls.

Lucy adds, 'She's right, Peter, the boys do both have a touch of Rose's red hair; they are so very fair skinned, you can't be too careful.'

Rose looks grateful for the defence. I'd be furious with Lucy for alluding to the fact that the boys have red hair, an issue we studiously avoid. I shoot Rose a sympathetic smile but she's too practical to let Peter's sulking bother her, she's moved on to matters of greater importance – wondering if the twins' bottles are in danger of overheating.

Extensive debate ensues. Where is the perfect picnic spot? We trek the whole of Hyde Park and eventually settle. We need shade for Rose, Daisy and the boys, but Sam and I are ignoring the government health warnings and want sun. We need to be near the roller-blade path (Lucy's request, although I'm not sure if this is because she is going to have a go, or whether she wants to ogle men's bums). We need a big space so that we can play Frisbee (Luke, Simon, Sam), but not too near noisy children (everyone but Rose). We can't be too close to quiet couples, in case the twins cry disruptively (Rose), and not too near a bin (me). We can't be too far from the ice-cream van (all the girls), or too near the loos (all the girls). After UN-style negotiations we finally find somewhere that pleases us all. Well, actually, Lucy says she isn't going to move another step and through fear of her temper we capitulate. Excitedly, we spread out the picnic rugs and food. It looks brilliant, just like one of those glossy spreads in a style magazine.

Despite summer sartorial elegance being a complete anathema to most Brits my friends know how important these things are. Daisy is radiant. She has that glow which cannot be obtained by anything other than great loving with a new man. She is wearing a lilac Elspeth Gibson lace dress, which she bought for a wedding last May. It's far too expensive to wear lolling around in Hyde Park, unless of course you are in that first flush of a new romance and want to look both seductive and feminine. She's pulled it off. Her hair is tousled and while she's only wearing a spot of lip gloss she has on a ton of eyeliner and mascara. She's obtained that smudgy, dishevelled look that says *fuck me and love me*. I look at Simon; it's working. I'm faintly uncomfortable when I catch them gazing at each other. They seem so wrapped up in one another that I feel I'm intruding. Sam gazes on wistfully. Poor Sam. Luke and I are beyond that nauseating touchy, sexy, can't-keep-my-hands-off-you stage. We've had that and now we enjoy a more permanent and settled affection, but Sam is still teapot hunting.

Sam is wearing the singleton's summer uniform: a white strappy T-shirt, from DKNY (cost a fortune, designed to look as though it's just 'an old thing'), a black Richard Tyler skirt, short, very, and a baseball cap, which of course is worn back to front. She looks like a waitress; this isn't a criticism, this is the look she wants. She's single, she shaves. Her legs are silky smooth and brown. She doesn't sit still for even five consecutive minutes; she's still proving that she's a good sport, a great hostess, a potential mum. No one is looking because Peter, Simon and Luke wouldn't dare look at another woman while Rose, Daisy and I are around. Sam isn't actively trying to attract our blokes, on the other hand, they are men and her entire being is validated through male praise. So when Luke says, 'Wow what a hit, you are really good at sport', Sam nearly wets herself with pleasure. I'd hate to be Sam, always having to try, even on a Sunday afternoon. Try to be the funniest, try to be the most well informed, try to be the most attractive. I'm grateful that all I have do is try to get a sun-tan. I smile warmly at Luke. He has no idea what I'm thinking but plants a kiss on my cheek anyway.

Lucy's wearing huge Armani sunglasses and white jeans, white T-shirt, and white mules. She looks immaculate and manages to stay immaculate all day, despite playing baseball, holding Henry, and eating a picnic. I'm wearing a black version of Lucy's outfit (although for certain I'll go home looking as though I've been dragged through a rabbit burrow sideways). Rose is wearing a practical but pretty, floaty, navy dress. She always wears dark, shapeless clothes to hide her body; which hasn't seen the benefit of an aerobic session or the inside of a beautician's for a couple of years. The guys are wearing guy stuff, canvas khaki shorts and T-shirts. The only variation is that Luke and Simon are wearing tight T-shirts and Peter's is baggier. I guess it isn't just Rose that can't find the time to get to a gym.

The food, alcohol and, most excitingly, conversation flows and the afternoon is blissful. We chat about our families, our jobs, our bosses, our gardens. It's a really easy afternoon. One where everyone gets on with everyone else. We naturally break into conversational groups (well, in Simon and Daisy's case there is plenty of tongue activity but not much articulation). Once we are finally able to wrench them apart, we naturally dissolve the original groups and regroup with someone new. It is all so perfect and comfortable. Simon and Luke discuss the things that boys do discuss when they know each other really well – sport and cars. Any occasional lull and they are able to fall back on telling a joke. Boy intimacy. Lucy talks work with Peter. Occasionally someone will walk over to them to refill their glasses and urge them to quit talking shop.

'Well, each to their own,' says Daisy as she comes back from offering another tapenade and salami roll. 'Lucy is so bloke-like in her ambition.'

We shake our heads, pitying her that amazing sense of achievement that she often describes when she clinches a great deal or gets a huge profit-related bonus, pitying her that quarter of a million salary and her enormous apartment in Soho.

The rest of us girls settle down for gossipy, chatty, truly intimate conversation. We never have any other sort.

Sam updates us on who she is currently snogging. Although technically single, she doesn't go without sex. She is in a sort of fairly inadequate way seeing two men at the moment. This sounds very glamorous but is depressing. Sam doesn't want to sleep with two men. She doesn't really want sex with anyone. She wants to make love, in an ongoing and mono-gamous style. Every week she goes to some club or other and meets some man or other. She is always hoping for commitment and he is always hoping for carnal knowledge. These aren't necessarily mutually exclusive goals, but they tend to be if the carnal knowledge comes first. It usually does with Sam, who is too terrified of looking like a killjoy to say no to sex. Last time we met at All Bar One, we'd devoted much of the evening to comparing and contrasting Dave and Mike. None of us had much enthusiasm for this particular game because none of us had much enthusiasm for either bloke. Including Sam, who says, 'The thing is, I'm a firm believer in a bird in the hand is worth two in the bush.'

Dave – handsome rugger bugger. Not that clever, funny or interesting, but does have good forearms (!). Met at a pseudo-student party, compulsory snogging. Two slow dances, asked her back to his flat, he had no money to pay cab. Sam uses cab ride to consider whether she should sleep with Dave or not. Would she look too easy? Would he still respect her in the morning? Rose supplies the answers: 'Yes and no in that order.' The question is academic. Dave suffers from barman's droop. Sam suggests he is a gentleman and sweetly old-fashioned (?). Does manage to perform next morning.

Mike – handsome banker wanker. Not clever, funny or interesting; still, he has a good job and nice skin. Met at a friend's dinner party. Only male, single guest. Enormous pressure, as other guests hope for public discussion on family planning or whether they should set up home in West London or North. Only variation on Dave's story is sex happens at her place.

Her stories sadden me. I am so grateful that I have Luke.

'I don't think I care if either of them call me again.'

We don't care either but it isn't very friendly to say so.

'Really?' asks Daisy.

'Really,' Sam confirms. 'The sex is fun but I don't think either of them are special so I think I'll just accept them for what they were – good sex.'

We nod our agreement, then fall silent and think about Sam's comment. There is something very exciting about a one-off sexual encounter. I remember. Of course they are invariably only successful if you really can stand up and walk away. Like Sam, I'd never quite pulled that off. I've always had a hard time separating sex from love. I've known plenty of men who say 'I love you' meaning 'I want to fuck your brains out.' And the women I know are more likely to say 'I want to fuck you' meaning 'I want you to love me.' I have no idea why it's this way, I didn't make the rules.

'I'm hot,' whines Sam. She does not mean hot, sexy-hard-body-stunning babe, she means hot, sweaty-thighs-sticking-together.

'I wish Richard Gere would just sidle up to me, with an ice cube in his mouth and melt it on my thighs. Slowly, very slowly,' she sighs. This is one of our favourite games. Erotic fantasy with unobtainable, unreal man.

'Or Antonio Banderas would appear from nowhere, with a bottle of sun oil,' adds Daisy.

'Exactly what would he do with the sun-oil bottle?' I ask. We giggle and then we go quiet again. We're thinking about it.

'Or George Clooney would turn up with a wicker fan to fan me.'

Rose's casting is commendable but her script is diabolical.

'But it never happens, does it?' I sigh, suddenly and inexplicably fed up. Why am I irritated? It's a beautiful day, I'm with my lovely friends, my wonderful husband and we are replete with delicious food and drunk with champagne. Yet I am . . . I don't know . . . I look around and see passionate couples kissing and lolling. It makes me feel . . . I don't know.

'Life isn't sexy men rubbing sun oil into your back, let alone thighs,' I grumble.

Sam stares at me, her saucer eyes expanding to dinner plates.

'Yours is,' she says in disbelief. 'Your life is a fairy-tale; you live in romantic bliss, highly developed, mature perfection.'

'I'm not talking about fairy-tales, I'm talking soap porn,' I mutter.

'Ungrateful bitch.'

I can't refute this, especially when she so eloquently argued her case. My life is a fairy-tale. I'm married to not quite a knight in shining armour, but a very pleasant architect in Levi 501s. We live, not in a castle with turrets, but a comfortable home in Clapham. Here I am in the middle of Happily Ever After. My life is lovely. I am very lucky. It's wedded bliss and really it is great, just great.

'You need a holiday,' says Daisy.

That's it. I nod my agreement.

'Yes, but it's unlikely with Luke being so busy. I don't quite understand why hot weather makes people want to build houses. I suppose we might get away in late autumn or perhaps go skiing in the winter.'

The solution isn't immediate enough for me.

'What are you talking about?' asks Lucy, as she walks over to refill her and Peter's glasses.

'Connie is bored,' says Sam.

'Not bored,' I correct. Bored seems too harsh. 'More I don't know . . .'

'Spoilt?' offers Lucy.

'Restless,' I finish.

'You need to take up a sport,' says Sam. I look at her, horrified.

'You need to shop,' says Daisy. This is a thought.

'You need to procreate,' says Rose. This is ridiculous.

'You could have an affair,' says Lucy. We all laugh. Her suggestion is horrifying and ridiculous. We laugh for a very long time. I mean it really is funny. Me, have an affair? Me? I have Luke and I'm so glad to be off the merry-go-round of the dating game. Lucy really makes me laugh.

'I know what you have to look forward to,' offers Sam. She sounds as excited as a five-year-old at a pantomime. I can't help but be infected.

'What?'

'We are going to Paris in September for the management conference. The official launching of Peterson Windlooper. It's only three weeks.' I vaguely remember reading some e-mail about this. Sam continues, 'Paris in autumn. It will be so romantic.' Her search for romance gives her a sense of purpose.

'There,' comforts Daisy, 'a conference, that's like a holiday.' Daisy is a teacher and has no idea about corporate life. Even so, it's a fairly accurate summation. 'Paris is a great place to shop.'

'And have an affair,' laughs Lucy as she sidles back to Peter to continue their debate on the introduction of the Euro.

Rose watches them. She's very quiet. I wonder if she ever misses the corporate life that she led before the twins were born. She had been really into her job. Which I find inexplicable, especially as she was an accountant. I watch her as she kisses Sebastian's head; she radiates pure love. Yes, she probably does miss it occasionally, but on balance she's made the right choice. For her.

'Peter is also working ridiculous hours at the moment,' she sighs.

I pick up Henry and cuddle him. Purring and humming in that stupid way that everyone does when they pick up babies. None of us quite know how to act in the face of a miracle.

'Still, you've got Sebastian and Henry to keep you company.' I nuzzle his stomach and smell his lovely skin. I look at Rose; she looks tired. She glances in Peter's direction to check that he can't hear her. He can't, he's arguing with Lucy, some point about the share index no doubt. He's making his point in an incredibly animated way.

'I'm not sure if that's the problem.' She circles the issue, trying to find a way to say what is on her mind without being disloyal to Peter. I understand. Once you're married it isn't as easy to share *everything* with your friends. Early on in my marriage I once made the mistake of whining to Daisy and Lucy that Luke was being selfish about something or other. I can't even remember what now. I really regretted it. Not that they tackled Luke and told him that he was a cruel barbarian undeserving of their friend. It was just that the next week, when Luke and I were all lovey-dovey again and I'd forgotten that he was a rotten bastard who could wash his own bloody socks, Daisy asked me if everything was all right.

And it was the tone.

That sympathetic, probing tone that I'd always loved suddenly seemed impertinent. Was she hoping that I didn't have a perfect marriage? Was she feeling sorry for me? Horror of horrors. Was she in some way suggesting that I'd picked the wrong man? Of course I know she wasn't. Daisy isn't like that but I wasn't comfortable. Since then I've always been really careful never, ever to moan about Luke. I prefer the girls to think everything is just brilliant, which largely it is. So I understand Rose's reticence in criticizing Peter.

'Go on,' says Sam. She's just so amiable, soothing and clement that is almost impossible not to respond.

'Well, since the boys were born,' Rose hesitates, 'he seems to prefer to be at work than at home. At work, or fishing, or at the gym. Anywhere other than with them . . . with us.' No one answers her because we've noticed this too. When Rose isn't with us we discuss *at length* what a selfish bastard he is, and the fact that he doesn't do his share with the boys, and that Rose is looking tired. We just hadn't realized that Rose felt the same.

'He's working hard for you and the boys,' argues Sam.

Sam doesn't think Peter is wrong to work long hours. She thinks they should be out hunting dinosaurs. But then Sam isn't married. In fact her longest relationship is a couple of months. She's never got to the tedious stage of eating alone and putting their dinner in the fridge, channel-hopping in the knowledge that nothing will interest, watching the hands of the clock drag round to after eleven and thinking that there must be something wrong with the clock battery. She doesn't understand the frustration of your husband arriving home too frazzled to string a sentence together, ignoring his reheated dinner and collapsing into bed without even so much as a peck on the cheek. I do, however, understand.

'He works very hard.'

'I know. I know,' replies Rose, instantly guilty, and then quietly she adds, 'but I work hard, too. Sometimes I wish he'd help out a bit more.'

We fall silent. Although usually we have a macabre interest in each other's misery (in the nicest possible way) it is too sunny for a serious debate on the deconstruction of utopia – married bliss. Henry begins to cry. We're grateful for the diversion.

'His nappy needs changing,' says Rose, already standing up to take care of him.

Following on from the conversation with her sister, Daisy obviously wants to be reassured about the 'Happily Ever After' so demands, 'Tell us about Luke proposing.'

'You've heard it all before,' I say with a laugh.

'I know, I know, but we like hearing it,' Sam and Daisy chorus, '*pleeeeeeease.*'

'You are insatiable romantics,' I tease, but I'm delighted and tell them anyway.

'Well, we are walking in the West Highlands.'

'What are you wearing?' asks Sam.

'Err, hiking boots, naturally.'

'Oh yeah, of course.' She looks embarrassed.

'And, surprisingly, we'd been really lucky with the weather. Perfect walking weather. Bright, dry, fresh days. Aqua sky, sun warm enough to wear shorts.' Luke has great legs, big and covered in blond hairs, quite Australian looking. 'Our plan was to walk from Loch Lomond to Fort William – '

'Well, when you say "our plan",' interrupts Daisy.

'Good point. It was Luke's plan and I was really doubtful that I'd be able to do it.'

'But of course you couldn't say as much,' says Sam excitedly. They know this story as well as I do. Like children they need to hear their fairy-tales being told the same way every time they hear it. I magnanimously concede to their enjoyment. Their grisly interest is because they use my story to perfect the details of their own proposals. It is a game that we all play; or at least, I used to play it but obviously can't any more. Every time there is a new bloke we imagine how he will propose, what the wedding will be like, which qualities our children will inherit from him. This game is more common than Monopoly and if it could be boxed up a games manufacturer would make a fortune. The details of the dress, the ring, the wedding speech vary, but the nub of the plans stay the same, i.e., loved-to-death bride takes centre stage.

'My ankle was really playing up. Huge, blue.' I'm laying this on pretty thick. 'But I couldn't complain. I wanted to be perfect for him.' They nod. They understand it's elementary.

'You are in agony,' Sam says. The word agony is said as though I'd just endured a six-week session on the rack in the Tower of London. The essential element of this game is that the heroine (me) really suffers, so that in the end when she gets what she deserves (in this case Luke) we can feel good for her. This isn't because the girls are the milk of human kindness, they are imagining their own sufferings. When they imagine my success, they are really imagining their own. I love being the centre of their adoration and interest. Luke interrupts the scene and gives us each a Cornetto. He grins knowingly as he hears what we are talking about and disappears back to Simon. Possibly to warn him.

'Go on. So eventually you have to take off your boot,' urges Sam.

'And Luke sees your foot. He is extremely worried, so worried that he had tears in his eyes.'

'*Shhhhhhh* Daisy.' I'm nervous that Luke will hear her. Not because I have embellished this part of the story, I haven't, there had been tears of concern in his eyes when he'd seen my big, blue, swollen ankle. But if he finds out that I've told the girls he'll be mortified.

'And he said?'

So I tell.

I tell them how he'd asked me if I thought he was capable of looking after me and I'd laughed, confirming that no one was better qualified. And although I pretended that I didn't know what was coming, I did. But at the same time I didn't. I didn't dare assume. Because it was the most scary, exciting, wonderful, horrifying moment of my life. I was hoping against hope that he was going to ask me. And my hope was combined with reason, to the extent that I was nudging towards knowing, but it was still the most scary, exciting, wonderful, horrifying moment of my life.

'So then he said that he would be honoured if I'd let him love me and cherish me for the rest of my life.' The girls smile at each other, like you do when you are six and your mum tells you that Cinderella's shoe fits. All gooey and marshmallowy.

'And then he produced the ring.' We all admire my ring again, as though this is the first time, not the millionth time, we've admired it. It has three diamonds in a row, all the same size.

'And tell us about how he chose the ring.'

'He told me that he had looked at hundreds of stones, marquises, squares, ovals, triplets. Then the assistant pointed out these stones which are called "round brilliant". He'd instantly known that this was the ring.'

'What is it that he said?' asks Sam. But I don't need to be embarrassed, they know the routine. Daisy rushes to fill in the details.

'He thinks that she is absolutely brilliant, sparkling, clever, exuberant, shiny, bright, all rushed together.'

'Like a diamond.'

They sigh.

3

I meet Sam at Waterloo. My only concern is negotiating the crowds in WH Smith and the channel tunnel. The station is heaving with people who, I assume, spend their days performing heroic acts; cures for deadly diseases; feeding starving children – as their rude pushing and jostling can't be motivated by a desire to get to the office to transport parchment. I am trying to balance three glossy magazines, a family-size bar of Galaxy, an overnight case and my laptop, when Sam says, 'That John Harding will be there, you know.'

It takes me some seconds to place him. As soon as I acknowledge him in my mind, I acknowledge him in my knickers too. A small dizzy sensation. It reminds me of swimming in the Indian Ocean, my feet being nibbled by fish, at once tingling, exciting and uncomfortable. John Harding is a horn. An utter tart. Irresistibly so. I'd met him, briefly, at a conference last April.

'He fancies you.'

'No, he doesn't. Not especially. He fancies everyone.'

'He really fancies you. You lucky bitch. Why you? You are happily married, you don't need another man.' Sam sighs, 'It seems it's only ever married women who are inundated with new and intriguing offers.'

'Men cannot quell the innate competitive instinct, it's

something to do with hunter-gatherer times. A wedding ring is the biggest universal turn-on since stockings.'

Sam laughs. 'Maybe. But you have blossomed, marriage suits you. You have that glow that I am so sick of seeing on other happily paired-off women.'

'In that case Luke got a bargain.'

We giggle at my vanity. Sam forgives me as she is aware that it is often counterbalanced by a really healthy dose of insecurity. To take me down a peg or two, she adds, 'It is *odd* that so many men come forward trying, with more or less vigour, to knock you out of your ivory tower.'

'Not that odd,' I defend, 'anyway, I always just laugh at them.'

'You didn't laugh at John Harding from Peterson Wind.' His name causes a sensation in my M&S briefs again, a six-week puppy on acid.

'They bore me. They are so faulty.'

'John didn't bore you. You seemed fascinated.'

'It was a bit of harmless flirting.' I try to steer Sam towards the escalator and away from the subject.

'Didn't he send you an e-mail to follow up after you first met him?'

'Did he? I can't remember.'

'Yes. He did. I'm sure.'

'I deleted it.'

'So he did send you one?'

'Shut up, Sam.' I nearly drop my *Vogue* as I bluster, 'I doubt I'll see him, there are a thousand delegates attending this conference.'

He is the first person I see.

I stumble upon him accidentally, as I am dashing through the crowds – huge, boisterous, stylish crowds, comparable to those at the Harrods sale. Having spotted Sue at a distance I am excitedly pushing my way through the pounding press. My childish glee at seeing my friend is blighted as I bump into his blue eyes. He blinks and I shudder as his eyelashes brush and lick my entire body. Earth calling Connie. Come in, Connie. Are you responding? Too damn right I am. Standing there in front of his stunning, neat, slim, defined body. The long, pale eyelashes gently resting on his high and graceful cheek-bones, it all comes rushing back to me. I remember that he has freckles, which I adore. Odd. I wouldn't have freckles up there on my list of 'must have on perfect male specimen'.

He is nervous and confident all at once.

The ball is in my court. Hadn't I left him at the bar in Blackpool? Hadn't I ignored his e-mail? On the other hand he is tremendously vain. Twenty-nine years of being adored and roughly fifteen being totally irresistible do encourage a certain confidence. He has a chiselled intensity that epitomizes a certain type of northern man; working class and noble all at once. I cannot imagine his skin in hot weather. He looks as though he will only be at home in a chilly, bitter environment, gamely running around a football pitch, or enthusiastically jumping up and down on the spot waiting for a pub to open; occupying his hands by clapping them together, rubbing forcefully or lighting a cigarette. He is raw and rough. He is the man that D. H. Lawrence had in mind every time he penned a hero. Imagine the filthiest, sexiest man you've ever seen. The man in the lift who undressed you with his eyes. The stranger in the street who held your gaze and left you feeling creamy. That deeply unsuitable and unscrupulous stranger is John Harding.

John blushes.

'I'd never have come over here if I'd known you were here.' Certainly not the coolest opening gambit I've ever used. In fact it's right up there with 'you're not as ugly as I expected you to be', once used on meeting one of Sam's boyfriends (her fault for describing him as having an outstanding personality). John blushes again. I am delighted that I disturb him enough to make him blush but I am confused by my illegal exhilaration. I immediately turn on my heel and violently speed my way back through the throng to my seat.

The conference room is like the dozens of other conference rooms I've endured in the past. It is a shame that such a beautiful room, designed for dancing and chatting, has been sold into conference-venue whoredom. Lattice chandeliers and white tablecloths look incongruous with the high-tech spotlights and speakers. Luxurious chairs and plush carpets fight ferociously with the suits, laptops and business vocab. The air-conditioning hums incessantly, interrupted by the odd cough or clink of glassware as delegates pour glass after glass of water. A couple of delegates sleep, heads on the desk, generating small pools of dribble from the corner of their mouths, one wakes up oblivious to the plastic Bic pen stuck to his head. Meaningless words float in and out of my consciousness: 'creating greater momentum', 'consulting firm of the future', 'integrated market offerings for optimal servicing'. What are they on about? My entire body, mind, being, concentrates on the fact that he is there in the same room as me. I scan the faces that wave and wash in front of me. They sit suited and booted, one indistinguishable mass. Management consultancies have quite a strict sense of what their employees should look like. Although it is not stated in any policy book, the style is so distinctive and the desire to belong so dire that a natural uniform develops. All the guys wear their hair short – no beards or moustaches – with white shirts and dark suits. On the surface he is just the same but somehow he radiates difference. I gaze from row to row, scanning, dismissing, until my eyes relax on where he sits. He shines, he glows. Dizzy with illusion. This time I fear not my ability but my desire to run away from him again.

The newly merged Peterson Windlooper flexes its muscles with a horribly demanding timetable. The conference finally comes to a close at 7.15 p.m., fifteen minutes before the beginning of the evening reception. I hurriedly throw my pencils and leather Filofax back into my bag and rush back to my hotel room. Personal hygiene or personal style? Fifteen minutes is hardly enough time to get showered, choose something to wear and reapply make-up. I opt for a shower as I am particularly and rather unnaturally sticky. In fact I'm Tigger at a rave. My head is spinning, I can't think! I won't be able to eat! I am sure of that already. I can barely breathe! I am thinking in exclamation marks. I'm in trouble.

Hurriedly, I scrunch my hair, teasing it into trendy spikes, rather than submitting to my galling curls. I pull on a clean white T-shirt and then put back on my business suit that I've worn all day. The suit makes me look leggy and more importantly, by wearing what I've worn that day, I achieve the casual, not having tried too hard look. I'm hoping to impress him. Which makes me shiver. Of course this is dangerous, of course I can't resist.

The assembly room is heaving. I recognize the corporate cocktail for disaster – copious amounts of alcohol and ambition. Rather than standing on the sidelines, deriving pleasure by laughing at the antics of my desperate colleagues, I am pulled to the apex. I pick up a glass of champagne from a passing waiter's tray, drink it very quickly and put down the empty glass, then immediately help myself to another. Sam watches me fearfully.

'You look gorgeous.'

She ignores my blatant attempt at diversionary flattery. Her huge eyes widen further as she nods questioningly towards the champagne.

'I just need a drink,' I shrug a bit huffily. I don't really want a baby-sitter. Sam, a divine friend, laughs indulgently but gently warns, 'Be careful Connie.'

'Yes. I know,' I reply. 'Look, if I appear to be in danger of doing something stupid, not looking after myself adequately, will you come and look after me?'

'Promise,' she affirms. I'm lost. If I'd wanted to resist I wouldn't have had to ask for Sam's help. Although on the surface I'm putting checks in place to stop me charging towards corruption, I know I can outmanoeuvre Sam if necessary. I want to create the impression of a respectable struggle with my conscience, but in my heart and head I know that there won't be a struggle.

Respectable or otherwise.

I know this because I always make snap decisions, whether it is about entrées or husbands.

I choose to sit with Sam, although Sue is sitting with John. I could have sat with Sue (John) except that I am holding off. This is nothing to do with hesitation, more anticipation. I know that if I hold back for a while he'll want me more. I've often acted the total bitch to increase ardour.

The evening rushes by, a series of Technicolor images and vivid, pungent smells: expensive perfume mixes sweetly with perspiring bodies, the smell of lamb gravy and Colman's mint sauce is tinged with the taste of metallic mass-catering trays. The noise around me is deafening; hilarity and excitement bump against indiscriminate wanting and general anticipation. Packing a passport has inexplicably led to scenes of gross debauchery. Women, who usually limit themselves to the odd G&T, are suddenly chasing shots better than George Best, and challenging each other to arm-wrestling competitions. Quite unassuming colleagues feel compelled to do the cancan on table-tops. The national anthem is burped out in baritone by people wearing party hats. All standards have flown out of the window. Chatter, constant chatter, buzzes and rushes around the room, accompanied by the dull thud of plates dropping on to white tablecloths, the clink of bottles hitting the rim of glasses, knives and forks clattering against teeth and china, and the pop of corks bursting forth. People strain and shout, desperate to deliver their punch-lines. Laughter, raucous and disproportionate, bounces around the tables. The laughter of successful escapees. No longer restrained by the formal, polite, small talk of strangers, or even the friendly cordiality of colleagues, the room oozes unrestrained, unashamed riotousness.

We are, in every sense, up for it.

The champagne kicks the back of my throat, a cold, unquenchable, and addictive dryness. A thousand, billion bubbles dance excitedly on my gums.

'No more champagne,' I complain to Sam, as I drain the last bottle on our table. She hands me the white wine. A second later the white is finished, too, so we move on to red. I fake interest in the conversation at my table. Although the banter is high quality and well delivered and my retorts are as racy and pacy as ever, I am only devoting a proportion of my attention. My neck is longer and my body thinner, my skin clears to a creamy fondant, the alcohol makes me blush, so I am a strawberry fondant. I lean forward, elbows on the table, fingers linked to cradle my chin. Uncomfortable but flattering. I remove my jacket. Too hot. Too many horny bodies in a small place. My arms are bronzed and toned. I am attractive. This incredible metamorphosis does not draw my attention away from him.

'Stop it.' Sam kicks me under the table.

'Stop what?'

'That blatant craning.'

Embarrassed, I try to look away but it is hard. I am conscious of him in the pure sense of the word. I know when he is sitting, when he is standing, when he is drinking, or eating or looking at me. I know when he is laughing or flirting and I know that he is always wanting. Me. A number of times my indiscreet staring is rewarded by my gaze resting on his glare. It soothes me to know he is looking at me. It soothes me to know that he is there at all. Somewhere here in my world. I don't know why it soothes me and I am too drunk to consider it. He is a totally delicious horn. I'm lusting after him. People always rush to say that they have never felt like this before and I always view such claims with scepticism. That insistent clambering to justify through differentiation. God how normal.

Having said that, I am sure I have never felt like this before.

I studiously avoid him, while constantly hunting him. Never quite with him, I am careful to remain in his eye view. He can't avoid me but he can't have me. The room degenerates into a more riotous state. The jokes and wine flow copiously. When nearly everyone is bouncing from table to table, flirting, antagonizing or socializing, I go to him. He sits alone with coffee cups and chocolate mints, discarded corks and dozens of half-empty wine glasses. I know he is very sociable and wonder if hanging back from other company is a sign that he is waiting for me. No false modesty, I sit next to him. He lights a cigarette and passes it to me and then lights another one for himself. I haven't smoked since I was eleven, in a friend's tree house, but I immediately take the cigarette from him and inhale. It hardly seems the right moment to tell him about the dangers of lung cancer.

'It's inevitable, you know,' he asserts. The pounding in my cunt and the dryness of my throat forces me to admit that he is probably right. I am frighteningly alive and awake.

'No, no, it's not inevitable,' I stutter. 'It's not. It's not,' I reiterate, without conviction.

'It's strange that you keep telling me you don't want me, but by talking to me at all you are saying that you do.' He laughs to himself. 'The lady doth protest too much.'

He sounds like a man who is certain that he holds the upper hand. I stand up and bump into the table.

'Whoops, one too many,' he comments, grinning. We both know that, as he is hoping for a shag, there is no such thing. I make my way back to my seat. Playing a game, wondering not *if* but *when* he'll approach.

My head is cartooning.

I nudge my dessert around my plate but somehow repeatedly fail to get the fork into my mouth.

'Lost your appetite?' Sam's eyes flash concern. 'Easy, slowly. You are flirting outrageously.'

'Do you think so? I think I'm doing it rather well,' I quip.

'You're married,' she states with what I consider to be unnecessary honesty. I glare at her. She tries again. 'Look, flirting is all right as long as you know how far to take it, when to stop. To draw the line.' I smile, wiggling in my seat. I know what is coming to me and I squirm. I thank God that it is!

'I think I'll have one more.' Sam tries to pour some red wine into her glass but misses. 'Shit.' She pours salt on to the tablecloth creating little mountains in the red sea.

'Not for me,' I say, as I pour myself another, 'I've had enough.' We giggle.

'You've had more than enough, you've drunk loads.'

'So has everyone else,' I defend.

Although it is only 10.30 p.m. getting glass to mouth, without spilling the contents, has become a major challenge for my motor skills. The waiters are trying to clear up around us and the management are encouraging us to stop drinking, so that we will turn up at the conference the next day. However their refusal to pay for any more wine is counter-productive.

The majority of us wander through to the hotel bar where the drinks are frighteningly expensive; our intention is putting them through as 'expenses incurred during mentoring'. Suddenly, amongst the confusion, he is next to me. He puts his right hand on my head, turns my head to face him, kisses me. There in front of everybody.

Warm, full lips; that pulse.

I burp back the champagne and it fizzes round my mouth, the bubbles and air are like the sperm of an unexpected blow-job, astonishingly intimate. The kiss is lingering but still. Certainly not a kiss exchanged between two friends, more than that. It silences the crowd. The women furious with envy that John has chosen to kiss me, the men grudgingly admiring as they see that I kiss him back. I look for Sam; she's not around. His lips are soft and firm at the same time. Kissing him is so different. Different from Luke, I suppose.

It's a good kiss, full of promise and intent.

'I'm going to ditch this dump.' He rolls his eyes disparagingly in the direction of the hotel bar. It usually irritates me when someone suggests moving venue. I am generally three sheets to the wind by the time the idea is mooted and much keener to stay put. A move always culminates in a bar with even more artificial pot plants, even more cheesy music and more expensive alcohol. But the grass is always greener. However, when John says this I think it is the best idea I have ever heard, ever.

Brilliant.

Astounding.

Sam's decided to call it a night but Sue is amongst the

fifteen or so that are going into the centre of Paris to find a 'decent bar' and a night club. Sam looks appalled as I hop into the taxi.

'Looksafter 'er, Sue,' she slurs. Sue nods and then leans out of the cab to be sick, relieved that only a small amount of it sprays back into her hair. I insist that I am entirely sober, tell Sue that I really love her, I always have and suggest that we find a karaoke bar.

We fall out of the cab, pleasantly surprised that for once we have not ended up in a really tacky bar. Indeed, some clever soul at the front of the convoy of taxis, carrying the rowdy bunch of will-be-animals, actually had a clue about where we were heading. We grossly over-tip the driver, who is furiously shouting, 'Engleesh pigs.' Although, at that point, he isn't aware that someone has thrown up in the back of his cab; I reluctantly agree that there is some justice in the accusation. The driver of the cab behind ours is smarter, he is forcing one of the change navigators of this century to wipe up his own vomit with his Armani tie.

The bar is small, smoky and packed full of locals. A result. We try to tone it down a bit so as not to lower the tone. I immediately spot John, who waves me over to his corner table.

'Piss off to another table, make room for her,' he says considerately to his mates. There are about half-a-dozen people sitting around the table; I already know that I never want to meet them in a corridor at work.

He turns to me.

'So, how many people have you slept with?'

'Isn't that a bit forward?'

'Oh, you've lost count,' he grins. He is cheeky, confident and wild.

Like at Blackpool, conversation is limited to sex. How sexy he thinks I am. How sexy I think he is. We talk about how often, who with, when and where. We competitively compare. He outdoes me on numbers, I outdo him on variety. I describe, with gratuitously satisfying detail, conquests (numerous) and consequences (hilarious). I feel sexy and experienced, not in the least vulnerable or slutty. He understands it all. He is just like me, if anything he's worse. He has had sex with the most diverse and erotic array of women imaginable, which is exhilarating. Challenging.

'It must be great to be born a bloke.'

'Why?'

'It is easier to be evil and get away with it if you don't belong to the fairer sex.'

'Unlucky.'

'Yes, isn't it?'

He vacillates between begging me to sleep with him, and chastising me because I say I won't. He forcefully states the inevitability of my seduction one minute and then throws his arms up in the air with despair the next. It is a luxurious and irresistible form of interrogation. I cannot refuse him. I don't want to. I feel deliriously irresponsible, infatuated, irrational. I adore him.

'Admit it, you know exactly what I'm talking about. You're just not used to people acknowledging it.' I am describing that really amazing feeling of knowing when you are a step ahead.

'God you're vain.' He chuckles.

'No more than you.'

'Guilty as charged.' He looks at me, pauses. He looks away and back again. He shakes his head and grins. I wonder what he is thinking. I think he is in love with me.

'You like games, don't you?' he teases.

'Yes,' I reply, adding flirtatiously, 'especially those I win.'

'Draughts?' Hmmmm. I was expecting doctor and nurses or mummies and daddies. He pulls a wooden box out from what seems like nowhere. We are in one of those bars that supply cards, chess and draughts to allow people to amuse themselves while they drink. I reckon it is designed for people who have nothing to say to each other; John assures me that it is designed for men who want to introduce the subject of strip poker.

'Would you like to be black or white?' he asks.

'I'm white,' I say.

'But not completely.'

'You're black.'

'Come,' he smiles, 'not completely.' He speaks very slowly and very clearly, and his words lick my conscience clean away. Deftly, I start setting up the white pawns. He puts a black counter in one hand and a white one in the other.

'Choose for who gets to make the first move.'

I tap the hand which uncurls to reveal the black. He smiles with his eyes. I shrug, battle not war. We are fairly evenly matched but I find it almost impossible to drag my eyes away from him and towards the board. My distraction makes me thoughtless and impulsive. He has more experience to draw upon and he plays a ruthless game of tactics and skill. I delight in surprise takings even if they jeopardize the security of the

79

more important pieces. He's playing a longer game. With every piece lost a measure of Jack Daniel's is downed.

'Are you playing to win?' he asks incredulously after I lose another piece and put one more in peril after an impulsive move.

'Always,' I giggle, lifting up the glass to my lips. I feign anxiety and confusion by biting my bottom lip, squeezing the blood out. I think the effect will be provocative. I am relishing my sudden, highly developed sexuality.

'We are playing where you must jump,' he reminds me, 'and you know now that I will take all I can.' I am counting on it. 'First you take me,' he says in a slow and luxurious tone, 'and then,' he pauses, 'I take you.' He jumps my king. I want him to jump my bones.

'Oh, how stupid of me not to see that.' I flop back into the wicker chair, momentarily wearing an air of defeat; actually I'm not too bothered. I am trying to work out all that *double entendre* bit. 'It was staring me in the face.' I twist my hair around my index finger, hoping that this looks cute and girlish.

'But even if you had seen it, you wouldn't have done anything else.' He is definitely after a shag.

'Couldn't I have helped myself in any way?' I giggle, loving the sophisticated flirtation induced by thirty-five units.

'No. Once you started the form of attack that you were so determined to follow, you could have done nothing else but see the consequences through.' Hilarious. He must see the obvious analogy.

'You're drunk,' I say to no one in particular and at the same time to everyone in the bar.

'Yes, of course, but even when drunk I am very, very serious.' The 's' of the serious falls into the air and hangs there.

'Your move, the game is not over yet.'

'No, indeed not.' He looks at the board where there are two white kings and one pawn and three black kings and one pawn.

'Most evenly matched. The night could be yours yet.'

'Do you really want to win?' I ask, moving my king.

'Yes.' He slides his piece across the board, pauses and then removes his finger.

'So you want me to lose,' I reason moving a piece.

He quickly responds, 'No I don't want that. We can both win.' He jumps another piece.

'A draw is dull and inconclusive,' I say, sharply. My move.

'And so who do you want to win?' His move.

'You.' I drop the syllable into the air and lift my eyes to judge his reaction.

He moves again taking my last piece. 'You have your desire.'

Then we dance. Right there in the little bar, with about thirty people squeezing on to a dance floor the size of a handkerchief. He is male and Northern so he doesn't spin me round doing a solo rendition of 'Dirty Dancing', but he is a brilliant dancer. Shallow as it may sound, this is important to me. It's a point of distinction, not many men are good dancers, although most are convinced that they can show John Travolta a thing or two and that Michael Jackson is just begging them for lessons. And it shows promise. Good dancers are *so* horny. I am sure that I smell of sex, my knickers are wet, dripping for him, I can probably wring them out. I simply want him with an appalling, agonizing intensity that should shame me, but instead excites me. We dance, suggestively grinding our toilet areas. Coolly swaying hips, leaving little to the imagination. The music speeds up and we maniacally thrash our bodies around the floor. I envy the beads of sweat that sit on his forehead, that slide down his temple and cheeks. I want to slide down him. We return to our table where a group of blokes are noisily arguing over a game of whist. We decide to use the noise as a cover and we slip out unnoticed.

It is a nippy, clear night, the cold air runs up my sleeves and bites my body. He puts his arm around me to keep me warm and hails a cab. He is just so capable. Every action oozes sex appeal, which can't be learned, taught or topped. As usual the French cabby drives at breakneck speed. However, instead of sitting with white knuckles hanging on to the seat in front of me and cursing that there isn't a seat-belt, I actively will him to hurry. Ben Hur's chariot would not have been quick enough for me. We don't speak in the taxi; there's nothing to say.

We run through reception, him holding my hand, which I think is very forward of him and therefore a point in his favour.

'My room,' he asserts. It is some time since I've been with anyone new and although I might have forgotten some of the nuances, I remember the basics. It isn't caffeine that is on my mind. He fumbles with the key while I rub my aching feet on the back of my calves. The fat, round bit under the big toe stings from being cramped into fuck-me shoes. The skin on my face feels tight and tired. I *should* feel like shit. He opens the door to his room and I have a choice.

I go in.

Or I don't.

He slams me against the wall and urgently and repeatedly kisses me. My left leg wraps around him. My hands are exploring his body, his are closing the door and taking off his shoes. There is no hypocritical false modesty. I fall on to his bed and he lies on top of me. He inches me out of my jacket which smells of sweat and sticks to me. It drops to the floor, cool air brushes me, lifting me, releasing me, sweeping my arms. I kick off my shoes, my toes wiggle their own little jig. His kisses are neat, deep, focused, probing. He begins to brush my skin, stroking, touching me. I ache for him. I want him. I keep hearing myself say *no*. This is definitely the monosyllabic word that my voice keeps uttering, but my body is saying *yes*. My back arches for him, Y, my thighs quiver, E, my head spins, S.

YES. He caresses my shoulders and neck, my waist, my stomach and then the outside of my thighs. By the time he briefly flitters over my breasts I am wilting with anticipation, I want to push his hand down my trousers. My cunt is salivating. He slowly, slowly moves in on my breasts, circling my nipples that have sprung to a point. LUKE.

'Stop.' I push him off, stand up, walk around the room. It doesn't phase him. He silently watches me as I light a cigarette. The combined attempts in the tree house and the Parisian bar have not convinced me that it is actually pleasant, so I stub it out.

'I don't have the face for it.'

'What, adulterous sex?' he asks, misunderstanding me.

'Smoking. I don't look cool when I smoke, or even hard. I

look comical.' This bizarre truth has probably saved me from dying a horrible death. Although I'm prepared to hamper the development of my spine by wearing a Wonderbra, and to sport varicose veins as a result of wearing twelve-inch shoes – at least those health hazards improve the overall package. He interrupts my thoughts.

'You are amazing. I want you,' he states. I look at him and he is staring at me as though he's been on a desert island for fifty years and I am the first woman he's seen. He breaks the sexual energy just a nano-second before it breaks me.

'Want a drink?' Casually he flips open the mini bar, grabs a beer, pulls back the ring and swallows it down. He burps, then wipes his mouth on the back of his hand. 'Sorry.' He grins. He is a small boy caught playing with matches. 'Sorry but frankly the risk is worth it.' He grabs a miniature whiskey, cracks it open, drinks it back in one. He pulls out another from the fridge and casually throws it in my direction. Surprisingly, I coolly catch it with one hand.

'Christ, your tits are fantastic. You are so . . .' He stops and shakes his head. My tits hear him. My back straightens and my chest puffs out. Months of pilates haven't managed to produce such a ramrod posture. I look down at them. They do look good. They look like the breasts I furtively examine in the gym. The litmus test; am I more or less pert? More or less full? Am I, at least, pert and full enough? It's not just breasts, but stomach and the flatness thereof, thighs and the square inches of cellulite, bum, the droopiness of. All women do this, while heads are turned upside down drying hair, or while casually asking if anyone has a pound for the locker. It's not blatant. It's not brazen. It's nothing like the way John is looking at me now, with open admiration and longing.

'I've got to go to the loo.' I try to push past him but as I do so he stops me and holds me tightly. Maybe I have died and I am already in heaven. If that is the case, then fine. I can live with this, so to speak.

I go to the bathroom and scavenge around for clues of who he is. I discover that he is clean and fussy (brought his own soap, not content with the hotel offering, also has body wash, deodorant – which is a big bonus – shampoo), he wears contact lenses (daily disposable suggesting vanity and a fast, convenient lifestyle which he is prepared to pay for – then again maybe he is just allergic to the hard lenses), he is well paid (designer soap, designer body wash, designer shampoo etc.)

It is a strange intimacy.

I sit on the loo and try to calm down. The cold porcelain is somehow comforting, it is at least familiar. *Luke.* My pulse is racing, my heart thumping out of my chest, I can almost see it. I make a plan. This is the plan. On returning from the bathroom, I will sit on the settee and keep away from the bed. It is still possible that we can just be friends, that we can talk and laugh and then that I can politely say good night, and go back to my own room.

Alone.

I practise my exit – 'It's been fun but I have to go now.' Cheery and brief. I might just hold my resolve long enough to make it to the door. 'Thanks for the drinks but I better be getting off now.' No, best not to allude to anything provocative. 'If things had been different, then maybe. But they're not so I'd best go. Good night.' Too regretful. 'Well, another time, another place, but I'd better leave now.' Too cinematic. Bugger. Before I can get anywhere with my script he calls through.

'What are you saying, Connie? I can't hear you properly.'

'Err, nothing.' I pee and hurry back to his bedroom.

What a shock.

He is naked.

He is magnificent, he is huge. He stands smiling at me, pleased with himself, with what he can offer me. He is so manly, so large. He is so boyish, so large. He is so sexy, so large. He is so *large*. Not that big is everything. I'm actually a fully signed-up member of the quality, not quantity, school. However his teasing strokes and kisses have been more than enough evidence that the quality will be resounding. The combination is tops.

He is throbbing hard. It is so sexy to be wanted in such a raw and obvious way. His huge, throbbing, wanting, manifested in a huge throbbing, err, erection. It's a really beautiful cock. I edge past him muttering, 'It's been fun but I have to go now.'

He moves a fraction and smiles.

'Thanks for the drinks but I better be getting off now.'

Only a fraction but enough for the tip of his knob to brush my thigh.

'Well, another time, another place, but I'd better leave now.'

It feels as though a laser has burnt through my skin.

'If things had been different, then maybe. But they're not so I'd best go. Good night.'

But I don't move towards the door. He excites me in the

very centre of my being. I already know the unmistakable smell of his skin – childlike, newly scrubbed after a tea-time bath. The tip of his penis, silky and hard at the same time, is like a stuffed rabbit's paw. He leans forward and kisses the corner of my mouth. I mumble, 'It really *has* been fun but I *have* to go now.' He kisses me again and nods. This is a low move, agreeing with me.

'Thanks for the . . . everything . . .' I kiss him back. ' . . . but we better be getting off now, I mean, let's get off now.' I shake my head and pull away. 'I mean, I've got to be getting back now.' He leans closer again and begins to rub the back of my neck with his thumb. He silently stares at me. I barely whisper, 'Well . . . another time . . . another place but I better leave now. If things had been . . . different, then certainly but they're not . . .' He corners me with his nakedness, which I think is brutally honest. Resistance is token. My heart isn't in it.

I keep my clothes on but I must have shrunk because my clothes are like a tent around a boy scout, plenty of room to manoeuvre for mischief. He finds a way to every inch of my body. He kisses me in all the usual places, inching up my T-shirt to kiss my stomach, waist, breasts, inching down my trousers to kiss my hips and pelvic bone. Inching open my shirt to kiss my neck and shoulders, head and hair. And he kisses me in the unusual places: my eyelids, my eyelashes, my nose. I kiss him too, and lick and suck and consume. By the time he slips his fingers inside me, I am drenched by my own excitement. Glacial fingers on white hot flesh. I come immediately, spurting out on to his hands. The exquisite release sends shocks somersaulting through my spine. I grab hold of his cock, moving up and down, swiftly and expertly, until he comes on my stomach.

We drink, talk, laugh for the rest of the night and a substantial part of the morning. He comes a number of times and so do I. I look at my watch, it is 5 a.m. Lust and lager finally overpower me. I close my eyes.

He holds me.

Shaking with excitement and exhaustion I locate my shoes and jacket. He is still sleeping soundly. Beautiful. I bend over him and kiss him. My head falls off and rolls under the bed. It wakes him. Animal-like he flings his arm around me.

'What time is it?' he asks.

'Seven.'

'You off?'

'Yup, places to go, people to impress.'

'Don't go.'

'I've got to.'

He falls back to sleep before I close the door.

The dots on the carpet won't stay there. And the walls are morphing. I find my way back to my room and turn on the shower. I get in and then realize I am still in my socks. Dressing becomes a MENSA challenge. I follow the smell of bacon and eggs until I find the breakfast hall. As I begin to focus I notice that everybody is suffering for their night of debauchery. They have faces like slapped bottoms. I, by contrast, am superbabe.

'You're all over the place,' snaps Sue, as I spill coffee on to my fried eggs and trail my jacket sleeve in tomato sauce. I just want to be all over him.

'Not like you to have a fried breakfast in the morning,' Sam notes. She is right – I've had about three fried breakfasts in my entire life. I'm always worrying about saturated fat. Well, maybe things are going to change. Maybe I am too strict with myself and maybe there should be some changes.

'I like fried eggs,' I defend. Muddled, I add, 'Unfertilized.'

Sam rolls her eyes. 'Are you hung over? I should never have let you go out on your own last night. The conference has only just started. You'll feel like shit sitting through these boring presentations with a hangover. They are bad enough when you're feeling OK.' She means well.

I have been to numerous conferences and business meetings that involve long, arduous hours and excessive alcohol. Invariably, by the second day my teeth have furred, my breath smells like an old beer keg, my eyelids are heavy and my hands and feet are freezing. So it isn't unreasonable that Sam thinks that this is just another conference-induced hangover. I doubt whether anybody would attend these things without the incentive of getting uncontrollably drunk. I have drunk four, five, six times the amount I normally drink, but this time I feel alive, bright and my stomach is empty. I feel exhilarated, spirited, known. Entirely known, the good bits and the horrors. I feel so sexy. So sexed. Every muscle aches. Every nerve is stretched taught with the effort of being so wildly sexy.

'I'm not hung over.' I'm still drunk. I never want to be sober again.

'What happened then?' asks Sue as she decapitates a boiled egg. Sam looks confused.

'Happened?'

'Yes, happened with John Hardon,' snaps Sue.

'Harding,' I correct.

'I think I got it right the first time, didn't I?'

I take a deep breath and then begin to spill the gore. They stare at me in silence. Uncomfortably I play with the tomato sauce that has formed a scab around the bottle neck.

'What?' I ask hotly.

'What about Luke?' They ask the same question, but in very different ways. Sue is disgusted, Sam is concerned.

'Don't you feel guilty?'

'Guilt has gone AWOL. I called in the military police but they can't track her down,' I laugh.

'I fail to see the joke,' says Sue primly. 'Think how hurt he'd be if he found out.'

'Well, he won't.' They stare at me. 'It's not as if I want to trade Luke in for John,' I defend.

'In some ways that would be more forgivable,' tuts Sue. I realize that I'm not going to win her over. I turn to Sam, who, historically, is more indulgent.

'It's not an affair.' I say the word contemptuously.

'What is it then?' she asks carefully.

'Well, we didn't have total sex.'

'I'm not sure those big red A signs come in different shades of red to reflect the severity of the indiscretion,' quips Sue.

'He might be my destiny.'

'Do you really believe that?'

'I don't disbelieve it,' I hedge, 'I can manage it at least for the duration of the conference and after then, well, I'll think about after, after.'

'Be careful,' begs Sam. Appallingly romantic with everyone

and ridiculously indulgent with me, she struggles to find levels of sexual promiscuity that she can be comfortable with. Something that will mean I haven't been unfaithful to Luke. She does a sensational amount of spin doctoring. President Clinton's aides could take advice.

'Kissing is OK, without tongues,' is the starting position. My face confesses. 'Sometimes tongues are OK, as long as it is just kissing.' She comforts. It is like a holiday point system in reverse. Eventually she proclaims that him touching my breast is OK, as long as I didn't enjoy it. We finally agree that infidelity is swallowing.

Sue chastises. 'The whole situation is commonplace and irritating. There is nothing romantic about infidelity. He's a grubby little Northerner on the make. Despicable, predictable, lowlife.'

I'm already bored with her moralizing. 'You dislike charming men, on principle.'

'Which principle would that be?'

'You're afraid of their good looks, athletic builds, charming manners. You only pretend not to like them.'

'They are so obviously confident,' she spits.

'Well, they can be, can't they?' I reason.

We fall silent. We seem to have lost our appetites. Forlorn cornflakes and shells of boiled eggs seem to be moralizing and mocking. I rub my temples and sigh.

'Maybe you're right, Sue. I wish I'd never met him. I wish he'd go away.'

'Well, sleep with him, then, that will be a sure-fire bet.' She begins to gather her lecture notes; Sam stands up from the table too.

'Are you coming?'

'I'll catch you up.' They leave me to my thoughts.

A spade is a shovel. I've been unfaithful to Luke. I was unfaithful the moment John kissed me and I kissed him back.

I didn't think I was capable of such a thing.

But I am.

I watch Sam and Sue flounce out of the dining hall. They are arguing. This situation is unacceptable; I cannot carry on. It's a disgrace. It must stop. I am referring to the gossip. I leave my eggs and then skip back to my room. I ditch my conference pack, lock my door, turn left, get into the lift, go to floor ten, turn right and knock at his door. I have to knock a number of times because he is still in bed. Sleepily he opens the door. He looks surprised to see me and delighted.

'Gorgeous, come back to bed. It's still warm.'

His knob springs up again, raring to go. Can't blame it, I feel just the same.

'I'm cutting class.'

'Oh yeah,' he sniffs and rubs his nose on the back of his hand, lights a cigarette and farts, all at once. Who says men can't multitask?

'Best thing.' He leans towards me and tries to kiss me but I avoid him by dodging under his arm. This isn't easy because even the smell of his sweat makes me feel weak with want.

'I can't face being down there hearing everyone boasting about last night's acts.'

He looks at me suspiciously. 'What do you mean?'

'Oh, you know the ones,' I say, mock casual, 'I drank twenty-five pints, shagged two Parisians, a Swedish tourist and still had a J&B nightcap.'

'No, no, that's nothing. I drank thirty-five pints, all Guinness, shagged two Parisians at once, a Swedish tourist, her grandmother, had a J&B nightcap and still didn't puke.'

We both laugh, very aware of the testosterone sharks that would now be swimming around the conference room.

'You know it's all lies though, don't you?' he says. I look at him quizzically. 'That guy did throw up.'

We laugh again and when we stop laughing I ask. 'Do you do that?'

'What, throw up? Well, sometimes – it depends on what I've mixed.'

'No,' I interrupt. 'I mean the bragging, the morning after, doubling points system.'

He looks perplexed. Embarrassed, I try to explain.

'You know, double the points with each mate you tell. So what sets off as a simple act in the missionary ends up as some depraved shocker involving animals and lawnmowers.'

'I know the points system. I know what you're asking,' he says evenly.

'Well, do you?' It is better to know where I stand.

'Yes, normally, I would be down there with the other blokes, dissecting my exploits.' He looks at his watch. 'Perhaps not this early, but yes, Connie, I am just like them. I have sex with complete strangers and I talk about it.' He looks a bit confused. 'Isn't that half the fun?' He puts his arms around me and I shiver. Damn, he is gorgeous.

'I am an absolute *GQ* lad. Utterly *Loaded*. I am a womanizer. I've told you that I've slept with literally scores of women, I can't even remember some of their names. Usually I sleep with them once and then I don't want anything else to do with them. I usually tell anyone who will listen exactly what we did and I also rate the performance out of ten. I am selfish, fickle, and lazy. I won't lie to you, I won't pretend this isn't how I've been in the past. Let's face it, you can ask around and quickly get the measure of me.'

He breaks away to stub out his cigarette; he immediately lights another one.

'I'm very different from your husband, Connie. He's no doubt a decent, honest bloke.'

I've never heard those words sound so off-putting before. He pauses.

'However, Connie, with you it's different.'

Different.

I'm *Different*!

I fight through relief and delirium to tune back into what he is saying.

'I have no desire to tell anyone about last night. Anyway if I did I'd be a laughing stock. You wouldn't let me penetrate and I wept over your hand-job. You're a married woman and I respect that.'

He pulls me close to him and strokes my head. I bury my face in his delicious chest.

'You are very like me. I saw that last night. You want to play the way you feel it. So do I. It will be our secret, all right?'

He tilts up my head and kisses me. My breasts hum like bees. I am sex. I feel ticklish, as though a small insect is beating its wings in a bid to escape.

'All right,' I say, swallowing the lump in my throat.

'Now, wait a few minutes, I'll get showered and then we'll go into Paris.'

We get a train into the centre of Paris. On the train, in true 90s style we do a post coitus crash course in getting to know each other.

'What's your favourite colour?' I ask.

'Blue. Yours?'

'Depends on my mood. Silver, red at the moment, often green.'

'Have you any brothers or sisters?'

He has one elder sister.

'What is your favourite food?'

'Curries. Yours?'

'Fish and chips but I never eat them. I eat pasta. What's your favourite film?'

'*Butch Cassidy and the Sundance Kid.* Yours?'

'*Dangerous Liaisons.*' He raises eyebrows. 'Do you read?'

'Yes.' He seems mildly insulted.

'What do you read?'

'Well, my favourite poem is Kipling's "If".'

'I don't believe you.'

'I can recite it to you if you like:

> *"If you can keep your head when all about you,*
> *Are losing theirs and blaming it on you,*
> *If you can trust yourself when all men doubt you,*
> *But make allowance for their doubting too . . .'''*

And so he goes on but I am lost. I slip out of my undies if men recite the football results but if they know poetry, I'm done for.

95

    ' "... *Yours is the Earth and everything that's in it,*
       And – which is more – you'll be a Man, my son!"

My mother taught me it.'

'I think it is "And *what* is more",' I offer.

He looks as though he feels sorry for me, 'I think you'll find it is, " And *which* is more".'

Since, at that moment, I want to have his babies, so consumed with lust am I, I decide to concede the point, but make a mental note to look it up later when I get home. After all, I am the English graduate.

'Constance Baker – what's your maiden name?'

'Green.'

'Ahh Greenie.' He is one of those blokes who have to give people nicknames, however banal.

'Ahhh Hardy,' I reply and we both laugh; I mean it is just hilarious.

Suddenly serious, he asks, 'Why are you married? Give me three good reasons.'

'Because . . .' I look out the train window and watch fields and lives rush by. I'm struggling to get it absolutely right. 'For one, it means that you always have someone who is *for* you, wherever you are in the world; whatever crap you're dealing with you always have someone who is a hundred per cent with you. Even if they are not standing right next to you they are for you. You're never alone. And then . . .' I trail off. I guess I'm aware that he is within his rights to say *What about last night? Was he with you then? What about now? Are you putting his best interests forward now?*

'One reason's enough.'

We both go quiet for a while. We read the graffiti on the seats.

He breaks the silence, 'What's your favourite day of the week?'

We find one of those little French cafés that are in films. The ones with hot chocolate, wicker chairs and rude waiters. He orders breakfast and we decide that hair of the hound is in order; a bottle of beer for him and a glass of red wine for me. Then we resume our discovery. We tell each other about ourselves. Not just the funny bits; making people laugh is easy, but all the bits. He roars with laughter at the stories that I haven't practised, packaged and prepared. He tells me about the terrifying pubs he frequents, where there is more metal in people's faces than the till. A dog on a string is as necessary a fashion statement to those punters as a mobile phone is in the wine bars I frequent. He is from Liverpool, he moved to London a couple of years ago. He lives in East London, I imagine him in trendy Clerkenwell, a huge, white, open space. I imagine us spending Sunday mornings in bed. We wouldn't read the papers the way Luke and I do, he'd strap me to the bed and take me from behind. Luke and I live in a very lovely, but fairly conventional, Victorian Terrace in Clapham. It's lovely. It's fine. We do not own a nest of tables, or a sideboard which groans under the weight of knick-knacks; we have Heals' furniture and the odd tasteful statement from Conran, our barometer of success is the lack of brass rubbings, potted plants and single-bud vases. It is tasteful, settled, sanitized, controlled. Suddenly it is lacking something.

John and I laugh as much as our hangovers will allow. We

fall over each other's words, both trying to articulate a really peculiar smell or memory.

'Remember school gyms, all dusty and sweaty?'

'The stench of cheap disinfectant?'

'Slimy, yellow soap and rough paper towels?'

'Worse, school dinners. Gristly meat and Mash-Get-Smash by the barrel.'

It strikes me that this is just like it used to be before I got married, only better. Which is peculiar, perplexing. Marrying has given me freedom. I'm in control. I'm not for sale. There is no sense that I'm trying to trap him. I can behave just as I please. I don't care if he thinks I'm a pig for choosing hot chocolate with double cream and the chocolate flaky bits for breakfast. Or if he thinks I am an alky for having wine. Or if he thinks I am simply odd for intermittently sipping both. It is quite unlike any relationship I have ever had with a man before. I hold opinions because I believe them, not to be cool, controversial or compliant. I hadn't realized that I had so many views, thoughts, ideas, but suddenly – being with John – my deeply private self comes tumbling out, rushing to the surface. Luke knows the balanced, decent woman that forgets to pay bills, but always remembers birthdays. He does not know the woman who has just made an entrance. The one who wants to give blow-jobs in the back of cabs.

'What music do you listen to?'

'Dusty Springfield.' Usually cringemakingly embarrassing, unless you're gay or on HRT, I feel it is OK to tell John this. He grins.

'I love Tom Jones, he's my hero.' He studies me closely, 'When you were a little girl, what did you dream about?'

'What do you mean?'

'Well, don't tell me that when you played with your Sindy dolls you said to yourself, "One day I'm going to be a management consultant".'

I laugh. 'You're right. I wanted to be a film producer or a photographer of the stars.' I fling my arms wide, wiggle my hips and laugh loudly.

'So what stopped you?'

'Good question.' I immediately stop laughing. 'I don't know. It takes a lot of determination and time to do something like that. I got caught up in life. Mortgages, responsibility, realism. I buried my passion and got myself a proper job.'

'Swapped your camera for a calculator?' I nod. 'Were you any good?'

'I still take photos. Some of them are OK.'

I never talk about my ambition to be a photographer. I haven't even told Luke. It seems too improbable.

'Well, Greenie, what are you up to?' he asks after I spend some time describing Luke, our home, our friends, my job.

'Be specific.'

'Well, from where I'm sitting you are the composite 90s woman. You seem to have it all. A husband who does his share of the housework, more than putting the rubbish outside. He seems to respect you, love you, he has dress sense. You have great mates, plenty of money, a nice home. You could be lying, but I don't think you are. So tell me, what are you up to?'

'I need a lover, latest designer accessory, didn't you know?' I joke.

'What are you up to?' he repeats slowly, vain enough to

know that he must be more than that. Fair question, I consider it. I can't find an answer. 'You are irresistible,' seems a bit like showing my hand. My second glass of red wine before 11.30 a.m. helps out.

'OK, if not an accessory, you are more of an experiment.' He raises an eyebrow. 'I want to see if I can want so much it destroys me. I want to see if I can let go, wave a cheerful goodbye to self-control.' I do not bother checking if this is true. It sounds cool. It sounds big.

'Oh.'

Four hours, two hot chocolates, one bacon and eggs, four beers, a bottle of wine and a packet of cigarettes later, we set off on a directionless ramble. We walk along the river, holding hands; he touches me all the time. We stop and buy oranges from a wrinkled man with a road-side store. He has white hair and sun-blistered skin which lies in folds, framing a toothless, smiling mouth. My senses are on red alert, I can smell stale sweat on the vendor's cotton shirt and soil on his hands. Unlike in England he does not put the fruit in an incongruous blue plastic bag, but instead he sniffs the oranges, wipes them on his dirty trousers and hands them to us. We wander on and pass a fun-fair. Smells of burgers and fried onions bang up against sickly, sweet candyfloss; the clear damp air is cold and black. I can smell the oil and paraffin that lubricate the heavy machinery. We mess around on a couple of rides, trying to squeeze into the undersized swings. My bum is freezing on the steps and seats, my hands numb as I hold on to the steel safety bars, yet my face is flushed and my upper lip sweaty. He looks at his watch.

'Shit.'

'What?'

'It's late.' He looks genuinely disappointed.

'Who is it that said, "all good things must come to an end"?'

'Well, whoever it was – what a miserably accurate fucker.' I try to laugh off the swelling pain in my chest. An indefinable tightness.

We slowly make our way back to Le Metro and then back to the hotel. He helps me pack and I help him. Then he walks me back to the train station. We say very little. Small talk is obscene. John comments, 'Frustrating not to have the vocabulary to describe the smell of wet pavements after a summer storm, the dank sweetness that is so individual and peculiar.'

We have pre-arranged trains and seats and we aren't on the same one. Surprisingly, he kisses me goodbye.

'I hope this isn't going to get all complicated by our caring for each other,' I say with a grin. He shrugs. I hope not. Oh, I hope so.

The journey home is quite different from the one to Paris. For a start my tiredness is unprecedented. I'm utterly but, not quite, literally fucked. And although almost immediately I cannot remember precisely what he'd said that made me laugh so much, I feel doused in a general sense of well-being. I feel wonderful, exhilarated, amazing, a winner.

For about ten minutes.

Then my head begins to hurt and I feel tearful. I'm sobering up.

Sue tuts, 'Pull yourself together.'

I scowl at her. 'I'm tired.'

She scowls back, 'You're behaving like a five-year-old after a party. You've demonstrated your ability for rough and tumble, noisy, dangerous, destructive games and now you are sulking because you don't want to go home.'

'Wow, Sue, you must know some cool five-year-olds,' I snap. I would have argued further but she is spot on; such arguing I leave up to men, who argue even when they agree with your point.

Sam pats my hand. 'Try to eat your sausages.'

I get home at about ten, to an empty house and a note from Luke reminding me that he is going fishing for the weekend, with Peter. Damn, if I'd remembered I would have stayed in Paris with John.

Maybe it is better that I didn't remember.

I am appallingly, achingly excited. Who can I tell? I ring Daisy; I have, after all, known her for ever. If anyone is going to make sense of this, she is. I pour myself a large glass of Meursault, empty a bag of popcorn into a bowl and take up residence by the phone. Over the years we have done this regularly, every time either of us have news; for *news* read sex life. Over the last eight weeks or so I've spent countless evening in my soggy chair listening to Daisy going on and on about Simon. How clever he is, how sexy he is, how revoltingly handsome, etc. Now it is my turn. Like old times, pre-Luke times, I get to take the hot seat. I call Daisy, hoping Simon isn't there. If he is, I'll be treated to a cursory 'Yes, no, fine' monosyllabic conversation. If he isn't there it will be the Full Friendship Monty. I'm looking forward to the day when they get used to each other. Then I won't have to listen to the banal dribble of the newly besotted.

'Did I ever tell you that he has the most beautiful toes?'

'Yes, I think you did mention that.' Six times!

'Did I? Gosh, I must be getting really boring.' Girlish giggle. Yes, you are. 'No, not at all.'

I tell her the bare bones. But not about the bare bodies. Perhaps I would have told her more but Daisy doesn't react as I expected.

'God, Connie, isn't that funny? He sounds just like all the guys you used to go out with.'

'Does he?' I'm genuinely surprised.

'Hell, yes. Do you remember that medic? What was his name?'

'No, I don't remember a medic.'

'Yes, you do. He was Irish, with eyes like marbles, jet-black hair, very fit, a complete louse. What is his name?'

'Fergus,' I fill in helpfully.

'Yes, that's it.' I had, until that point, forgotten all about Fergus.

'And that lecturer, now what was his name? Something traditional? Thomas or David?'

'Paul,' I supply.

'Yes! Another utter bastard, complete womanizer. And the sailor.'

'Andrew. He was a Marine.'

'Yes, same thing, more women than tattoos. Still you always did go for "mean about town" types; being such a flirt yourself, you lived for the challenge.' I wish Daisy would shut up.

'I can't remember that.'

'Oh, Connie, come on! That's why it was so great when you fell for Luke. Such a relief. I mean you were envied for your ability to bag such delicious men, but to be honest it was a bit discouraging that even you couldn't keep them. What chance did we mere mortals have? Do you remember how pleased your mother was when you met Luke? She rang my mum to gloat. She practically sang, "He's not a drummer, no. No drugs, No, there's no wife. Yes, a regular salary."'

I smile to myself. Daisy chatters on, oblivious to my silence.

'John sounds just like the prats Sam wastes her time with.'

'Does he?' I'm stunned. Has Sam ever dated anyone quite so sexy and interesting?

'Yes, "a disturb". Connie, you should recognize it, you coined the phrase.' It stands for disrespectful, irresponsible, short termist, utterly rotten, bastard. I'd coined the phrase to describe the majority of men we'd collectively dated over the years. I tune back into what Daisy is saying. I can hear her munching down the phone line, thoughtfully chewing Twiglets. She recounts a number of Sam's disastrous romantic liaisons.

'But John is not a bit like Jed, William, Tim, Karl or any of those others,' I interrupt. Now it is Daisy's turn to sound surprised.

'Isn't he? He sounds like them from your description. Very into sex, utterly delicious looks, talks about being a free spirit. What half-decent bloke would make such a play for a married woman?'

'Lots,' I defend.

'*Decent* bloke,' she insists. 'It's obvious that he just thinks of you as a challenge. You must be so pleased that you weren't tempted.' Err. 'It must have made you feel so smug to be married to someone like Luke, so you can just tell this guy to take a hike.'

'Yes,' I mutter.

'I mean, we've all had more dishonest and dull fucks than any of us care to remember. It is your relationship with Luke that made me realize what I want.'

'Is it?' Curious and vain, I like being inspirational.

'Definitely. You've restored my faith in the Happily Ever After. It is because of you and Luke that I decided that I wasn't going to compromise. I want to be loved and respected and cherished. I want to be able to laugh with my bloke as much as I laugh with you and the girls. I want a best friend. I want the kind of partnership you and Luke have. I want . . .'

Daisy can be enthusiastically verbose at the best of times, and this is not the best of times, not considering the topic she is waxing lyrically about. Like an atom bomb, once set off, she mushrooms. Admittedly the consequences are not on the same scale, but I'm not in the mood.

'Daisy, there's someone at the door, I'll have to go.'

'Oh. OK then. Take care. See you at All Bar One.'

'Yes, take care. Bye.'

I put down the phone and sit still, listening to birds and watching the last bit of daylight eke its way down on to the patio outside. I love this time of day. Even in London early autumn evenings seem so peaceful. I look around the sitting room which is awash with warmth and familiarity. Our beautiful home. I stand up and walk towards the mantelpiece, where the predictable wedding photo takes pride of place. Only a year ago, we were maniacally smiling at the camera man, thoroughly content, blissful. In fact, we have been that way up until very recently; three days ago to be exact. I'm gripped with panic. Hell. What am I thinking of? How can I be so unrestrained and unreal. I have to put John out of my mind. Out. Carry on as though it never happened. Forget him as soon as possible.

Yet I'm thrilled and I cannot, hard as I try, summon up any regret.

The weekend lasts about six months. I clean cupboards, I sort knicker drawers and jewellery boxes. I hoover under the bed and on top of shelves and wardrobes. I tidy the desk draw, introduce a filing system for our post. I scrub, wash, dust, brush, disinfect, de-scale, de-mould and de-fuzz every single square inch of our, already immaculate, house. Once I have played the 1950s happy housewife role and the house is glowing, I spring-clean myself. I file, cleanse, detoxify, brush, cut, shave, pluck every follicle, pore and hair on my body. I visit the hairdressers, attend two gym classes and have a massage. There are still about four months of the weekend to fill. I then throw out sackfuls of clothes that I no longer would be seen dead in and immediately spend over a £1000 on a suit and shirt from Joseph. I have never spent this kind of money on myself before. I feel so horribly guilty that I spend even more in Paul Smith buying a jacket for Luke. I have abandoned all normal routines that add up to life. I don't sleep and I don't eat. I don't think.

Luke comes home late on Sunday afternoon with a huge trout which, undoubtedly, he's bought from Sainsbury's.

'Hi, darling, did you miss me?' he asks putting his arms around me.

'Yes,' I answer truthfully. As he kisses me I wait for the guilt. I wait for the overwhelming urge to confess. I wait for my stomach and knickers to somersault. I wait in vain. Nothing happens. Disappointed, I pull away and go to bed.

Finally it is Monday morning but it is without the usual Monday morning blues. I almost run out of the house at 7 a.m., desperate to get to work, away from home. Now officially in the same company, John and I will be sharing a building and although I'm not *expecting* to see him, as we are assigned to different projects, I *might* see him. I'm convinced that he'll send an e-mail, the way he did after Blackpool. What will I do if he does? What will I do if he doesn't! I weigh about 7 stone, my eyes are shining, my skin glowing. I am a goddess. Except for my chin which has nearly fallen off with the amount of kissing we did last week. Rather ill-advisedly I've slopped on a ton of emergency Vaseline – big mistake, now I have dry patches intermittently broken up by a crop of really choice whiteheads. Besides *that* I feel like a goddess.

My unusually good mood stretches to Tube travel, where I merrily nod and smile to all the other passengers, letting people go in front of me and offering up my seat. Odd behaviour at the best of times in London, but on the Northern Line on a Monday morning I'm in danger of being committed to an asylum. I breeze into the office, past the security guard, Bob.

'Morning,' I sing.

'Got your badge, Connie?'

'Err no, but you know I work here, Bob.'

'Not the point, Connie. Can't be too careful. I can't let you in without someone else signing for you.'

'Who else is here?'

'No one, too early. You'll have to go next door for a coffee. I'll come and get you when someone arrives and they can sign you in.'

This deeply infuriating scene is played out about once a week. It usually culminates in my screaming at Bob that he is a jobsworth and that after I've finished with him he won't have a job to be worth. Bob and I secretly like these little fracas. We both realize that it is the most exciting part of our working day. He always looks positively disgruntled if I have my security card with me. Today I smile at him and tell him I'll come back at 9 a.m. I leave him confused and disappointed. I go next door for a coffee and a croissant, which I can't eat but rather pick at in a love-sick manner, until Sam comes to collect me up. She pushes my croissant into her mouth, asking all at once, 'Finished with that? Good weekend? What happened to your chin?' She stops and stares, horrified. 'Is that a post-snog fall-out chin?'

I spend all morning in a state of painful agitation. Sam keeps casting me concerned looks that she upgrades to a positively anxious look when I fail to eat my mid-morning KitKat.

'So, Connie, what's the story with you and this John bloke?' she asks insightfully.

'There isn't one.'

Just then my e-mail bleeps. I immediately flick to e-mail but it isn't from him, it is a reminder that my time sheets are late. Sam shakes her head but wisely leaves it at that. I repeat the same routine 135 times throughout the morning. As I sit at my desk I vacillate wildly as I try to understand and justify my outrageously indulgent indiscretion. I'm not sad that it happened but it has to be a one-off, never to be repeated. Not that anything really happened, we didn't even have full sex. I'm not going to talk or think about him again. Who can I talk to? If only I could talk to someone. Perhaps I'll confide in Sam? Luke must not find out. Not because he'd leave me. He wouldn't leave me, but I don't want to hurt him. Being bad is bad enough, getting caught would be terrible. Nothing *really* happened, anyway. It was just a mistake. It could happen to anyone. All I have to do now is forget him. Ha, who?

As I think this, I doodle 'John' all over my desk diary. Angrily I score out his name. With unadulterated horror I admit I have not forgotten him. I do not despair of him, nor do I despise him. Luckily, I am too happy in my real life to allow him, this glittery and attractive fake, to exercise any serious pain or disruption. He is without doubt like a strong alcoholic drink: pleasant to enjoy, forgotten when swallowed.

John, John, John.

I should have had sex with him. It would have been better to have had sex with him and acknowledged that it didn't mean anything and then move on. Get back to normal. Stop obsessing. It is because I *haven't* slept with him that he's become such a big deal. Maybe I should take him as a lover. A full-blown lover, none of this adolescent fumbling with clothes on. Deeply frustrating. I could manage a fling without hurting Luke. What the head doesn't know the heart won't grieve for. I'll only have to do it the once. It won't *mean* anything. It is just sex. Curiosity. He'll definitely call, because we haven't shagged.

1.10 p.m. – no note.

1.50 p.m. – still no e-mail.

2.20 p.m. – he has not called.

2.50 p.m. – still no word.

I'm not bothered. It is understandable. He probably doesn't have access to his e-mail. I am a *bit* surprised, you'd think he'd send something. I'm not going to write to him – that would be *so* uncool.

3.15 – well, maybe just a short impersonal note to ask if he got home safely.

3.30 – a woman should never do the running, it will be better to wait. He will send something soon.

3.45 – then again, he is in a difficult position. I'm the married one.

4.20 – I don't want to make it too hard for him.

At 4.50 I locate the newly branded, internal telephone directory and call him.

'Can I speak to John Harding please?'

'He's not at his desk, can I take a message?'

I quickly and impressively hang up. I wait another ten minutes and then I ring again.

'Can I speak to John Harding, please?' I say this with my best Australian accent so that his secretary won't recognize my voice.

'Oh, you again, didn't you just call? He's still not at his desk. Can I take a message?'

'Err, I think we just got cut off.' Even I'm wincing as I say it.

'Uh huh.' She doesn't sound convinced. An unwelcome

image of his secretary pushes its way into my head. She is about 5 feet 10 with legs up to her eyebrows. She is extremely cool, she dresses from head to toe in Kookaï. It actually fits her, she doesn't look like a Tiny Tears doll in Barbie clothes – my experience of Kookaï – and oh, God, no. Yes. No. I can see it . . . she has sex with him on the desk, without even messing up her hair. Of course she does. Why wouldn't she have sex with him? Anyone in their right mind would have sex with him. He is gorgeous. Except for me because I am a fool, a fool!

'Can I take a message?' she asks pleasantly enough. She would, wouldn't she? I mean, she is satiated. In fact she sounds a bit distracted; can it be that they are actually having sex now? While she is fobbing me off with 'not at his desk'. *On* the desk more likely. Just before I yell 'Put him down you harlot', I manage to get a grip and remind myself that it is pretty unlikely that even he would be bashing it out on the desk at 5.00 p.m.

'Can you tell him that Connie called.'

'Does he have a number?' The innocent question sounds impertinent.

'Err, no,' I say and hang up. So cool. Not.

I berate myself. Let's recap the golden rules of combat. Never make the *first* move. Never, ever call him. If you must call, speak, do not hang up. Do not leave a befuddled message – open to ridicule, do not forget your own telephone number! I slowly begin to pack away my laptop and tidy up my desk, I am mortified, deflated.

Just as I turn into the lift, and the doors begins to close I hear my secretary say, 'You're after Connie? I'm sorry you've just missed her. She's just left for the evening.' I hammer on the lift door, alarming everyone else, squeeze through a three-millimetre gap and then hurtle, Seb Coe-like back through the floor, to arrive, panting, in time to see her put the phone down.

'Who was it? Who?' I demand.

Nonplussed she says, 'Didn't leave a name.'

'Well, did you recognize him? Did he sound familiar? Was it an internal call or an external call? Scouser by any chance?'

'*She* didn't leave a name.' I have a feeling she knows more than I'd want her to. She puts her coat on and sashays off the floor. 'It's twenty to six, you stopped paying me ten minutes ago. Goodnight.'

The phone rings and android-like I pick it up.

'Good evening, Constance Baker, extension 3469.'

'Greenie.'

I come in my pants.

Serious organ jumping.

'Hardy!' Ecstatic.

'Greenie.' Erotic.

'Hardy.' Suggestive.

'Greenie?' Hesitant.

'Hardy.' Dull now.

'It is you, isn't it?'

'Have you missed me?' Tactful, teasing, sensitive . . . not really, straight for the jugular.

'I am dying for you. I want you. I have to have you. I need to fuck you, Greenie.'

I am so flattered I would have conceded there and then if

he'd been in the room. Tension and excitement is erupting from every pore.

'I've been thinking about that poem.' I mumble into the phone – bloody open plan!

'Which?'

'Kipling's "If".'

'Oh yeah, what about it?'

'About taking gambles and risks and stuff.' I try to mix code-speak with cool. I think I fail.

'Hmmm?'

'Well, if *you* can make one heap of all your winnings and risk it on one turn of pitch-and-toss, and lose, and start again at your beginnings and never breathe a word about your loss – '

'Yes . . .'

'That bit about never breathe a word.'

'Yes.'

'Well, I can if you can. I mean I will if you will. Or rather I won't if you won't.' Shit, I'm blowing this. 'What I mean is, I want to fuck you.'

'Excellent. Well, I look forward to "forcing my heart and nerve and sinew to serve their turn long after they are gone".'

Goal. Goal. Goal. *Goal. Gooooaaaaaalllllllll.*

4

We haven't discussed exactly where we are going to go or what we are going to do. So I don't know how to dress for my date. It hasn't been easy to arrange, what with alibis at work and home. Work think I'm on holiday, Luke thinks I'm on a training course. John's boss thinks he's attending an out of town meeting. Normally I hate deception but I've happily embraced all the clichés that oil the wheels for an illicit affair. The important thing is to see him, soon. I haven't seen him for twelve days. He hasn't left my mind for a minute. I bathe in Body Shop sensuous bath oil, shower, scrub, shower again and then rub on Clarins anti-cellulite cream. Will it work in two hours? I apply five moisturizers. One for the neck, one for the area around my eyes, one for the side of my lips, one for my cheeks and one for good measure. I put on full make-up – too obvious – I take it off. But I have to look as though I've made an effort, I wail in despair. I reapply, striving to look 'nude'. Underwear. *Agghhh*. I usually wear pop socks and grey/white M&S briefs. Luke doesn't notice if he comes home to me and I'm naked, draped across the *chaise longue*, or dressed in a full-length, Walton Family, winceyette night-dress. I remember what torture most underwear is. Designed for male titillation and female discomfort. Still, male titillation is quite important to me, right now. I try on suspenders and corset (I reject it – too tarty), then stay-ups and lacy, matching (special occasion only) La Perla bra and briefs. I try the lacy bra and briefs combination in four colours: white (too bride-like), red (too saloon girl), black (too *Rocky Horror Show*), cream (too starter set). The frantic putting on and taking off of underwear leaves me hot and sticky, so I shower again. I finally decide on white, cotton, Calvin Klein thong, no bra. I pull on three black tops, four white tops, two pairs of black trousers and a navy pair, brown pair, khaki pair and a beige pair. I settle on the third white top and a black skirt. I pull the garments off and then on again in agitation. Another top is dragged over my head; I pause, look in the mirror, tut with impatience and wrench it off. I entertain myself by getting horny imagining him deep inside of me. It will be such a relief to get it over with; I know that as soon as I have sex with him I'll forget him. I can almost see myself wrapping my legs around his body and him pushing down on me, the heels of my feet digging into his spine. I remember Paris, his eyes wide open, staring at me. And his smile, a bloody cheeky grin, as he rolled off me.

We meet at Euston. I spot him when he is still some distance away. He refuses to walk in a steady adult way, instead he hops, jumps, bounces towards me, grinning broadly. He is smaller than I'd remembered. He kisses me. My pelvis jumps into my mouth. It doesn't matter, Chanel No 5 isn't sold in litre bottles. He is sooooooooooooo sexy.

'You look fuckable. I've brought a picnic.'

I'm sure that winning the lottery would be dull in comparison to this. Delighted, I look for a hamper, imagining crusty loaves, ripe cheeses, black olives, hummus and autumn berries. Now I'm with him I feel hungry again, for the first time since Paris . . . starving. I can already see us sitting on a rug, feeding champagne to one another from our mouths. He holds up a couple of carrier bags, he has eight bottles of beer. For a split second I'm disappointed. Oh well. It doesn't matter. I'm here for sex, not romance, aren't I? I don't need Brie and grapes.

'Fancy a walk? Hampstead Heath? A bit of heterosexual fornication is small play to what usually goes on there.'

I nod. It is far enough away from my stomping ground for me to relax, and anyway if he'd suggested it I would have followed him to the moon for a shag.

It's a bright, early autumn day. There is a solid, deep-blue sky that looks more like sea than sky. Bright sunlight dances with the leaves on the trees, the smell of burning wood drifts over the park. We walk aimlessly, holding hands and carrying a bottle of beer each, although I've studiously avoided it for thirty years. I hope it doesn't bloat my stomach or make me fart.

The Heath is almost deserted except for the odd housewife, pensioner and drug addict. A young mum pushes an empty push-chair and her son runs by her side. He makes short steps and is finding it difficult to keep up with her long ones. His red wellingtons, slightly too big, splash in murky puddles of rainwater. Small, cherub-faced, plump and careless, he bends down to pick up a shiny, brown conker from the wet pavement. His gloves, attached to his coat by strings, trail on the ground and leave a silver snail-like path as they drag behind him. Seeing this kid makes John behave like one: showing off, he expertly bounces another conker like a football. I join in, kicking with a haphazard, unpractised, approach, sloshing leaves and mud everywhere. We both think this is hilarious.

'Come on.' He leads the way, running to a pocket of trees in the near distance.

This is it then.

My throat is dry and tight, my hands clammy. We fling ourselves to the ground under the trees and at once start pulling at each other's clothes, swiftly, expertly undressing one another. I'm naked from the waist up and my skirt is bunched up to my hips. He takes off his shirt and jumper and is wearing his trousers on one leg. I indulge myself and allow my eyes to drop slowly from his face, down to his shoulders, down to his neatly tucked stomach, down to his evident passion, past and down to his legs which are splashed with mud. I lie, facing him. After leisurely surveying, I return my eyes to his face: he is examining me. Without embarrassment, but with fearless pride I wait as his eyes fall from his lips, to my breasts, to my bush. In a second he swoops and kisses me there. Slowly, so slowly he kisses and licks and bites, until I whelp with pleasure. Gently I roll back, my bare flesh touching the damp earth and cold grass, occasionally a sharp stone sticks into my back or buttocks. I have to keep edging back on to our now very damp and crumpled clothes. I can smell the sweet grass and feel heady and sick on it. Slowly, slowly his tongue roams over my body. He kisses me and discovers zones of pleasure that make me weep and gush simultaneously: the centre of my palm, the inside of my elbow, the back of my knees, my ankle. He nibbles my stomach and sucks my tummy button. When I think that I can't take any more and that I'll burst with desire if he continues his butterfly discovery, he thrusts suddenly. He falls, he pushes, he burns, grabs and pulls until I moan with a scarlet mix of pain and desire.

I am exhausted with ecstasy, but know that I have to reciprocate the attention. We are not married and so there isn't the option of gratefully smiling, flicking out the light and turning over to sleep. I have to perform. I push him on to his back and mount him. He makes me feel so sexy, an undisputed expert. He moans, wriggles, slithers beneath me, writhing for me, then he shakes and becomes breathless . . . finally he screams. A peace-shattering scream which sends an overhead bird flapping from one tree to the next; in the distance a dog barks. With the scream, I fall sweating and exhausted off his hot body.

I think he liked it.

I check his face, it's hard to read.

My hair is wet with sweat and is sticking to my neck, my tits are damp with his kisses and my stomach and thighs with his love. We don't know what to say to each other so we hold one another, very tightly, until our breathing calms and slows. We inhale and exhale in unison. His hands smell of sperm and mud and grass; I do too. I'm sure I'll never be so clean and clear again. Instinctively I cup his face in my hands; it is an ecstatic, assured glow, so devastatingly positive. So now there is no fudging, no avoiding the issue. No spin doctor can hand out a prescription on this one because I am an adulterer.

'What love-making,' he sighs contentedly.

I roll away from him and lie on the cold grass. To test his sincerity I say sharply, 'What a euphemism, it's a fuck.' He looks at me and there is a mountain of confusion, the size of the Rockies, Alps and Everest combined.

'If you are more comfortable with that description.' Then he visibly brightens. 'I guess you're right.' He's just bought the Emperor's latest couture. I'm not certain if this is what I intended. I'm not a *femme fatale*. We don't say much to each other as we get dressed. We make jokes about the time he took to iron his shirt that morning and the state it is in now. I rather hope that we can go back to the hotel I've booked and do it all over again but he says that he has to get back home. We smoke a cigarette and buy a plastic cup of tea from a caravan near the edge of the park, then head back to the station. Although the temperature has dropped severely and it's starting to get dark, neither of us complain. We keep warm by hanging on to each other. Beer is surprisingly potent, normally a hostage to doing the 'right thing'. I don't worry for a second that we'll get spotted playing hookey from work and marriage.

We part at the Tube station. I'm going south, he's going east. Squeezed between an enormous black woman and her shopping and a nervous, young executive and his laptop, I allow myself to think about his parting shot, 'I'll call you.' I wish he hadn't said that. Or, since he had said it, I wish I'd asked when or said no, I'd call him. I get off the Tube and check the messages on my mobile, *You have. One. New message.* 'Hey Sex, told you I'd call.'

I arrive home. Still grinning. The house, as I expected, is empty. Luke is never home until after eight. Which gives me plenty of time to shower off the mud and other evidence before he gets home. My relief turns to irritation by the time

I push my sperm-stained jumper into the washing machine. No wonder I'm playing away. I've been forced into this by his neglect. I'm always on my own. I cheer myself up by playing John's message. Eight times. I pour myself a conciliatory gin and bitterly think, even if he had been home he probably wouldn't have noticed my unkempt state. I sigh and crawl into my wrought-iron bed. I'm exhausted. A vivid picture of John, tying me to it, performing all sorts of base acts, pushes its way into my head. Where did that come from? I shove the image to the side.

What exactly is he tying me up with?

On Thursday, Luke goes to his Spanish class. I do try not to think of sex on a Spanish beach with John.

It's Friday, Luke comments that we haven't seen much of each other and that we should go out. We go to the cinema to see some arty French film. Subtitles and I've forgotten my glasses. Even if I had been able to see, I doubt whether the plot would have held me. I try *not* to think of John's funny, French/Liverpudlian accent. Luke and I are in bed by 10.30, he is asleep by 10.40. I lie awake staring at the ceiling. It is a good thing that I have such a full life that I don't waste time thinking about John. Saturday, I go to the King's Road with Daisy while Luke tinkers with his motorbike. I don't need new clothes but I plan to treat myself to countless slutty dresses, the type I imagine John likes his women to wear.

Daisy is in love with Simon so my presence is superfluous. I could have been walking next to her wearing a billboard claiming 'the end of the world is nigh' and she wouldn't have noticed, therefore shopping with Daisy isn't as much fun as it used to be. The trips are irregular (fitted in between Simon's golf matches) and frustrating (they never culminate in a purchase, only in a decision to 'give it some thought' or to 'come back later and see which Simon prefers'). Today has every sign of following this irritating, more recent pattern. I sit outside the changing room while Daisy tries on sixteen pairs of identical grey bootleg trousers. After trying on the first and third pair, for the fourth time each, she suggests we get a coffee to give her time to 'think it over'. I smile conspiratorially with the Saturday girl but she is very disenchanted and sweeps past me disdainfully. I marvel that she can manage to be disdainful while carrying sixteen pairs of trousers.

'John Lewis as usual?' asks Daisy.

'I fancy a change.'

I huddle Daisy into a smoky café, one we pass every Saturday but have never entered. The café is full of deeply intimidating people, all of whom are devastatingly beautiful, or up-to-the-second voguish, or a combination of both things. Daisy hesitates at the door. I think she might bolt. I know what she is thinking. I shrug, I'm feeling experimental, brave and appropriate.

'We've as much right to be in this café as anyone else,' I hiss as we nudge into the two seats nearest the door. Eventually, well after we have had the 'do you think we should go to the counter or is it waitress service?' debate, when I'm beginning to think that it isn't a café at all, but in fact someone's front room, a tall French waitress approaches our table. Like the clientele, she is impossibly attractive. She has large, grey, almond-shaped eyes, a waist about the width of my wrist and straight glossy hair that moves with her head. She silently takes our order. I really hope black coffee, filtered and caffeinated is an acceptable choice. She sashays back to the counter, nods silently to the bar boy and hands him her illegibly scribbled chit. I consider that there is a possibility that the note reads 'move quickly, tight pecs, we want them out of here'. I watch suspiciously but the bar boy doesn't so much as glance our way; instead he slops filter coffee into two glass beakers. Languidly the waitress puts them on our table and then leaves us to it. Daisy and I watch her hair swing gracefully, hovering between shoulder and chin.

'She probably doesn't have a personality,' whispers Daisy, tugging at her curly fringe. We both know she doesn't need one. I pick up a sachet of sugar cane and then change my mind, opting for Canderel.

'It does make you think though, doesn't it, Daisy?'

'What?'

'Well, with so many really good-looking women in the world, how do ordinary women get their men to stay faithful? Or even how do really beautiful women get their men to stay faithful? There are no guarantees.'

'Con, Luke's mad about you. He'd never look at another woman!'

Daisy might be right, Luke wouldn't look at another woman, he hardly looks at me, but John will look. More than look. I shudder and try to fork-lift the thought out of my head. What does it matter to me if John is a womanizer? It doesn't matter. I won't be seeing him again anyway. I said it would just be the once. I mean where can it go? I'm a married woman. Luckily, with Luke, I don't have to give infidelity a thought. Well, at least not his.

'What's up, Con? You seem distracted.'

'I'm just tired. I've something big going on at work, a project I started a couple of weeks ago. I'm not getting much sleep because of it.'

Daisy nods, relieved. 'I thought for one awful moment that there was some problem between you and Luke.'

'Don't be mad.'

'Yes, you are right. One certainty, in this crazy life, is that you and Luke have a great marriage.'

I don't like the way this conversation is going. 'How's your coffee?'

'Fine. I mean, I really envy you, Connie. You really do have such a great marriage. Luke is so nice, especially in this world full of bastards.'

'Hmmm. Err, which trousers do you think you'll get?'

'I mean, he is so patient, clever, understanding – '

'I liked the ones in Whistles – '

'He really listens to you.'

'God, it's smoky in here, isn't it?'

'I think that Simon is really similar to Luke.'

Better, better territory, Simon rather than Luke. I try to encourage her in this direction.

'How are things going with you and Simon?'

'Really well. He's so good. He's intelligent, thoughtful, creative. Just like Luke.'

Infuriated, I sigh. She is right of course, Luke is good. Good in the clear and honest sense. I know little about John but I know enough to have established that John is not good. He is bad. Bad in the clear and honest sense. He is not good enough for me, yet I've never come across anything as good, in the vital and wicked sense. Luke is good enough but not enough. Suddenly, I notice that he's dull. I'm doomed to a life of once-a-week sex. Luke fiddling with my nipple as though it is a light switch, fifteen minutes from start to finish. The only sex toys in our lives are pyjama bottoms and the only novelty is if we do it before or after we've brushed our teeth. John, my lover (I tentatively try out the word) is not as kind, not as selfless, not as known. Damn it. Not as known. That's why he is in my bed and head, oh, and the fact that he is unimaginably sexy. I sip my black, strong coffee. I've married a man who can offer me a constant, and very respectable, nine out of ten. I love him. He is kind, tender, intelligent, compassionate. How could I not love him? Our friends are known to burst forth in spontaneous cries of 'You guys' and clapping their hands with glee, thinking about what a wonderful couple we are. Fuck John for showing me that ten out of ten is still out there. Even eleven. But I can't kid myself – by sleeping with John I'm not succumbing to my heart, but a far louder organ. I only have to hear his name and I come. I think of his eyes and my tits sit up pert and expectant, begging him to cup and suck. I wish I'd never met him. He's disturbed everything, ruined everything.

I have these thoughts as I talk to Daisy about what time she should come to dinner tonight. I notice that her hair curls attractively around her neck and the guy sat on the table next to me is staring at me. The couple opposite are obsessed by each other. Suddenly I'm aware of sex. Mine, John's, Mr Six-Pack behind the bar. It's weird.

It is our turn to have everyone round for dinner. It is frequently our turn or Rose's. It is rarely Lucy's turn and almost never the turn of Daisy or Sam. There are very good reasons for this: comfort – Rose and Peter, and Luke and I, live in very spacious homes that are designed for entertaining; cuisine – Rose and Luke are both excellent cooks and Peter and I both do an admirable job of setting the table and cooling the wine. Lucy is also a chef *par excellence* and has an elegant and spacious home. She used to do a lot of entertaining but invariably only when she was trying to impress some man. She'd invite us round to show him that not only is she a hugely successful career woman but that she can balance her exhausting schedule with leisure time and close friends. Lucy wrote the blueprint for having it all. Inevitably the man in question was not just impressed but affected and moved. With immutable predictability, before the chocolate soufflé made an appearance, Lucy and her victim would have moved on to a whole different type of dessert. And we guests would be left to the struggle with the percolator.

Daisy is a teacher in North London, so there are two obvious reasons that we don't often dine at her place: the Northern Line, enough said, and the fact that she lives in a matchbox. A very studenty matchbox at that. All damp patches on the bathroom ceiling, a shortage of loo roll and a veritable plethora of brothel beads and various bits of hangy material, that divide up already minuscule rooms. Besides which Daisy doesn't have enough chairs for us all to sit on, well, not all at once. So dinner either degenerates into a rather haphazard game of musical chairs; whereby someone always has to be jumping up to get salt or pepper, or matches, or more wine, so that someone else can sit down. Or, a row breaks out because Lucy sits on someone's knee. Not mine or Sam's, but Luke's or Peter's, or most dangerously, the date of Sam or Daisy.

Sam's flat is perfectly lovely for dining but she shares it with the flatmates from hell. She used to share it with Mike. Mike was really dishy and for a while we had hopes that Daisy and he would become an item. The signs were all there. He slept with her on an infrequent basis, failed to call her for weeks on end, and whenever she met someone else he begged her to come back to him. Which she always did. However our hopes were crushed when he announced that he was moving out of Sam's flat to get married. A very awkward situation, especially when Sam asked Daisy if she could borrow a hat of hers for the wedding.

Now Liz has moved in. Liz hasn't attempted to seduce any of Sam's friends but it turns out that it is simply because we're not her type. We're all apparently too frivolous and she's looking for a woman with a bit more moral meat. Liz is an ardent feminist, even though she knows it isn't fashionable any more. To be fair, she's a really interesting woman, full of thoughts, ideas, facts and viewpoints. She can be very pleasant and informative company.

As long as you are not a man.

And you don't like men.

Men are the enemy and women who like men are traitors. They should be tarred and feathered. Liz holds (and frequently expresses) the opinion that men are selfish, lazy, two-dimensional relics and since the invention of sperm banks and

126

the Black & Decker they are now without any real purpose. Possibly their demise as a sex would be of no real economic, moral or practical loss, but to most of us it just seems such a shame. I mean Luke is a man and I'm grateful, Sebastian and Henry will grow up into men and they are adorable (of course there is the argument that Sebastian and Henry won't grow up, that no man does, and that their little baby selves are as good as it gets), our fathers are men and a number of them are tolerable. And there is John.

Liz labours under the impression that the whole reason for a dozen adults to sit round a table is to discuss religion and politics. Drrrrrr no, Liz, it's to get pissed. With missionary zeal she attempts to advance our awareness. No amount of polite diversionary tactics work, the atmosphere is always strained.

'What a lovely dress, Daisy, is it new?' Rose tries.

'Do you know what you are reinforcing by wearing a dress with a neck line that virtually meets the hem line? You are reinforcing all chauvinistic views that a woman's role is to decorate rather than create or debate.' Liz spits angrily.

Daisy stammers that she saw it in a Karen Millen window and isn't trying to reinforce any particular view, she just liked it. Peter usually jumps in with some well-thought-out counter-argument that makes us laugh.

'Dyke.'

And then Rose has to start all over again. 'What lovely sauce, Sam, you must give me the recipe.'

So tonight it is our turn. Dinner parties are taken seriously in the Baker household. Luke, quite unlike any other man I've ever met, actually does do the cooking. He doesn't just say he does the cooking and then leave it to me. He doesn't put on a huge display – a theatre – when he cooks. He doesn't only do the cooking when people are around to praise him either. He genuinely cooks, and does it in a quiet, methodical, sensible way and the results are always delicious. I do the inviting and the table-laying. I put the nibbly bits into bowls and I place said bowls tastefully around the sitting room for our guests. I also do the cleaning up. Luke is a man not a saint.

Luke is poring over the various cookbooks that we own. I say 'we' because Luke's parents, with tedious regularity, insist on buying me cookbooks for my birthday and Christmas presents. I think I created a rod for my own back when I actually asked for Marco Pierre White's, *White Heat*. Obviously I had no intention of actually cooking anything from it. I just wanted to salivate over the moody shots of bad boy Marco. He is a bad boy, very like John. Serves me right because I am now the proud owner of *Delia Smith's Winter Collection*, *Delia Smith's Summer Collection*, *The Sunday Times Complete Cookbook*, *Master Chef 1995*, *Master Chef 1996*, *Master Chef 1997*, *The Ultimate Barbecue Cook Book*, *Sainsbury's Low Fat Gourmet* (a contradiction in terms if I ever heard one), *Sainsbury's Astrological Cookbook* (honestly!), *Sainsbury's Fish Cookbook*, *Sainsbury's 1000-recipe Cookery Book*, Michel Roux's *Sauces*, *River Café Cook Book One* and *River Café Cook Book Two*. Each year I thank them enthusiastically and then the following Christmas, when they buy me another one, I always wish that I hadn't been quite so enthusiastic. Still, I doubt that Mrs Baker Senior is over-thrilled with the M&S toiletries that I buy her every year or Mr Baker Senior is all a flutter over the slippers that I buy him; yet they are always polite enough when they receive them. The *raison d'être* of Christmas is to fill each other's homes with gifts neither finds useful nor beautiful. It keeps us and our purses occupied as come November we have to fight our way through tack and crowds to buy the gifts. Then in January we have to fight through reduced-price tack and even more ferocious crowds, as we return the gifts we are given. That's civilization.

'I think I've been over-cooking the tuna for our guests. According to this book, it barely needs searing,' says Luke. He's having this conversation with his wife because he doesn't know I have sucked another man's dick. I do know this however. And I hate that we know different things for the first time in over five years.

'Do you think it is enough to love, even if you are not in love?' I blurt dangerously.

'We could pepper them, that would be nice.'

'Does lust have anything to do with real love?'

'Or basil. What do you think of basil?' Basil, who's Basil? His name is John not Basil. We stare at each other from our different constellations. I try a more conventional approach.

'What are we eating tonight?' My interest is feigned, feigned to a record-breaking level. It is the least I can do if he is prepared to cook.

'I thought we'd start with Sardinian wild-fennel soup and then spiedini of monkfish and scallops with wood-roasted Jerusalem artichokes and celeriac for main. What do you think?' I don't really hold an opinion as I have no idea what or where the spiedini is on a monkfish, so I venture a non-committal, 'Sounds yummy.'

'What are you doing for pudding?' he asks.

This is part of the deal; he does starters and main but to give him an opportunity to get slaughtered I take over for pudding. I don't mind because as a rule the food that Luke has already dished up is so exquisite that the accolades are flowing. I can serve up Wall's Viennetta and get told I'm a brilliant chef.

'Ben & Jerry's,' I reply. For a nanosecond Luke shows his disappointment.

'Two flavours,' I defend, 'chunky monkey, your favourite.'

'What's the other flavour?' he asks trying to sound grumpy but I know he isn't angry with me.

'Chocolate, for the girls,' I smile.

'How many are there tonight?'

'Full complement.'

'What? All the girls have dates to bring?'

'Well, Lucy isn't bringing a date; but, yes, everyone is bringing someone. You sound surprised.'

Luke often suffers as one or other of the girls calls me in the middle of the night, furious or broken-hearted over the latest disastrous love affair. Luke is always brilliant in these situations. He makes tea and offers his handkerchief. He has a whole string of platitudes that he rolls out like, 'The man's a fool, I pity him', 'It is his loss' and 'Do you want me to punch him?'

He rotates them. He also tells my girls that they have great legs or look knockout just when they need to hear it. They all simper and lap it up. Luke approaches the news that my girlfriends have got new boyfriends with some trepidation. He seems to think it is only a matter of time before he'll be called upon to put the kettle on.

The preparation for our dinner parties is usually a laugh. Luke puts on his huge white chef's apron (or pinny, as I like to tease him). I pour a couple of massive glasses of wine and put on the stereo. While he chops and slices and boils and trims (which I find very attractive, it's the knives), I dance around the living room pretending to be Tina Turner (which he finds very attractive, it's the underwear). By the time we open the doors to our guests we are usually *non compos mentis*, either dizzy with the wine or sex. Not tonight. I'm relieved that Luke is too involved in the monkfish for any monkey business. I am carefully avoiding having sex with him.

Daisy and Simon arrive first. They are glowing and giggly, which I find annoying. They keep looking into each other's eyes the way you do in the beginning, when you can't believe your luck and you try to understand that the other person really is believable, by continually checking that they are there. *John's eyes are unsurpassable. He stares at me with that intensity.* They've also developed a really annoying habit of answering each other's questions and finishing each other's sentences. I find it peculiar. I pour Simon and Daisy a large gin and tonic each while Luke rushes back to the kitchen to season fennel leaves. I'm patently unnecessary. I watch Simon and Daisy gaze at each other passionately over the slices of lime and amorously touch hands as they both dive into the nut bowl. *Paris.* If it is possible to throw lustful vibes at one another while discussing finding a parking space, they manage it. Simon is of average height, *a little taller than John* and above average humour. This would not have seduced the type of woman who likes a tall, dull man, but seems to suit Daisy perfectly. To compensate for his height deficiency or to exaggerate his humour proficiency, he is extremely affable and grins constantly. He is an interior designer, which is how Luke met him. Simon has quite a reputation and Luke tells me he is 'going places'. I finally drag Simon away from giving Daisy erotic and eager caresses and force him into conversation. I am, after all, about to feed him; the least he can do is distract me from my distraction. I discover that before he started his career in interior design, he'd been an art director and held a powerful and profitable, exhilarating and enviable position in one of London's top advertising agencies. He explains that it made him nauseous. He couldn't bring himself to believe in the all-powerful client or the greater wisdom of the Account Management Department, which he regarded as spineless. He was at first irritated and then appalled at the careless abuse of his reputation; so he resigned, retrained and then set up his own business. In the absence of Daisy's mother I feel it is my duty to establish all of this.

Peter and Rose arrive next. Rose goes into the kitchen to help Luke, and Peter settles down to a manly chat with Simon. He also wants to check out Simon's eligibility. Men define themselves through their work and therefore they define each other through each other's work. To a man like Peter (who works in the City doing some clever thing, like Lucy) a chap cannot be a decent chap unless he has a respectable job. Therefore the endless trail of poets, drummers and bartenders that Daisy has brought home have not cut ice with Peter. After all, whoever Daisy selects as her ultimate mate in life will be related to Peter. Peter, however, is too well brought up to just ask, 'So what are your prospects young man?' It does sound a bit keen. But then it is essential that Peter can define

Simon, so he can relax. Luckily, Simon is good-humoured enough to know that Peter's endless questions about golf, fishing, tyre tread, rowing machines, household insurance and endowment mortgages, are not just small talk but a way of gathering clues as to what Simon actually does for a living. Simon puts Peter out of his misery by telling him he is a designer and also telling him the odd story about tax and car insurance to show that he takes life seriously. Peter visibly softens and Daisy orgasms on my sofa. I'm bored. My friends are boring. They care about MOTs but not Kipling's 'If'.

The bell rings. I'm grateful. Lucy bursts into the centre of the gathering, announcing grandly, 'I am so sorry I'm late,' although there isn't a single intonation in her voice to corroborate her statement. It is one of Lucy's traits to be late and to apologize profusely and insincerely. Lucy has kindly brought me flowers, which serve to further enhance her appearance. She sashays over to me and presents the lilies with a flourish, her limbs tapering in all directions like ribbons on a May pole. I suddenly feel dull and clumsy. By contrast, all the men light up like the Regent Street Christmas lights. Her 'date' for the evening is Tarn. Tarn is slight, physically perfect and homosexual, Lucy's living accessory. Her tall, slender blondeness is a stunning contrast to his short, neat, darkness. Tarn and Lucy cheerfully use each other as dates and make up numbers whenever necessary. 'Necessary' is when Tarn needs a straight partner. He is a lawyer in a fairly conservative chamber and often needs a beauty of the female variety to accompany him. Lucy usually asks Tarn along when she is involved with a married man and needs an exposable date. It's odd that she's invited him tonight, when neither circumstances apply. But I'm happy to have Tarn along. It adds to everyone's kudos to have a gay friend. And his presence embarrasses Peter, which makes me titter. Besides which, Tarn is interesting in his own right, sexuality aside, which is more than can be said for most.

Luke is getting a bit concerned that the flavour of the Sardinian wild-fennel soup will be impaired if Sam and her man don't arrive soon. It is extremely convenient that 'Sam' rhymes with 'man', if for no other reason than it saves us the bother of learning her boyfriend's names. The generic term is easier considering the rapidity with which she swaps them. She arrives late and tearful. While Luke pours her man a drink and she helps me serve up the soup, I discover that her man, Mark or James or Paul or something instantly forgettable, didn't want to come at all. They've argued all the way from her house to mine. They've stopped the cab three times. Firstly, when she shouted, 'Well, don't come then, you won't be missed.' Again when he shouted, 'All your friends will be expecting something of me, it's such a pressure,' and finally at the off-licence when they stopped to get some wine. Apparently the problem arose when Sam asked Mark/James/Paul what his surname is. This led to all sorts of questions about commitment and accusations about her tying him down. It does seem imbalanced that she knows which side of the bed he prefers to sleep on, *John prefers the right*, but not how to introduce him in public. I sympathize as much as it is possible to sympathize when your mind is concentrating on carrying ten bowls of soup up to the dining room without spilling any on the floor or your guests.

Despite this rather inauspicious start to the evening the

dinner goes well. I can't eat but the food by all accounts is delicious, and although I've had nothing to do with it I happily accept the compliments on my husband's behalf. The wine is plentiful and a good year, I can vouch for this personally, despite my inability to digest solids. The drunker I get the harder I fight the urge to tell everyone that I'm in lust. I can't for obvious reasons, I'm married to the host. So instead I'm forced to listen to Lucy relate the details of a recent date with a wealthy magazine editor.

'Very pleasant. I was wined and dined but not sixty-nined.'

'Why not?' asks Rose. The question is not unreasonable.

'He talked about money too much, he's such a cliché,' replies Lucy, not even bothering to take offence at the assumption that she sleeps with all her dates.

'You can't say that,' I argue.

'Why? Because he's Jewish? If he was Roman Catholic I'd complain he is irresponsible about contraception or that he has a hang-up on the mother/whore dichotomy.' *John is Catholic, in a nominal sense.*

'You are so harsh,' I say fondly.

'And Muslims, what's your objection there?' asks Daisy, curious.

'Sexist and restrictive.'

'Protestant?' asks Sam's man, his tone is hopeful.

'Bullies,' Lucy replies without even treating him to a glance.

'I'll be specific, C of E?' he persists.

'Mummy's boys, terribly oedipal.' I love her when she is like this. It is such fun.

'Church of Scotland?' laughs Luke, as he shakes his head in despair.

'Heathens, they like the cold, they are tight-fisted and don't know any good restaurants. However I am quite interested in that kinky no-underwear thing.'

'Russian Orthodox?'

'I never kiss facial hair.'

'Agnostic?'

'Weak.'

'Atheist?'

'Hedonistic.'

'Lucy, you can't operate by categorizing everyone by prejudiced stereotypes.'

'Yes, I can. In fact, it is an absolute must, it makes life so much easier. Anyway, after that concise tour of the world's religions and male embodiment thereof, I guess being told how much dinner costs isn't too awful. Maybe I will call him.'

Rose leaves the room to call the baby-sitter and Lucy takes the opportunity to tell the rest of us the news that she has been dying to tell us all evening. She's slipped into another liaison with another married man. I think I'm going to implode as I force myself to remain silent. Me too. Me too. Me too. But the other way round. Rose is very intolerant of Lucy's liaisons with married men. My own view had always been that such relationships are pointless and heart-breaking, god, was it only days ago that I had such black and white sanctimonious, infantile, ill-considered viewpoints?

'Why do you do it?' Sam asks, exasperated. She dates to marry. Married men can't marry you, so in Sam's eyes, they are a waste of time.

'Well, all the nice men are married or gay,' Lucy defends petulantly, blowing kisses at Tarn and Luke.

'Come on, guys, let's go outside for a smoke. I get the feeling that the ladies want to gossip.' Luke's ironic intonation is only just suppressed. Sam's man, who is of course fascinated by Lucy, seems reluctant to leave.

'Believe me,' says Luke, 'if you miss the instalment this week, you will pick up the tale next, it's always the same story.'

'Bloody cheek.' Lucy playfully throws a discarded cork at Luke.

'Let's go, they are becoming violent.'

The guys leave us and we are grateful. We are able to scoop big dollops of ice-cream out of the tub with our fingers. This makes up for the pathetic portions we limit ourselves to in mixed company. Except for me, I can eat in front of Luke. I mean, I fart in front of him. We have no secrets. Rather we had no secrets.

'Is that really why you date married men?' asks Daisy, who is genuinely interested in Lucy's psychology, 'because all the nice men are married or gay? I mean I've just met Simon and he's neither.'

'You haven't known him long enough to be sure,' snipes Lucy cruelly. She sighs, 'No, not really. I don't believe *all* the nice men are married or gay, although it is something I say often enough. I've done *fag hag* in my teens but the advantages are limited. Gay men wash and they are, as a general rule, useful when it comes to advice about getting stains out of fabrics.'

'You have IKEA to thank for that,' I point out.

'I date married men because they are easy. They are grateful and quiet. Not demanding at all. I don't want domestic bliss, which is lucky because it doesn't exist.' Lucy doesn't care about not being with someone over Christmas, she usually works through the holidays, or, less pathetically, spends it with us.

'Married men are usually reasonably good lovers, as they've usually been broken in by their wives. They never complicate things by wanting to get to know, really know, you.'

'Don't you ever think of their wives?' Sam asks, although she knows the answer already. Of course she doesn't.

'Do you remember when we were at university and we considered it a cardinal sin to as much as kiss a bloke that was seeing some other girl?' says Daisy.

'Yes, such a slippery slope,' laughs Lucy bitterly. She fiddles with her cigarette packet. As I won't let her smoke in the house she has two choices. She can join the guys for a smoke in the garden, one of her favourite pastimes, or stay with the girls and talk about herself, another one of her favourite pastimes.

We are quiet and we can hear the chaps in the garden.

'Why do women have orgasms during sex?' asks Peter. 'To give them something to moan about.'

They laugh drunkenly and we laugh too.

As I wash the car on Sunday, I wonder what car he drives. When Lucy arrives and drags Luke and me out for a Sunday afternoon walk around Clapham Common, I can't help but think of my last visit to a park. I try not to think of him, only I can't concentrate on anything else. The plan had been: work hard, go to university, make nice friends, get a good job, have random sex, meet someone special, have exclusive sex, marry, live Happily Ever After. I have careered off life-plan A to Z, headlong into the surrounding barricades. It seems unlikely that I'm going to make it to the chequered flag. I vacillate between desperately wanting him to call and hoping that he won't. I've told him not to. I'll die if he calls. I told him that was that. Problem is, I really fear that this is *it*. I'll die if he doesn't call.

'It's me.' I feel the taut elastic band of tension snap as I move towards a blonder, cleaner, filthier self. It's Tuesday, I've waited for this call for a lifetime.

'I'll call you back.' I put the phone down and grab my handbag. 'I'm going to get a sandwich. Do you want anything?' Sam shakes her head.

'Not unless you stumble across any eligible bachelors in Pret.'

'It's unlikely.'

'I know.'

Once outside the office I call him back from my mobile. Bob watches me suspiciously. The phone rings once before he picks it up.

'Hey, Sex.' I'm delighted, he must have programmed my number into his phone. 'How are you?'

'Tired,' I reply. Thrilled. Exhilarated. Amazed.

'And sore, too, I shouldn't wonder.'

'I didn't get much sleep this weekend.'

He goes silent, I've hurt him. 'I don't mean because of sex with Luke,' I rush to explain and therefore I shout. Some bloke from my office enjoying a fag break, raises his eyebrows. I huffily try to look unperturbed at his eavesdropping.

'Hmmm?' John sounds pained, confused.

'Because I'm excited,' I say coyly.

'Why?' He adds something else but I miss it because a taxi driver starts to bawl at a courier on a bike.

'What did you say?' I yell.

'Say something sexy,' he instructs.

I feel stupid; it is only 10.45 in the morning and I'm standing outside my office, where it is generally accepted that I am a responsible, respectable, married woman.

'You start.'

'I want to rub you up and down until you say stop. I want to play with your body and make you real hot. Let me do all the things that you dream of.' It isn't poetry, it is a bit of a cliché but it is already working. I'm squirming. 'Would you like that?'

'Very much.' I feel flustered and awkward, so I turn the conversation. 'What have you been up to?'

'Had my hair cut. Had a laugh chatting up the bird that does the shampooing.' He tells me that the poor love-sick trainee rescued his hair out of the mucky dustpan, stuffed it into an envelope and put it in her jeans pocket, near her bum. He goes on and on about her being really flirty whenever he visits the hairdressers.

'Excited at the reception desk.'

'Sounds like a sad *Time Out* lonely hearts ad.'

He tells me about her giving him extra attention when she massages the shampoo in, never charging for conditioner, always there with a cup of coffee and the latest copy of *GQ*. It is quite a funny conversation. I'm not threatened by hearing about the other women he flirts with. I mean, it's not as though he's sleeping with them. They aren't real competition and anyway I can hardly insist that he remains faithful to me, since I'm with Luke. I'm not jealous or anything. I'd like to poke her eyes out.

'How old did you say she is?'

'Errr . . . 'bout seventeen, I imagine. Hard to know with Continentals.'

'You're nearly twice her age.'

'How old do I look? Do I look thirty? I'm not thirty yet you know. I don't feel thirty.'

'You certainly don't act it,' I assure.

'Anyway, you're only as old as . . .'

'The woman you feel.'

'Ha ha, the old ones are the best.' He giggles, largely to himself.

'My point exactly.'

'Your point. I thought we were talking about my point.'

'Whey hey.'

'She has fabulous tits and such a nice bum.'

'She will have, won't she? Not only is she just seventeen but she's Italian.' I'm consoled by the fact that they only defy gravity until they marry and then everything hits the pavement. To ensure that he realizes I'm not in the slightest bit jealous or disconcerted, I agree that there is something about youth that is a distinct and undeniable turn on.

'Maybe it's the ready willingness, the firm expectant loins or the fact that they are always curious and then grateful. Or maybe its because they don't expect any conversation.'

He doesn't respond but falls silent. I'm irritated and stare at the cracks in the pavement. They don't swallow me up.

'Don't be like that. Look, the reason I called is that I

have some good news. My girlfriend, Andrea, is away next week. I can see you any night you want, every night if you like.'

Girlfriend!

Girlfriend!!

'Girlfriend?'

'What? I can't hear you. This is so frustrating, the line keeps breaking up.'

'I didn't realize you had a girlfriend,' I stutter.

'Surely you're not jealous, Greenie? You're the married one.'

I'm silent.

'You are jealous. Oh, Connie, how touching.'

He's rarely called me Connie. I dissolve.

'I thought you'd be pleased. This way I'll never be the type of bloke that turns up on your doorstep declaring undying love for you, making a nuisance of myself. You must be relieved.'

'Yes.' No.

'Are you jealous?' He sounds thrilled.

'No.' Yes.

'Look, I've got to go, I'll call you later about meeting up next week. I need to know your beautiful body again.'

'Are you jealous of Luke?' The question pours out frantically.

'Very.'

He hangs up.

I drag myself back into the reception, I snail into the lift and crawl to my desk. He has a girlfriend.

'What's up?' asks Sam. 'You look as though you've bought

the winning lottery ticket, left it in your jeans pocket and then put them through the wash.'

I cradle my head in my hands.

'I've just heard that John Harding has a girlfriend,' I hiss across the open pig pen. Six people pick up pens and pretend they are not listening to me.

'The cheek of him, the way he flirted with you in Paris.'

Sam, as a very loyal friend, has a convenient memory. She has downgraded my Paris indiscretion to him flirting with me. Thank God she doesn't know how things really stand, or more pertinently, lie.

'The cheek of him!' she says again and angrily hits her delete key.

'I wonder what she's like?'

'What does it matter to you?' asks Sam, rationally and unhelpfully. 'You must be relieved you never let it go too far. He's obviously a bastard. Any man who can pursue with such persistence, when they have a perfectly lovely girlfriend sitting at home, must be a complete bastard.'

I stare at Sam who has turned back to her budget scenarios. I don't like what she said. It sits uncomfortably. If he is going to insist on having a girlfriend at all, I want her to be perfectly horrid – a hard, calculating, two-headed monster – at least. I don't like the idea of her 'sitting at home'. Home is established, and sitting is passive. Now, if she is out randomly shagging other men, then that would be fine. What perturbs me most is the fact that I have a perfectly lovely husband, if not sitting at home, then certainly pottering around in the shed. If John is a bastard, then I am obviously a class A bitch.

Sam interrupts my thoughts.

'At least if he had been really-keen-die-in-a-ditch for you then I might have understood his dogged persistence. But since he just fancied you, liked the challenge, wanted a shag, then he has no right to be so disruptive.'

'My point exactly.'

'But it doesn't matter because he hasn't managed to be too disruptive, has he?'

I am silent.

'Has he?' she persists.

'No.' I sigh glumly and return to my electronic solitaire. People put down their pens again; assuming the conversation has come to a close, they no longer have to pretend to be occupied. Sam and I remain silent for some time. The only sounds are the shuffling of papers and the pounding of fingers on keyboards. I can almost hear the cogs of our minds whirling around. The problem is I've slept with him now. Less than a week ago I'd taken him as a lover. It seems childish to decide, at this early stage, that I've made a mistake. I won't call it a day. I can't call it a day. Besides which, Sam has offered me a glimmer of hope. She said that if he'd been really-keen-die-in-a-ditch and we had been one another's destinies, then it'd be OK for him to pursue me and for me to accept. Or she said something very like that.

'How will I tell?' I whisper. Universal picking up of pens.

'Tell what?' She is refusing to lower her voice. She thinks she can shame me.

'Whether he's really keen, willing to die in a ditch for me?'

'He'll act like Luke.'

'Thinking back to the way he looked at me in Paris I'm almost certain that he would die in a ditch for me.'

'Don't be stupid, Connie.'

'He acted as though he was crazy about me.'

' " Acted" being the operative word. Believe me, I've been out with a dozen men like him. You're asking for trouble. Forget it, before it goes too far.'

She is wrong. He said I was his favourite smell. He said I was irresistible. That I am entirely fuckable *and* that he can talk to me, too.

'Maybe he's feeling threatened and vulnerable. I mean I'm married. He's not only a he, but he's Northern. He's unlikely to wear his heart on his sleeve. I wouldn't like it if he did.' I'm warming to my theme. Sam's mouth hangs open.

'He has to appear nonchalant but he's not at all.'

'So you've shagged him, then?' Sam's been round the block, vicariously and actually, too often to be shocked by infidelity generally, but I can see mine saddens her.

'We are destined. He just doesn't know it yet.'

'What about Luke?' she screeches.

Luke?

'Luke and I met, liked the look of each other, started seeing each other, told each other that we loved each other, got engaged and got married. It was very easy.'

'Delightfully easy.'

'Too easy. That doesn't seem like destiny does it? I mean there are no lost epistles, no dividing continents, no missed planes, no "other person". John might be my destiny and I have to know.'

5

I have been an adulteress for six weeks. The situation is serious, a national state of emergency. John is all-consuming and although I manage to do the things I've always done, everything is different. Life BJ (Before John), when I went to work Monday to Friday, I resented every moment I was there and complained. A lot. Now, I love work. Every moment is one of unprecedented expectation. I practically make love to the phone every time it rings. I declare war on the phone when it's not John and I ask the phone to marry me if it is. Will he e-mail? Will he pop by my desk? Sometimes he walks by, raises an eyebrow and says 'Hi', a secret acknowledgement that we are insatiably bonking one another's brains out. It is so romantic. On the other hand, my evenings have become a lot less productive. Like clockwork, Monday used to be All Bar One with the girls. Get pissed and tell each other intimate secrets that our partners would kill us for sharing. Now All Bar One is becoming a drag. I have no one to talk to.

I've only confided in Sam, which I am hugely regretting. Sam is too nice to have such tales of duplicity thrust upon her. She hates meeting Luke now she knows what I'm up to. She goes red and stammers as Luke greets her with his usual friendly peck on the cheek. Daisy, who observed Sam's obvious discomfort, asked me if I thought Sam had a crush on Luke. I'm terrified that Sam's lack of guile will give me away. It's only a matter of time before she wails and beats her chest, shouting, 'I know nothing. Pull out my fingernails but I'll tell you nothing about Connie's horrific, adulterous affair.'

I've considered confiding in Daisy but how could I destroy her idea of the 'Happily Ever After'? She needs to believe in this with absolute, unwavering commitment. More selfishly, could I stand her disapproval?

No way would I tell Rose. I can imagine her sanctimonious reprimands, or worse, her charity.

Lucy would be a good person to confide in as she is excellent on the subject of men and an expert on the subject of infidelity. She is extremely clinical about sex and relationships. Lucy wouldn't give me a hard time. I just haven't had the opportunity to see her on her own. She's really wrapped up in this new man of hers. If not emotionally, then certainly physically. My lack of confidantes has left me feeling removed and secretive. I am not used to keeping secrets and I'm not very good at it, so as a precaution against alcohol-induced 'fessing sessions I avoid getting pissed with the girls. They think that I'm trying for a baby. Clearly, staying sober, when all your mates are hell-bent on getting paralytic, is not a clever way to make friends and influence people.

John is the only one really in on the secret and I can hardly call him and say, 'Let's just run over the details of last time we met – what exactly were you wearing? What was I wearing?' I can hardly say, 'And when you said that you thought I was exceptional, what exactly did you mean? More or less exceptional than your girlfriend? And this girlfriend thing: she can't be very important if you are sleeping with me and countless others, can she?' Hmmm. Finding out about the countless others was soul-destroying. I comfort myself that the number is not countless exactly; he is constrained by time and energy. But it has quickly become apparent that there are certainly quite a few others.

Besides me.

And besides his girlfriend.

They are mostly one-night stands; he doesn't often bother with repeat performances. Under normal circumstances I wouldn't accept this. Certainly, when I was single if some bloke offered me the opportunity to be part of a chorus line I'd tell him to take a hike. However big his dick was. Or cute his smile. But these aren't normal circumstances. I am in a tricky position. It is difficult to complain. I'm the married one. I can hardy adopt the moral high ground or make a pitch for commitment. I'm not the regular girlfriend; she is the one entitled to do the nagging. Anyway, his inability to stay faithful to his girlfriend is actually a source of comfort, rather than concern, to me. Clearly this is another indication that she is not his destiny, which gives me a better crack of the whip, if I should decide I want to be ring master. On that subject I am still irresolute. I can't imagine leaving Luke. So when I think of destinies I mean *I have to see this through to some sort of conclusion* destiny, rather than *I have to have this man or die* destiny. The problem is I cannot imagine what that conclusion will be.

Doing without him is not a viable option.

Tuesday and Wednesday are still gym nights but I no longer visit reluctantly. I've embraced the gym as my new best friend.

Stray shagging has made me very conscious of my body and although I'm not Roseanne, I'm not Elle McPherson either. Luckily, living a life of deception has proven to be a really good dieting technique. It gives a whole new complexion to the F-Plan. I go to the gym with a religious fervour, not only Tuesday and Wednesday evenings but four or five mornings a week as well.

On Thursday, Luke and I still go out for a meal, providing he isn't working. Naturally my lack of interest in food and my newly acquired status of adulterer, has had a colossal effect on the intimacy and cordiality of these evenings; in other words, they're not as much of a laugh as they used to be. We don't seem to have too much conversation. No more riotous giggling as he blows bubbles through his nose or I mispronounce brasserie as 'brassière'. It's understandable that we no longer make each other laugh until we're asked to leave a restaurant, but I do sort of miss it. Although I'm really lucky that John is such a comedian. I'm always laughing with him now.

Friday, we do what every other married couple in the Western World do on a Friday, i.e., have a TV fest. Watch *Coronation Street, Brookside, Friends* and *Streetmate*, eat pizza, ignore the telephone and not move from the settee.

Not for anything.

Except the pizza delivery man.

Now the TV fest also lacks the intimacy of old. I get uncontrollably hot over the Scouse accents on *Brookie* and never before had I noticed how poignant soaps are. The rest of the weekend is an endless expanse of tedium, throughout which I do grievous bodily harm to time until I can get back to work.

Saturday morning, obligatory fight with the other trolleys in Tesco (awful). Saturday afternoons, obligatory fight with the other shoppers on the King's Road (fabulous). Saturday evening, dinner party with girls and our various partners. Sunday morning, sleep. Sunday afternoon, roller-blade (well, that's what we did this summer, last summer we played baseball, we take our lead from *Wallpaper*). Then Sunday night is spent squeezing really painful spots and ironing Luke's shirts. We still do the dinner thing on Saturdays and the blading on Sundays but the warmth is lacking. Luke is busier than usual with his work, his car, his fishing, whatever, so he hasn't noticed a change. He spends literally hours in his shed. What he does in there is quite beyond me. When we first got married I was fiercely jealous of his shed, I raided it, expecting to find well-thumbed porno mags. I emerged with nothing more incriminating than a pile of his old clothes that I thought I'd thrown out and he'd rescued. Rose told me not to think of the shed as a threat but instead be grateful – 'he isn't trailing mud into the house and he is in calling distance if you need to get something from a very high shelf'.

The main change to my week's routine is that it can no longer be routine. There is always the possibility of an unexpected rendezvous. My all-consuming interest in *him* means that I find it hard to concentrate on the minutiae of life – such as carrying an umbrella, ironing a shirt or returning library books. This detail is not grand enough for me, not interesting, simply not him. I forget to eat. I have barely slept since Paris. When I do sleep I am too agitated to sink into steady unconsciousness but instead delight in being sustained by dizzy, sexy dreams. Just thinking about him makes me come, so I indulge in obscene amounts of mental masturbation; I have filthy thoughts as I sit on buses, trains and in cars. I fantasize as I walk down the street, play with my food, watch TV. I have such heady thoughts about him. I'm fucking delirious.

I'm extra fucking delirious now, as I walk towards the Hen and Cock, a grungy pub off the Caledonian Road. We never go anywhere really smart. Mostly he takes me to grubby pubs, like the ones he described in Paris. Still, I am certainly safe from bumping into any of my friends. It's five past eight, which makes me five minutes late. Quite an achievement as I've been ready over an hour. I shove open the heavy wooden door, side-stepping the vomit splattered on the pavement. It takes a nanosecond for my eyes to adjust to the dim lighting. I see an ageing sex symbol in a tight leopard-skin top behind the bar. She nods at me, possibly acknowledging that I am the only other woman in the joint. She is playing out the stereotypical part of the tart with a golden heart and letting some mangy looking dog on a string lick out Guinness from a glass. I watch as the glass hardly hits the water in the sink before she puts it on the shelf again. I make a mental note to myself not to order anything to drink that comes in a pint glass. The place is not so much is 'spit and sawdust' because there is no sawdust, only sticky lino. Sticky lino, grimy glasses, loos that are positive health hazards. Initially, these venues of dubious reputation intimidated me. I missed my choice of twelve wines and eight designer beers. I didn't think that salt 'n vinegar crisps would be able to replace mozzarella on sun-dried-tomato bread, as a bar snack. But now I'm grateful that I don't have to fight my way through crowds of trendy wankers with rounded vowels and wallets. These pubs with old men in stained trousers are more real. I'm ecstatic.

He is there when I arrive. I clock him and my heart stops. He smiles and it starts again. Every time I see him I am freshly surprised by his beauty. He scans round the pub with an expert, practised eye, locating the fag machine and the dark corners. He doesn't lead me directly to the dark corners, too obvious. Instead he chooses a location that is centre stage, for us to perform on. He likes to show off, he wants us to be seen. I sit with my back ramrod straight, proud of him. He's unusually handsome, no, stunning. We are alarmingly beautiful.

'How was your day?'

'Shit.'

'Yours?'

'Crap.'

'That's because you have a talent and you are wasting it.' I nod. Whenever I'm drunk I think I can be the next Annie Leibovitz.

'I hate my job,' he says as he drains his pint before we've even settled into our seats. 'Want another?' He indicates my empty glass. I nod.

He comes back to the table with refills and says, 'But it pays a fortune now I'm managing this big job with London Underground. Details of which I can't go into because of client confidentiality. If I tell you. I'll have no choice but to shoot you.' He grins and goes on, 'To be honest, if I tell you, you will probably terminate through tedium. I won't need to shoot you.'

I laugh. Like mine, his job is an infuriating cocktail of pride and shame. I try to cheer him up.

'Yeah, you've done well.' Management consultancies usually hire Southern, Oxbridge types. BBC English and a lifetime of protection through conformity and a family name. Tools that help them grow the life-armour of arrogance. He has succeeded with his Liverpudlian accent, comprehensive education and enormous chip. As we both find our work tedious we don't talk about it much, which is not to say we don't talk about anything solid. We behave like students, profoundly putting the world to rights over a pint and a pie. I hadn't realized that I'd missed the irresponsible optimism; I certainly don't miss the damp accommodation or the essay crises. We talk about feelings and thoughts and experiences, which are raw and red and real and truthful. I have no interest in 'gap analysis' and 'charter of intent'. The only gap I'm worried about is the gap between our meetings (I never allow myself to think beyond that) and as for charter of intent, well, I think I'm pretty clear with regard to his intentions.

I change the subject and mood by carefully recounting to him some delicate, long-forgotten memory. He likes it. He tells me about his dreams. He fidgets on his chair, finding it surprisingly easy to tell me the most fabulous and morbid things about himself. He's amazed that I'm equally interested in both. I expect his breathtaking successes and understand his shameful compromises. He talks about his background and I understand his description of the stale smell of fags on heavy curtains and lingering smell of Pledge polish. I strain my eyes and brain trying to show him that I feel it too. I try to show him that my mind is open, by sitting leaning towards him, legs wide, hands gesticulating to make my point. I frequently repeat the words 'The point is' as I struggle on the one hand to make sense of my life, while on the other hand, or more accurately with the other leg, cunt or breast, I am shoving my life into a state of pointless disarray. Our conversation progresses. Part way through my profundity I forget what I'm trying to say as I've drunk a fair amount.

I'm attracted to his irresponsibility, his manliness, his sexiness, his disposable income, his disposable respectability. He is a walking stag weekend. He is a funny, disrespectful, fast, confident, irreverent go-cart race and pub crawl. I never have to discuss lagging the loft, replacing a tile on the roof, fixing the washing machine, or washing the kitchen floor (especially those sticky stubborn corner bits). I never even have to ask him to put petrol in the car. We happily spend a fortune getting pissed. It never matters whose money is spent achieving this oblivion. We both want to demonstrate that we are irresponsibly generous (flash). It is so shiny. So dream-like. It is like going under an anaesthetic or doing class A drugs (not that I ever have but I have a vivid imagination). A floaty, special, shiny, irresponsible, exciting, amazingness.

Fun.

I am so excited, so sexy, that my cheek-bones rush to meet my eyebrows, my muscles grow a couple of inches longer; well, actually, they stretch. I am taller, really. Honestly, I am. Not a foot taller but a couple of inches I'm sure. My nails grow longer and they don't split as often – at all, in fact. My hair becomes shiny, manageable and curly. Glossy not frizzy. Not straight, which I lust after, but shiny. And although it isn't the first time I've heard, 'You fascinate me. You're brilliant.

You're amazing. You're beautiful', it has never sounded better.

The atmosphere thickens with cigarette smoke and desire, we begin to squirm in our chairs. We become tense and edgy as we concentrate on the most expedient way to find somewhere private to bang out our needs. Expediency, not discretion, is now the driving force. This is to be expected from him but frighteningly dangerous for me. I've adopted his screamingly irresponsible behaviour. Am I willing to get caught? We drink more and more. We become less and less cautious, then he starts to look for an opportunity to move me somewhere private. Halfway through the evening I am already thinking about how it will end. Sometimes we will get into a taxi and begin to hungrily pull at each other's clothes, both making clumsy grabs at each other's crotches. Other times we lunge at each other in the bar or pub. He puts his hand under the table and finds the hot space where my legs meet. I edge closer to him, urgently pushing myself into his hand and then I reach under the table, too, grasping for his stiffness. Never disappointed, there it is, hard, long, thick and ready. Sometimes we rush out of the pub impatiently, not waiting to finish our drinks, dash down a backstreet, where he drops his trousers, I fall to my knees gratefully, as if praying, and take his cock into my mouth. We writhe and scream and moan and come. We have angry, insistent, overwhelming sex. It's deep and fast and done in illicit places. It's the craziest, dirtiest thing I've ever done in my life. I feel soused and renewed with each truthful fuck.

Throughout September I'd been weighed down by morals and a sense of responsibility to Luke. I'd vacillated between wanting to throw caution to the devil and wanting to cling to my beliefs. This served to increase John's ardour. He inched off my clothes, slowly, slowly and at the same time my conscience seemed to dissolve. He stripped it away, as though he was peeling onion skins, but it didn't make me cry. My vadge imploded with desire. I willed him to break me.

He too, must lack a confidant because he speculates with me about what exactly he finds so compelling and fascinating about our affair. His training as a management consultant wins through and he puts theories on the table.

'Maybe it is because we are ultimately inaccessible to each other. Really unobtainable.'

'Maybe.'

I often tell him that I won't leave Luke for him. I mean it. I won't even stop loving my husband for him. John spends a lot of time telling me how he hates the idea of settling down or being responsible. I won't strangle him with a wedding band or trap him into making false promises of commitment, which would nag his conscience and destroy his security. I can't. With John I am my entire and naughty self, with the undiluted confidence that he will never expect too much of me. He can be his entire and naughty self, with the undiluted confidence that I will never expect anything of him. We are both extremely aware of the advantages of my being married. He tries another theory. 'You are beautiful but not the most beautiful woman I've ever had.' He stares at me through cigarette smoke and sexual vibes.

'You do have a good figure. You like it, which is bloody sexy. Invisible cellulite and angst about breast size is a complete bore.' He grins, then having a second thought: 'Well, not a complete bore, every hole's a goal.' He shakes his head.

'But, Connie, I've had some stunning bitches and they have never, ever touched me like you do.' He theorizes, 'You're possibly the brightest woman I've ever met. You challenge me, it's refreshing, exhilarating.' He leans across the tiny table and puts his elbow in spilt beer. 'Somehow it's infectious. You are the catalyst for my most stylish behaviour. When I'm with you' – he looks up to check he has my entire attention, of course he does – 'I know, with a life-defining certainty, that I'm better, better than I normally am.' He blushes slightly and says, 'You do know what I'm talking about, don't you?' I nod. He is still somewhat cautious about talking about feelings. As a woman, I have a thirty-year head start. 'I feel hungry' does not count.

'Yes, I know what you are talking about. When you are with me you suspect that you are totally irresistible.'

'I can pull any woman I want,' he agrees enthusiastically. I nod.

'And strangely, I'll probably encourage you to do so.'

I shrug and he kisses me. Suddenly he pulls back. 'Why do you always wear trousers, Greenie? I'd love to see your arse in a skirt. Your legs, too,' he mumbles. I love him fancying me so much.

'Please wear a skirt like you did when we shagged in Hyde Park.'

'Hampstead Heath.'

Sam is angry with me. Furious actually.

'You shouldn't be doing this.' She attacks her pizza with a vengeance and I think she's imagining that it's John. Sam tries to catch my eye and I try to stop grinning. I obviously fail because she tuts and returns to her pizza. 'You are living a lie. You could at least have the decency to be unhappy. In fact you should be tortured. Instead of looking so bloody gorgeous. It would have been fairer, more respectable.' I'm not sure what's bothering her most – my declining morals or improving midriff. 'You shouldn't be doing this,' she says again, shaking her head, then asks as though it is the first time she's thought about it, 'Why are you doing it, Con?'

'I can't not.' I pick up my knife and fork.

'What about Luke?'

'He hasn't the faintest idea,' I snap bitterly and put down my cutlery without managing to get anything into my mouth. 'Look. I know I am betraying my husband but I've never felt more alive. I really haven't got a choice. If you knew John better you'd understand. Do you fancy a glass of wine?' Before Sam answers, I flag the waiter and order a carafe of house red.

'Red at lunchtime?'

I ignore her.

'Go on, then, convince me.'

'Oh, he's just so totally amazing.' I grin.

'Yes, so you've said. Every man I've ever met that's hung like a donkey is amazing. Try to be more specific.' I look round the pizza parlour. How can I explain it to her?

He is the reason I was born a woman.

I look up at Sam and she is waiting patiently. The look on her face tells me that this won't cut ice.

'Well, he's different from the blokes we know.'

'Really?' she says flatly.

'Really!' She can't rein me in. 'He has dreams and passion. He has a heart.'

'More heart than Luke?'

'Just different. He didn't have the advantages of fancy family connections, he's really had to work for everything he's achieved.'

'I've never met anyone who works as hard as Luke. You're always complaining that he works too hard.'

'We're not talking about Luke!' I'm exasperated. 'John came to London and played all these poncey bastards at their own game.' I wave my hand around the restaurant, taking in twenty identical suits, eating identical fresh pasta delicacies and drinking the latest in statement beer. Sam shushes me. She is being touchy because, to my certain knowledge, she's dated at least three of the other diners. I nearly shout, 'He's played them at their own game and won.'

'Yes. John seems the type to be good at games.'

'They all have money and motors and – '

'Muff. Lots of muff, various muff.'

'It doesn't bother me, Sam.'

'Well, it should.'

We sulk. But I'm better at sulking than Sam so I'm not surprised when she reluctantly mutters, 'So what's his family like?'

'Irresponsible father, who John regards as a bohemian.'

'Left his mother for a younger model?'

I nod. 'As is natural, under the circumstances, he's developed a very strong bond with his mother.'

'Which will mean she'll make a very interfering mother-in-law.'

'I have no desire to find out.'

'John will be like that guy, Toby, I dated. He will never think his wife's gravy is as good as his mum's.'

'Look. He's not like that.' I think I can win Sam round. She's too romantic to resist for long. 'You'd like the stories about his family,' I encourage. Sam meets my eyes, I think she's thawing. 'John's extended family is large, boisterous, close, working class. They like each other so they do things together.'

'Like getting drunk?' asks Glacier Queen.

'Maybe, so what's your point? We get drunk together.' To prove it, I swallow back the rest of the red and order another carafe. 'I like families that do things together.' I don't care whether she wants to listen. I want to talk. 'He's told me about these family get-togethers. They sound – '

'Amazing.'

'Exactly! At the beginning of the night the mood is celebratory. Everyone is up for it and the evening seems to be full of stretching possibilities. Invariably, by the end of the night, after several renditions of Tom Jones's best, when they've moved from the stout to the Jack Daniel's, the room is awash with depression.'

'That will be the Tom Jones.'

'You can almost feel it, touch it, that nagging mist of regret and sadness. His mum will remember his dad, the uncles will list the faults of their wives, past and present, and his sis will shout that all men are bastards.'

'Fair enough.'

'He told me that Hardings aren't good at marriage and the relationship thing.'

'That's a warning.' Sam starts to tell me about a number

of emotional fuckwits that she's been out with. She's very gullible. I glaze over and while doing an admirable impersonation of listening, I remember our conversation from only the night before.

He'd explained, 'Ahhh, but it's all right, you see. Because just when everyone is getting a bit pissed off and miserable, one of my uncles, or perhaps me Nan – never me mum directly, she doesn't have to, she knows she can depend on one of the others to do her bragging – will turn to me and nod and say that it can't be all bad. They ask me to explain exactly what I do at work every day.'

'You must struggle with that,' I'd quipped.

He'd raised his eyebrows, a wry admission of the accuracy of my joke.

While Sam is still going on about some absolute no-hoper that she's currently trying to drag down the aisle, I continue John's story in my head. I imagine them smiling round at one another, never tiring of his stories and wrapping themselves in his self-deprecating humour. They'd nod to each other knowing he is being too modest, and look from one to another as though trying to decide exactly who it is he takes after. Just for a short time they don't mind the worn carpet that needs replacing or the outrageously bad luck they've had on the horses that day because in front of them is the font of all their pride. I imagine that sometimes, depending on exactly how much has been drunk, one or two of the Hardings will cry a tear of pure joy. John's success changes the atmosphere, and again the room is full of possibility and Tom Jones.

'Can you imagine how disapproving Rose and Daisy will be if they find out?' Sam is trying another tack.

'If Daisy ever comes up for air again. She's having too much fun to give two hoots what anyone else is up to.'

'But your wedding vows?'

'I don't care about my wedding vows.' She looks aghast. I know she thinks I'm ungrateful. I know I have what she wants. 'Sorry.' I try to turn the subject to the things that really do concern me. 'Do my thighs look fat in these trousers?'

'No, you look great.' She sounds weary. 'This infatuation is just another fashion statement.' I look at her, she's lost me.

'All of Europe is worshipping Cool Britannia, exalting anyone who epitomized a bit of rough. Blokes like John are very in. I've noticed you playing up your Sheffield heritage, even though you managed to lose your accent on the coach down here, ten years ago.' I scowl at her but she doesn't care. She carries on. 'Even *Vogue* has started to run editorial on cut-price fashion, "Snip on the Street" and cover restaurants farther afield than SW3. Personally I think it is a disgrace. I'm thinking about cancelling my subscription. John isn't real. He's entirely about tight clothes, skinny limbs, pop music, smoking, drinking, being cool.'

And her point is? I call the waiter over and ask for the bill.

It's November and I think I'll explode if I don't talk to Lucy soon. The idea of bits of guts and gore all over our newly decorated home is absolutely unacceptable. We meet at a terrifically trendy restaurant because Lucy prefers this to a casual supper at Cafe Rouge or All Bar One. She likes to go to these smart places to be seen. She is terminally indifferent to seeing others.

As we sashay into Le Pont, half-a-dozen people try to catch

Lucy's eye. Some are colleagues, others are people she barely knows. It doesn't matter if it's her godmother, her reaction is always the same. She has none. At best she acknowledges their desperate nods and waves with a vacuous, wide smile. She's perfected this smile to give the impression that she doesn't recognize them, even if she does. She's explained to me how much more cool this is. Anyway, tonight I don't want us to be disturbed either, so I'm pleased with her ice-maiden routine.

The waiter leads us to a centre table. I guess he wants to show us off. Lucy looks gorgeous, as ever. She's wearing a slate-grey, box-pleat Nicole Farhi skirt, a white agnès b. T-shirt and a Lamberto Lasanis cashmere cardigan, finished off with Mandrian leather, kitten heels from L. K. Bennett. I'd look like a cross between Ms Jean Brodie and Miss Marple but Lucy looks chic, not school-marm. Throughout my years of knowing Lucy I've been educated in the language of labels, so I too have made an effort. Not quite Bond Street, but I look cool in my Jigsaw trousers and Pied à Terre suede boots. I carefully place my ridiculously expensive Tanner Krolle handbag on the table. A new purchase that I'm sure Lucy will appreciate. She acknowledges it – 'Smart bag' but then nods to the floor indicating, by the way she raises her eyebrow, that I've make some terrible social *faux pas* by putting it on the table in the first place. She doesn't throw me.

My confidence is soaring.

I know that I've never looked as good as I've looked for the last two months. I feel younger and more stunning by the minute. I know that it isn't just Lucy that the waiter is showing off. We settle into our seats, declining bread, accepting water, ordering food and opening the bottle of champagne that a couple of guys have sent over. This kind of thing always happens to Lucy. She's great when it does. She knows just how to accept it without appearing either overly grateful or condescendingly blasé.

'Don't let them come over,' I whine. 'I want to talk to you.'

Lucy pats my hand. 'Under control.' She efficiently ushers away the waiter. As peace begins to descend around the table she says, 'OK, fire.'

'I'm having an affair.' I find saying the words out loud is an extraordinary relief. Tension flows from my body. It's also shocking. Tension crashes back into every organ. I may detonate. The words make it real, which is exciting. And terrifying.

'With whom?' Lucy pours some champagne and clinks my glass. Unperturbed. Un-fucking-perturbed!

'I won't tell you his name. It's John.'

'Tell me all about him.'

'He's irresistible.'

'In what way? How exactly? Is he tall, dark and handsome?'

'No, yes and exceptionally so. In that order.' I squeal, delighted. The floodgates open. I take her through the exact details of our meeting, and every subsequent date and phone call that John and I have shared. I recount every single emotion I've felt, outfit I've worn, meal I've eaten, in his presence. Then I give her a soap-opera script of everything he's ever said to me. We dissect it. We discuss it. We consume it. And we drink a load to celebrate.

Lucy's reaction to my infidelity is elation. She is pleased that I've moved closer to something she understands. Lucy is used to juggling numerous balls and hearts. Many of her lovers are married. She is dismissive of the holy sacrament of matrimony and refers to it as 'an unholy sacrifice, matrimony'. I think that her elation is rather bad taste. She was bridesmaid for Luke and I, shouldn't she at least be a little bit shocked? Then I remember that it is precisely because Lucy is unshockable that I've chosen to confide in her. I've had a stomachful of Sam's disapproval.

'At last you've grown up, I thought you'd never get real.' She refills my glass. 'People are not born to be monogamous. Oh, it's great to have you back! It's like the old days.'

I cock my head to the side. 'What do you mean?'

'Pursuit. It's your *raison d'être*.'

'You're saying I'm like Sam.'

'No, her pursuit is tinged with desperation.'

I'm relieved.

'Yours is tinged with arrogance.'

I'm pissed off.

I need her opinion. 'There are seven million people living in London. Assume half are women, and discount girls under seventeen and women over forty, which I think is about his range, adjust for the fact that half of those are below average looking and he won't touch them, and again assuming that those who are pregnant or taking holy orders won't touch him, there must still be over a million women for him to choose from. How will I keep him?' I ask her, then a more horrifying thought hits me: 'Imagine the odds when he goes abroad.'

'Connie, you can't seriously imagine that he is that attractive.'

'He is,' I reply simply. I poke a hole in a bread roll but don't eat any of it. She is staring back at me, unmoved. I try to explain. 'I know the taste and texture of his skin, every inch of it. I know the exact shape of his cuticles on every digit. I can tell you exactly where his freckles are. I've licked in between his toes. I know the smell of his hair and his sweat. I know the *different* smells of the *different* sweats, brow or body.' She's impenetrable. 'I not only know the shape and taste and smell of his genitals but I'd recognize his arse-hole in a line up.' That gets her. She nearly falls off her seat.

'Shush.' She checks the restaurant.

'Now do you understand when I say he's all-consuming?'

'It sounds exhilarating. It sounds like great sex.'

'It's not just sex.'

'I didn't say "just sex". I actually don't believe in "just sex". I think sex is very important. But you haven't said anything that tells me what it is apart from sex.'

Momentarily I'm stumped.

'OK, OK. Yesterday I was walking down Oxford Street.'

'Oh, Con, how could you?' Lucy asks horrified.

'OK, pretend I said Bond Street, if it will offend you any less. It's like this. There are a hundred million people teeming up and down that street. And those people, they are every shape and size and variety and colour and height and weight and social status. The women range from buxom to anorexic and the men from nerd to Adonis.'

'Yes.' She waves impatiently. 'I can imagine what it is like.'

'But do you know what the one thing is that they have in common?'

She stares at me; unusually she is lost for words.

'Not one of them is him. Not one of them can make my heart beat faster, encourage me to fling my clothes and morals aside, induce me to break my wedding vows. He's extraordinary' – I pause to take a breath – 'do you think he is my destiny?'

Lucy tuts, largely ignoring the question. 'I understand. I'm still seeing my married lover as a matter of fact.'

'Really?' It's been quite a prolonged liaison. I wonder who she is sleeping with and why. With Lucy there is always a rationale, a fully weighed up 'why'. The drink is going to my head too quickly and I can't clearly define the difference between us, but I do know that mine isn't a calculated affair, sensible or pre-considered.

I. Simply. Can't. Resist. I try to explain.

'I'm loving this but it is a disappointment to my grand plan. I still believe in marriage and I want to be monogamous. Life has gone topsy. It's tearing me apart that I am actively, certainly, methodically, destroying all that I want to believe in. I feel it almost physically, a rip deep inside my body but I'm powerless to stop myself.'

'It would be inconvenient.' I glare at her. 'We are the same,' she insists, 'I know what you are talking about, Connie. He's like a pudding: wicked, bad for you, unnecessarily excessive and leaves you feeling sick. Enchanting.' I'm uncomfortable when she says this. Because she is spot on.

Although we drink a stack, Lucy doesn't tell me much about her married lover. She doesn't tell me how they met, what he looks like, how old he is, what they talk about. She does tell me that she reads his horoscope. She describes how her fingers leave sweaty marks on the glossy paper. Dirty patches that are her signature, a signature that dries and disappears after only a few moments. She angrily explains that if the horoscope hints at domestic bliss, she rips out the offending page, her hands shaking with rage. She crumples it up into a tight, furious ball and tosses it into the wastepaper basket. Annoyed by a horoscope that might tempt him into betrayal; ironically, betrayal is being with his wife. She refers to his children. I gather that he has at least two, possibly three. I glean that they come together every day. They find a way.

'If not in a bed, then offices; I went into his office earlier this evening and we bashed it out, there and then, on his desk. I howled so much that he had to push a shirt in my mouth in case I disturbed anyone and brought them running.'

'So you work with him?' I'm surprised.

'Yes.' She quickly goes back to describing the sordid details of their relationship, which is brilliant because that's what I want to hear about.

'We do it in toilets, cars, against walls mostly. A quick, deep, lustful banging. His trousers around his ankles, my skirts pulled up past my thighs.' She whispers this naughtiness and we compare venues.

'And as he does up his zip he only just stops himself saying how bloody marvellous it is that he should find himself such a devoted, expert, uncomplicated lover who possesses an immense amount of unshakeable confidence. I can see it on his face. He's saying what a relief.'

'Oh, Lucy, I'm sure it means more to him than that.'

'Are you? Well then you are a fool. We're old enough to know that this is about need and attention. He angrily screws me because his wife is too tired or too uninterested in making love.' She drains another glass. 'Still that doesn't mean I can't have fun. It's even possible that I might get to keep him. I may turn his infantile desperation into a dependence on me. Even angry screwing can become love of a sort. I'm a patient girl, I know the score.'

My gob is well and truly smacked. Lucy is talking about *love* and keeping him. Lucy! The waiter interrupts us as he brings our salads.

'What's his name, your chap?'

'Pete.'

'Oh, how funny. We now have two Peters. Rose's Peter and yours.'

'Mine is definitely Pete, not Peter.'

She makes me laugh. She can't bear to have anything in common with Rose, even something as simple as a partner's name.

'So, by the sound of it, this Pete won't be making it into your book of funny stories, "passes that I have known and loathed"?' I slur. It really isn't easy to say this as I've had the best part of a bottle of champagne. Lucy goes very quiet. 'He's different, isn't he?' I ask excitedly. If so, she isn't going to let that cloud her judgement.

'God, Connie, how can you believe in such clichés? They are never different. There is no such thing.' I don't believe her. I don't think she believes herself. She pauses. 'Let's order another bottle. There is no such thing as a great love, the *one*. Someone who understands one completely, suits one completely. There are simply chaps that are more, or less, convenient or amusing. It's all about timing.' She raises an eyebrow and pours us both another glass of champagne.

'Lucy,' I slur, 'you are so cynical. You're wrong.'

'Are you sure? They are all the same, insisting that I am the best or different.'

I'm taken aback and it must show on my face, as Lucy laughs at me contemptuously.

'You don't fall for that shit do you, Connie? Thinking that you are the best, the sexiest, *different* somehow.' My silence confirms her suspicions. I shift uncomfortably in my seat, Lucy's reminded me of something that, due to my safe and secure relationship with Luke, I'd forgotten. Their declarations-slash-deceptions are all the same, when they are thinking with their second head.

Lucy hoots. 'Oh, come on! This John bloke, you don't believe him? You haven't thought, for a second, that you are anything more to him than a lay? That this situation is anything more than a challenge?' She often gets nasty and bitter after alcohol.

'Lucy, just because the men you've spent your life with men who are equally finite and unreliable, it doesn't mean all men are bastards. Luke proves that.'

'It seems, to me, pretty reprehensible that you are using your faithful husband as a defence for the behaviour of your scurrilous lover.'

I blush and drain my glass. The waiter opens a bottle of Chablis and Lucy continues.

'We've both been around enough men to understand the subtext to male language and their psyche. We know that, "Its not a good time for me to get serious" means "I have another woman." "My mates mean a lot to me" means kiss goodbye to Friday-night dates. "I never meant this to get so serious" is "I just wanted to sleep with you, not speak to you." "I don't deserve you" is "I don't want you." "My wife/girlfriend/fiancée doesn't understand me" – chances are she understands too much. "My wife/girlfriend/fiancée is my best friend" is of course "I'll never leave her, I just want to have sex with you." Finally, "Let's be friends" is "I don't fancy you any more."'

I am silent. I guess some of this does sound familiar.

'I thank God,' Lucy continues, 'that I've listened to enough of this to know how to play it back convincingly. Women rarely say these things to men so they never recognize the appalling clichés that every woman sees as clearly as fluorescent loo-roll floating down the Thames. I will not take responsibility for their vain, selfish, cheating actions. I'm not married. They are.'

As soon as the words are out of her mouth we both see the consequences. Lucy hasn't added, 'And you are too.' She doesn't have to. It's clear that her vain, selfish, cheating men are no worse than I am. I am no better.

'Err, look, Con, I'm sorry.' Lucy lights a fag. 'Errrm, I'm sure it's different for you.' I am too amazed to bother reminding her that she doesn't believe in *different*. There is a prickly, uncomfortable feeling hovering around my neck, shoulders and head.

It is shame.

We both drain another glass and agree to have pudding. We very, very rarely have a pudding. We keep them for birthdays and those days when one of the gang has been dumped (but not for Sam, otherwise we'd all be huge). We don't say another word until the brioche lands on our table with a thud. The table is a hive of activity. I am tearing the label off the wine bottle and Lucy is furiously puffing on her ciggie. Lucy's face is red. I feel sorry that she's embarrassed, and so I rescue her.

'Sooo,' I slur, 'have you ever tried to exercise any restraint? At any point did you think, "Oh, he's married I shouldn't do this"?'

She shakes her head impatiently. 'Not at any point, quite the reverse, full steam ahead. You?'

It's impossible to comment, console, or condemn. I am floundering around in a moral no man's land, ambiguous and directionless. My introspection is sadder.

'No, I have not. I ask myself when will it stop? How did it start? But I can't bear the idea of it ending and I make no effort to draw it to a close. I want him so much.'

'Is that wise?'

'Probably not.' My tongue clasps the roof of my mouth. I can't be more articulate, so I settle on, 'I really want him.'

'Be specific,' she challenges.

'I want him to long for me. I want him to fall in love with me. There isn't a challenge for either of us in getting someone into bed. Both of us can do that with anyone, everyone, we want. But getting someone to love you . . . Better still, letting them know you and them still loving you, that challenge is huge.'

'Luke knows and loves you.'

'Oh yes, Luke,' I say dismissively, 'not enough.'

'Works both ways you know. Play with fire and you will have to call in the paramedics.'

'Oh, I'll never fall in love with him.' Trying to sound more certain than I am. 'I love my husband.'

'Really,' says Lucy, scattering ash all over the bread-and-butter brioche. 'So why are you so cruelly determined to risk so much? From what you've told me Connie, he doesn't even want you that much.'

I am horrified. 'Where do you get that idea from?'

'From you.'

'He does!'

'No, Connie, he doesn't.' She says this with some determination. 'How often have you actually met up?'

'Who keeps count?' I laugh.

'Women do,' Lucy argues, 'so, how often?'

'I don't remember.' I play with my napkin.

'Yes, you do.'

'About eight times.' Six.

'Eight times in two months!'

'It's difficult. I'm married. Remember?'

'You said that Luke has been away a lot recently. I can guess the pattern, three times in the first week, twice in the second week, once in week four, five and seven.'

'I have no idea. I haven't plotted it like a share price,' I snap, desperately trying to remember exactly when I have seen him. I shake my head. No. Lucy is definitely barking up the wrong tree there.

'Sweetie,' she says, putting her hand on mine, 'it's not that I'm not delighted for you. I mean your first affair, it's a big thing. And he sounds simply marvellous, what with his huge cock and enormous eyes. But this destiny thing.' She shakes her head. 'Just try to keep it in perspective.'

'You don't understand, Lucy. I'm married. I wouldn't have done this if it didn't mean something . . .' I search for the right word . . . 'enormous.'

'Are we still talking about his cock here?' asks Lucy. She can be very crude. 'Where would you put him.' I stare, non-comprehending.

She elaborates. 'If he was for keeps? How would he fit into your life?'

OK. As it is Lucy, time to be frank.

'I've known from the beginning that I can't keep him. Honestly? I'm not even sure I want to. He's not about perman-ence, that's his very attraction.' I look at her to see if she is following me. 'Instead I cram as much of him as I can into a short time. I memorize his looks, his gait, his words, his clothes, his views. I push and squash it all into my mind. It's like the week before A-levels when you know that you have a finite time to cover as much of the syllabus as you possibly can and you know that after the exam you'll never have use for that information again.'

Lucy adds, 'Yet it is true to say that little facts will always be with you and pop into your head when you're least expecting them.' She is looking dreamily into the middle distance and I get the feeling that she isn't really concentrating on me. I'm determined that she will.

'The difference here is that the cramming and swotting hasn't satiated my appetite. To extend the metaphor, I now want to do a Masters in the subject of John Harding. I study his form in an attempt to capture him exactly as he is. He wears his trousers too long, he keeps his hands in his pockets, he balances his weight on his left hip. I look closer, his socks don't match. I store these memories deep in my head where they are safe.'

'And we call it knowing them,' she finishes for me.

'Lucy,' I slur, reaching over the table, urgently trying to make my point, 'it's exquisitely exciting and enthralling. I cannot be without him.'

Deadpan, she says, 'You might have to be. Let's get the bill.'

As I get in a cab I begin to sober up. For the first time since I met John I feel almost morose. Lucy doesn't know anything about men! I mean if she knew anything about men, would she still be single? I'm the married one.

Hhhmmmmm?

Christ what a mess. I lean my head against the cold window of the cab and watch the lights of London whiz by. Exhausted, I begin to drift off to sleep. My mobile playing the distinctive 'Happy Birthday' melody that John programmed for a laugh, wakes me.

'Greenie.'

'You called!'

'Returning yours, how goes it?'

All the frustrations of the conversation with Lucy fall from me. I try to sober up so that I can concentrate on being witty and engaging. He beats me to it.

'I want to fucking fuck you.'

He's struggling and stuttering with excitement. 'You turn me on so much my cock aches. My cock is straining. I'm hard just talking to you. I'm putting my hands inside my clinging Ys, now, this minute, and I'm rubbing my cock.'

I squirm on the leather cab seat, thrown into immediate

confusion. He makes me feel invincible. I've never been so sexy, never been so desirable, in my life. It at once excites me and shames me. When Luke and I talk dirty it doesn't seem real, it seems as though we are playing at grown-ups. This is real, really real, really horrifying.

'Where on your cock?' I lean forward and close the glass partition between me and the cabby.

'You know the very sensitive rim at the end.'

'Of course I know it. I found it for you.'

He laughs.

'Where are you?'

'I'm in a cab, on my way home. I've just had dinner with Lucy. You know she said the strangest thing – '

'Turn round. Come to my place.'

I waver, I look at my watch. It is ten to one. I really should go home and let the cat out, also Sam will think it odd if I turn up in the same outfit two days in a row. On the other hand, Luke is away on some architects' seminar.

'You're staying at mine tonight.' It isn't so much a question as a command.

'What's your address?' I scrabble around my handbag and eventually unearth a blunt eyeliner. I try to concentrate on my brain to hand motor skills. I give the cabby the address. He rolls his eyes.

'Do you know it?'

'Sure do, darling. Best lap dancing club in East London.'

'Oh.'

Thirty minutes later, the cab pulls up outside the club. I see John, my insides do a flip. He pays the extortionate cab fare and lets it go.

'I thought we were going to go on to yours?'

'We are. We can walk from here but I have to have you now.'

The cold night sweeps over me and I shiver with anticipation. I should have eaten more than a salad, I only played with the brioche, now lack of food means that the alcohol is flowing like blood, directly to my brain. We walk briskly, talking about something or other. Our hands find one another's; his long fingers knit into mine until we lock tight. He leads me into a doorway. Our mouths are on each other's immediately, roughly. I pull at the zip of his trousers and his hands urgently search under my shirt, for my breasts. Hard nipples and the weight of him leave me without the need for other sensations. My heart pounds in my thighs, then I feel him burning into me. Filling me, climbing up inside me, choking the breath out of me. When it is over, he pulls up his zip. 'Come on, let's go back to my place.'

His house is a bit of a surprise, not a white loft-space but a tiny two-up, two-down in a scruffy part of the East End. He forces open the door, pushing his way through mountains of junk mail. A stale smell hits me. I wonder if he's hired this place to bring me to. He probably has a wife and three kids ensconced in a nice house in Fulham. The smell is revolting, and momentarily I prefer the idea of a wife and kids, rather than him being responsible for this smell. John seems unaware of the vile odour of decaying vegetables, sweaty socks and that indefinable smell of male locker rooms. Alternatively, there are corpses rotting under his floorboards. By contrast he always smells of designer soaps and expensive aftershave. I wonder, what is the masculine equivalent for the saying 'All fur coat and no knickers'?

The house is full of solid second-hand furniture. A sturdy 1930s three-piece suite and several art deco bookcases. The armchairs are masked by floral stretch covers and the settee is blooming mustard-coloured stuffing. I stroke the dirty surfaces, happy with the invitation back to his flat. It seems to make the relationship more real than hotel beds and alley walls. We stagger up the stairs to his bedroom. He vaguely waves at the bedroom floor and mumbles an apology for the mess in the room. Chaos prevails; undies and outer clothes lie where he's dropped them, in sweaty piles. Books are stacked to calf height and the wavering towers look decidedly precarious. Several half-empty coffee cups grow fungus. Dozens of empty beer cans are scattered around; they double up as modern art sculptures and as ashtrays. A large pine bed dominates the room. It's unmade. He begins to pull off the linen.

'I'll change the sheets.'

'Save us the embarrassment of finding a stray, foreign pube.' For all that I'm acting very blasé I read this as an extreme compliment; men have to be very keen to change the bed covers.

Other pieces of furniture include: an open fireplace, more bookshelves, a couple of bean-bags and a large wardrobe. There aren't any photos or keepsakes, only ashtrays full of copper coins and paper clips. The floor is stripped and partially covered by a threadbare rug. The room's effect is at once both impersonal and sensual. It suggests that an impoverished poet can find comfort in sex here. I don't have time to take anything else in as he pounces on me.

Right on cue, as per the appointment card, I wake up, far too early, with a humdinger of a hangover. I lie still for some moments wondering if God is using the house as a yo yo. I decide not to risk getting up but fall back to sleep. I wake up a second time to the sound of a file rasping against wood. I cling to my head, a new strain of hangover. One at a time, I force open my eyes, letting light surge in. I am pleased it is electric light, necessary in November, as it is less offensive than cheery natural daylight. Chris Tarrant is blaring out of the clock radio, which is on the floor near the wall; it has obviously been thrown there. It keeps going silent and then a few minutes later roaring into action. I don't like this welcome to the day: an aching head, the sound of Tarrant and what is that grating? When I wake up at home Luke is practically out the door on his way to work, but he never leaves without making me a cup of tea and running my bath. I feel disorientated waking to the smell of cigarettes and stale beer plus the inexplicable sight of John crouching over his pine bed with a knife.

'Are you going to kill me?'

He briefly kisses me.

'Morning, Sex. Won't get very far cutting your head off with this.' He waves his tool (the knife); it looks like a knife from a dinner set, but I can't swear to it, because my eyes aren't yet up to the complexities of focusing. Even if he isn't going to cut off my head, it is about to fall off anyway.

'What the hell *are* you doing?'

'Notches.'

'Notches?'

'It's a new bed.' He grins.

'How many notches do you have?' I ask fearfully.

He stops his woodwork and turns to me, 'You're the first, Connie.'

Na Na Na Nana Lucy. Shows what you know!

I hope that we will play hookey together and spend the day in bed nursing our hangovers; he quickly disabuses me of that fantasy, he has a big meeting at work which is too important to miss.

'You can stay here though,' he says obligingly. 'Actually you might have to wait an hour or so until the hot water comes on again. I had a bath.' He is dashing about the house with a bowl of cornflakes in one hand and a shoe in the other. 'Have you seen my tie?'

'Which one? This one?' I indicate the silk Hermès that he used to tie me to the bedpost the night before. I've never done that before. It was quite good fun but he'd been too drunk to actually tie any knots. Still, bows are fine.

'Better untie that or it will be ruined.' He picks up another tie from under the bed. 'Here's a key; when you've locked up, just post it back through the letterbox.'

'Aren't you worried I'll get one cut?' I joke. As if! This place smells so bad he'll have to pay me to come back again. He doesn't see the joke and momentarily looks worried.

'Do you want one?' he asks in a manner that *could* be mistaken as *nervous*. I shake my head; is that relief I see on his face?

'Does your girlfriend' – I force myself to say her name – 'does Andrea have one?' my mouth asks without permission from my brain.

'No.' The 'no' doesn't comfort me. It is not a 'no, she's not that important to me', it's more of a 'no way are we going to talk about Andrea'. I resent the way he protects her from me.

'You do want me? Don't you?' Fuck, how did that happen? What am I thinking about? As soon as the words are out of my mouth I regret them. I know I sound like a woman unsure of her position, a woman unsure of when she'll next get a phone call. Mentally I kick myself for allowing the things Lucy said to unnerve me. She can be such a bitch.

She is probably jealous that I am so happy.

Although Lucy isn't normally the jealous type. I am much too hungover to concentrate, I shake my head. He pushes his left foot into his shoe and sits on the bed to tie the laces.

'Of course I do. What kind of question is that?' He isn't looking at me as he says it, but then he is late and in a hurry to get to work. 'I called you last night, didn't I? I carved you a notch, didn't I?' He turns to me and ruffles my hair. 'We're having a laugh, aren't we?' He gives me a peck and then runs out of the door. From the stairs he calls, 'Don't forget to post the key.'

Alone in his house I start to get dressed. The lack of basic hygiene means that I don't want to hang round too long. I dress hurriedly and decide to shower at work.

Where is my bra?

Shit! Why did I ask if he wants me? That was stupid. Far too heavy. And unnecessary, because it's been obvious from the first moment in Paris, he does want me, that this is somehow meant to be. It's obvious. I am here in his house aren't I? This is real enough for me.

I kneel and look under the bed to try to locate my knickers. What have I knelt in? I don't like to think. Beer? Baby oil? No knickers, maybe they are in the bed, tied up with the sheets.

Even if we don't talk about the big things and we haven't agreed who's calling who next and when, I am sure that he understands. Ours is more of a deep, silent understanding.

Now stockings, where would they be?

Thing is, after coming on all heavy, now if I talk to him about destinies it'll seem impossibly cloying. What a blunder! I can't believe I've done that! Bloody Lucy.

Trousers? They lie in a crumpled pile behind the door. I shake them out. Hmmm, not ideal for work. They smell terrible – fags, sex and beer. It was a mistake to continue drinking when we got back here. I might have had a chance of feeling half-human today, if it hadn't been for the beer and red wine. Oh no, red wine; I spilt that down my white Calvin Klein top when we were trying to have sex in the kitchen. I rummage through his wardrobe to see if I can find anything of his to wear. I can't. I'll have to go to Next on the way to work. I look out the window. It is an icy November morning. My nipples spring out in protest. I'll catch pneumonia.

Slowing down is a mistake. I take a deep breath and fight back the tears. What a bloody, fucking mess. I try to calm down. It is not a problem. It's simply that I temporarily forgot the golden rules: men are very simple and straightforward (not a criticism, a light relief to our constant soul-searching). Men are only ever with you when they want to be. They won't stay with you after they stop wanting to be.

Closed chapter.

I don't need to ask him if he wants to be with me. It's obvious. I pull on my hat and search for my gloves.

Frantic, dirty, dizzy and sick, I close the door behind me and obediently post the key back through the letterbox, without even considering keeping it to get a copy made. Well, without seriously considering it. I have no idea where I am or where the nearest Tube is. We're having a laugh aren't we? God yes, I am having such a laugh.

I stumble into the office at five to ten.

'You're late,' comments Sam. She gapes at my crumpled yesterday clothes. I know she's not worried about what time I clock on, just if I've copped off. I've had the journey from hell and don't want to get involved in this discussion; luckily I am saved when my phone rings.

'Connie, it's me.'

'Hi, Lucy, how are you?'

'Fine. Listen, has Luke called you?' She sounds brusque, which is as near to agitated as Lucy ever gets.

'Luke? No, why should he?' Sam is making a terrible attempt at looking busy.

'Because he came home early last night. I gather you never made it back.'

My heart stops.

I've been tumbled.

Time to face the music.

Time to walk the plank.

Time to wake up and smell the coffee.

Time to stop listening to Sam's moronic clichés. I tune back into Lucy.

'I have to be on the trading floor in four minutes, so pay attention. When I got back to my flat there were a couple of messages on my answering machine. Nothing too heavy, just asking what time he should expect you. Didn't you get a message on your mobile?'

'No,' I say. I did listen to my messages but fast-forwarded all those that weren't John's. There might have been one from Luke.

'I told him that you'd passed out but you'll have to ring now and pretend you've just woken up at my house.'

'OK.'

'And, Connie, remember to use your mobile in case he 1471s.'

'Yes. Thanks.'

I call Luke.

'Baby, how are you? I was so worried.' His voice oozes concern, which is at once a relief and irritating.

'You needn't be.'

'Needn't I?' His voice wavers.

His words hit like stones. 'What sort of question is that?'

He doesn't answer but turns the conversation. 'Connie, let's go out tonight.'

'I have to work tonight.' It is true. I know that the pounding hangover will mean that I'll achieve little today and will undoubtedly spend this evening catching up.

'Well, can you leave it?'

'Not easily.'

'Oh well, I guess we can always do it next week.' He sounds disappointed.

'Yes, we can always do that.'

I put the phone down and Sam stares at me. Her glare withers my intestines.

'What?' I ask innocently.

'You know what,' she says, pretending to be my father.

6

A break with tradition, we are not going to spend Saturday afternoon spending *spondoolies* but spending energy instead. We are going for a ramble. Sam has decided I need a distraction ('You're bored. That's the root of all of this. You aren't challenged. You need a break from your routine'). Although I don't agree with her diagnosis, I concur because I am obsessively pursuing a better physique. Besides which, it is late November and I can't bear the idea of battling with the Christmas shoppers that have been populating Selfridges since August. Sam manages to persuade Daisy and Lucy to come along; they are also pursuing better physiques more or less vigorously, respectively. Rose is delighted to be invited, too, and so offers to drive us out to the country.

Lucy and I spot Rose's red Volvo at the same time and watch it curl around the corner. We wave maniacally. Rose flashes her smile, huge and welcoming, and them immediately settles her face back into a worried expression, as she concentrates on finding a place to park in the heavy, Saturday traffic. Sam winds down the window of the passenger seat and yells at an unsuspecting passer-by,

'Show us your grundies!' He is about nineteen, probably going to a football match, not really ready or willing to encounter a group of man-eating thirty-somethings. Sam throws her head back, laughing raucously at her own cheek. Rose, of course, feels sorry for him.

'He's blushing. Leave him alone.' Christ, there is an unreasonable amount of compassion squeezed into that woman.

Lucy pulls open the car door violently and throws her bag inside. She climbs in and folds her long cK-clad legs after her. She does this in one swift easy movement. Daisy and I, in the meantime, struggle with loading all our bags into the boot and then sardine in after her.

'Gosh, it's amazing to see how light one can travel without children,' comments Rose. If anyone else had said this I would have thought the comment was sarcastic, as I survey enough sweets and spare clothes to feed and dress the Russian Army.

I am in the middle seat. This means I have to wear my head at a jaunty little angle, of 45 degrees, for the entire journey to Essex. No one offers to take turns to sit in the middle. Rose would have happily sat in the crappiest seat, but her fear that none of us is insured to drive the car, overwhelms her sense of politeness. The journey will be uncomfortable for me but agony for her. She likes to be the one who suffers most.

Quick air kisses all round, sharing of Evian (precaution against dehydration) and Mars Bars (necessary for energy), taking off jackets, a decent amount of elbowing, questions about everybody's week at the office and Rose's babysitter, then we settle into the journey.

'Is that really necessary?' Lucy asks Sam. 'The pseudo-laddish behaviour?'

'Oh yes,' assures Sam, 'it's a girls' day out, with obligatory innuendo and infantile behaviour.'

'Good point,' concedes Lucy, 'pure filth.'

'That's an oxymoron.'

'Don't call the lad a moron, you've never even spoken to him.'

General sniggers. I know that Sam is being overly jolly in an attempt to coax me out of what she wrongly identifies as my 'adultery stage'. She's trying to show me that I can do crazy, zany things with my friends and don't need a lover. Although I appreciate the effort, I do not allow that a Mars Bar has any advantages over his dick, not even a King Size.

The journey to Essex is brilliant. Admittedly, we get lost a couple of times, well five actually. But no one cares. As an all-women vehicle we have no hang-ups 'fessing-up that we said right, but meant left. We can pull over into lay-bys and study maps without feeling an iota of shame.

'I'm glad I wasn't born a man,' comments Daisy, as she climbs back into the car, having asked for directions for the third time. She's just discovered that we are heading in the wrong direction by about 180 degrees.

'Why is that?' asks Rose. 'I'm curious. They seem to have got the best deal from where I'm standing, or more often, from where I'm hoovering, cleaning, shopping or burping babies.'

'They aren't allowed to ask for directions though, are they?' says Daisy. 'Simon seems to think that as Christopher Columbus and Captain Cook managed without doing so, it is beneath his dignity.'

'How much further?' asks Lucy, 'I need the loo.' No one is foolish enough to suggest that she should have gone to the one at the Little Chef. Lucy doesn't use public conveniences, under *any* circumstances. It would be acknowledging that she is as mortal as the rest of us.

We have just finished a rather rousing, if somewhat tuneless, rendition of 'Girls Just Wanna Have Fun', when Sam shouts 'Here we are, that's it! Pull over to the left, Rose.' I see a pub, pretty much the same as twenty or so other pubs I've seen on the journey here. But according to our *Country Walks Near London* guide the Green Man pub is *the* pub, where we start and finish our walk. It's an enchanting pub, panelled in dark mahogany, which is cosy and comforting in the winter and, I imagine, cool and shady in the summer. The stone-flag floor is worn by the hundreds of years' worth of reluctant dragging of drunken feet. We are tempted to stay put and spend the afternoon there. But Sam insists that we take to the hills, well, to be pedantic, country lanes. It is a shockingly cold day and I can see my breath on the air. Sam assures us that it will be all right as soon as we start walking.

'You'll work up a sweat.'

'What a horrible thought,' comments Lucy.

We amble along, doing country things like identifying birds:

'It's a seagull.'

'It is not a seagull, it's a goose.'

'Rose, what type of bird is that?'

'A grey plover.'

'See.'

'See yourself.'

Stepping in droppings:

'Watch that.'

'Watch what?'

'Too late.'

And getting spooked by harmless cows:

'It's a bull.'

'It hasn't got horns.'

'It's a young bull.'

'It has udders.'

Yup, we are definitely communing with nature. Six and a half miles of country lanes and coastal lines seem a lot longer than the six and a half miles from Harrods, through Knightsbridge, to Sloane Square, up King's Road and back again. That is the problem with the countryside, there are no designer boutiques. However, Rose offers alternative entertainment. She is quite instructive about birds that feed off eel grass, muddy tides, and the history of smuggling. And she starts quite a lively debate on the wrongs and wrongs of fox hunting. The only right any of us can come up with is when Lucy says, 'The chaps do look rather dashing in their liveries though, don't they?' Good point, hard to disagree. I find myself breaking away from Sam, Daisy and Lucy and walking with Rose. It is sort of pleasant to learn new things, even if they are absolutely useless things, like the mechanics of chemical crop-spraying or how Britain's farmers are to be compensated for the effects of mad cow disease. I make a note to remember some of it to drop into conversation next time I'm in the pub with John. Although it strikes me that it may not be his thing.

'What are they *doing*?' asks Rose. She points to the girls who are some way ahead of us; they haven't stopped to listen to Rose explain the science of oyster-catching. They are huddled together shouting to a mud-flat of geese.

'Did you lock the door before you came out?' asks Daisy.

'Have you started a pension fund?' yells Lucy.

'Are you sure your insurance covers leaking radiators?' adds Sam.

'What are you doing?' I ask, once we catch up with them.

'We are deliberately flouting the Country Code,' says Lucy, with some glee. 'We are worrying geese.' By way of an explanation she adds, 'We couldn't find any sheep.'

'Have you got a television licence?' I add.

'Do you think he loves you as much as you love him?' cries Daisy.

'Have you thought that there is a possibility that you'll never meet Gander Right?' probes Sam.

'How do you know if you've married the right man?' I mumble.

'Is there a possibility that your husband's having an affair?' whispers Rose. I turn to her.

'So it isn't just the geese that are worried?' She doesn't answer me but walks on. Lucy throws a parting shot at the thoroughly overwrought geese.

'Don't you wish you'd joined an aerobic class?'

We move on. Salt wind in my hair and thousands of sea birds for company, I use the time to pursue my favourite hobby – thinking about John. I draw up a whole new list of outdoor fantasies. John chasing me along the beach, me stumbling, him falling on top of me. John chasing me along the cliff, me stumbling, him falling on top of me. All the scenarios are basically the same. I'm a slow runner and he's a fast worker. I'm interrupted when we come across the Saxon chapel of St Peter's-On-The-Wall. Sam and Daisy dash inside to practise walking up the aisle, they are singing, 'I'm Going to the Cha-a-a-pel and I'm going to get Ma-ha-ha-ried.' Although it is likely to be marginally warmer inside the chapel, I linger outside with Lucy, choosing to smoke a cigarette instead.

'Aren't you coming in?' asks Rose. 'It's very interesting.' She reads from a plaque, 'It's stood here facing the marshes for well over 1300 years. St Cedd, a Celtic Bishop trained on Holy Island in . . .' I tune out. I'm in danger of reverting to my original opinion of Rose. She's boring. Everyone is boring.

Lucy turns wise sage on me. Which is infuriating.

'Scared you'll be struck by lightning?'

'Don't be ridiculous, Lucy.' I don't think I'll be struck by lightning, exactly. But I haven't been in a church since I married Luke. Not a fact in itself that I should be proud of. I check my mobile for messages. Lucy's watching me, closely.

'No signal,' I explain with a sham, twisted grin.

'Use mine. It's working perfectly.' She offers me her phone. I glare at her, turn away and start to stride along the path in the direction of the Green Man. I need a drink.

As godparents it is obligatory that Luke and I attend Henry and Sebastian's first birthday celebration. I am sceptical.

'They'll never remember it. What's the point?' I moan, grumpily, as we climb into our car. I can't seem to shake my bad temper. If only John would ring. If only I could talk to him. We haven't spoken since I stayed over at his place. I know it is my own fault. I was too heavy. Asking about Andrea and the key. It is a cold Saturday afternoon, two weeks before Christmas and I still have about a billion things to do, to prepare before that joyous day of family squabbling and the giving and receiving of unwanted gifts. I haven't sent any cards or bought any presents. This level of disorganization is unlike me and amounts, in my mind, to a state of emergency. Not the actual failure to do my bit for retail sales but the fact that I don't care. Of course this state of emergency passes Luke by, unnoticed. He is a boy and he's never, in his life, done any Christmas shopping before Christmas Eve. In fact, since he met me, he simply hasn't done any Christmas shopping. Whatever gene it is that allows men to abdicate responsibility for festive preparations is contagious. I no longer care if the turkey will be big enough to do sandwiches the next day. I have no interest in whether or not we bought Auntie May sherry or brandy last year. It's likely that I'll do all my Christmas shopping at Texaco, too. Air pumps and Castrol oil all round.

'You'll have a brilliant time once you're there,' Luke says, giving my hand a little squeeze. I pull it away and put on my glove. 'You love kids and they'll be loads of them there. Guess what the best bit is?' he teases, merrily.

'What?' I ask, brusquely.

'We don't have to bring any of them home.' He smiles at me and I force myself to smile back. It is hard not being nice to him, it's hard to be nice. Luke is exactly the same as he always has been, nice. The problem is that I'm not nice any more. And as I haven't got the decency to feel guilty I concentrate on feeling disgruntled instead.

Why hasn't he called?

Men never ask women what they are thinking, they don't have to. Unprompted, we share the very deepest parts of our

193

minds and souls, or chatter about trivia. By contrast, women constantly ask men what's on their minds. This is because we genuinely want to know if they are thinking at all. If asked they offer the unfulfilling response, 'nothing'. The accuracy of this answer leaves us sulky and resentful. The nothing is earwax, navel fluff, or football fixtures. Therefore it is disappointing in the extreme that during the car journey to the party, Luke fulfils my lifelong fantasy by asking, 'What's on your mind, Con?' And instead of being able to chatter animatedly about the inconsequential amusements that normally fill my head, I am forced into a sulky reply.

'Nothing.'

We finish the journey in silence. I want him to push me. At the same time, it is my biggest fear. What would I do if he asked me straight out, 'Connie, are you screwing someone else?' I like to think that I couldn't lie to Luke, my best friend, my true love. I'd like to think that I'd come clean about my true lover. But it strikes me as inconsistent, to say the least, that I have scruples about lying directly when I am betraying him in absolutely every other way. But then I'm riddled with exhausting contradictions right now. I'm furious that Luke hasn't noticed that I am undergoing this unimaginable transformation. I want him to jealously demand where I'm going and who with? Why don't I want sex with him? Why am I constantly buying new clothes? (Although maybe that isn't exactly condemning evidence) but certainly my visits to the gym are. On the other hand I am crippled with an overwhelming sense of my unworthiness. Luke loves me and he trusts me; it would never cross his mind that I'd be doing anything remotely delinquent. His confidence in mankind, and in me especially, is at once the thing I most love and despise about him.

Rose and Peter live in a large four storey, Victorian terrace in Holland Park. Paid for with the fruits of Peter's stunning and sustained success in the City. It's the type of house that is featured on Christmas cards. Huge, white, impressive, impenetrable. The type of house that makes most of us feel horrendously inadequate. Daisy flings the door open.

'Oh, it's just you two.'

Luke and I exchange grimaces. 'Thanks, Daisy, what a welcome.'

'Sorry.' She looks momentarily guilty. 'I was hoping you were Simon.'

'Is he late?'

'Fifteen minutes.'

I want to tell her that that's not late. That's positively prompt. She looks at her watch anxiously and then wanders away from the door, back into the sitting room.

'Come on in, can I take your coat?' Luke sarcastically imitates the perfect hostess. Rose bustles out of the sitting room, nearly knocking over the monstrously large Christmas tree that dominates the hallway. She looks like the Pied Piper, as about a hundred kids are pulling at her skirt, demanding the loo, sweets, drinks, toys. I feel claustrophobic. I can't imagine what it is that makes Luke think I ever liked kids. She welcomes us with a harassed, happy smile. Luke swoops down and picks up some fat kid who is crying. As he hoists the weight-challenged monster on to his shoulders I ask, 'Where did all the spare children come from?'

'It is a children's party,' says Rose, apologetically.

The house is awash with garlands and greenery. I can smell mince pies and mulled wine. There is an obscene amount of glitter, baubles, holly and goodwill. It looks a lot like a Next catalogue shoot. Or maybe Next meets Early Learning. I am surprised that none of the men are wearing kilts and I genuinely expect someone to suggest that we all gather around the piano for a sing-a-long. We trudge through to the sitting room. There are children everywhere: under tables, on tables, on chairs, under chairs, behind curtains, on settees, in cupboards, hanging from lampshades, climbing up the Christmas tree. Very few of them are happy, none of them are quiet. The majority are screaming or crying, or punching, or teasing, or nipping.

'Everyone's having a brilliant time,' shouts Sam, without a hint of irony. But then she has a very pink face and her champagne glass is empty. Luke and I exchange a glance and we silently agree that Sam's survival tactic is sensible. He goes off to find some alcohol and I call after him not to forget that he is driving home.

'Where's Lucy, we don't see much of her nowadays?' asks Sam.

'She's working her arse off,' I reply.

'I miss her,' says Sam, who is always sentimental after a couple of glasses of champagne.

'You're in the minority,' adds Rose, in a rare moment of cattiness.

'Ouch,' chorus Sam and I. Rose immediately turns scarlet, instantly regretting her foray into the Alexis Carrington school of manners. She tries to defend herself by adding, 'It's just that she can be so negative, so cutting.'

'She's not cutting, she's clever,' says Peter kissing his harassed wife on the forehead. He is trying to smooth over her social gaff of slagging off one of our friends so early in the afternoon even before we have a drink in our hands.

'I miss her too,' says Luke, terminally pleasant. I take the gin and tonic gratefully that Luke proffers then move on. Luke wisely disappears to Peter's den. I understand the fathers are congregating (read hiding) in the den, smoking cigars and congratulating themselves on their sons and heirs.

I manfully separate Becky-from-ballet and Tom-from-Tumble-Tots, who are viciously thumping each other to within an inch of their lives. No one seems bothered that there could be a bloody and foul murder on Rose's shag-pile carpet. Children are ferociously beating each other, tying each other up, biting each other and generally training to be enthusiasts of spectator sports. I squeeze my way on to the settee, pushing in between Arabella's mother and Ben's mother. They are sitting discussing the colour of poo and the texture of Heinz baby food. I think I've got that the right way round. There is an undeniable specialness about motherhood but why is it that everyone assumes because we can do it, we all want to? Women who have had babies spend hours telling those who haven't about the discomfort of the pregnancy: varicose veins, hideous bloating, back ache, chucking your guts up every morning, no alcohol but lots of coal with gherkins. And the actual birth?! Shitting a football *cannot* be made to sound pleasant.

'Planning any children?' Arabella's mother looks at me hopefully.

'No,' I reply, guiltily, thinking I have somehow failed her expectations.

'Are you trying?' she whispers conspiratorially. Ben's mother leans closer, interested.

'No,' I reply, guiltily, knowing that I have failed her expectations. They stare at me horrified, as though I am some kind of a monster. What am I supposed to say? 'Bit tricky at the moment, my husband would think it was immaculate conception and my lover would . . .' What would John do? Run a mile I suspect. Not that he's exactly up close and personal as it is! I swallow back my gin and gratefully accept the glass of wine that Daisy hands me. I search around for some other conversational piece to try on these mothers. I consider explaining my theory on Mother Nature being a bloke. Transvestite Nature for certain. I refrain.

'So, no children,' Ben's mum continues. 'Are you one of these career women?' She tries to sound supportive but sounds pitying.

'Not really. I hate my job.' I know I sound as though I have more in common with Ben (aged three and a half) than his mother but I cannot force myself to be pleasant. I am bored. I am scared. I don't want this. I don't want to be in a job I hate, waiting to have children, who will undoubtedly hate me, just so I can live out my failed ambitions through them. I gulp down a second glass of wine and watch Eloise's mother scoop up puke and Robert's mother use her beautifully manicured nails to remove a bogie from her son's nose. This is boring. I am not ready for this. There must be more. I'm rescued from the embarrassment of not being a mother or a career woman by Sam pulling me off the settee and into the dining room.

'Santa's here,' she grins.

'Err, Sam I don't know how much you've had to drink and I don't like to be the one who breaks it to you, but Santa doesn't exist.'

Sam rolls her stunning eyes, exasperated. 'I know that. I found out when I was twelve.'

'Twelve?'

'Simon is dressed up as Santa. It's a surprise for the kids.'

I'm grateful for the diversion. I have to admit, it's brilliant. I hardly recognize him.

'Are you hot?' I ask. He is acting quite strangely, fidgeting and moving from foot to foot. I wonder if he's been drinking or if he has stage fright.

'I'm fine,' he assures me and then he screams, 'Where's my sack, where's my sack!' in a more than mildly hysterical way.

Sam and I round the kids up and get them into a reasonable semblance of order. Introducing discipline is relatively easy, bribery springs eternal. Even these cynical cyber children are artless enough to be interested in Father Christmas. Only one of them complains that he's already seen the real Santa at John Lewis. When we line up all the kids, there are only about ten of them plus half-a-dozen babies. How can they make so much noise? I thought that we had the combined casts of *Annie, Oliver Twist* and *Babes in the Wood*.

Daisy isn't in on the Santa gig and she is thrilled when she recognizes Simon *ho ho hoing*. She goes all misty eyed and I just know that she is imagining trips to Baby Gap and scenes from Calvin Klein adverts. I know because I used to do it all the time when I first met Luke. I don't now. Adultery doesn't make an appearance in Calvin's advert. It's not very 90s. Simon asks each child if they've been good that year (and they all happily lie through their teeth). He then delves into his huge sack and produces a present – Teletubby water-pistols and Barbie ankle bracelets – rather than the clementines and chocolate coins that Rose wanted. Their happy excited faces could have melted the heart of even the most cynical person in the room. Which, as Lucy hasn't turned up, is me.

When all the kids have gifts and they are beginning to fight about who has received the best of the identical plastic novelties, Santa Simon shouts, 'There's one girl who hasn't told Santa what she wants for Christmas yet.' He takes Daisy's hand and makes her sit down in Santa's chair. She is the colour of a bottle of burgundy.

'Now, Daisy, have you been good this year?' he asks.

Sam whispers to me, 'Besides the incident in the park', and we both giggle. Rose gives us a stern preacher's look and, duly chastised, we shut up.

'Quite good,' giggles Daisy.

Santa Simon says, 'Well, as much as I hate to disagree with you, I think you've been more than quite good. You're wonderful and so I have a special present for you. If you'll accept it.'

'I wonder what it will be?' whispers Sam excitedly.

'Tickets to fly somewhere exotic is my guess,' I whisper back.

'Bitch.'

Sam is a great friend.

The room is tight with tension. The women are delighted

by such a romantic gesture and the men are mortified. If Simon is going to set a precedent with such open shows of affection, there is a serious danger that they'll have to return their perfunctory perfume gift packs and electric egg whisks and buy something that their women actually want.

'In fact,' says Santa, 'you are unbelievably good. I never thought that I'd meet anyone quite so good, special and amazing.' His voice thickens with emotion. 'So I would be honoured, ecstatic, if you'd accept my gift.' He pulls from his sack a small box, a ring-shaped box and the room holds its breath.

'Will you make me a very happy man. In fact,' he giggles self-consciously as he uses the cliché, 'the happiest man alive and agree to be my wife?'

'*Aghhhhhhh*, yes, yes, yes,' screams Daisy, shoving the huge diamond on her finger before he gets a chance to change his mind. The room burst into cheers and applause. Someone starts singing, 'For they are jolly good fellows'. Daisy is kissing Simon, and then Rose. Then Rose is kissing Simon (not in the same way as Daisy did, understandably), Simon is shaking Luke's hand and Peter's hand. Daisy is kissing me and Sam. Sam is crying, so is Becky's mum, Arabella's mum and Eloise's mum, although none of them had even met Daisy before today. Champagne corks are popping. It is Daisy's brilliant, shiny moment.

I urgently push through the crowds and run to the bathroom. I feel the champagne in my mouth for the second time, my chest is tight. Suddenly hot and dizzy. I heave and then splash water on my face and then lean heavily on the bathroom door.

'You OK?' Sam is banging on the door. 'Are you feeling ill?'

I open the door and let her in.

'Very.'

'Booze, pregnant, jealous or guilty?'

I glare at her.

'Was I ever that besotted?' I ask as I sit on the loo seat and put my head in my hands.

She softens. 'More so. Don't you remember?'

'No, I can't remember Luke ever creating that stomach-churning excitement, I can't remember him being all-consuming.'

Stone again, 'You are a passion junkie.'

'I am not.'

'You are. It was exactly like that with Luke, except better because he stroked your tummy when you had period cramps. Don't you remember you wanted him so much you used to pull out all the stops? You took up golf. You babysat for his sister every Friday night for six months. You once sent flowers to yourself to make him jealous.'

I smiled at the memory. 'It worked.'

'Too damn right it did, our office was like a florist for a month. Don't you remember how you used to both speak, fall silent for hours and then start the conversation somewhere else but a place you'd both arrived at? You think the same way. Don't you remember finishing each other's sentences? Remember how excited you were when you found out that he adored Arthur Miller and he could quote it to you. Your favourite playwright. Con, I wasn't even there for most of this and I remember it, because you told me. You told me that from the moment you saw him, you knew you'd marry him. You wanted to marry him. You said he completed you.'

I remember some of it. I remember speaking of it. But I can't remember feeling it. I sit up and face Sam, repeatedly running my hands through my hair. 'Every time I think of John my stomach lurches.'

'Stomach?'

'Fair point. The feeling is lower than that. But I am a woman. I am not supposed to be led by base instincts, that's a male domain. He is so good-looking, stunning, wanton, sexy. Thinking of him is enough to make me come. I am attracted to the shape of his neck. To the sudden, jerky movements that he makes when he walks. To the smell of his skin. The touch of his hand.' Sam sits on the corner of the bath and takes hold of my hands. My voice is tight and my explanation ekes out like a plea. 'He scalds my conscious and unconscious mind leaving a messy sore.' Sam can't understand me. I have what she wants. Now I have it twice. But she's my friend. One of the best friends I have, and so she wants to help. She whispers, 'Although possibly the sore would soothe and heal, if you just stopped picking at the scab.'

'Possibly,' I admit. Part of me is tired of the deception and silences and mistrust and agonizing. Witnessing Daisy's uncomplicated rapture made me long for that easy innocence I've chucked away. Tentatively I ask Sam, 'But can I ever piece back together what Luke and I had?'

Happy Birthday To You, my mobile whistles from my handbag. Crazed, I shake the contents on to the tiled floor: lipstick, pens, keys, tampons, purse, receipts scatter in every direction. I ferret manically until I pounce on the phone. I ignore Sam's mystified and disappointed face.

'Hello, hello,' I peal urgently.

'Hey, Sex. How are you. Can you talk?'

I sink back against the bath, awash with delight. My face is nearly splitting. Sam sighs and lets the bathroom door bang behind her.

The others may not have been seeing much of Lucy but I am, so that I can indulge in eternal chatter about John. Lucy isn't exactly patient ('Connie, what did you used to talk about?'), or even understanding ('I mean, when you were interesting.'). In fact, she is often downright pessimistic ('If this one doesn't work out, you can get yourself another.'). Still at least she doesn't moralize. She has always approved of indulgent, hedonistic, behaviour ('You have to be kind to yourself.'). Her philosophy of self-preservation used to offend me, now I recognize it as a sophisticated take on life, a reality. Who am I hurting? I am very careful that my alibis are watertight, I never meet John if Luke is free and I am the soul of discretion when I am with John. I never, ever talk about Luke. Really, I am being as fair as I can possibly be. Under the circumstances. Lucy approves of the way I am handling the situation ('I think you have the ability to get quite good at adultery. Providing you drop your romantic expectations.').

It is convenient to shop with Lucy because even Christmas crowds part like the Red Sea. We trail around Harvey Nics, I'm behind her, trying to keep pace with her determined step. The lift stops on the fifth floor, which houses the food goodies. Teas, coffees, puddings, pickles and cheeses, every shape, size and variety imaginable. The choice is overwhelming. Delicious products packaged with astounding flair, astonishingly expensive. We agree on about twenty-five 'necessary luxuries'. I finger an exotic hamper, crammed full of indulgence.

'What do you think for Rose?' Before she answers I resume my original conversation about John. 'He told me that he feels uncomfortable with the chasm between who he is and who people expect him to be. What he feels and what people expect him to feel. When he tries to explain himself it's so clear to me but most people don't get it. He is so misunderstood. He is so much more than what people can see.'

Lucy looks at me as though I am from another planet. She sighs impatiently and then pronounces her verdict. 'Sounds like a pretentious wanker. Con, he is an emotional cripple; worse, he is a self-obsessed emotional cripple. Rose would prefer navy towels.'

I walk away from the hampers and check the store directory for bathroom accessories. Actually he hadn't quite said it the way I'd recounted it to Lucy. He'd said something more like, 'I'm just like how I am. And I like me this way, I don't want to change into something someone else expects me to be. I can't explain it. Dunno why I can't explain it, Con, but you get it. Don't you? You are just like me and this thing we are doing is just for attention. We are being indulgent. We don't like not getting what we want.' He was standing naked, except for his socks. He held his arms to the air and then let them flop as he pounced on me, bored with the conversation about expectation and self-realization.

'He's not an emotional cripple. Well, no more than most men. He's got the potential to be very deep. He'd be fine if he read *Marie Claire*.'

Lucy stares at me bemused.

'Don't,' she says with some authority, 'don't romanticize him. He's the kind of bloke that thinks every hole's a goal.'

I nod. I think I'd heard him use this phrase.

'He certainly doesn't follow the script for a devoted and hot lover. He never takes you anywhere.'

'I don't mind.'

'Well, you should.'

'He always has the intention. We often meet up agreeing to go to supper, after a quick one.'

'Except you mean a drink. He's not big on the romantic gesture either, is he?'

I feel tired.

'Does he ever send you cute notes by e-mail? Has he sent flowers anonymously, or even openly?'

'He bought me a book once and he'd written in the cover, a romantic note about us acting out the contents.'

'Which book?'

'*American Psycho.*'

'Hardly Cathy and Heathcliff?'

'I was a bit apprehensive about calling him for a few days, after all those decapitations.' We laugh.

'He goes for just one with the blokes, every night. Somehow that "just one" always turns into several hours' drinking.' She puts a packet of truffle risotto into her basket. 'He tries to pull the waitress, the girls on the next table, all of them. If that doesn't work he goes to the cashpoint machine to withdraw some more money and he tries to pull the women in the queue.' She adds some squid ink pasta. 'But by this time he can barely stand, so any boyish charm he did possess has washed away. He then goes to some tacky nightclub. He wears his tie around his head and he can't even pull the sixteen-year-olds that are visiting from Essex. Even girls who are desperate for a part of the big city are offended by his indiscriminate, indiscreet, cretinous behaviour.' With each sentence she angrily flings a delicacy into her basket. She stops selecting and turns to me. 'Then as he struggles home, he calls you. And you think that is love?'

'It's not like that,' I insist. 'I've never mentioned "love". Only "destiny".' I feel exposed. 'My number is programmed into his phone,' I defend.

'He's a bastard, isn't he?' she asserts rather than enquires. Her wealth of experience makes her an authority.

'Of course he is; I wouldn't be attracted otherwise.'

She nods at the truth of this.

'What's wrong with you anyway? I hadn't realized you objected at all.' I say 'objected' in a rather haughty voice.

Lucy sighs, 'I'm not looking forward to Christmas.' She turns back to the preserves and picks up a jar of Gentleman's Relish. She puts it down again disdainfully. 'It's not a good time for mistresses.'

I'd never known Lucy care about Christmas before. She always, rather sensitively, refers to the celebration of the birth of baby Jesus as sentimental, superstitious crap.

'Do you want to talk about it?' I ask sympathetically. Lucy hesitates. Obviously not, so I resume.

'Would you be angry if I said John is misunderstood?' I leaf through a cookery book, wondering if this is the one Luke's parents are planning to buy me.

'Furious.'

'Would you hit me?' I smile trying to lighten her mood.

'Yes.'

'I'm in danger of being on the receiving end of physical violence.' She doesn't smile, instead she holds her face in solid indifference. 'This is serious Lucy. Can you imagine if he is my destiny, if I've married the wrong man?'

'Is there a right one?'

'But I'm so happy, Lucy!' I argue.

'No, you're not happy. I've never seen you more unhappy. You get no pleasure out of the things and people you used to delight in. You're desolate, depressed, frustrated, angry. You vacillate between a glorious rage and simple rage. You're furious. Furious at yourself, at Luke, at John. Kick it into touch, Connie. It doesn't suit you.'

'Of course it suits me. I've never been so thin. It can't be a bad thing if I'm losing weight.'

Lucy rolls her eyes. 'Bollocks, Connie. You haven't been happy since you met him. Tortured – yes, angst-ridden – yes, skinny – yes. But not happy. Go to weightwatchers, it's kinder.' She pauses, serious again. 'Let him go, Con.'

'That is definitely advice.'

'OK, all right. I'm advising you, shoot me. I'm trying to do a good thing here, Con. I'm not moralizing.'

'Well, you'd hardly be in a position to do so, would you?' I snap. I'm being mean, I know, but I don't care.

Lucy purses her lips. 'Exactly. I know what I'm talking about. Connie, you don't want to become me. Try talking to Luke. Give John up. You don't want him for keeps. You're just playing at this because you're bored. Let it go before it all goes wrong.'

'Goes wrong?'

'Before you get caught or dumped. Just tell me, how can this have a successful outcome for you? Just think about it.'

'Tra la la la la laaa. Le la la la laaa. The angels they are singing.' Luke wakes me up with his singing. He carefully places a Christmas breakfast tray on the bed. Smoked salmon and scrambled eggs, mince pies, fresh orange juice, coffee, his Christmas card and a sprig of spruce. Christmas fare. He kisses me, a nice warm kiss. Fine. A fine kiss. I make a big show about how I have to get up now and we are going to arrive late at Rose and Peter's unless we hurry.

'Don't panic, Con. I was just kissing you. I wasn't suggesting sex. I know that you are training to take holy orders.'

He leaves the room and I feel a twinge of guilt. I know I've spoilt the atmosphere. I'm running low on excuses to avoid sex. Headaches that last four months are generally regarded as pretty serious. *Aghhh* I can't think about this now. I rarely *think* about what I am doing. My schizophrenic existence doesn't leave me much time to. I day-dream, fantasize, and occasionally, worry. But I do not think. My best fantasy is the one where my two separate, parallel lives do not painfully clash and mesh.

In the life with Luke, I live in our large Clapham house. I'm a clever, bright, dutiful wife. A wife that is in love with her husband. Delighted, not just content. Focused and single-minded. Eating croissants, drinking reasonable amounts of fine wines, exercising thoroughly. The wife I was before. The wife I have been.

The other life is dirty, filthy, sexy. A life of shagging against walls and on tables. Smoking cigarettes, nursing hangovers, doing drugs to keep me thin. The life I'm leading. We exist in a crazy, hedonistic, sparkly, nowness.

I can't marry the two. And now I've lived for four months with a foot in each camp. It's giving me cramp. This is extremely unsatisfactory.

I don't want him to go away.

Yet I can't see a future for us.

Luke and I ostensibly celebrate Christmas like all our other Christmases. We buy a tree from the flower stall on the Common, drag it home and although there is rain falling, not snow, it is almost a perfect picture postcard scene. We dress the tree with large tartan bows, red and gold tinsel, baubles and lots of those little wooden ornaments. We eat mince pies, listen to two contrasting concerts by carol singers: beautiful, soul-piercing carol singers that perform in Westminster; and a performance by the local pre-teen thugs, who are not so much rosy, but have peculiar red spots high on their cheeks, a result of the cheap and lethal cocktail of cider and aspirins.

Luke and I buy presents, wrap them, buy, write and fail to post our cards. An entirely appropriate Christmas. The one difference is that I refuse to spend the actual day with either Luke's family or mine. My three sisters and their spouses and offspring are all visiting my mum and dad. They can field the questions on fertility from ageing aunts. Luke's brother and his fiancée are visiting Luke's parents. They're prepared to travel a fair distance to avoid handling turkey giblets. My mother is too perceptive, I can't risk her seeing Luke and I together and besides I would suffocate under the married-bliss-vibes that both clans exude. Instead we spend the actual day with our adopted family. Rose, the hostess with the mostess, has thrown open her doors to half of London. It's unlikely I'll be made to feel uncomfortable with the resonance of married ecstasy there.

Rose's father, Mr Kirk, answers the door.

'Bloody marvellous to see you,' he says as he energetically pumps Luke's hand. He leans in closely and warmly kisses me. A bit too close and a bit too warm in my opinion. Christmas is a great excuse for old hounds to gratuitously seize flesh that has been unavailable to them for decades.

'How the devil are you?' he asks, smiling warmly. We stand on the step, freezing and longing for a drink, assuring him that we are quite well. We politely enquire if he is sound in body (the evidence for the condition of his mind is apparent).

'Tip top. Thanks for calling.' He closes the door. Luke and I exchange giggles. I feel relaxed with him, for the first time in a long time. So relaxed, that I promise myself that I'll try to enjoy Christmas Day. To enjoy Luke. We ring the bell again.

This time Mrs Kirk answers the door. Mrs Kirk is Rose, plus thirty years. Yet her limitless patience, naive optimism and outstanding good nature fits a woman in her sixties much more comfortably. Odd. She isn't frustrating, you don't want to shake her and say, 'Wake up and smell the decaf.' She is ethereal and charming.

Rose runs through from the kitchen, flushed and cheerful with sherry and season. For once she isn't wearing leggings and a sloppy jumper. She has taken a risk by wearing a clingy red, velvet dress with red hair. The dress is surprisingly flat-tering despite the fact that 'clingy' is a potential pitfall for every woman, except perhaps Cindy Crawford. But it works and if only she could be persuaded to ditch her Alice band and wear a spot of make-up, then she'd look pretty good, pretty damn good. Daisy and Simon are both being desperately trendy in black polo-necks and trousers. Or at least I think that's what they are wearing; as they are a homogenous mesh it is difficult to be sure. Seeing their blatant longing for one another sends me scrambling for my mobile.

Is it switched on?

It is.

Fuck. So much for the promise I made myself. I *will not* think of him for the day, or at least until the Queen's speech. Tarn is impeccable in a Connolly ribbed sweater; 'marl anthracite,' he informs me. I have no idea whether he is talking about his jumper or an exotic holiday location. I must ask Lucy. *John would look a complete horn in that sweater.* Peter is looking smart-casual in a sophisticated, relaxed, spot-on sort of way. I wave to him as he plays in the garden with the twins. Lucy looks stunning. Rather unusually she is wearing a colour. A baby pink, cashmere cap-sleeve jumper and cardigan with pearl buttons. It undoubtedly cost the equivalent of an average family's monthly income. Lucy proves the adage 'You get what you pay for.' She looks a million dollars. Immaculate, alluring, amazing, if not a bit sulky. Which is a shame because everyone else seems to be getting on so well.

Christmas lunch is Christmas lunch and there are very few variations on a theme. By 25 December I have usually drunk my way through a cellar of wine, consumed a veritable mountain of sprouts and more turkeys than I'd expect my true love to send on any day of Christmas. Not that my lover has sent me anything for Christmas. At this stage, I think a really nice meal would be an undressed green salad, washed down with a couple of glasses of Resolve. However Rose's Christmas lunch is always worth saving a bit of space for, in fact a lot of space. It is distinguished, as it is unparalleled, in its size and deliciousness. We start with roast pumpkin soup which is dripping with melted cheese. Which, as a rule, I do prefer to frozen prawns with mayonnaise and limp lettuce. Next, Rose serves kiwi sorbet. Then a pheasant (that by the size of it has suffered an identity crisis – it thought it was a baby elephant) and pork with crackling and roast apples, seasoned delicately with thyme and parsley. No one-lump-or-two-gravy disgraces Rose's table, she serves a citrus, rum and raisin sauce. No soggy sprouts or hard carrots; instead we gorge on sautéd caramelized fennel, spiced red cabbage with cranberries and perfect roast potatoes. Next we have mascarpone cheesecake with fruit and nuts served with crème fraiche. Just in case any one of us find ourselves stranded on a desert island for the next twenty years, with no nourishment other than the reserves that we are wearing about our person, we finish with Christmas pudding and mince pies.

I check my mobile fourteen times. I call his mobile five times.

The others bang party poppers, pull crackers and laugh at the jokes. They even wear the tacky paper hats, except for Lucy who comments that it is a common mistake to expect to increase your festive fun by wearing a ridiculous paper hat. We drink a lot, an awful lot. Champagne, sherry, mulled wine, white wine, red wine and port, which explains why we laugh at the cracker jokes.

After lunch the men and Lucy stagger to the sitting room to smoke cigars and drink brandy. Mrs Kirk and Rose begin to clear the table, Daisy (surgically removed from Simon) continues to force chocolate mints into her mouth and I, in an effort to appear industrious, begin to drain glasses and tear up paper crackers. I forlornly look at my mobile. Mrs Kirk notices; she is unaware of my problem so offers her blanket compensation, 'Have another biscuit, or Brie? A smidgen of Brie?' She proffers a heaving tray. The combined efforts of a herd of cows and a herd of goats. It hasn't been touched. Why hasn't he called?

'Waiting for a call?' asks Daisy.

I jolt at her unexpected precision. 'Errr, yes. My mum.' Daisy looks sympathetic.

'You should have said. Use Rose's phone. It's hellish not talking to those you love on Christmas Day.'

Why hadn't I thought of that!

I rush to the hall, ensuring I close all the doors between me and the game of charades. My finger hovers above the phone.

And stays there.

I have no idea where he is. He could be in East London in the health and safety infringement building he calls home. Or in Liverpool with his parents. My thoughts get blacker. Or with Andrea. And blacker. Or with her parents. Does Andrea have parents? And a home town. And friends. And a favourite clothes shop. I've never considered it. I hurl the thought to the back of my head. This is not the time to begin.

'Have you called him?'

'Christ, Lucy. I nearly died of shock.'

She sits down next to me. We both stare at the phone.

'I can't. I don't know where he is.'

She laughs pitilessly. 'Take a hint, Connie.'

'What?' I snarl. 'What do you mean by that?' I feel so miserable, I don't expect she can say anything that will make me feel worse. Lucy, I've noticed, has not once checked her mobile today, nor has she sneaked away to make any calls. She is unfeasibly cool. But then she is also more organized. I bet she's arranged to meet her lover tonight. He is probably going to have to force down a second round of turkey and sprouts, just so they can eat together.

'Do you think he is at least thinking about me?'

Lucy doesn't answer but pokes me in the ribs. Luke had just walked into the hall.

'Anyone fancy a walk?'

We fight our way into scarves, gloves, hats, boots, coats and earmuffs ensuring that we all look sufficiently like Michelin men, then we roll out on to the streets of Holland Park. It is freezing cold, which is invigorating and strangely pleasant. We walk up Aubrey Road and head to High Street Kensington and then along to Kensington Gardens. The streets are deserted, which is a refreshing change after the months of battling past Christmas shoppers. It takes a long time to get to the park. There is a serious chance that we won't get there before Burns Night. I walk between Mr and Mrs Kirk. Keeping them both upright is a challenge, even sober Mr Kirk is not that steady on his feet. Still, it doesn't really matter how long it takes us, as we laugh and joke the walk away. After our long bracing stroll we return to Rose and Peter's for more food and a game of cards.

I curl up in bed on Christmas night and I know I should be

exhausted and ecstatic. But I am exhausted and dissatisfied.

'You OK?' Luke's voice appears out of the dark, breaking my thoughts.

'Fine,' I mutter and nudge further towards the edge of the bed. Christmas then, is a series of beautiful vignettes. I've taken photo after photo. All three films say the same thing: a perfect textbook Christmas, surrounded by my friends, giving and receiving beautiful presents, eating delicious food, drinking copious amounts of alcohol, and not having a single row about returning ill-fitting gifts.

A perfect Christmas, on paper.

He hasn't rung. Not a word. And I've had my mobile on all day. If my phone were broken, it would be wonderful, because my heart wouldn't be. I've considered signal failure, poor reception, flat battery. I ruled out all these possibilities by using Rose's home phone to ring myself. The signal is clear, the battery is buoyant, the message collecting facility is ticketyboo, ticketybloodyboo. He hasn't rung me. I know what this means. So I'm not ecstatic. I am not thrilled to my core.

'No really, are you OK?' Luke sits up and flicks the bedside light on. I try to blink away the intrusion. I consider the question. The only time my nipples have stood to attention the whole bloody Christmas is when I walked to the park in sub-zero temperatures. No, I'm not OK.

'Yes. I said. I'm fine.' He looks hurt and I'm ashamed. 'I've drunk too much. I'm tired.' I offer another lie as an explanation. We fall silent.

'Look at me, Connie.' Carefully Luke rolls me over to face him and I haven't the energy to resist. 'Is there something you are not telling me. Is there something worrying you? Is there something I can help you with?'

His eyes bore into me. Singeing my conscience. I'm surprised that his aim is so direct. I had thought my conscience had shrivelled to such a lilliputian blob that he'd never find it. The deception is foul, exhausting and wrong. But coming clean is unthinkable.

'There's nothing you can help with,' I answer as truthfully as I can, then I spin away from him and resign myself to another night feigning sleep.

Merry Sodding Christmas.

7

The 3rd of January. My unopened e-mails number in their hundreds; I'm finding it nearly impossible to pretend that I care. My in-tray is a lighthouse, flashing warnings of impending danger and the need for immediate attention. I ignore it and settle down to the serious work. I call him, get his message box, I don't quite know what to say, so I stall for time and I send an e-mail. I know that it is hopeless to be angry or cajoling on an e-mail, so instead I opt for the casual teasing route:

> Hardy,
>
> How predictable that you failed to call me, and tedious in the extreme. Is this your new seduction technique – bore me into submission? I think your chances of getting me into bed would be much improved if you spoke to me. My New Year's Resolution this year is to remain faithful to my husband. I'm not going to sleep with you again.

Then as an afterthought I add,

> but it would be nice to be asked. At the moment I have nothing serious to resist.

I think that I've managed to hit the necessary note of casualness. For a week there is no reply. I justify this to myself. Maybe he is still on holiday, skiing or visiting family. I don't know and admitting that I don't know, even to myself, is humiliating. However, the alternative is intolerable; he has the mail and isn't going to answer. Oh, why didn't I think to track it? Then, at least, I would know if he'd received it. Me and my in-tray are wobbling precariously. I wonder which will collapse first. I am drained. How long can I endure wanting him this much?

On Thursday I get a reply!!!!!!!!!!!!!!!!!!!!!

Lover,
  I've had a good, long, hard think about us this lunchtime
and a few things came up/arose/reared their head/(etc. etc.
insert (!) your own phallic reference here).
Finding it very difficult to type this because . . . .

a – trying to keep it pithy, witty, and relevant at the same time.
b – I currently have a monstrous, aching, throbbing erection,
just due to the fact that I'm typing a mail to you.
c – I desperately need to perform all sorts of degrading acts
with you urgently!. . . . immediately! . . . *NOW!*

  Anyway, I've kept this note brief and incomprehensible so
that you have to contact me for a further explanation. Will
send another missive shortly – i.e. tonite.
  Love,
  Long John

He has written 'Love'. 'Love, Long John.' I will never need

to eat again. I will never doubt him again. There! He does want me! He's going to send another note tonight. Well, there is no point in being coy. I wait a seemly minute and a half and then write back.

Hardy,
   Interesting that you should choose the term 'Lover' because strictly speaking this is not an accurate form of address at the moment.
   NB. I am prepared to open negotiations regarding opening my legs.
   I like your naked wit (I barely remember your naked dick?) But not sure whether you are struggling with trying to mail me or nail me? I would be interested to understand what are you planning to do about desperately needing to perform all sorts of degrading acts with me? Please do not let this disintegrate into an all gob no grundies situation.
   Con

My phone rings on average 35 times a day. I receive 50 to 70 e-mails. I have countless conversations. By my calculations he has roughly 135 to 220 opportunities a day to make contact with me. He has had eleven days. That is 1485 to 2420 opportunities that he's failed to take up.

Fuck him!

I wish I could.

I continue to flick through the job columns, half-heartedly.

Fuck him!

The phone rings and interrupts my lack-lustre attempt at instilling my life with a sense of purpose.

'Greenie?'

YEEEEESSSSSS!

It isn't easy to find a date when we are both available; things get busy at work after Christmas, especially for him. So when we do meet at the end of January, as much as I want to give him a really hard time about not calling me, I somehow never find the right opportunity. The evening is so marvellous that I don't want to ruin everything by moaning. At 6.30 p.m. he marches into my office, charges straight up to my desk and kisses me.

'You look bloody horny.'

I am thrilled. He's on time. The fact that he has arrived without a bag, therefore doesn't have a Christmas present for me, becomes unimportant. I push my gift for him further under a pile of paper on my desk. I'd found an early edition of Kipling's poems, including 'If'. I don't want to give it to him now. He'll be so embarrassed. Seeing him is enough of a pressie. All the pain and sorrow of the Christmas holidays washes away. All the times I've been crucified when a message on my mobile isn't from him are forgotten. The fact that he hasn't called, visited or sent a card, dissolves from my mind. My cunt is jumping again and I want him.

We go to a bar, the type of bar I like. The type where young men have stains on their trousers and the people, although not friendly, are at least beautiful. We fight our way to a small table, risking hand-to-hand combat with another couple who are jostling for a seat. We win the table by intimidating them with haughty glares. We excitedly drink a bottle of champagne in under twenty minutes, then he buys a second one.

'How was Christmas?'

'Christ, yes. Christmas. Err. Happy New Year, Greenie,' he says, clinking my glass. I am so relieved. Explanation, he is too bohemian to have noticed Christmas. He finishes telling me about the gifts he received, then he says, 'Funny thing happened over Christmas, Greenie.'

'What was that?'

'I spent three consecutive days with Andrea. Day and night.'

My heart takes residence in the toe of my leather thigh-high boots. They have been going out with each other for two years, on and off. So three consecutive days should really have been expected, yet I know this first is important. It is significant. I know this in my head and as my heart has moved residence, it seems she has a pretty clear idea too. But my La Perla pants are oblivious. They are still twitching expectantly. He's often told me how he's incapable of spending a full weekend with her. How she annoys him, irritates him, that he needs his privacy. The fact that he doesn't like her consistent presence secretly delights me. John frequently amuses me with his outrageous stories of debauchery, and his honest accounts of his exploits protect me. Other women are demystified and cease to be a threat. He has me, his casual shags and his girlfriend (a sound bird, but not 'the one'). I don't care how many women he has sex with, as long as he is having sex with me. And as long as it is only sex he is having with them. And as long as he uses a condom. I have deliberately avoided asking about her. Andrea. When curiosity has reared its charming but senseless profile, I've bashed it down with a solid dose of practicality. What the heart doesn't know. There is nothing he could say that I'd want to hear. If he says she is beautiful, I'd implode with jealousy. If he denies her beauty, I'd think he was a fool or a liar. If he tells me she is fun, I'd want to know what they make jokes about. If he confirms she's dim, I'd *know* she is more beautiful than me. I don't want to know.

It unnerves me that he's managed to overcome his aversion to roll-over stay-overs.

It is essential that he doesn't think I am concerned.

'Really. Weren't you bored?'

'A bit, yeah,' he says, looking embarrassed. 'I got myself into a bit of a mess actually.'

'Really?' I brighten. This will be another tale about one of his other spare-time women. A tale that proves that I still hold premier position.

'Yeah, Andrea and I are lying in bed after sex, chatting and stuff.'

So it is going to be an Andrea story, not a spare-time-woman story. Hell.

'I am flaring my nostrils . . . you know, it's a sort of post-coital joke.' He flares his nostrils to demonstrate, but he needn't bother. I know about his flaring nostrils, charging bull thing. I've been on the receiving end of it. I am a bit surprised that he says he and Andrea were *chatting* after sex. We never even talk in bed. No, thinking about it, we did in Paris. But never since he told me about Andrea. I know that by accepting that he had a girlfriend I forfeited the courtesy of him bothering to get to know me. I'm temporarily accepting his low standards of intimacy, because I'm convinced that eventually he'll be interested enough to ask, 'So what did you do today?' I shake the thought away and I try to concentrate on the story he is telling.

'Andrea is normally quite a silent lover but that night she amazed me by letting out a low moan. A deep throaty sound, gurgling up from inside of her, which refused to be suppressed. I was pleased, knowing that my performance must have been reasonably impressive. As you know, Greenie, I like to please my women.'

He shoots me a fast smile, which I try and fail to return.

'The irony is that it is you who is making me feel so horny and capable.'

I am unsure whether to be flattered or furious.

'You wanting me so desperately has increased my potency and desire. I feel that I can fuck every female that I know. I feel that I should. That I owe it to myself.'

'Do it,' I say, and stand up to get another round in. I've often said as much to him, but I feel odd listening to his stories, sad. At the bar I breathe deeply, trying hard not to hear what I've already heard. He is *not* chucking me. Is he dumping me? I think he *is* binning me, even if he hasn't realized it himself yet. OK. OK. No need to panic. Shitfuckpiss. Sorry, God. I knock over a bottle of Moscow Mule. 'Sorry, Barman.'

I return to my seat with a couple of beers. 'Well, go on. So you are being this great lover and she is being a grateful, noisy lover. Doesn't sound very complex to me. It sounds commonplace.'

'Ahhh, but I haven't got to the complex bit yet. Because she is being so unusually responsive, I start to get a bit carried away and introduce some of the things that we do. She really likes some of it and says so. This is the funny bit, Con, I am all frenzied and confused, you know?'

'Yes. Lust,' I say, dully.

'And I say to her, "Well, you taught me." She stops me and grabs my head, making me look her in the eye. She says, "No, I did not". "Yes, you did," I argue. Honest to God, Greenie, for the life of me, I couldn't think who taught me. I knew you'd think it was funny.'

But I don't.

'You don't love her,' I try.

He looks indignant and angry. 'I do.' His words slap my face.

'OK,' I back down, as soon as I see his anger. I try something else. 'But you are not *in* love with her.' His face relaxes, he is willing to listen.

'How do you know?' Big gamble this one. But weighing it up, I see my choice is I can either say something big and dramatic, which doesn't necessarily have to be true (in fact it is probably safer if it's not true), or lose face. The former is infinitely preferable to loss of face.

'Because you couldn't do this to her if you were.'

'You do it to your husband.'

'I know.' I'm almost embarrassed. I am extremely confused and therefore I concede the point. True, conventional wisdom says people in love do not cheat on their spouses and partners. Seems fair. But conventional wisdom also said that I'd live Happily Ever After and would no longer need grubby sex with wickedly exciting strangers. Quandary, I have just played a double bluff and John may insist I show my hand. For the first time I have hinted that if he wants something more than a terrific shag behind a Portaloo, then maybe I am the girl. But even as I am offering him this bait and hoping to reel him in, I am unsure as to whether or not I want to have him for supper. I look at the empty glasses that litter the table.

'You're right, I'm not in love with her.'

The contents of my La Perla jumps into my mouth. Is this it? Is he is going to tell me he's in love with me? What will I do? Permanency? Luke? What about the amount he drinks? That will be an expensive habit on a permanent basis.

'I find no comfort in intimacy, it's claustrophobic.'

Oh.

'Constance, I am fickle, lazy and selfish. No one can hold my attention for long. Not even you. I get distracted, that's just me. A woman walking into the bar can distract me, a football game can distract me, something on the TV – '

I nod and finish, 'Can distract you'.

'Christ, Con, a piece of tinfoil fluttering down the street can distract me.' As he says this he does a funny little mime whereby he follows the progress of a piece of tinfoil, as it skips down the street. He is so active and funny that I can clearly see the shiny piece of foil. I need to reel him back.

'Have you ever had a soulmate?'

'Be specific.'

'Someone who challenges you. Have you ever dared to love someone more than yourself? Are you trying to go through life never knowing anyone? That way you'll stay untouched, uncontaminated, perfect.'

'I've read the books, Greenie. I know about denial. I'm not like that. It's crap.' He pauses for a long time.

'If you want to know the truth you are the closest I've got.

In Paris I was really happy. Thank God you are married.' He pauses again, finishes his pint, goes to the bar, orders more and then reconvenes. 'And what about you, Greenie? How are you with intimacy?'

'I am more honest with you than anyone else in the world,' I say. This sounds grand. Fitting. I have had a bottle of champagne and a couple of beers and this feels like the truth. I have no tolerance for small talk. I, more or less, demand big talk, which only has to be, more or less, reliable.

'The entire world, imagine that.' He has no reason to doubt me. My confession prompts him to consider his level of honesty with me.

'Christ, Greenie. I think that's true of me, too, about you.' He is surprised and somewhat dismayed that he feels compelled to offer me honesty. He expects other people to deal fairly with him but he's never felt duty-bound to reciprocate.

'Why is it that I find it easier talking to you than I find it talking to my mates?'

'Lucy thinks it's because you are an emotional cripple.'

I wake up with a shiver because the quilt has slipped down the side of the bed. Almost instantly I'm aware of his warm body next to mine. Smiling, I curl into him. In his sleep he nuzzles closer to me and puts his hand on my bottom. I prop myself up on my right side, to stare with wonder. Such eyelashes, such a perfect mouth and fine, jutting cheek-bones. I gently trace his noble features with my index finger. Notwithstanding the fact that I am obviously delighted to be here, I keep getting an uncomfortable sensation in my stomach as flashes of Luke come into my head. Not Luke bursting in on us and shouting: 'Unhand my wife you cad.' That doesn't strike me as Luke's scene. Actually, it doesn't strike me that it would be anybody's scene. Anyway, Luke is away on another frigging business trip so he won't know that I haven't made it home, so I don't have any problems there. The visions that come into my head are more mundane than that. Recently I've noticed that Luke is looking a bit tired and peaky. Is he taking his vitamins? Is he eating properly? We rarely breakfast together nowadays as I am invariably nursing a hangover, so I'm not certain. I wonder if he's packed his razor, he usually forgets unless I remind him. And he hates the ones the hotels supply. Never mind, I'm sure that they have good razors in Sweden, or is it Switzerland that he is visiting?

I lie awake, for hours, listening to the radiator announcing that it is morning. In the absence of birds and daylight, this system seems reasonably reliable. I gaze at the long off-white curtains which billow in the draught created by the ill-fitting window. The breeze is cool and relaxing, a welcome contrast to the sweaty warmth of our bodies under the covers. I'm careful not to move too violently, in case I wake John up. I roll over to watch him sleep.

I am almost certain that Luke will have taken a warm jumper.

As I watch I begin to doubt that he is really asleep. His breathing, last night, was regular and deep. Now it is barely perceptible. He is awake and holding his breath on life. I play along with his silent farce. I don't want to talk either, I'm too tired to be entertaining.

He rolls over in the crisp white sheets. He stretches his cat-like body. He is rolling over with some trepidation. By now, I know that this is because he changes his women as often as

228

the sheets. He is thinking, Will she be fat or thin, blonde or dark? Never quite certain. Trepidation and anticipation. The exciting moment of rediscovering what he's pulled. Who has he brought home?

Turning.

He's thinking, So a blonde – good. Focus, focus, he shakes his head slightly and immediately winces, regretting it. 'So let's have a look. Blonde, good. Slim enough, nice tits, focus, focus.' It is coming back to him, not in flashes, like people always say, but in slow motion. The presence sleeping next to him is, in fact, a repeat performance. He's woken up to me before.

'Fuck, we drank a lot last night. How much?'

'We shared two bottles of bubbly, then we had four pints each.'

'Flash bitch.'

'You love it.'

I stretch too and glance at him; he quickly shuts his eyes. He doesn't want to hold my gaze. In lurid, Technicolor smudges it's coming back to him. Is he regretting opening up to me? Is he dismissing it, trying to ignore that he's moved the relationship on by telling me I am different, perhaps even exceptional? Is he wishing that he could rewind?

I don't want to kiss him until I've cleaned my teeth, yet I want to reconnect in some way. There are suddenly a million miles of confusion pushed into the few inches of sheets that lie between us. Separating us. I gently trace the definition of his muscle with my finger but he shakes me off. We stay silent, in contrast to all the talking of the night before. I get out of bed and stumble to the bathroom. I know he's watching me. He'll be able to hear me plonk my bum on the loo and pee, which is excruciatingly embarrassing. This is the first time I've ever been embarrassed in front of him. I flush the loo, clean my teeth, emerge from the bathroom, swaying in the doorway. Then I say something inane and flop back on to his sheets. I can't say anything articulate as I am still trying to judge his mood. The morning after is never easy but it is particularly hard if one of you is waking up with a head full of shame, the other a head full of regret and both with a head full of dented brain cells. Severely limiting. I wait for him to kiss me. I wait about a thousand years. He doesn't. This may be because his breath smells of cunny and fags, with a little next-morning staleness mixed in but I get the feeling that he doesn't want me there at all, worming my way into his sanctuary.

I'm not worried.

I am very worried.

I watch him as he gobbles his breakfast cereal, moving the bowl closer and closer to his mouth, spooning the stuff into his face, faster and faster, like everything he does in life, racing. Eventually he just drinks from the bowl. I do this too, but only when I am alone. There are two dirty cereal bowls besides the one he is using. I raise my eyebrows but don't ask the question. It is possible that the bowls are his, from two other days. He grins. They might be. Or they might be the debris from another love picnic. I don't shower there, I don't eat breakfast. I just want to go home. I need to get back before Luke flies in.

'I'm off now. I'll call you.'

*

It had been Lucy that complained that she hated January. 'It is a flat and grey month and worse, everybody accepts that it is. No one parties, everybody abstains, nobody flirts, or dines, or drinks or thinks. I hate it when flirtation stops.' We'd been in All Bar One, a day or so into the new year. I think her bad mood was a result of the hangover that she'd been nursing for three consecutive weeks. She'd arrived late and was unwrapping herself, discarding coat, hat, gloves, earmuffs. We stared glumly into our glasses, our silence was our agreement. Except Sam who had piped up, 'Well, I'm going to make sure January is a fun month. It's my birthday on the 29th.' We'd glared at her, darkly. Why is it that she is so optimistic, when all the evidence indicates she should be the opposite?

Unreasonably, I'd been quite touched by her buoyant outlook, which sat in stark contrast to my own and so I'd offered to host a sleepover for her birthday.

'It will be a giggle,' I'd assured brightly and falsely. It would, at least, fill a part of the ever-increasing gaps of time that stretch between my evenings with John. So now, here I am, knee-deep in alcohol, balloons, alcohol, streamers, alcohol and small sausage things on sticks. Luke's cleared out. Run for cover at the squash club with Simon.

'Cocktails, haven't you heard, are certainly making a come-back. I read it in the *Evening Standard* the other night. They are popular among not only the young and fashionable set but also the more mature and sophisticated,' I quote.

'And which set are we?' asks Sam.

I roll my eyes. 'Accept it, kiddo, the latter.' I, self-appointed cocktail queen, have planned ahead. My hostess book informs me that a supply of glasses, ice mixes and garnishes must be available. They are. I've read and heeded the advice that cocktails ought to be consumed as soon as they are made. I intend them to be. The book also encourages experimentation. 'The Cocktail Game, A to Z' is certainly that. The idea, theoretically, is a sort of truth or dare but in this case it is truth or drink.

Game rules: by turn, we each ask the person to our right, the most intimate, impertinent or outrageous question that we can think of. If anyone refuses to answer a question, they have to drink a sip of alcohol (or the entire glass as the game becomes more riotous). If someone challenges the veracity of an answer (which is usually a hoot of laughter and a screech of 'you bloody liar'), and their case stands up, you have to drink. If their challenge is not accepted then whoever challenged has to drink. These are the official rules. The rule that we generally play to is simply 'there are no rules'. Besides the above, reasons to drink are: if your answer is too tame you have to drink, if your answer is shocking then the person who asked the question has to drink, if someone reveals something that no one knew before, everyone has to drink – a kind of celebration, if someone shouts 'Have a drink', you have to drink.

Basically, you have to drink.

I line up the stock: brandy, gin, whiskey, vodka, light rum, vermouth dry and sweet, Cointreau, Baileys, crème de cacao, for Sam and Rose, soft, girls' drinks.

'Bloody hell, we'll all die if we drink this lot,' laughs Daisy, 'I'll never sober up for the wedding.' Daisy wedding has now officially replaced AD and BC as a Western calendar.

'We don't have to drink it all,' I argue, although I do think that as I've gone to so much trouble we should try, 'and we do have tomorrow morning if we don't get through it all.' General nods seem to suggest that this is OK then.

'I've also got orange juice, lemonade, mineral water and tomato juice.' As I list each product I pull them out of the Tesco Metro bags and reverently place them on the kitchen table. Sam starts to help me pull out more bottles . . . 'Cream, Angostura bitters and grenadine, of course.'

Lucy joins in. 'And the garnishing is so important, I bet you have lemons?'

'Check,' I confirm.

'And limes.'

'Check.'

'Strawberries?'

'Check.'

'Olives?'

'Check.'

'Maraschino cherries?'

'Check.'

'Salt?'

'Check.'

'Sugar?'

'Check.'

'Eggs?'

'Check.'

'We can't catch you out, can we? I have to admit you are the hostess with the *moistest*,' says Sam, in her Adelaide from *Guys and Dolls* accent. We all laugh.

'Come on, then,' urges Rose, who is surprisingly fond of a cocktail, 'get mixing.'

I've done my research. I've bought all the necessary equipment. I deftly collect together a shaker, a strainer, mixing glasses, measures, spoons, juice extractors, tongs. I whiz around the kitchen collecting teaspoons, chopping board, knife, corkscrew, can-opener, clothes, swizzle sticks and straws. I love the look of pleasure on Sam's face and the look of surprise on everyone else's.

'Wow, this must have cost a fortune,' says Rose.

'And so much time,' adds Daisy. I rapidly open cupboards, frantic to locate the glassware. We put as many glasses as we can lay our hands on in the fridge. Martini glasses, champagne flutes, red and white wine goblets, tumblers, highballs, brandy balloons and liqueur coffee glasses. We hold back about a dozen glasses and immediately half-fill them with crushed ice. Some of the ice escapes and scatters on to the floor. No one bothers to pick it up.

'OK,' I say darkly, trying to create an ethos of reverence around the game. 'The A to Z begins. A is for Alexandra Brandy. Ice, brandy, crème de cacao and cream all into the shaker, a spot of nutmeg, a strawberry.'

'Lovely,' smiles Rose, who picks up the Martini glass and downs its contents in one. Everyone stares in disbelief. Feeling their eyes burning into her, Rose pauses, she holds the empty glass halfway between her lips and the coffee table, as if in an attempt to disown it.

'What?' she asks hotly.

'We didn't even ask you a question,' Sam points out.

'You didn't even refuse to answer,' Daisy adds.

'Oops,' Rose says and smiles her sweet, girlish smile, 'well, it is so lovely.'

'Quite right,' I say. It doesn't bother me, as the ultimate objective of the game is to get everyone plastered and sipping might not be the answer. Unquestionably, downing shots will be fine. I am quite keen to rush towards oblivion myself.

'Well, you've broken the rules so you will have to have another now, as punishment,' argues Lucy.

'Fair enough – ' Rose accepts her fate – 'B is for . . .?'

'Black Russian,' squeals Sam excited, 'I'll do that. Vodka, kaluha and a cherry.'

There are loads of Bs to wade our collective way through. Bloody Mary, Blue Spring, Brandy Crusta, B&B.

'A what?'

'Brandy and Benedictine.'

'Ughhh, lethal, it will send me to sleep.'

B52 and finally, Boo Boo's Special.

'Now you are making them up.'

'I'm not. Pineapple, orange and lemon juice, Angostura bitters and just a dash of grenadine,' I defend.

'Sounds almost healthy,' says Sam disapprovingly.

We relax and sit like cushions, scattered and untidy. I have abandoned the rule of not smoking in the house and so it looks like an opium den. We each rush to make the next drink and also think of the next question, yet our heads are already beginning to feel . . . floaty.

'Are you seeing anyone at the moment, Sam?' asks Daisy tentatively. Quite a brave question under the circumstances. Sam is now officially our only single girl, well, besides Lucy but Lucy is beyond any categorization that fits the rest of us.

'I am actually. I'm snogging a Beckham look-alike.'

We visibly sit up.

'What does he do?' Me.

'What's his name?' Daisy.

'How old is he?' Rose.

'Is he married?' Lucy.

Sam grins. 'Art Director at Abet, Mood and Wickers, Warren, twenty-eight, no.'

'Abet, Mood and Wickers, I'm impressed.' Daisy.

'Twenty-eight. I'm jealous.' Me.

'Single, I'm glad.' Rose.

'Warren, there is always a drawback.' Lucy.

We laugh. After some serious interrogation we discover that he is South African, blond, happy to go down on her. By the end of 'B' we have established that Sam and Warren have, on average, sex nine times a week but that is to be expected as they've only been going out together for a couple of weeks. Daisy looks a bit fed up when she admits that she and Simon have sex roughly once a week.

'Sometimes twice,' she defends.

Sam immediately cheers her up by saying, 'But you're practically married, Warren has no intention of marrying me.' We all nod our agreement and have a free group swig to celebrate and console. Lucy is laughing. I look at her and am hit again by her beauty. She looks staggeringly splendid at the moment. She's recently had her hair layered around her face – maybe that's it.

The cocktails are about as strong as Tyson and much less familiar than Fergie is to the tabloids. Slowly we nudge forward, towards that amazing time when we will all swap intimacies, the latest and unknown secrets. Well, actually, I hope that my secret will stay exactly that, but I am interested to know what is going on in everyone else's life.

'OK, Sam, this question goes to you,' says Lucy. We all pity Sam, Lucy's questions always cut to the chase. Having said that, we are all quite relieved that she hasn't chosen us as her victim.

'Have you ever done trios?'

'Boy or girl majority? Do be specific,' Sam says, grinning. Cool.

'Girl?'

'Yes.' Sam calmly inhales.

Whoa, Whoa, wild screams of excitement. Drink.

'What would you have said if I'd asked boy?'

'Yes.' Sam calmly exhales.

Whoa, Whoa, wild screams of envy. Drink. We all enjoy a good compare and contrast so Sam instructs, 'Down a drink if you've ever slept with a man born in the 50s.'

Lucy and I drink.

'I obviously haven't pitched this hard enough – how about the 40s?'

Lucy drinks again.

'*Noooooo*,' we scream aghast.

'It was in the 80s,' defends Lucy.

'Oh, that's fine then, he was a child molester,' tuts Rose.

'No, he was forty-five, I was nineteen. Perfectly legal and actually very instructive.'

Daisy puts us back on track.

'Down a drink if you've ever slept with a man born in the 60s.' We all have.

'70s.' Three of us.

'80s.' Predictably enough, Lucy has. Riotously we circle her like a band of Red Indians hooting and screeching, 'Toy boy, toy boy.'

'That's indecent.'

'He's eighteen!'

Rose quips, 'Don't even ask about the 90s because we'll have to report her.'

'So where are we?' asks Sam. I pick up the cocktail book but the words are jumping off the page. We've sipped our way through a Campari, champagne cocktail, crème de menthe (which made Daisy retch, 'It's bloody toothpaste!'), a daiquiri, a Drambuie (and believe me at this stage it is challenging just saying them, never mind drinking them), and finally Sam has just finished off the eggnog. We are sharing these drinks, encouraging one spirit to fraternize with another in a reckless way.

'Weruppppptoooeffff,' I articulate carefully.

'Wotzeff?'

'FaaalllllleeeeennnnAnnngel,' I squeal.

A Fallen Angel sounds brilliant, really profound. It moves us away from the strict rules of the game, which by now have become complicated beyond comprehension.

'It's yoooour turn to drink.'

'No itzs snot. I ask the quesdon.'

Instead we change game to, 'If I was a cocktail I'd be . . .'.

Sam starts, 'If I was a cocktail I'd be a Ritz Fizz.'

'Fair enough,' I agree, reading from the book. 'Another sparkling champagne cocktail sure to enliven the evening. Use chilled champagne. Any liqueur.' Actually, I read that, I say, 'Anoooother sparking champin cocktail sure to en-liv-en the evnin. Use chill champin. Any lick your arse.' Lucy mixes the drink and exasperated, takes the book from me. Despite my recent intensive course to build up my threshold I am still pitifully poor at holding my drink. Sam sips at the Ritz Fizz, and yells, 'You'd be a Shirley Temple, Daisy.'

'Oh definitely.' we chorus our agreement.

'Can't I be something a bit sexier?' she pleads. Lucy stops pouring the ginger ale and considers the request.

'No,' she replies, definitively. Daisy's crest falls. Then Sam checks the ingredients. 'Daisy's right, she can't be a Shirley Temple.' Daisy's crest soars. 'It has no alcohol in it. You can be a Fluffy Duck instead.' Crest plummets.

'It sounds delicious,' assures Rose, 'rum, Cointreau, cream.' I have to say Rose is being a surprisingly good sport about all this excessive alcohol. I thought she'd disapprove and that this would tinge the atmosphere. I was wrong. Rose is frantic-ally leafing through the book to try to find a cocktail that suits her personality. She sighs as she gets to Z.

'There isn't one called "Dowdy Housewife".' Her already very flushed face becomes more puce and tears are threatening.

'You OK?' I ask. Rose has been drinking at an unpreced-ented speed tonight. Nearly keeping up with the rest of us. Rose looks at me, straight in the eye. Her ferocious glare is particularly disconcerting as she generally has a limited range of emotions: extremely pleasant to mildly flustered. She uses words like 'cross' and 'happy' and consequently we use them about her. Rose is not a woman that you associate with words like 'ferocious' or even 'hilarious'. She is tempered, even, serene. She drinks back the fluffy pink cocktail that she is nursing and then immediately starts to mix another one. A woman with a mission. She's hardly concentrating on the ingredients and the resulting concoction must be rough, as she winces as it spills down her throat. Still, I get the feeling that she doesn't care. She's actively striding towards oblivion.

'Rose?' Sam sounds concerned too. The party atmosphere is leaking away.

'I'm fine.' But before the words are completely clear of her mouth, her angry face collapses into a booing wreck. It sort of melts like wax as she dissolves into shaky sobs. Daisy rushes to catch her face in a Kleenex, and orders her to blow. Rose is too obedient to do anything other than blow. Sam rushes to put a protective arm around Rose. But it's a fragile and impotent shield.

'I think Peter is having an affair.' Her words fall out into the confessional room. Scolding the earlier frivolous revelations for not being big and real enough.

'Nooooo,' Daisy, Sam and I rush to reassure. I say, 'Not Peter, don't be silly, Peter wouldn't have an affair. You're too happy.' My subconscious is a nanosecond behind my mouth and the independent, cocky bastard notes that this is what people would say about me and Luke. I hate Freud for inventing the subconscious, it is so sanctimonious.

'Really, do you think so?' asks Rose, who looks hopeful again. But then she remembers something and adds, 'But maybe *he's* not happy.'

'Nonsense,' Sam snaps (nonsense is a Rose-associated word, Sam wouldn't think of using it otherwise), 'of course he's happy.'

240

'What makes you say that?' asks Lucy. I stare at her, uncomprehending. That's low. That's brutal. Even by Lucy's standards. 'What?' she mouths to me, she looks offended. 'I'm just saying . . .' We don't let her. Instead we drown her out by insisting to Rose that Peter is the very picture of happiness.

'He looked perfectly happy when I saw him last night,' I assure.

'You saw him last night? Where?'

'At our house. He came to see Luke.'

'Really, truly?'

'Really, truly, I mean, yes, definitely. Why?'

'He told me that he was seeing Luke last night but then he stayed out really late. I was worried so I sat up for him. I thought he'd only be out for an hour or so. When I heard a cab pull up I looked out the window. I am sure that I saw a woman in the cab as it pulled away.'

'Did you ask him about it?'

'He said that he was with Luke. He was dismissive of my question about there being someone else in the cab and told me to get to the optician.' Magnificently drunk, Rose didn't have to face the acute embarrassment that she should feel. Her husband was exactly where he said he would be, with exactly who he said he would be with. How paranoid! Really, she doesn't have enough to think about.

'He was with Luke,' I reassure.

'Until what time?'

I knew that Peter had popped by to see Luke because they were sitting in the study, enjoying a beer when I came home from Lucy's. I'd waved through and then gone straight upstairs for a long soak in the bath. I went straight from the bath to bed. I assume they'd gone out for a pint. I wasn't *exactly* certain of my husband's movements, I don't need to be, I trust him. My blasted subconscious reminds me that I'm too busy hiding my own whereabouts to pay much attention to Luke's. I answer Rose truthfully, 'Gosh, I don't know exactly. Luke came to bed late, he woke me up. He smelt of alcohol. I bet they had a session.'

'Really?' She's delighted. 'I feel so silly. Peter kept saying check with Luke.' Daisy and Sam start to pour more cocktails. Acknowledging that Rose is totally overreacting.

'Luke doesn't lie,' Sam reasons.

'No. He doesn't.' Rose smiles, happily convinced. She takes another slug of her cocktail; obviously this time it doesn't taste so bad. I make a mental note to be a lot more careful with alibis. God, if someone as simple and trusting as Rose is suspicious, because Peter innocently gets hammered with the boys, then it will only be a matter of time before Luke starts to ask questions. I shift uneasily and catch Lucy's eye.

'Where were we?' asks Daisy; struggling to revive the party atmosphere, she pours yet more alcohol and changes the CD to something noisy and pointless.

'We were trying to find a cocktail that suits Rose.'

'How about a Tequila Sunrise,' offers Sam. 'That will suit you.' We nod our encouragement.

'There's one called Zombie,' offers Lucy helpfully. The rest of us glare at her. 'Or an Old Fashioned Whiskey,' adds Lucy, as she jabs the fire. I nudge her with my foot. Christ, can't she behave? What is wrong with her? Drink.

'Well, we won't have this problem with you, will we?' Rose retorts. 'There is a whole array of appropriate cocktails. Harvey

Wallbanger, Screw Driver.' Rose smiles as she makes her suggestions, but I definitely get the feeling that she isn't trying to be friendly.

'You can be a White Lady,' Daisy says to Rose, desperate to break the tension. Lucy lights her cigarette and I think she mutters, 'Rusty Nail.'

We spend the rest of the night listening to Nina Simone, Billie Holiday and Diana Ross warble their sad way through countless love affairs – which is fantastic, every one of them relates to my current situation. At about midnight Rose goes to bed, happy with the thought that as neither of the boys can interrupt her sleep, there is just an outside chance that she'll get nine hours.

'Well, Daisy, have you settled on a colour for your bridesmaids?' asks Sam. This isn't a disinterested enquiry. We are all down for bridesmaid duty.

'Not yet, I haven't given my dress much thought either. We've been so busy telling everyone the news.'

'People pleased are they?' asks Lucy flatly.

'Delighted,' gushes Daisy. 'I couldn't be happier.'

'Oh,' says Lucy. Weddings aren't her thing, she can't understand why people are pleased about the announcement of another poor sucker being pulled into the matrimony vortex. 'Going well is it?'

'Wonderfully.'

'We can tell, you look so content.'

'Content, you mean fat?'

'No, she means happy,' says Sam

'Well, everyone puts on a few pounds when they are, you know, content,' adds Lucy.

'You're saying I'm fat. Where? My face? My thighs?' Daisy starts grabbing bits of her anatomy as though she is speaking to a child who is unsure where her thighs are.

'Not fat,' I assure.

'No one said anything about fat,' Sam adds.

'No?'

'Not exactly,' Lucy.

'Not exactly!'

'It suits you.'

'*Shoots you, Sir,*' we all chorus, giggling riotously. Lucy opens a box of Ferrero Rocher that Rose bought Sam for her birthday. We all know the rules – if you haven't paid for the food then they aren't real calories; food consumed while standing doesn't count either.

'Don't worry about it, Daisy, soon you'll start arguing about the wedding, everything from guest lists to first dance. You'll lose a stack of weight then,' I assure.

'Thanks, Connie,' says Daisy delighted.

Lucy falls asleep in a chair and Sam, Daisy and I begin to drink copious amounts of water to try to abate the inevitable, raging hangover that we have booked for the next day.

Alcohol makes Daisy brave, or pensive, or insane, because she suddenly turns to me and says, 'How long have we known each other?' Before I can answer she responds for herself, 'Twelve years, that's how long. And in that time we have had zillions of evenings like this. Over the years we have told each other everything about ourselves. Everything of interest and actually also the boring bits, too. If you were to combine the hours that we've spent talking and whispering and giggling I think you'd have the time equivalent to a sentence for a minor fraud case. Well, actually maybe not so minor. But you know what, Connie?'

'What?' I ask robotically, but actually I sense from her tone that whatever what is, I really don't want to know.

'I don't think I know you at all at the moment. Not really, Connie.' I am horrified.

'What do you want to know about?'

'Well, for all you tell us about' – she waves her arm vaguely – 'sex and stuff, you never talk about anything that matters.'

'Sex matters,' shouts Lucy. We all jump, as we'd incorrectly assumed that she'd passed out.

'I mean you never talk about love.'

I stand up to throw some more wood on the fire. I am suddenly angry, disorientated. The alcohol that buoyed me up for the last few hours is suddenly drowning me.

'You never talk about Luke any more.'

'Yes, I do. I'm always telling you about the proposal, and when I met him, and you see us all the time. It would be very indulgent talking about us all the time.'

'We don't see you all the time. Not together. You're never together any more.'

'It's true to say that we are going through a bit of a rough patch,' I confess. Daisy looks confused. I feel confused extra strength. We all stare at the fire. I am hoping that Sam will help me out. She doesn't.

Daisy lies down, resting her head on my lap. She persists, 'You told us about meeting, dating and the engagement, but now you've closed the doors. You shut us out.' It surprises me that Daisy sees it like this. I didn't shut them out, I just moved out of the commune. After I got married I sometimes felt as though I was the one shut out; they were all being single, young things. Doing the things single, young things do. Shopping, shagging, clubbing. The things I'm doing now but can't tell them about.

'What's it like? What's it really like being married?' asks sleepy Daisy. I guess she has a very active interest at the moment. I sigh. I've spent plenty of time thinking about this one recently.

'Good question, Daisy.' I don't know how to answer. I struggle to find the words. Being unhappy is pretty easy to describe. We are all able to talk about being dumped or disappointed. That's why we are so practised at doling out sympathy, being there for one another. But when you are happy, you don't sit around trying to articulate it, you are too busy being it. You are just . . . happy.

'I don't know what your marriage will be like, Daisy,' I say, patting the top of her head. 'I have every reason to believe that you'll be very happy.'

She yawns. 'I know I will,' she affirms and shuts her eyes, desperate, no doubt, to fall into the land of nod where she can dream about tulle Alaska-bake dresses and bridesmaids dressed as fairies.

I check that Daisy is asleep. She is. I ease her head up and put a cushion in place of my legs. Sam helps me to cover her with a duvet.

'It seems pointless to wake her just to put her to bed upstairs,' I comment.

'Yeah, much better that she gets a bad back from sleeping on the floorboards. She'll feel it's a more thorough sleepover experience,' Sam comments.

Because I am very drunk I decide that it is essential that we clear away the glasses. This faulty logic has often forced me to complete countless games of Trivial Pursuit and 1000-piece jigsaws. This drunken determination always ends in disaster. The glasses often ending in as many pieces as the jigsaw, but at the time there is no dissuading me. Sam knows this, so with a resigned air she picks up a tea towel. However, the combination of the amount I've had to drink, and the fact that I wash up by candlelight leads to very poor hygiene standards.

'These frosted ones are pretty,' Sam offers.

'They are not frosted,' I say, taking it off her and sulkily dunking it in the water again.

With uncharacteristic tenacity she continues, 'Well, are you happy?'

'Hey, haven't we stopped playing truth or dare?' She stares at me. I know Sam disapproves of John but before I go into automatic pilot, telling her that she doesn't understand, or see the good bits and therefore can't comprehend how important he is to me, I hear myself say truthfully, 'I'm heartbroken.' As heartbroken is a concept that we each think we have the most familiarity with, there is no thunder, no dramatic bars of piano music, no one faints. I pass her another smeared glass.

'Has he left you?'

'Not yet. I think he wants to. But that's not why I'm heart-broken. I always expected him to leave. I'm heartbroken because I wanted to believe in it all.' I wave towards Daisy's pile of bridal magazines. 'It's so complex.' I rub my forehead, leaving soapsuds on my temples. 'My marriage was wonderful. Too individual and private to describe properly. I never thought I was capable of having an affair. I never thought I wanted one.'

'What happened then, Con? What went wrong?'

'I did. I guess I blame movies, books, fairy-tales, magazines and pop songs.'

She looks confused. 'I think it's simpler than that. I blame John Harding.'

'Who's John Harding?' I drop the glass I'm washing as I twirl round and face Daisy. She is standing in the doorway, rubbing her eyes. We are, all three, lost for words and I can hear Toni Braxton's 'Unbreak My Heart' drift through from the stereo in the sitting room. Surely Daisy can handle the truth. I look at her sleepy, girlish face, still full of hope and wonder. Then again probably not.

'My lover.' I don't quite manage the bravado I was hoping for. Daisy gawks at me, her mouth hanging open; she staggers slightly and I think she is going to faint like a Victorian lady in a Broadway show.

'You fucking hypocritical bitch.'

That's one way of looking at it.

'You stupid fucking bitch.'

And that's another.

8

The ending, like the affair, lacks decorum. It is rough and filthy and exciting and undignified. I call.

'Luke's away. Are you free?'

He hesitates for the longest time and eventually says, 'Err, no, I'm going to the pub.'

'Who with?' My voice is unreasonably high as I battle to avoid sounding like the chief whip in the Spanish Inquisition.

'On my own.'

'Well, I'll come and keep you company,' I say with false joviality. I have no shame.

'I'm meeting the lads there.'

'Oh.' Is he? 'But you agreed last week that we would meet today.' It's a thin line between clingy and angry. I want to remind him of his commitment but I don't want to sound entirely desperate.

'Did I?' He sounds vague and uninterested, which I know he is.

'A quick one.' I mean a drink but he misunderstands me.

'Look, Con, I think we should cut out the sex and just be mates. This just doesn't make sense. You're married and I'm going to make a go of it with Andrea.' When he says her name I feel sick.

'OK, then, if we are mates we can have a drink together.'
Even I don't believe it.

'No.'

'Please.'

'No.' He wavers.

'Why not, if we are friends? Look, I'm happy to be your friend. You like your friends better than your lovers anyway.'

He laughs, 'Oh, Connie, you know me so well.'

'So? Look, I'll drive over to your place and we can go to the pub. If I have the car, I won't drink, so neither of us will do anything you will regret.' I force a laugh but I don't feel funny. Not being wanted is never amusing. Eventually, after a lot of persuasion, he agrees. I have recovered the situation. He is muddier and sadder but he has, in some small way, come back to me.

The car journey is hellish. It is dark, the traffic is appalling and I don't know the way from Clapham to Clerkenwell. Perfect conditions. I drive dangerously and nearly do irreparable harm to a number of passers-by. I feel faint and clammy and agitated. I vow to myself that when I get there, I will be different. There will be no sex, no confusion, no anger. If *mates* is what he wants, I'll give it a go. Or at least I'll pretend to, until I can convince him that I am a Sex-Diva that he cannot live without.

I can't find anywhere to park near his house, so I park in Australia. I run to his door, arriving sweaty with anxiety and anticipation.

'It's me,' I utter tonelessly into his intercom, mindful not to let the edgy excitement that I feel leak into my voice. He says nothing but the door opens immediately. He's been hovering, waiting for me. He flings open the door and more or less pounces, knocking for six my intentions to parrot, 'Oh, I'm so fine with being your friend, I wish I'd thought of it.' He pulls me into his hall, kissing me passionately.

Not expertly.

Still, his unexpected enthusiasm delights me and more than makes up for his sudden lack of ability. He tugs roughly at my clothes and I reciprocate by pulling at the buttons on his shirt and within seconds we are both undressed. Within minutes he has come on my breasts.

His urgency at once flatters and disappoints me. After he has come he does make half an effort to entertain me, lapping happily . . . but the oral sex has become just that, oral sex. He could be setting a table down there or writing a shopping list, it is that exotic. I'm pretty good at fooling myself most of the time but for some reason I am not able to this time. Sex may end in bed but begins in the head. My head knows that he's moved on. I look at his transparent skin and his amazingly elegant cheek-bones that frame his outrageously exquisite eyes and I feel dull. The eyes are still unfair, wickedly blue, but they are changed. They do not burn with lust or curiosity or desire or love. His eyes are glacial and bored. He is just as sexy but I am amazed by the entire lack of feeling. Does he know who I am? In the past when he'd licked my thighs and lapped my clit, I'd been extremely appreciative that I was lying down. Convinced that if I hadn't been my legs would have buckled and I'd have ended up flat on my back anyway. Now I am horrified that I am lying on my back, as I wonder how I will ever stand up, under the strain and shame of not being wanted. I push his head away. I wipe his cum off my breasts with his T-shirt and slowly begin to fold my body back into my clothes. I turn away to button up my blouse, suddenly wary, suddenly shy of him. He watches me pull on my leather trousers. My guaranteed-hit trousers. Spurting on tits seems alarmingly like a miss.

'Nice trousers.'

'Thanks.' I force a bright smile as I turn to him, sitting down to pull on my suede ankle boots. What happened to 'You look drop dead' or 'You are the sexiest bitch alive, I want to eat you'? Why is he commenting on my trousers?

'Where'd you get them?'

He is not a girl, so he can't be interested in the answer to that question. Unless, oh, horror of abhorrence. I have to know.

'Joseph. Are you thinking of getting a pair for Andrea?'

He looks at the floor and is not able, willing or bothered enough to deny it.

I sigh and pick up my bag.

'Where are you going?' He seems genuinely perplexed.

'Well, I think I'm finished up here,' I snap abruptly. 'You said that you wanted to go for a drink with the boys – well, go. I'm off.' Naturally, I don't want to go. Naturally, I want him to take me in his arms, and kiss me, and tell me he is sorry. I want to start the evening all over again. And this time, the imaginary time, I ring him to tell him Luke is away and he offers to take me to a restaurant. He picks me up and when I get in the car (after he's opened the door for me) there is a huge bunch of white roses, with tightly closed buds, my favourite kind. In my imaginary start-again day he tells me I look wonderful and he gazes at me longingly and he treats me well. He treats me the way people that genuinely care for each other treat each other. He treats me the way . . . the way Luke treats me . . .

I feel overwhelmingly morose and moronic. Unscheduled tears well up in my eyes. Angry tears. I am angry at myself, angry at John, angry at Luke, angry at the whole damn set-up.

'I can't just go to the pub. Not after that.' He points to the floor where he hurriedly had me. 'I can't just go out with the boys.' Slowly, *reluctantly?* he adds, 'We'll go to the pub.'

So we go to a dirty, intimidating pub, with no other women and no decent wine. I order a Diet Coke and he orders a half, indicating a swift and certain exit. Even I, with my unreasonable sense of invincibility, begin to understand that it is garbage-chute-wipe-a-tear-baby-dear-say-goodbyee-another-suitcase-another hall-time, and yet I long to believe that I've put my marriage in jeopardy for something more than a lusty shag, a feckless fuck. Isn't there just a chance that he still wants me?

No. Fool.

Yes. Cynic.

No. Do you want to be humiliated further?

Yes.

No.

If I am left caressing even the most minute glimmer of hope, within a month I will be able to magnify it into a galaxy of promise and intent. I need all doubt and uncertainty to be taken away. I require it spelt out, I want to hit rock bottom. I almost crave the words 'You repulse me' or as near as he dares to go.

'So why the restraint? Charming as a novelty but really rather out of character,' I snipe bitchily. It is important that he continues to think I am unassailable, that he hasn't touched me beyond a mild irritation.

'Restraint.' He moves his cigarette half an inch, indicating, as he always does, that he is interested, and that I should carry on.

'Coming on my tits, not inside of me.' Painfully clear, I think.

'Well . . .' He squirms on his chair, trying to avoid answering me.

'Oh, I see. Sex without penetration isn't infidelity. That' – I can't bring myself to be explicit – 'That thing we've just done, isn't being unfaithful to Andrea?'

He nods sheepishly.

'You fucking hypocrite,' I snap, possibly showing my hand.

'Maybe, but you taught me the rules, Con.'

Shame, he has a point. At the very beginning, in Paris, I used the exact same argument. Our relationship was based on challenge. He wanted to get me into bed and I wanted to get him to fall in love. As soon as I'd slept with him my allure instantly vanished. He'd won months ago. He won in Paris, just when I thought the cards were being dealt. I don't like losing.

'What's changed?' I ask.

'This just doesn't make sense,' he offers. He doesn't say: 'This doesn't make me happy' or 'I'm jealous of Luke' or 'I've gone off you' or 'Your insatiable appetite is making you indiscreet, which is tiresome.' Instead, he keeps on insisting that what we have doesn't make sense. He says it forcefully, calmly and repeatedly. He is not hysterical or impassioned or drunk, simply resigned, determined. He stares at me, with his *fuck-me* eyes that have turned into *you-bore-me* eyes and he says again, 'What we have doesn't make sense.'

'Sense!' I spit the word back at him. 'Sense, what does sense ever add up to? A detached house which you will fill with furniture, knick-knacks and arguments. Keep your sense for Andrea.' I never wanted sense. I wanted passion, a lack of temperance, anger, love, filth. I pull my lips together in a tight, controlled line of misery, as my brain desperately tries to get my heart to accept that I've lost. This thing we've had is gone. I want to wail. I feel cheated. I watch him as he lets my words lick his consciousness and he nods.

'Look, OK, so I want sex with you but that's it. I find no comfort in intimacy, it's claustrophobic.'

'Well, if that's the case, aren't I the perfect answer? A married woman that can never get involved. I'm offering exactly what you said you wanted, unconditionally. You charm me and I want to keep you around. I simply want you as you are, your damaged, faulty self. I want this on a regular but infrequent basis. I know you'll eventually choose a more tempered permanence but you'll always long for the exquisite exhilaration, which is self-destruction. We can come clean with each other.'

I am surprisingly cheerful. I am enjoying this. Even if he ditches me in the end, at least it is dramatic. At least it is exciting and big. There is a long silence and for a moment I think that I've reached him, so I add, 'You wanted intimacy in Paris.'

Then he plays his ace card, he beats me at my own game. He draws upon popular culture.

'What's the phrase they use in films, Con, "a few stolen hours"?' He smiles the widest smile and then struggles excitably to find the correct words. 'Con, what we had in Paris was more vibrant, definitive, exhilarating, than anything I'd ever felt before or since. Of course that stupefying happiness was because I'd bagged an unlikely conquest.'

He laughs and I don't know if I am supposed to believe him. 'I dunno, it was probably the excessive alcohol or the unusually balmy nights of the Indian summer.'

'No' – too excited to be embarrassed I babble on – 'I know, and you know, too, John, in the deepest part of your soul, where we keep the secrets that we are most ashamed and afraid of, that you fell in love with me in Paris. You know that you can't reason it away. That you simply loved me. And although you keep this thought secluded in a largely undiscovered recess, it does from time to time surface. The fact that you discovered you have a heart and soul which will beat in time with your cock scares the living daylights out of you. To you the unleashing of possibility is the unleashing of vulnerability.'

Despite his constant professions of having a minute attention span, he sits through this lecture. Which is rather courteous of him. He plays with a Tetley Beer mat, concentrating on tearing around the T and the B. Breathless, I let my daring words swim between us. He nods his head a fraction and for a moment in time I think he is going to agree with me.

'Maybe. Or maybe, Connie, you really are just another tart and I don't give a shit.'

Thud.

That is me hitting rock bottom.

He grins and finishes his drink. He is walking towards the door, without acknowledging anything that I've said, and without negotiating over taking me back to his flat. He doesn't seem to understand the monumental consequences of accepting that it is over. The consequences are obvious to me. If it is over, I've been wrong.

I've lost.

He walks me to my car and says, 'It's been great. Hey, don't look sad. You'll meet someone else.' He is oblivious to the fact that he is someone else. 'One day, maybe we'll meet up, you know, have a beer.' He is being artificially bright and his chirpy politeness fills me with wrath. 'I knew you'd understand.'

I don't watch him walk away from the car. Not because I am being big and brave but because it is final. I turn on the engine and for the first time since I passed my driving test, over a decade ago, I conscientiously mirror, signal and man-oeuvre. I drive directly to All Bar One, I do not pass go, I do not collect £200.

Lucy and Sam are sitting amongst the smoke and sawdust. There is no need for me to explain my unexpected appearance or my obvious distress. Lucy takes one look at my face and says, 'You've never been very good at letting go.' I put my head on the table and concentrate on ignoring her.

'Men are traditionally better at letting go,' observes Sam.

'Well, he's ace at it. I need pudding. I'm in shock.' I grab the menu and momentarily perk up.

257

'I'll join you,' says Sam, salivating at the choice. We order chocolate mud cake and banoffee pie.

'Shock?' asks Lucy, 'Why are you shocked? I've been wondering how you were managing to ignore flashing neon lights.' I gawk at her, not comprehending. 'The lack of telephone calls, the lack of e-mails, the vacillating between intensity and indifference, not to mention the vacillating between blondes and brunettes.' We sit silently until the puddings arrive. I dig my spoon into the mud cake and cram a crateful into my mouth. Instantly I feel better.

'Well, I've read the signs now. It's just that I am a bit late. About five months, two weeks, three days too late. About. To be exact. I think he stopped wanting me in Hampstead Heath, sometime between putting away his dick and pulling up his zip.'

I give them the details about undiscovered recesses.

Lucy sighs, 'Where do you get it from, Con?'

'Films.'

'Oh.'

'He confused things in January, by hinting that there might be more to it,' comments Sam. She looks at her banoffee pie, as if it has the answers. Luckily, we have Lucy on hand to offer some clarity.

'His emotional speech was the result of accumulated alcohol and sentimental Christmas songs. The equivalent to Daisy auditioning for *Stars in Their Eyes* via the security cameras at Peterson Windlooper. Didn't you notice that he's never called you except when he is returning your calls, or when he is utterly pissed, or randomly randy?'

'No, Lucy, I didn't.'

She flicks her blonde hair over her shoulders. I glare at her. Saddam Hussein is more sensitive than she is.

'You're right, Lucy, after that first time he never said, "Stay" or even "don't go". He didn't call for a month. But that didn't help, it only made me want him more.'

'I bet if he'd suddenly turned hopelessly devoted, you'd have get bored, you always used to,' comforts Lucy.

'Well, it would have been nice to have been given the opportunity to find out.'

'So what's your next project?'

'Project?' I reiterate, shocked.

'Yup, project,' confirms Lucy. 'Men have always been your project. I think that's the issue. When you married Luke you finished your 5000-piece jigsaw and now you don't know what to do except break it up again and start again. What's the next big thing?'

'That's ridiculous,' I snap. 'Isn't it, Sam?'

Sam doesn't answer my question but says instead, 'Maybe if you were a bit more fulfilled at work, then . . .'

'I have a good job.'

'You have a job that someone else would think was good, but you only became a management consultant because of the male to female ratio of the staff. Once you married you had no motivation to be there.'

'Oh, thank you very much for your understanding.' I hastily make to gather up my handbag and huffily pretend I'm going to leave the bar. Sam and Lucy are unperturbed, they know I have no intention of leaving. We've all known each other far too long to care about a mild bout of self-indulgent histrionics. They know what I want to hear.

Lucy: 'He's a bastard.'

Sam: 'You deserve better.'

Lucy: 'You have better.'

Sam: 'Don't blame yourself. It takes two to tango.'

Lucy: 'Well, it looks like your dance card's empty.' Lucy starts to veer off the comforting script here and instead reverts to 'telling me like it is'. She has every right to do this as she is a very close friend. I hate her.

'I can't believe you accepted he had a girlfriend and the fact that he took other lovers, didn't it cross your mind to tell him how unacceptable it had all become?'

'Of course it didn't,' Sam defends me. 'She was looking through carnality goggles and listening through infatuation ear-muffs.'

'Where did I go wrong?' I wail, as I finish my chocolate mud cake and start to edge my fork into Sam's banoffee pie. I am flat with disappointment and regret. 'Maybe I should diet? Grow my hair? Have it cut?' The girls stare at me in silence.

'You look good.'

'You look brilliant.' It is true to say that never before have I spent so much time and money at the beautician's. I am toned, tanned, pumiced, exfoliated, manicured, pedicured and cleansed to within an inch of my life. Normally a neat size 10, I recently hit that previously inconceivable nirvana, size 8. Anyway he was keen on my bod. I remember his voice, 'I love your tits, Connie, you are so fucking sexy.' (Not sexy enough as it turns out. Well, you know how sexy is – going for a song nowadays.)

I shake my head. 'Maybe if I hadn't rung him as much over Christmas. I should have played it cooler.'

The girls are silent. Sam chews on a banana and Lucy deeply inhales on her cigarette.

'Perhaps I should have shown him more of my feelings? Maybe if I'd been more up-front.'

Sam tries to smile sympathetically, Lucy tries not to throttle me.

'I'm not sure what I should have done, what could I have said that would have held his attention?'

Lucy smirks and says, 'I've got the answer.'

I look at her hopefully.

'Maybe if you'd said nothing. Been absolutely mute from September to February, only opened your mouth to take in his cock, then you just might have hung on to him.'

I try to treat her with the disdain she deserves. I play the past months over and over in my head, but I can't think how I could have acted differently. Not on rewind, pause or fast-forward. The take is always the same.

I leave them to their Chardonnay and I drive home. I park in front of our large Clapham home and I howl.

I sob.

I cry for John, for Luke, for me. I beat my hand down on the steering-wheel, envying my husband's certainty.

I'm not going to work. I am sick. I am broken-hearted, miserable, mournful, desolate, despairing, devastated, disappointed, disconsolate, inconsolable, prostrated, sorrowful and wretched – that has to be worse than flu. Besides which,

261

I am very tired. I haven't slept for months and now I feel as though I could sleep for England. My friends, colleagues and associates don't seem to realize that I'm keen to do a good impression of Tutankhamun. The phone never stops ringing but I ignore it and when I can't ignore it any longer, I take it off the hook. After about five minutes I am disturbed by a high-pitched tone and a very prim voice informing me, 'You have failed to replace the handset correctly, you have failed to replace the handset correctly.'

'I know,' I yell as I yank the lead out of the wall, 'but that is the least of my problems!'

Luke is staying at some castle in Scotland. A stockbroker friend of ours has bought it for the price of a small car and has commissioned Luke to renovate it. Luke wanted to stay there, to see it in all lights. Since it is February and Scotland, I reckon the ranges of light he will see are, dark, mid-dark and very dark, but he was insistent. He isn't due home until Saturday morning. I wish he was here, he'd cheer me up. He's the only person who can ever laugh me out of my disappointments. Like that time I'd wanted my haircut before we got married. He kept telling me not to do it, or at least not before the wedding.

'Why not? I think I'd suit it short,' I'd argued.

'I'm sure you'd look beautiful, long, short, bald. It's just that all those bridal magazines, that you so avidly read and quote, advise you not to do anything too dramatic with your hair just before the wedding.'

I ignored him of course, and regretted it. I cried for about four days and refused to go out of the house. He bought me a joke orange clown wig and tugged on my remaining hair to stimulate growth. I did sort of get used to it by the time the wedding came round but I don't know how I'd have got through those first few days without him. Typical that he isn't here now when I really need him!

At about six o'clock I hear a key in the door.

'It's just me,' Luke shouts. He bounds up the stairs but I don't bother to sit up. 'I came home as soon as I heard the news,' he declares.

He sits on the side of the bed and I freeze. He's heard!

'Are you in there?'

He lowers the sheet from my face and pushes a huge bunch of white roses in front of my nose. The leaves rustle and the scent drifts. I can feel his icy hand on my forehead, 'You're not ill as well, are you? Poor darling.'

I gawk at him and say nothing. He waves the roses; they are the most colossal bunch I've ever seen.

'A consolation prize.'

This is surreal. My husband is buying me roses because my lover has dumped me. It seems improbable. I slowly sit up. His cold lips hit my warm ones. I don't know why but a large tear falls down my face. It isn't that the kiss is unpleasant, quite the opposite actually.

'Hey, don't cry, pumpkin.' He keeps pumpkin for very special occasions. 'I know you are disappointed, that's natural.'

Is it? Yes, I suppose it is. But his reaction is far from natural. I am stupefied, I still say nothing.

'But maybe in this case the best woman won. Hard as it is to take.' He strokes my hair. How does he know Andrea?

'And she's worked very hard for it.'

Me too, I silently cry, but I am still too astonished to risk speaking. Should he be taking this quite so calmly?

'She's so worried about how you will react, she's been calling you all day.'

Who has? Andrea? Does she have my number? This is perplexing.

'Call her,' he says, handing me the phone.

'But I don't know her number,' I stammer.

'You are ill. It's in memory, just press four.' Luke smiles his huge, enveloping, patient smile.

'I'm calling Sam?' I ask uncertainly.

'Of course, who else would I be talking about?' Luke is using the tone that he uses when he speaks to small children. 'To congratulate her. It's the right thing to do, especially since she's going to be your boss now. Head of Department, that's quite a promotion. I'm sure you were in the running, too, darling, but she has been there a lot longer than you. I'll go and put the kettle on, leave you to it.'

Luke leaves the room and I stare at the phone. I piece it together. Yes, Sam did tell me that she was applying for Head of Department. She'd taken me for coffee and very seriously asked me whether I thought it would impact on our friendship if she got the job.

'I won't even apply if you think it might come between us,' said Sam, her eyes wide with sincerity. 'You should apply, too, I think you've got a good chance.'

'Do you like this suit?' I'd asked her. 'It's new.'

'Yes, very much,' she'd replied, somewhat confused as to what the connection was. So she'd applied for the job and evidently she's got it. Well, good for her! I can't believe that my friends, and even my husband, think that I'd get this upset over a job! I never even got round to putting an application in. I call Sam. Luke comes back into the bedroom, puts a cup of tea on my nightstand and beams at me.

'We'll have to have a party to celebrate, Sam. This is brilliant news,' I gush down the telephone.

I catch Luke's eye and he mouths, 'I'm so proud of you.'

Lucy is going away for a weekend in Paris with her married lover. She is very excited about it and wants to talk of little else. I am being unfair. I won't let her. There is nothing more depressing than listening to a friend go on and on about her successful love affair when yours is in shreds. Especially when said friend is insisting on taking a mini-break in the same city as shredded love affair played out its promising beginning.

'It will be marvellous, three whole days together. No dashing home. No looking over his shoulder.' She's gushing.

'Then he said, "Nice trousers. Where do you get them?"' I blow my nose. Lucy realizes that as I'm not going to join in her conversation she might as well join me in mine.

'The bastard. I bet he is going to buy them for his girlfriend.' It's depressing that she jumps to the same conclusion I did. 'I hate it when they go back to their wives and girlfriends. It's so . . .' She searches around for the correct word.

'Degrading,' I offer.

She shakes her head.

'Disappointing,' I sniff, barely holding back the tears.

'Annoying is the word I am thinking of.' Lucy holds up a chemise, examines it and then dismisses it.

'Is red too obvious?' she asks as she holds up a red La Perla

265

bra and knickers set which, arguably, would have been at home in an Amsterdam brothel.

'Definitely,' I sigh. Lucy immediately drops them into her basket. Despite my black gloom I can't help but screech, 'That's £175 worth of bra and £80 worth of knickers.' I doubt she is getting her money's worth as they are both minuscule. Her smile indicates that perhaps she is getting her money's worth.

'Men like to know you've made an effort with your underwear,' she breezes. Maybe, but Luke would think I was crazy to spend that type of money on knickers; he fancies me even if I am in M&S. Now what was I talking about? Oh yes, John.

'You know, I once wore John's underwear for work and he always kept a pair of my knickers. I always left some garment with him. Not on purpose, it was just that I always seemed to be in a hurry to get dressed as I left.' I don't dwell on this train of thought for too long. 'Do you think it is extraordinarily sexy that he wanted to keep my underwear?' I ask Lucy, hopefully.

'Commonplace, darling,' she whispers conspiratorially and then somewhat pityingly she adds, 'where have you been?'

By the time we leave Harrods it's dark and pouring with rain. We stand, vainly trying to hail a cab. The circumstances are against us. Past experience proves that we might be waiting weeks before we get one. A spot of rain in London and everything slows to a halt. I am disdainful of softy southerners.

'A smattering of rain wouldn't grind Sheffield to a standstill,' I mutter. The rain is ruining my carefully applied makeup, although unaccountably Lucy still appears immaculate.

My clothes are wet and heavy and it is difficult to balance my numerous chunky bags. I am sure that it isn't raining anywhere else in London, except above me. I think about those peculiar black and white films with crude special effects where the rain follows the clown around the set.

I am that clown.

Normally Lucy is prepared to shove the other contenders for a cab under the wheels of a passing bus rather than stand about. Today, she is patiently queuing. She is obviously delirious. I wonder if there are any diseases you can catch in Harrods that manifest themselves in a personality transplant. I haven't given Lucy and her extra-marital affair much thought. But watching her now as she animatedly chatters about the George V Hotel and the Eiffel Tower, I realize that she's really fallen for him. If it was anybody else, Sam for instance, I'd have been quite concerned. Dating married men can only end in tears. But I know there is nothing to worry about with Lucy. She knows how to look after herself.

'Come on.' Lucy nearly pulls my arm out of the socket as she leaps over a dozen other people patiently huddled under umbrellas waiting for an orange light. Lucy has spotted one. She flings open the door and bundles me into the back seat.

'Where to, luv?' asks the cabbie. Lucy gives her address.

'You're behaving very maudlin,' she says critically. 'Is Luke away tonight?'

'Yes, on business,' I sigh my resignation.

'Well, in that case you can stay with me.' Lucy's clipped incisiveness is a relief, and as it turns out a contrast to the dithering cabbie who has no idea how to find Lucy's fairly prestigious and renowned address. 'The Knowledge' is an urban myth. Lucy barks directions at him which allows me the opportunity to sit back and wallow. I feel woefully sorry for myself. I'm angrily tearful. The cabbie, an amateur driver but an experienced psychologist, reads my mood and switches the radio channel from the slow blues of Billie Holiday, to a cheery, pointless ditty. He is well-meaning but frankly I want to indulge my misery. I wish do-gooders would jump in the Thames. The cabbie lights a fag. The cigarette smoke tickles my throat uncomfortably and reminds me of John. I want to cry. The delicate balance I call life is seriously smashed out of kilter. The rain drills down on to the cab and the manic windscreen wipers, however industrious, cannot clear the downpour fast enough. The lights look like a box of costume jewellery. It is her fault. It's Lucy's fault for going on about Paris. Ha Paris, hateful place. Why does she want to go to Paris? Nothing but endless fountains, countless elegant lampposts, innumerable tall clean trees, dozens upon dozens of grand cream buildings, wide avenues, fantastic food, delicious wine, what is there to like? More than enough charming bridges, more passionate couples than anyone can bear, what is the attraction? Paris, the loneliest city in the world.

'What are you thinking about?' enquires Lucy.

'Nothing,' I answer, as though I am a man.

'Look, it's to be expected you know?'

'What is?'

'Your feelings of self-pity and regret. Unfortunately the pain is often inversely proportional to the wanky behaviour of the beloved.'

'Lucy, you are such a comfort.'

'I'll give you three weeks, four at the outside and you'll be over him. But, be warned, between now and then you'll cover more emotions than American tourists do sights on a week's trip to Europe.'

'Really.' Piss off. No, not seriously. I am, of course, indebted to Lucy for her patience. In this past week she's shared countless bottles of wine and cups of coffee, while I've bored her rigid with oft-repeated questions.

'Do you believe he meant that?' I ask, as I remember a wonderful thing that John said.

'Yes,' sighs Lucy, pouring another glass of wine, 'but, Connie, you know as well as I do – '

'I know,' I interrupt her, 'it is only valid for the time it takes to get from their mouths to our ears.' She nods.

'Can you believe he did that?' I ask, affronted. I'm outraged every time I remember some terrible thing that John did to me, or more likely, failed to do. Like failed to call, or even to return calls, failed to be on time, or even turn up at all.

'Yes,' sighs Lucy, inhaling deeply, 'but, Connie, what I can't believe is that you put up with it – '

'I know, I know' – I hang my head – 'but – '

This time she interrupts. 'But you wanted him.' She says this in a whiney voice and for a moment I think she is imitating Sam, then I realize that she is imitating me. Despite myself, I laugh.

Lucy pilots me through the awful moments, as we visit denial, self-pity and regret. I then fly on in my package tour of emotional experiences and visit irritation. It is only one stop further on before I hit on anger. Whereas irritation was an Easy Jet overnight stop, fury is quite a plush resort and I stay for some time. Scarlet, fierce, ferocious anger. I become *very* angry. I become very *angry*. This is an ugly period. I lash out at my friends and loved ones. Hating Luke for not being John, hating John for not being Luke. Incensed with myself for being so bloody simple and falling for John and his lies. I am furious with Lucy for not warning me to stay away from him, then exasperated with her when she reminds me that she did tell me to stay away from him. I rip and break and smash and swear my way through bitter March. I feel permanently premenstrual. I rage against mankind. I start each day thinking it will be awful, which generally ensures that it is, even if it began with a fighting chance of being passable. I count my causes for concern as I go into work. I am irritated by idiots that leap into the Tube as the doors are closing, risking injury and causing delays. I am terminally exasperated by teenagers listening to music that pulses loudly and incomprehensibly. I am inflamed by couples who insist on talking to each other, or worse publicly displaying their affection for one another. I find that inconceivably rude. I am mortally offended by anyone who has too much luggage and insists on pushing their luggage into my legs. I don't like traffic wardens, librarians, ticket inspectors, cab drivers, shoe-shop assistants – they are all mean. I loathe anyone involved with BT, British Gas or the Electricity Board – they are all incompetent. I really abhor happy people.

'I keep seeing that piece of tinfoil skipping along the street blowing in the wind, spinning in a sparkly way and I see him chasing after it. A shiny, flimsy piece of tinfoil,' I stutter angrily, falling over my words with indignation.

'Bastard,' Lucy confirms, not for the first time.

'Fucking cheek of him coming on my tits,' I yell, as I hurl a book at the wall.

'Ya, gal, go,' says Lucy who is evidently very pleased with this development in the emotional scale. She picks up a book and flings it at the wall.

'Why are you angry?' I ask, confused.

'I'm always angry,' she answers grimly.

'Maybe I'm just another tart and he doesn't give a shit.' I can barely repeat his words, I spit them out. '*Another* tart, another *tart*. And he doesn't give a *shit. Not a shit!*' I noisily throw the empty Chardonnay bottle in the bin, put my hands on my hips and scowl at Lucy. 'What's more, Lucy! . . .' I am still yelling, she looks mildly apprehensive, but then again anyone else would have been peeing themselves following my display. Lucy has nerves of steel. 'What's more, we are out of white wine, we'll have to drink red.'

'Red's fine by me,' she grins.

Luke quietly suffers throughout this roller-coaster of emotion. He thinks my depression in February is to do with the prolonged winter. He thinks my anger in March is due to the fact that I missed the promotion at work. He reads lots of articles about women's hormones, then suggests that I visit the doctor to change my pill. When I glare at him he tentatively suggests I call a headhunter instead. Throughout, he is courteous, concerned, chivalrous and distant. He is extremely busy with a massive new contract. He's won a pitch to convert a theatre into a restaurant, right in the heart of the West End. The project is extremely high profile and both the media and industry gurus are carefully monitoring his progress. We both know that this is the big break we've always talked about and it has come earlier than either of us ever hoped. If things turn out well and Luke is judged to be successful on this project, he will get endless offers of work. He is very wrapped up in it. He works even longer hours than his already unfeasibly long hours and when he isn't actually at work, he is talking about it. I am very pleased for him. Naturally. Very.

And a bit jealous.

Well. How is it that I am going through all of this and he just hasn't noticed? And how come he has a cool, creative, satisfying job and I don't? How come my biggest challenge is designing a new model paper plane and then getting it into the bin without moving from my chair? How come he's absolutely failed to see what is under his nose? Another thing that annoys me is that he still seems to be very golden, very A standard but *we* no longer seem like the golden *couple* or the A *team*. I am tarnished and coming in with D grades. Every night I fall asleep resenting . . . stuff.

I wake up before Luke and jump nervously. I check the clock, it is 9 a.m., what day is it? I panic. Is it a weekday? Have I slept in? Then I relax as I realize it isn't a weekday. It's Saturday 19 March. Still, something is odd. I quickly turn to look at Luke, to check he is OK. Please, God, let him be OK. Please, God, please. Is he breathing? Of course he is breathing, of course he is OK. He is sleeping soundly wearing that gentle, contented look that he always wears in his sleep. I begin to relax and I lie back down again. Sleep is no longer the given it used to be. Up until meeting John I'd always slept soundly, cuddled spoon-like into Luke. After meeting John my sleeping became erratic, too heady and happy at first and then too preoccupied and tense. Regret, disappointment and anger are all awful bedfellows. Suddenly it dawns on me. I realize *that* is the difference. I have woken up at 9 a.m., not at 2 a.m., or 3 a.m., or 4 a.m., or 5. I have slept a solid nine and a half hours. I feel relaxed. My anger has subsided. I check to see if it is hiding under the bed. It isn't. I think about the other guises anger might be hiding in, but I am neither irascible nor fiery. Nor am I fretful or snarling. Anger has gone and it's been replaced by relief. Actually relief is quite a cheery chappie to have around, easy going, undemanding, unhurried and amenable. Relief keeps saying, 'Well done, Connie, nice job. Potential damage huge but you got away with it. Congratulations. Clever girl.' Then relief energetically slaps me on the back.

Fried breakfasts are sexy. I don't know why but they are. It could be that fattiness is associated with indulgence or it could be the association with huge, rugged truckers, like the Yorkie man. Relieved, I cook Luke a fried breakfast and take it up to him. I shyly put the tray down on the bed. The *bed*. Luke looks at me suspiciously, which is fair enough because I've only made him four fried breakfasts in his life and I have never brought them up to the bedroom. I watch him cheerfully tuck in. He thrusts bacon into his mouth and grins at me. There is some yolk on his bottom lip. On the right hand side. Impulsively I lean in and kiss it away. It turns into a slow kiss. We keep our eyes open and watch each other throughout. I tilt my head a fraction and kiss him again, gently biting his bottom lip. My breast pushes against his arm, my breathing

273

is quickening, he carefully moves the tray to the floor – the phone rings. We laugh. He nods, indicating that he doesn't mind if I pick it up. We're in no hurry.

'It's me.'

'Daisy.' I'm delighted. Daisy and I have had a very strained relationship since she discovered about my affair. Daisy's torn. She loves me but hates what I've done. She cried for a week asking me, over and over again, how could I have betrayed Luke. Sam pointed out to Daisy that it was none of her business and if anyone wanted to call me a 'Selfish, wicked, two-faced whore' then it should be Luke. Daisy then changed tack. She railed at me for quite some time as to why I treat her like a child? She insisted that I should have told her as I'd told Sam and Lucy (Rose doesn't count, none of us tells her anything). Lucy intervened by resorting to friendly chastising.

'Connie was trying to protect you. We treat you like a child, because you act like one. Now stop crying, get dressed and kiss and make up.' Both Daisy and I are too intimidated by Lucy to object. Daisy reluctantly hugged and said she was sure that I'd understand why I couldn't possibly be her bridesmaid. Relationships have marginally improved since she discovered it was all over; Sam told her that I'd finished it, a little scarlet lie.

'I'm going to look at wedding dresses today. I wondered if you wanted to come.' I expect one of the others had asked her to do this, Rose perhaps? It could be that I've been invited to referee Rose and Lucy. Sam is still attending fine art classes on a Saturday so won't be able to make it. Rose and Lucy, who rarely see eye to eye, would not make ideal shopping companions for Daisy, especially when the decision is as big as this. Whatever the reason, I'm pleased.

'I'd love to, Daisy.'

Lucy and I wait outside the bridal boutique for Rose and Daisy. Lucy leans against the shop window, smoking. She is wearing dark sunglasses, although the sun will not make an appearance in Britain for at least another three months. She inhales and exhales audibly.

'So, Connie, how are we feeling today?' she asks.

'Relieved.' I grin. 'It's not just relief at remaining undiscovered, although that is pretty compelling. It's the relief of remembering that I love Luke. There is a lot I still don't understand – like why I did it in the first place – but I am so relieved that I still love Luke. I think we can fix this.'

Lucy studies me. 'Relief isn't the end of it,' she warns me cheerfully. Damn, Lucy has a load of experience in this department, she's bound to be right.

'I'm really trying to make it up to Luke. It's surprising how quickly we've gone back to our old ways. Buying things for the house, attending work events, throwing dinner parties, making visits to aged aunts. It's amazing how quickly I've forgotten John.'

'Not really,' she smiles. 'You haven't heard from him, then?'

'No, he's insisted on behaving like a real person, not a character in a book.'

'What do you mean?'

'No grand gestures, no big bids to win me back, just plain silence.'

'Bad luck.'

'Yes, isn't it?' I grin, she knows I am joking. 'Look at me Lucy, I've rediscovered my sense of humour.' We fall silent. Lucy uses the shop window as a mirror to check her immaculate reflection. I rub my shoe up and down the back of my trouser leg, to try to induce a shine.

'You know, I've been thinking about this and in my considered and expert opinion, you could get John back. If you put your mind to it.'

Before she has a chance to share her strategy with me, I hear myself say, 'I don't want him back.' This is news to me. Brain did you register what mouth said? Brain is in accordance. Heart did you hear? Actually heart has never been too involved and is therefore happy to agree. Acid test, err, knickers, what are your thoughts on the subject? There is no reaction. No jittering small puppy feeling, nothing. To check I say his name. John Harding. No pang, nothing. Thank God. I don't want him any more.

'Well, what do you want?' asks Lucy reasonably.

'Nothing. Everything is just perfect again.'

'Is it?'

'Of course it is. I don't miss him at all.'

'Just be sure you aren't too hasty in wallpapering over those cracks, Con.'

I spot Rose and Daisy walking towards us. We move forward to greet the Kirk girls. Daisy hugs me tightly and I think I'm forgiven; perhaps I'll still get to be bridesmaid.

The shop bell *trings* to announce our arrival. That *tring* also propels us into another age, although not a definitive era. A time when women, normally extremely independent, can – without surrendering any self-respect – wear long flowing gowns, carry parasols and hide behind heavy lace, being at once demure and provocative. A time when everyone speaks in muted voices. When women manage to be both the centre and centred, and men are charming and attentive. By walking into the bridal shop we have access to a romantic utopia, even if it is only for one day, Daisy's day.

My heart at once hardens and then implodes as I remember my own trip to a bridal shop, only two years before. I remember feeling like a caterpillar entering a cocoon. Knowing that I was about to become something much freer and more tremendous on emergence. An entirely different shop and yet just the same. The same deep-pile carpets that massage feet, the same plush folds of silk and rosettes of ribbon that sway in the draught caused by opening the door. The silk moves slowly but with purpose, like an ocean tide licking a creamy beach. The *Love Story* theme tune is being piped out of some secret vent and although we self-consciously recognize this as an appalling cliché, we all feel woozy with the promise of romance and everlasting hope.

Rose and I exchange glances. Rose looks sad and defeated. She and Peter are squabbling on a more or less continuous basis. I want to squeeze her hand and assure her that couples do come through bad patches. Perhaps when the twins leave home.

Lucy shows no signs of intimidation, more irritation as the shop assistant asks her to 'refrain' from smoking. I watch her stubbing out her fag, I know her well enough to realize that she is imagining it is the face of the shop assistant.

Daisy hasn't moved from the doorway, she daren't. If she moves, it might all disappear, this hopeful, heavenly, possibility of a cleaner, sleeker, chic-er self. Not just on the day but forever after. I want to tell her, I want to try to explain, this is part of the game but it is not the home run.

Tentatively, she moves towards the closest dress and is just reaching out to touch the cushion hanger, when a shrill voice trills out.

The assistant explains that she is not a shop assistant but a bridal consultant. This distinction is the first of a long list of new vocabulary that is imbued into us. She describes the dresses as 'gowns', shoes as 'slippers', underwear as 'intimate apparel'. Lucy lets out a snort, which is ignored. We watch as the 'bridal consultant' *oohs* and *aahhs* her way into Daisy's good nature. Offering at once motherly indulgence and girlie advice. Daisy selects three dresses to try. All of them are slinky, tight-fitting, glamorous dresses. We look on doubtfully. The consultant encourages Daisy to swap the 10 for a 12 – 'These gowns come out so petite.' I am grateful for her tact.

Daisy goes to the dressing room alone. 'The next time a friend of mine gets married I'm going to warn her to buy new underwear for this bit,' she shouts through the curtain. Rose and I look at each other guiltily.

'You failed in your duties there,' says Lucy smugly, 'and to think, Rose, you are the matron of honour.'

God, it is cold war between those two at the moment. I wonder if Lucy wanted to be Daisy's chief bridesmaid and is miffed because Daisy picked Rose. Daisy, from behind the curtain, adds, 'Wax her legs, buy new shoes, reapply make-up.' Her self-confidence has set off on a downward spiral. Daisy has always been described as curvaceous, which is the bane of her life. She is very bonny with creamy white skin, a sprinkling of freckles, red curly hair and huge green eyes. In her better moments she grudgingly accepts her rather individual beauty, but most of the time she longs for a dark, glossy bob, which will look and feel like glass. And no chest. She wants to be elegant and tall with a long neck and large brown eyes. Eyes framed with thick velvety lashes.

Daisy emerges. We stand with jaws hanging open, eyes wider still. The dress isn't exactly tight, it is snug. She'll be fine unless she wants to sit down, or move too much, and it will probably be better if she doesn't wear knickers, to avoid unsightly panty lines. Daisy looks in the mirror and her grin collapses immediately. She hesitates and blushes. The colour starts at a small spot on the left-hand side of her neck, grows down her chest and up her cheeks.

'I thought I'd turn into Audrey Hepburn.' Daisy tries to giggle but is genuinely disappointed. 'Crazy huh?'

Rose smiles her motherly smile and puts a tender arm around her sister. They both face the mirror and look at Daisy's reflection. They see Daisy in a wholly inappropriate gown.

Lucy rolls her eyes heavenward and I squeeze her arm indicating that she must refrain from comment. 'I know, I'm not completely insensitive,' she whispers. 'Christ, I suppose it isn't Daisy's fault that she's succumbed to the crazy fantasy that is piped out from day one. The big whacko dream for suckers, the Happily Ever After. I blame pop songs.'

Lucy is being so understanding.

'Honey, that dress is for anorexic neurotics with no personality,' she grins, 'those girls make terrible brides.' Daisy tentatively turns to Lucy, unsure (as we all are) of what she will add. Lucy can, when she puts her mind to it, be the most charming and convincing counsellor. She bends her knees so that her eyes are level with Daisy's. She takes Daisy's face between her long thin hands and spreads her fingers up to replace a stray piece of hair behind Daisy's ear. I notice the gesture is rather Audrey Hepburnesque and wonder if Daisy thinks so, too.

'Simon loves your curves. He's marrying you. The same you that he's seen in thermals and with greasy hair. This marriage isn't about the wedding day, it's about you and him, not a dress.' How come she knows so much about marriage all of a sudden? A small smile from Daisy, sun peeping through rain clouds. Lucy grins seductively. 'Go on, admit it, how often has he told you that he loves your hips, your bot? Come on, he hangs on those massive . . .' Lucy leans very close to Daisy as she whispers, 'tits'. Daisy's face immediately becomes fire.

'*Shhhhh*,' she giggles, 'we are in a wedding shop.'

'Yes, a wedding shop, not the bloody church. I promise I won't say "tits" or any other profanity when I'm in the church.'

Lucy's description is both attractive and accurate. Daisy hastily pulls off the clingy empire line and discards it like a cheap pair of pop socks. She re-selects a gown that not only accommodates but accentuates her hourglass figure.

We leave the shop three hours later and over a thousand pounds lighter.

'How was the dress hunt? Bloody?' asks Luke.

'No, really very successful. She's chosen one.'

I kiss him. He puts his arms around me. And gazes at me. It's a bit embarrassing, it's so intense but I resist breaking away.

'Look, I hope you don't mind but while you were out I took an executive decision. I called Peter and said that we wouldn't be going over for dinner tonight.'

'Did he mind?'

'No, in fact he sounded relieved.'

'I don't mind, if they don't. Are you ill?'

'No. It's just that I feel we are on a treadmill at the moment. That we never spend enough time together. I mean alone together.' He leans his forehead on to mine and stares at me. 'I'm so busy and you're so . . .' He trails off. 'Do you know what I'm talking about?'

I put my arms around his neck and grin. 'I do, exactly. I think it is a brilliant idea. What do you want to do instead? Should we go to Tesco and buy supplies?'

'No, let's go out.' He's a little boy suddenly, excited with his plans and surprises. 'I've booked a table at La Belle Epoque. I've heard that it's like eating inside a Chanel handbag. So it might be a bit cramped but very stylish.'

I laugh and run upstairs to choose something to wear.

'What are you thinking about, Rose?' I ask, as I hand her a cup of tea. We are sitting in our garden with Henry and Sebastian. It's not exactly warm, but I prefer to risk catching flu than watch the boys actively destroy my home. We are eating cream cakes, they are eating soil.

'I'm trying very hard to remember him wanting me, really wanting me. I'm trying to remember when it stopped. What

I did to make him stop wanting me.' Rose is in shock. We all are. The night of our visit to La Belle Epoque, Luke and I had stumbled home to find Rose and the twins ensconced in our front room. She'd used the spare key, for which she apologized profusely but explained that it was an emergency. Peter had left her. For Lucy.

The ripples of devastation have lapped at us all. In one swift move Lucy has detonated all that was familiar. Naturally there has been a division of loyalties. Luke is not making much of an effort to hide his disgust, Daisy is making none at all and has dragged Simon to her side of the barricades. Sam is walking the front line, seeing it from everyone's viewpoint. I'm ambiguous, but this isn't because I'm generous, I have long since sacrificed my right to the moral high ground. In addition I'm abashed that my self-absorption means that I've failed to notice something so profound in Lucy's life. Lucy's *in love* with Peter? Lucy's in love with *Peter*? The girlie gossiping in All Bar One, the dinner parties, the picnics are no longer possible. We're left without ritual and routine. This, for me at least, is uncomfortable and, strangely, a relief.

'Oh, I'm sure he hasn't . . . stopped,' I console.

She looks at me. 'Don't kid yourself, Con. Pleasant of you to try to console me but don't waste your time. See things as they really are. He doesn't want me.'

I don't contradict her this time. She gazes at the boys. Sebastian is squashing ants and Henry is putting sand in his shoe and then pouring the contents on his head. I remind myself that these violent and dysfunctional behavioural traits were present before the children became a product of a broken home. Henry grins at me. I look beyond them at Luke. He is at the end of the garden, burning rubbish.

'I just wish I could remember when he did want me. I'd like to remember that feeling.' Then she sighs and shakes her head, 'But what would be the point? I know that he no longer wants me, so the memory is not only redundant but also repellent.'

She pauses, takes a sip from her tea and removes a worm from Henry's mouth. I don't interrupt her. I know she needs to talk it through.

'I've been thinking about long-term strategies.' She counts her options on her fingers. 'I could fling myself on the floor and beg him to stay for the sake of the children. I could lie low, ignore him for some length of time, treat him badly. It seems he gets a kick out of that sort of woman. I could see him, but disallow him to touch me,' she sighs, 'assuming he still wants to, which is unlikely, thinking about what he's been touching recently.' Rose pre-empts my polite comments. 'Be sensible, Con, look at me and think of Lucy. At my very best I was not half as attractive as she is on a rough day, and I'm hardly at my very best. In fact, I haven't been at my very best for quite some time.'

'But you're his wife,' I say truthfully, 'and you're the mother of his children. You've been together since you were twenty-two. All those years must count for something, Rose.'

'What do you mean? All that cooking and cleaning and rearing and remembering his mother's birthday and darning and sewing buttons on his shirts and ironing and attending his bloody boring work functions and massaging his ego and rearing his children and being nice? You think it counts for something, do you, Connie?'

'Well, yes, I do actually,' I answer honestly.

'Well, it doesn't.'

I guess not. After all, it didn't count for me, not at the time, did it?

Rose turns to me and very seriously asks, 'Did you know, Connie?'

'No. No, really I didn't. It seems so stupid now. I should have put two and two together. I knew she was having an affair with a married man. She even told me that her lover' – Rose shoots me a look and I stumble – 'boyfriend' – wrong again, I settle for – 'that he was called Pete. But I didn't know he was your Peter.'

'He was always going to be somebody's Peter, if he was a married man. Maybe not mine, but someone's husband, someone's dad, someone's love, sweetheart, hope, future.'

It is very hot all of a sudden. I wiggle on my deck-chair.

Rose has been remarkable about Peter's desertion. She has faced it with a quiet acceptance that has amazed me, and incensed Daisy.

'So, you're just going to let that bitch walk away with him are you? Without putting up a fight,' Daisy had yelled.

'I can't force him to love me. I can't force him to stay.'

Rose had arrived at our house on Saturday night. She didn't cry at all, although she necked a bottle of red and three straight whiskies, which did suggest that she wasn't totally unmoved. Luke and I had sat with her until she passed out. Then we went to bed and held each other. Very, very tightly. In the black silence I lay on his chest and he stroked my hair.

'Those poor children,' he'd whispered.

'They are very young, they'll be fine. Poor Rose,' I'd replied.

'It's so wrong.' Luke squeezed me a little tighter. 'How could Peter be so selfish?'

I felt like someone who has just crashed their Jaguar but has walked away unhurt. It could very easily have been Luke bunked up at Rose and Peter's. Sometimes it is disconcerting just how right Lucy can be. I figure it is her training in the city that gives her this sixth sense for so many things. Relief had not been the end of my package tour. I was acutely relieved that I was sympathizing with Rose and not the other way round. But as I lay in Luke's arms I felt crippled with shame. I was overpowered by the knowledge that I'd betrayed Luke and myself, my values, my hopes. Strangely I was grateful for the shame. It allowed me to be contrite.

'This is typical of Lucy, but I can't understand Peter,' mused Luke.

'No,' I mumbled and clung harder still.

The sad conversation with Rose contrasts with the elated call I received from Lucy.

'Why didn't you tell me that Pete is Peter?' I'd screamed down the phone. 'Hang on.' I dragged the phone into the downstairs coat cupboard and sat among packing boxes, cagoules and smelly trainers. Rose was still staying with us – this was a precaution against her hearing.

'I did. You didn't listen,' answered Lucy clearly.

'Weren't there enough married men out there for you?'

'Don't be a hypocrite, Con.'

Fair point. I heard Lucy light a cigarette, drain back her G&T, and pour herself another.

'I didn't plan it,' she defended. Her excuse sounded familiar.

'No?'

'No.'

'But you didn't stop it.'

'Look, Connie, if you want to call me a bitch, can you say it quickly but quite honestly, I don't think you are in much of a position to condemn.'

I sigh, 'No, I suppose not. But she's your friend. You knew when we were in that bridal shop that he was packing his suitcases to come and live with you. How did you manage to carry on the affair and still see Rose?'

'You're sleeping in Luke's bed every night, aren't you?' Her answer was cruel and accurate. It amazes me how brutal truth is.

'Don't tell me you're in love with him.'

'OK, I won't.'

Hmmm, now my curiosity was bubbling over.

'Go on, tell me. Are you in love with him?'

'I do love him.' The words settled between us.

'Oh well then.' I didn't know what to say.

'And he loves me.' Naturally.

'Did it have to be him, Lucy?'

'Apparently, it did. It always was. From the day we hung out of the hall of residence window waiting to see what Rose's boyfriend was like, I was impressed. No other man has ever affected me in the same way. I'm not even going to say that I'm sorry. Because I'm not. I'm thrilled. I'm ecstatic.'

This is Lucy! This is too much.

'That stuff about destinies, Connie. Well, you are right. There is such a thing. Pete is mine. I'm his. It is awful that other people are going to get hurt by this, but I'm worth it. So is he. I make him happy. Rose didn't. I'll make sure he's fair to her and that he is a father to the boys, but I love him.'

This turn of events has given me a lot to think about. Naturally, I've compared Peter and Lucy's affair to my own. On the one hand I admire their courage to ruthlessly pursue their own happiness and yet simultaneously I abhor their selfishness. I realize now that marriages, even those of my friends, can break down. I stalk the thought. If Peter managed to leave Rose and the boys without being ostracized from life, then I could have left Luke. If I had wanted. Luke waves at me from the shed. My heart hiccups.

I'm staying put.

9

Luke comes home from playing football wearing more mud than Kew Gardens and catches me watching my third classic movie of the day. He flings open the curtains, the April afternoon sun reflects on the TV, dazzling the stars.

'Ah ha. A near empty box of Milk Tray, half a box of Kleenex and at least three, no, four pots of tea' – he lists the debris I am immersed in – 'looks like a successful afternoon.' I shush him as Celia Johnson's clipped tones signal the end of *Brief Encounter*. I sigh and reach for the remote.

'Marvellous,' I confirm, '*Funny Face*, *Casablanca*, and finally *Brief Encounter*.'

Luke grins. 'We've saved a fortune in the King's Road since you discovered cable.'

Thinking about one of the lines in one of the films I ask, 'Do you think you are more obsessed with me and interested in me, than any other man has ever been, or ever will be?'

'No,' replies Luke, calmly.

'No,' I repeat, disappointed.

'No,' he confirms. Damn and blast his honesty. If only he would humour me. Then he adds, 'Anyone with any intelligence would be obsessed with you. I just got lucky that you let me be the one to have the most opportunities to show my interest.'

I look at his blond head bent over his bleeding knee and I suddenly feel very strange. Sort of sick and giddy. I don't know what to say, so I say, 'Oh, Luke. You're bleeding.' I jump up, concerned.

'Don't worry, it's only a surface wound,' he laughs, limping over to me on the settee.

'I'm not worried about you, only the carpet,' I tease to hide my feelings, as I fetch the TCP.

'Shit. That stings.'

'Must be good for you then.'

'I think this is more serious than we first suspected.'

'Why?'

'It's the knock on the head. I'm hallucinating.'

'Really?'

'I can smell cooking.'

'Pig. I thought I'd surprise you. I've made a fennel and vodka risotto.'

'The shock might finish me off. What's in there?' He points to the oven.

'Artichokes baked in foil with thyme.'

'How did you know where to buy herbs?'

'I'm not completely useless,' I say, pretending to be offended. Then I confess, 'Actually, I rang Rose – she also told me how to put the extractor on.'

'Pudding?' he asks incredulously, his open face hazing with confusion.

'Blackcurrant ice-cream.'

'Oh, Ben & Jerry's,' he smiles, relieved.

'No, home-made.' I can hardly keep the smugness out of my voice.

'I think you're ill,' he says with mock concern, 'I think you'd better lie down. And the shock has left me dizzy. I think I better lie down, too.'

So we do.

We get up to eat my supper and drink a lot of wine. We are tempted to stay in bed but Luke understands the importance of my cooking and knows that I will be disappointed if he suggests we skip supper, however much fun we are having in bed. It doesn't taste all that good, so I fill up on the hazelnut whirls which lie forlornly in the Milk Tray box, previously beneath my notice. Luke valiantly eats everything and even insists that he is enjoying it.

He talks to me about his game of football and although my interest is sub-zero I really try to concentrate on what the difference is between a forward and defender. He is in a particularly good mood because he managed a hat trick. I was not aware that they wore hats, let alone that they had to perform tricks with them.

'I might come and watch you next week,' I offer.

'Really,' he beams, 'won't you be very bored? Wouldn't you miss your black and weepies?'

'No, I'd like it.' I pause. I am glowing with his love-making. We really have made love. Not acrobatics, not gymnastics, not a sparring competition where we see how many stances we can each take. It was not duty, or guilty, or perfunctory. I lost myself to him. I began to confuse his body and mine as I melted into him. My body is his again. My heart is his.

My secret is mine.

'Luke.' I have to tell him. I have to confess. Honesty is the best policy. How can we ever be close again if I have this huge secret hanging over me? How can we ever recover the intimacy that we experienced in the very beginning? It is fairest all round. Only when he knows all of me can he decide if he wants to be with me. I panic as I follow this line of thought. What if he decides he wants to leave?

'What?'

'Nothing.'

'You all right?'

'Yes, why wouldn't I be?' Suddenly there is a vast expanse of silence, miles of the stuff, gallons of the stuff, an eternity's worth. I search for the words. The explanation. I hunt around the silence but draw a blank. How can I explain myself? I can't. We both listen to the clock ticking and Everything But The Girl playing on a neighbour's stereo. There are no right words for something so wrong. Silence is the best policy. What would I gain from telling him about John? Ease my conscience, destroy his peace of mind?

'Let's make a toast,' he says, refilling my glass.

'What to?'

'Here's to life.'

'Did you say "here's to love" or "life"?'

'I said "life".'

'OK. To life.' I am a bit disappointed.

'And love.'

'Here's to love,' I say smiling.

'It's one and the same to me.' He nods.

'What do you mean?' There's silence again. He traces my eyebrow with his finger.

'Connie, I know, I'm not big on the romantic gestures and I probably don't tell you often enough. Christ, you're such a romantic I don't think it would be possible to tell you often enough, but, I do love you. I love you. You *are* my life. Your love is my life.'

There is a monster lump in my throat and I want to say something as wonderful back but I can't think of anything big enough. Instead I squeeze his hand. Luke goes on.

'I know, I don't always say the right thing, or seem to be concentrating on you, but you are everything to me. I live for you. All the work I do is to build us a great life. It's my way of looking after you.' Luke, normally so quiet, is now on a roll. 'And although you are very complicated and I know that I don't always read you properly, I'll never stop trying. I want to explore your mind, all the different scenes. Because you are the most challenging, interesting, fascinating woman I've ever met.'

Did he just say *fascinating*?

'Did you just say "fascinating"?'

Luke blushes and begins to clear the plates. 'I just realized that we don't often tell each other that stuff any more.'

I listen to him scrape plates and let the cat out. He comes back into the dining room. I am sitting in the exact same spot he left me in. I can't move.

'Luke, I love you.' I mean it so much I'm terrified. He nods.

'Fancy a game of cards?' He's obviously had enough deepness for one evening.

'No, Luke.' I can't explain myself, so instead I am as generous as I know how to be. 'I'd like us to agree to something.' I drain the last drops of wine from my glass. 'I'd like us to agree that if we are ever making each other unhappy, we should call it a day. We shouldn't torture each other.'

Luke's response surprises me. 'Oh no,' he says, looking shocked, 'no. I'd have to find out why I'd started to make you unhappy or even stopped making you happy and I'd have to fix it.'

I stare at him amazed that he can move tenderness and generosity to such a new and exalted plane.

'Connie, I'm never going to lose you or let you go.' He holds my hand very tightly, as though he thinks I am about to run out of the door there and then. Which couldn't be further from the truth, because I know that I want to be exactly where I am now. I want to be holding this man's hand. I want to be this man's wife.

Much later we go to bed and my drunken slumber is interrupted by the sound of the fax machine downstairs chugging into action. I feel Luke stir too. The fax machine groaning into activity in the middle of the night is a rare, but not unprecedented, occurrence. I roll over and just as I am about to bury my head under the pillow, I notice that Luke is getting up.

'What time is it?'

'2.45.'

'Can't it wait until the morning?'

'No, I'm expecting a fax from Australia about the slate for the restaurant roof, this is probably it. I can't sleep knowing that it's in the in-tray, deciding my fate and the fate of thousands of others, men, women and children.' He raises his eyebrow with good humour and adds, 'Especially children, Con.' I fail to see the joke. He stumbles downstairs and I toss and turn, moving my pillow, trying to mould it into the shape of Luke so I can go back to sleep. I only just close my eyes when he comes back upstairs and into the room. I throw back the duvet to welcome him back to bed but he doesn't get in. He puts on the light, momentarily blinding me. As I blink away this rude interruption, I mumble, 'What's up?' Something clearly is. His face is white, granite. He throws the fax he is carrying on to the bed. It flutters and then rests.

'This fax isn't for me. It's for you, I believe.'

I know immediately that it isn't a work fax. Regret pierces, I gave John all my numbers; work, home, mobile, e-mail, fax, in the days when I was desperate for him to contact me. I know the fax is from John. Not that John has ever sent me a fax before, I just know. As I should have known that, sooner or later, my world would shatter into tiny pieces.

The fax is handwritten in large, illegible letters. It reads:

Greenie, I have to have you now.

The second 'have' is underlined a number of times.

'So, Greenie . . .' Luke hesitates as he uses my pre-marital nickname, a foreigner in our married home, 'what's this about?' His voice is barely a whisper. He offers me a look which is at once hopeful and accusing. His eyes are small beads of confusion and horror. 'I'm sure there's an innocent explanation.' Now his face is pleading. And at that moment I would have sold my soul to have been able to laugh and reassure him that, of course, there was an innocent explanation, or at least to have been quick enough to come up with a convincing excuse. An excuse that would allow us both to climb back into bed and fall back to sleep, in our safe, little world. As I open my mouth we both hear the fax lumber into action again. Luke speeds out of the bedroom and leaps downstairs.

I slowly get out of bed, put on my dressing gown and snail my way downstairs. I feel like Anne Boleyn sailing down the Thames, towards the Tower. When I get to Luke's office he is sat at his desk watching the machine churn out another fax. This one is even less legible than the first, but it is legible enough. It reads:

> **Greenie, I want you. I want you in every sense.**
> **Now! Now!! Call me, you have to call me.**
> **I have to have you again.**

Then as an afterthought he'd added,

> **I'm in the office.**

As I read the word 'again' I hear the nails being banged into my coffin. My mind swiftly orders the pieces of the puzzle. John's been out on the town. He's drunk gallons. He's tried to pull. He's failed. He's stumbled into the office to pick up his weekend work or call a cab. He's still randy so finally he's thought of me. I cannot think of a convincing lie that is going to whitewash this evidence. I look at Luke. He looks as though I've physically assaulted him. He is bruised and shocked, he is obviously in excruciating pain. The tiny thrill that I'd felt in my abdomen, that John had got in touch, is snuffed out in an instant. We say nothing as the fax churns into action for a third time. I glare at the incriminating machine, *just shut the fuck up*. The third and final fax reads:

Greenie, how does the song go? 'Let me rub you up and down until you say stop. Let me play with your body, make you real hot. Let me do all the things that you dream of. I can't forget the curves of your body and it makes me feel so naughty.'

It's a song! The bastard. It's a song! I hadn't realized up until then that the erotic, naughty talk wasn't even original. It's a song. Luke, still silent, waits until the fax is finished and then switches the machine over to telephone. As he does so, it immediately rings. He picks it up and I want to die. I can see from the way he knits his brow and pulls in his lips that he is enraged, stunned, pained, confused, yet he keeps all of this turmoil out of his voice as he calmly says, 'No, you can't speak to her. This is her husband and I say you can't speak to her, she's in bed.'

My head is reeling. I want to talk to John. Then I don't. I want to shout at John. And then I don't. I want to scream, why? Why now, you bastard? Why after weeks of silence? But I don't. I want to reassure Luke but I can't. I want to comfort Luke but I can't. I want to say to Luke that it isn't what it seems, but it is. I want it to be something different, but it isn't. I hold my breath, I am waiting for anger or for accusations, for tears, for insults, waiting for a chance to justify myself. A cold prickly tension creeps up my legs, the back of my knees are sweating. What an odd place to sweat. I can hear the immersion heater and a couple of drunks in

the street, laughing. I don't look at Luke but instead stare at the
faxes, intently wishing them away. They don't go away. They
get bigger. Finally I drag my eyes to Luke. He is leaning,
propped up against the doorframe, naked. Normally so tall
and strong, he is slight and wounded. He looks isolated,
betrayed. I can't say I am sorry. Not that I'm not sorry. I am.
I mean, I physically can't say I am sorry, my tongue sticks to
the roof of my mouth like church bread. My brain is giving
no direction whatsoever. It appears to have abandoned ship.

'I'd better go and pack,' says Luke. I am incapable of stopping him.

I run round the house looking for some cigarettes. I search
through Luke's desk drawer, as I know he keeps some spares
for guests. I frantically scrabble through keys, paper clips,
pens, erasers, elastic bands and calculators. Eventually I find
them and light one immediately; without pausing I run to
the wine rack, pull out a bottle of red wine, open it and glug
it back straight from the bottle. Then I look for a glass. I have
a momentary twinge as I consider which of Luke's wines I am
drinking. He has some bottles worth a couple of hundred
quid and I live in perpetual fear that one drunken girl's night,
we'll drink one of those by mistake. Then I think that the
question is rather academic – sheep, lamb and hanging
comes to mind. I run back to the sitting room and find my
Filofax. I urgently flick through the pages. Momentarily,
my mind has gone blank and I can't remember Lucy's telephone number.

All this unstructured activity is in sharp contrast to the past
two hours. I have been a known adulteress and a deserted

wife for 120 minutes. In those 7200 seconds Luke has packed a large overnight case and left. There were no histrionics, no bitter recriminations, no furious demands for an explanation, no chance of repentance. He hurriedly but methodically packed his bag; first laying out the things he needed on the bed, then reassessing his selection and then putting his choice in his bag. He'd packed as though he was going on holiday. I remained seated in the study but I tracked his actions by his movements overhead. He walks to the window and the floorboard near the radiator creaks; he is checking the weather; he walks back to his wardrobe; he is pulling out his brown Nigel Hall trousers and three white T-shirts; I hear him walk towards the chest of drawers, on the other side of the room. He opens the second drawer down, it is stiff so you have to jolt it about a bit to release it. He takes out his boxers and socks. I track his movements between the bathroom, the spare room and the laundry room in the basement. I can detail the contents of his bag, but not his heart, and I've made the mistake of thinking this is knowing him.

Lucy comes round immediately; well, almost immediately, she has to get dressed and apply her make-up. This is probably the only time in Lucy's life that she's ever seen the light of day this early on a Sunday morning. Used to being at her desk by 7 a.m. every weekday, she ferociously protects her rights to extensive amounts of slumber at the weekend. We never, ever suggest an arrangement which requires Lucy surfacing before 11 a.m. on a weekend. My SOS has registered. Heard loud and clear.

I open the door. She looks stunning. She looks exactly as she always does, which momentarily takes my breath away.

Isn't it strange? Shouldn't she look altered now that every-thing is so different? I hug her.

'Thank you for coming round.' I automatically add, 'You look great.'

She slides her sunglasses on to the back of her head.

'You look like shit. Poor baby.'

She is probably right. I've been drinking solidly for three hours. Lucy follows me into the kitchen and while I am keen to open another bottle of wine, she insists on making coffee. Another first.

'So?'

So I tell Lucy the facts and show her the faxes.

'A song. He tried to seduce you with some hackneyed bloody pop song?' she asks, outraged. 'I can't believe he'd do that. It's not even a good song.'

I rather think she is missing the point.

'Will you just forget the song. This is serious. He's left me. I want him back.'

'Can I clarify, which one?'

Bitch. I don't think I've ever liked Lucy less. I stare at her hoping that she will frizzle up, like frying bacon and disappear, vanish or evaporate, or dissolve or something.

'To think I wanted you to come round to comfort me,' I snap.

'Honey . . .' She hands me a tissue. I'm crying? When did I start to cry? 'I don't, as you well know, *do* sympathy. I don't do it. I don't expect it and I don't even believe in it. If it's sympathy you want, give Sam a call, or Daisy. I do survival. To help you survive I need to know what's going on in that mixed up head of yours.'

'I don't know what's going on,' I howl. Then I cry. I cry for hours. I cry my way through forty pots of tea and two man-sized boxes of Kleenex. I cry my way through three boxes of cigarettes, more than my combined total consumed in my lifetime thus far. I cry while Lucy goes to the shops and buys two slabs of Galaxy. But she can't tempt me to eat – I'd have to stop crying and I can't. I cry while the morning light turns to afternoon light and I do not come up for air. When it is physically impossible for me to cry any harder, longer, more, I fall asleep. Lucy wraps a duvet around me and strokes my hair.

'Poor baby,' she mutters.

'Don't leave me.' I'm alarmed. I can't bear the idea that I am going to wake up but even in my drunken, sodden, distraught state I figure that I will. Waking up will be bad, waking up alone will be terrible.

'I'm not going anywhere.'

I don't think I've ever loved Lucy more.

I wake up with a jerk. I leap from the settee where I collapsed. When? Yesterday? Why? Not properly conscious, I cry, 'Want me, want me.' I run to the window expecting to see snow on the ground. The room seems so white. White duvet, white space, white except for my skin. The whiteness makes my skin appear grey. And my mind? My mind is black, a dirty, truthless fog. I feel a thick stench of shame and grief all about me. As I identify this stench, I realize why I am on the settee.

Luke has left me.

When Luke left the house this morning (is it only this morning?) my heart lurched. My heart heaved. It jumped and escaped, it was severed from me. But now it has returned.

I know it has come back because it is hurting so much. A terrible pain, like drilling on a gum or repeatedly banging your funny bone. I feel someone is squeezing the life out of me by clasping my heart so tightly. The grip is agony. Lucy comes into the room.

'You're awake,' she observes and passes me a vodka that she's obviously poured for herself. Very good of her. Very self-sacrificing.

'Have I been here all day?'

'Yup, it's quarter past eleven.'

'At night?'

She nods. I take the vodka. 'Thanks.' I am just human enough to be grateful. 'Has he rung?' Hope rushes into me, nearly knocking me completely over.

'Who?'

'Will you stop doing that! Obviously, I mean Luke.'

'Well, it's not so obvious from where I'm standing,' snaps Lucy. She is always terrible if she doesn't get enough sleep. 'It is only a couple of months ago that you were crying for John.'

'I didn't cry,' I point out. She knows me too well. She raises her eyebrows. I'm forced to add, 'Much.'

'No, but you swore and shouted, ranted and rowed. I'm just not sure if you know what you want.'

Fuck off, Lucy.

'Well?' she persists, 'do you know? What do you want, Connie? Which of them is real?'

'Fuck off, Lucy.'

So she does. She says that she hasn't sat around all day waiting for me to wake up to be insulted. No doubt Lucy has been expecting me to wake up, put on my spangly boob tube and get down to a club to find myself a brand-new husband. That is Lucy's idea of getting over it. Getting on. You get knocked down and you get up again. Higher up the second time, so that no one can reach you to knock you down again. That is her theory. But she has never been deserted by a husband, well, at least, not her own. Doesn't she understand that my husband has just left me? My husband! I am alone! She tells me to have a long hard think, and that I know where to find her when I want to be constructive. Constructive! Well, that call will be a long time coming. Lucy might not be very familiar with the concept of waiting by a phone that doesn't ring. But I might be about to introduce her to that experience. I think about that. Yes, it will be a service to the community. Thousands of men throughout the metropolis will be grateful to me for wreaking revenge.

I open another bottle of wine and another packet of cigarettes.

I hear the doorbell ring but don't move. I am in bed. It's Tuesday, I've been in bed since Sunday. I can't imagine moving ever again. Except for more wine, cigarettes or the occasional trip to pee. The bell rings again, and again. Silence, and then it rings again.

'It's me,' yells Sam through the letterbox. I still don't move. 'Lucy called me. She's worried about you.'

'Is she?' A seven-year-old says in her sulkiest voice, 'Funny way of showing it.'

'Are you going to let me in?' asks Sam.

'I just want to be alone,' says Greta Garbo.

'Look, I understand you don't want to come to work but it might help to talk,' tempts Sam.

'Nothing to say,' says the Wicked Witch of the West.

Where are my clothes? Where am I? Where is my head? I move. Ouch! That is where my head is. I slide back the sheets, stale sweat out, cold air in. I inch downstairs acting out the scene from Michael Jackson's 'Thriller' video, but not the twirling agile break-dancing bit, the bit where the zombies are awoken from the dead. I open the door.

'Poor love. You look like shit.' What is it with my friends? I glance in the hall mirror. But Sam is right, I'm not at my best. She fights her way through the bottle bank that I have accumulated.

'Is this all you've done since Sunday?' She gestures towards the empty vineyard. I nod. It is amazing how much time you have to drink, as soon as you stop wasting time on things like eating, washing, dressing, speaking.

'Has Luke called?'

I shake my head.

'Have you called him?'

Odd question, I shake my head again. This is too much.

'I'm going to be sick.'

I am, very.

I vomit for England, which is quite a relief. I figure that I bring up about half the alcohol that I've consumed. I'm surprised that there aren't butt ends swimming around in my puke. Sam holds my hair and mops my head. When I finally stop turning myself inside out, she runs me a bath and puts me in it. This isn't so much an act of kindness, more to do with the fact that I smell vile. I have green teeth and a sweaty body; she can't stand being with me. Half an hour later I emerge from the bathroom wrapped in a large towelling dressing gown, with a towel round my head.

'Good girl,' says Sam encouragingly, as though she is congratulating a seven-year-old for washing her hands before lunch. I go into the dining room, see a steaming bowl of tomato soup. Invalid food.

'So?'

So I tell it all again. Sam nods and only interrupts with 'uh huh', 'uh huh', 'thought so'.

'Has he called?'

'No, I told you he hadn't.'

'I don't mean Luke, I mean John.'

I'm confused. 'John? Why would John call?'

She reads from the fax, 'Because he has to have you now. Because he wants you, he wants you in every sense, blar blar because he wants to rub you up and down until you say stop. Blar blar can't forget the curves of your body and it makes him feel blar blar.'

'That was the other night,' I explain patiently. 'He'll have been drunk. He doesn't *really* want me.' Why is Sam wasting my time talking about John? I try to explain it to her, without offending. 'It was another one of his games. He never has really wanted me. At least not for a very, very long time. More importantly I don't want him. I don't want him to call . . .' I pause . . . 'which is lucky because he won't. He'll be scared of Luke. John is history.'

'Christ, Con. You're in a mess.'

I don't think Sam deserves a medal for her perception.

'Have you told Luke that it is over, that John is history?'

'No. I hardly think that is his point. I didn't tell him anything. He didn't give me a chance.'

Sam sighs, 'Connie, he gave you the biggest chance of your lifetime. It's you who's been tight-arsed with the chances.' I glare at her. Oblivious, she continues, 'People always say that you don't know what you have until you've lost it.'

Yes. Thank you, Sam. Thank you for that.

'That is such a cliché,' I yell.

'Well, clichés only become clichés because there's some truth in them, and they are oft repeated *and* proven correct. Imagine how many people have loved and lusted before you.'

I can't see her point and if I do, and I've got it right, I don't like it.

I've lost him?

'Call him. Say you're sorry. Try to explain. Oh, Connie, at least think about what you've done. Think about it.'

I am grateful for the interruption of Daisy arriving. Daisy hugs me tightly for about an hour.

'You poor, poor thing,' she sighs as she shakes her head. 'How awful. How dreadful.'

'Yes, isn't it?' I mumble, grateful for her uncomplicated sympathy. She blows it by adding, 'Still, if I'd been Luke I'd have left you, too. Well, I'm sure that you can sort this out.' Daisy looks at Sam, expecting a chorus of affirmation. I wait patiently as well. None comes.

'Err, Daisy, you were pissed off when you found out Con was having an affair and you're not her husband. I very much doubt that Luke sees this as an easy-fix.'

'But the point is, she's not having the affair any more and she's sorry,' says Daisy reasonably, 'aren't you?'

'Very,' I nod vigorously.

'Oh well, that's all right then,' comments Sam.

'You know what your situation reminds me of?' Daisy obviously thinks Sam is being unnecessarily mean so she valiantly tries to cheer me up, single-handedly.

'What?'

'*Tess of the D'Urbervilles*.' She's lost me. 'Where Tess is seduced by the D'Urberville cad but then later realizes that Angel is the love of her life.'

'Tess ends up dead,' points out Sam with unnecessary frankness. Daisy blushes.

'Yes, that's not a good example. It's more like *Anna Karenina*.'

'Leaves her husband and then dies.'

Daisy is struggling. 'I know, I know. It's like that film where that couple are really meant for each other, but she has a fling with the neighbour. But it's OK because he forgives her, and they sort it all out, and they get back together and have twins.'

'Who's in that film?' I ask, suspicious that she's making it up.

'Errr, Helena Bonham Carter, Ralph Fiennes, Robert De Niro, Cameron Diaz, and errr, Rock Hudson, I think.'

They leave! Why are people always leaving me? First Luke, then Lucy, now Sam and Daisy. Admittedly, they stayed for five hours but then Sam said she has some work to do and they left. What is going on here? Isn't the story supposed to begin with a sad, lonely, mixed-up thing, who has no friends, drinks and smokes too much and then isn't it supposed to end with a party? Isn't it? Aren't I supposed to be in the arms of a tall, blond, handsome sex lord right about now? Hello, God, calling in law and natural order. Are you out there? Are you listening? What's going on here? Stop the world I want to get off. Where's the crazy, funny, babe? Where are the laughs? I'm more than shortchanged, I'm carrying Ethiopia's national debt.

I sit in a tight ball of despair.

Sam is right, of course, I should call Luke. If only to find out where he is staying. I pick up the phone and then immediately put it down again as if it has scalded me. What should I say? What can I say? I could go for the brutal, brazening-it-out approach, 'Hi Luke, it's me, Connie. That's as in con artist rather than constancy. Yes, about that fidelity thing, well, you were labouring under a misconception. Much better that the truth is out. Wouldn't you agree?'

No, I don't think so.

I could try the 'I'm really, really sorry' approach. After all, I am. But suddenly 'sorry' seems such an inadequate word. I'm all out of ideas. I pick up the phone and practise speaking to it. 'Hi, Luke.' Hi? Hi? Hi hardly seems appropriate under the circumstances – far too flip. 'Hello', 'Good day', 'Watcha'. I began to ring his mobile. My fingers are shaking as I press the numbers. Such a simple process that I am used to doing two or three times every day has suddenly become over-whelming. I listen to my heart, *boom titty boom. Boom titty boom*, thumping inside my tight chest. I can almost see it pounding.

'Hello.' It is him. I hear his voice and it stabs me.

'Luke? It's me.'

Silence. No 'Hi, me', which is what he's said every time

we've spoken on the phone for over half a decade. All he says is 'Yes?' This is excruciating.

'I just wanted to call.'

'For a chat?' Sarcasm doesn't suit him. I feel I don't know him. He is cool and calm. He tells me he is staying at Simon's. He tells me that he wants to come and pick up some more clothes. I ask him if we can talk and he says that he doesn't think I can have anything to say that he wants to hear.

'I want to explain,' I wail.

'Can you, Connie? Well that should be interesting. I'm waiting.'

Suddenly thrust to centre stage, I forget my lines. How am I going to explain? I can't explain it to myself.

'I'm waiting, Connie.' I think he's enjoying this. The barbarian.

Finally, I find my voice. 'Not over the phone. I can't explain it over the phone.'

'Connie, you'd be struggling to explain this one face to face, by letter, phone, e-mail, *fax*' – he spits this word out – 'Morse code, Braille, smoke signals or any form of communication known to man, invented or yet to come.'

He is right of course. He always is. We are silent. I'm scared he'll put the phone down. This is more frightening than anything else in the world right now. I don't mind that he is angry, I just need to be connected to him, even if it is through millions of cold cables. Nothing would be as bad as him hanging up.

'Just tell me one thing. Are you having an affair?' Except perhaps that question.

'No,' I insist firmly. I think I hear him sigh at the other end of the phone. Is it relief? Is it disbelief? Is he tired? How badly have I hurt him?

'Have you ever had an affair?'

You said tell you one thing! I hold my breath. Should I lie? Can I get away with it? Can I invent anything that would be even remotely plausible and can we rewind the last three days? My mind goes blank.

'Yes,' I whisper. The silence is deafening. It slams round my head and heart. In the absence of guile (having a nap, been on overtime recently), conscience has crept out flanked by 'the right thing to do' and 'time to come clean'. To be honest I'm not keen on any of them. They always cause trouble.

'I can explain.'

'I doubt it.'

'I need to talk,' I insist.

'Oh God, here we go again, what Constance Green needs. Well, I'm sick of it, Connie. What about my needs? Right now, what I need is to go away and think about all of this. Alone. I don't need you and I don't want you.' I can't remember him ever thinking so badly of me. I guess that's what happens, sleep with someone other than your husband and you lose his respect. Yup, sounds pretty straightforward. But the clarity of the situation did not become apparent until afterwards. Why was that? He puts down the phone.

And my heart breaks.

All the pain I ever felt before, the falling off my bike when I was a kid, failing exams, Simon Le Bon getting married, impacted wisdom teeth, having curly hair, not getting the job I really, really wanted and deserved, and even John coming on my tits, they were dress rehearsals.

This is pain.

Knowing that I've hurt the person I love more than anyone else in the world. Knowing that the damage I've caused is irreparable. Knowing this knowledge is all too late, is pain.

My friends stop calling round. They take me at my word when I continually insist that I want to be on my own. Which I don't think is very nice of them.

Alone, I become semi-delirious. I feel I am walking a fine line between bewilderment and heightened consciousness, fact and fiction. I'm sleeping a lot, it's all I am capable of. But now, even my sleep is contaminated by my sense of fuckeditupness. It becomes impossible to distinguish dream from fear, truth from lies, answers from dream, truth from fear. But that could be the alcohol.

The telephone rings.

'Luke?' I say eagerly, as I pick it up.

'No, sorry. It's me, Rose.' Rose never quite dares play the 'It's me' game, in case we fail to recognize her. Her apology is because she knows that the only person I want to talk to is Luke.

'Hi, Rose,' I say, with some trepidation. I've been dreading this. The worst thing about being a bad person is talking to good ones. No, God, please. I know I have sinned, I am very, very sorry. And I am going to make amends, God. I haven't quite worked out how yet, but I promise I will. You can age me prematurely, you can send a plague of lotus notes, you can let the authorities catch up with me for avoiding my council tax, but please God, not this. Not a sanctimonious lecture from Rose. I won't be able to stand it.

'Sam tells me you are' – she hesitates – 'off sick.' Rose sounds nervous. I am sick, most of the time, as I continue to jump into the bottle. It seems easier than growing up.

'I wondered if you wanted some company? I'm going to take the boys to the park and I wondered if you wanted some fresh air. I'll understand if you'd rather be on your own but – '

'Rose, that would be great,' I say, and, surprisingly, I mean it. I haven't left the house for ten days, not even when I ran out of milk. I just drank the emergency supply of powdered stuff that I'd bought in case of nuclear disaster. Getting some fresh air is a homely remedy, but a proven one.

'Fine.' Rose sounds delighted. 'I'll pick you up at eleven.'

I look at my watch. Eleven! My heart plummets, this only gives me an hour to get ready. I look in the mirror. It is bad, very bad. I haven't brushed, let alone washed, my hair since Luke left. Oddly I've been perpetually cold since he went. Too lazy to take my clothes off and wash them, I've stockpiled. I'm wearing about six layers of alcohol- and sweat-encrusted garments. I am a bit embarrassed as I realize that my knickers are ten days old. My skin is grey, with interesting hues of black under my eyes. Ten constant days of crying has left me wrinkled and puckered. I look like some of the vegetables in my fridge.

And I'm not the worst of it.

The house is abysmal, a serious health risk. I am ashamed. I begin to load the dishwasher, scraping away the debris from Luke's and my last meal together. I soak the risotto dish and put away the vodka bottle. I throw out the foil that I'd lovingly baked the artichokes in. I clear the dirty wine glasses and put the bottles in black sacks. I empty the various vessels that I have since turned into makeshift ashtrays: milk bottles, discarded beer cans, saucers, pans, bowls. I throw out the rotting vegetables and moulding bread and empty the bins. I open the windows and drag the hoover across the floor, and then finally I put the sheets in the wash. The ones that are stained with blackcurrant ice-cream and smell of him. This nearly kills me. But I don't cry. I'm not sure why I don't. Maybe I am wrung dry.

I haul myself into the bathroom and start to undress. It is like unwrapping a mummy, not a pretty sight. I throw my clothes into the corner; for a moment I think there is a real possibility that they'll walk out of the door in protest at having been so badly treated. I run a hot, deep bath and climb in. I scrub and scrub trying to shift the dirty feeling I am carrying. I wash my hair but can't bring myself to style it; instead I scrape it back into a ponytail. I drag my body into tracksuit bottoms and pull on a polo-neck jumper. I am just tying my Nike laces when the doorbell rings.

'Oh, Connie. You look . . .' Rose pauses.

'Like shit?' I fill in helpfully.

Rose blushes, she doesn't like expletives.

'I am going to say very thin.' I don't have the monopoly on surprises, because Rose's transformation is much more dramatic than my own. I hardly recognize her. She is wearing a caftan, which I think is vile but she obviously loves. She is wearing a ton of costume jewellery and make-up.

'Peter always hated the hippie-gypsy in me,' she comments, grinning. 'The boys are in the car. Are you ready?'

Rose and I walk the boys around Richmond Park. Stopping

to look at the deer and to feed ducks. We buy coffee from a caravan and sit on a bench sipping it. So my début back into the living world isn't very glamorous, but it's a bright day and the cute dependency the children radiate takes me out of myself.

For a while.

Rose has, so far, studiously avoided talking about Luke and me. It is only when we sit down, with the kids safely ensconced in a sand pit, that she turns to me.

'So, how are you?'

I am very grateful to be asked.

'Horrible, terrible,' I manage to squeak before I start to cry again. So much for being wrung dry. Rose hands me a tissue.

'Hmmm?'

'He won't talk to me. He won't take my calls. How will I cope without him?'

'Luke is very unhappy, too,' says Rose and her voice, which usually irritates me, soothes me – strange that.

'You've seen him?' I pounce on this information. I know he's still staying with Simon and the temporary nature of the arrangement suits me. 'How does he look? Is he eating? I wish he'd talk to me. I need to see him so much.'

'What happened?' I stare at Rose amazed. She is curious. She wants to gossip, just like the rest of us. 'I mean, without knowing all the facts it's hard for me to comment . . .' She pauses, waiting hopefully. After Daisy had found out about my affair I'd begged her not to tell Rose. Which, eventually, she agreed to. We all censor what we tell Rose, she is after all an older sister. Rose is human, she must be dying to know the nitty gritty. I find myself telling her the truth before I've even worked out whether this is to my advantage or not.

'I had an affair.' The words sound ludicrous. Not at all cool, as they'd sounded when I told Lucy way back in November. 'It just happened. I couldn't resist.'

'Really?' she sighs. 'Yes, I imagine that resisting would have been very uncomfortable for you.'

I surprise myself by not taking offence; instead I try to explain. 'I thought, incorrectly, that he was different. I thought he was so different that he must be my destiny.'

What am I doing having this grown up conversation with Rose?

'Do you still think that?'

'No. Now I know that I just fancied him. Intrigued a bit too. Flattered. Nothing more serious.'

'Do you still want him?'

'No.' I am definitive.

'Do you want Luke?' I don't reply directly although the answer is very simple.

'He's gone.'

'It puts it all into perspective, doesn't it?' she asks.

I've always hated perspective. It's so dull. But I know now what it's for. I know with absolute clarity and certainty that I want only one thing in the entire world. I want Luke to come home. I want this so much that I dare not breathe.

'What's the point in wanting Luke?' I say to Rose. 'He's too proud and stubborn to come home.'

'And too hurt,' adds Rose. 'You fool, Connie.'

'I know. I can't think of anything else. I can't do anything without him,' I say dramatically.

'Yes, Sam mentioned to me that you've put in a sick note for over two weeks. Do you think that is wise?'

'Please don't tell me life goes on, Rose. I can't stand it. My life will not go on. Not without Luke,' I say firmly.

'Sam's life is going on,' she says, tactfully. 'She's working all hours, now her department is one down. She needs you.'

I haven't been needed for a fair while, and even in this state of self-loathing the idea attracts me. Still I'm not going to be won round that quickly. I argue sulkily, 'I can't face going back. I hate my job.'

'That's been apparent for some time.'

'Has it?' I am surprised. How come people know important things about me before I know them?

'Yes. You should think about what you really want to do with your life and then do it. But in the meantime you have a mortgage to pay.'

The enormity of what Rose is saying hits me. She thinks of me as someone who is single and has to be responsible for their own mortgage. How horrifying!

'Luke needs time, Con. He's very confused.'

'Unfortunately, time is one thing that I do not have,' I say, petulantly.

'Yes, you do. You have lots of it. So, you are *sure* you want him back?'

'Of course I'm sure. Wouldn't anybody want him back?'

'Well, yes,' admits Rose, 'but most people would never have allowed him to go away in the first place.' Rose has secretly always had a soft spot for Luke.

'How can I get him back?' This shows how desperate I am.

I'm asking Rose for advice on men! Which is pretty pointless. What has come over me?

'You have to be sure, because he loves you, and if he's not what you want it's not fair to let him think he is. You've done that once. You've got to think this through.'

Think it through! Think it through! That's all I've done, think about things. Why do people keep asking me to think about things?

'Can't someone else think about it for me?' I whine, lazily kicking a stone between my left and right foot.

'No,' says Rose, with surprising firmness.

'But you do still think he loves me? You do think I can get him back?' I ask excitedly.

'I think he loves you. I have no idea if you can get him back. He's a very proud man,' she says with far too much honesty.

Sam greets me like a survivor of the *Marie Celeste*, turning up after a few centuries' absence, rather than someone who has been off sick for just under two weeks. It is a good thing that I have come back, since work is frantic. I don't even have a chance to nip out for a sandwich at lunch. I watch Sam as she energetically plans and plots, processes and prepares presentations. She is absorbed. She is glowing. I look at her and around at the other people in my team and I realize I'm different from them. They live for their work. I work to exist. Not exactly to pay my mortgage, as Rose so depressingly suggested, but at least to buy my Gianfranco and Patrick Cox. Like my colleagues I am throwing myself into my work but I know it is not my life. I am doing this to block out my life.

When was I last so absorbed? What absorbs me? I can hear Rose instructing, 'Think about what you really want to do with your life.' Luckily, I am far too busy to have any time to actually do this. Finally, at 8.30 p.m., Sam pronounces, 'That's it, guys, the presentation is impressive. It's polished. Well done.' It is good. Even the work that I've contributed but I can't understand why that's important to them.

I begin to put away files and close down my PC.

'Fancy a quick drink? I'm meeting Lucy,' Sam tempts.

'Yes. I'm calling a council of war,' I grin. I definitely, definitely want Luke back and it is time to meet with the girls to decide exactly how I am going to achieve this. I am excited. I am hopeful. They never let me down. We always console, guide, advise one another through our crises. I am looking forward to being swaddled in their sympathy and condolences, then being uplifted by their foolproof plans.

I push open the bar doors and the familiar smell of wood steeped in red wine hits me. I love it.

'I want Luke back,' I announce grandly. It is big. They must be thrilled. I pour the first of what, no doubt, will be many glasses of Chardonnay. Sam nods and smiles sympathetically. Lucy lights a cigarette.

'Do you mind if I ask why?'

'He's my husband.' I say this very slowly, as if I am talking to a dumb animal.

'Correct me if I'm wrong, Connie, but hasn't Luke been your husband throughout this entire episode?'

'Look, I made a mistake, OK.'

Silence.

'A big one, I admit it. But what was I supposed to do? Stop

noticing other men? Forget the fact that there are hundreds of thousands of men out there, which up until the point I said "I do" were potential soulmates.'

'Yes,' says Sam.

Lucy doesn't see things in the same way. She shakes her head and comments, 'Your logic is so faulty. Look, I don't care who you sleep with. I just want you to be happy. And you're not. And I think it's time you found out why not and how you could be.'

I am despondent. But I decide to be a little patient with them.

'Do you remember the Antonio Banderas game?'

'Erotic fantasies with unobtainable, unreal men,' confirms Sam.

'Well, it was like that.'

'*Fantasy!*' yells Lucy. I haven't seen Lucy since the fateful fax day and although we've swapped answering machine messages, I get the distinct impression that her flavour of the month I am not. I nod.

'Yes. John was a fantasy. I'm not sure I ever really knew him.'

'Oh well, that will be a consolation to Luke,' confirms Lucy sarcastically, as she reaches for the wine. The table falls silent again.

'Why are you being mean?' I am genuinely stumped.

Sam shuffles uncomfortably on her seat and fingers the ashtray nervously. 'It's just that maybe you should have been a bit more cautious. Pride comes before a fall.'

'Yes, thank you, Sam.'

'We don't want to judge.'

'But?'

'But . . .' She glances at Lucy, obviously hoping that Lucy will help her out. She should know Lucy better than that by now. 'Well, you still seem to be looking at this from a single point of view . . .' she hesitates and Lucy interrupts.

'Yours.'

I sigh and try again. 'I realize now that John meant nothing to me.'

Lucy: 'John did mean something.'

Me: 'I was just bored – '

Lucy: 'So your next project is getting Luke back.'

Me: 'Why are you always going on about projects?' No one replies. 'You don't think he'll have me back, do you?' They don't answer but suddenly the table top is the most fascinating thing on the planet. Lucy studies it as though it is the *Financial Times* Share Index and Sam is pretending it is her engagement ring. Uncertainly I ask, 'Do you think it is *possible* that he'll take me back?'

'Possible is infinite, probable is more defined,' says Lucy with killing accuracy.

'Call him,' offers Sam, as she pats my hand, but I can tell from her tone that she isn't putting money on it. Where are the guarantees? Why aren't they helping me? I stare from one to the other in amazement. Lucy opens a packet of crisps and offers me one. She sighs. It is a very articulate sigh. She thinks I am hopeless. She goes to the bar to order another bottle and some food. On her return Sam provides a change of conversation. She has just split up from a two-month relationship with a lawyer.

'We had the most silent break-up ever. I offered him a range of options, from large white wedding to let's just be friends, and he still didn't answer. A new all-time low.'

'Can't see him making much of a living as a barrister,' Lucy points out.

'Well, that is the final straw for me. I'm giving up men.'

We stare, horrified. I wonder if she is following the advice of her latest self-help book. She rang me the other day to advise that, 'If you have a bird and you love that bird, you must open the cage door. It will fly away but if it loves you it will come back.' Wise bloody words from a woman who normally doesn't so much as open the patio doors on a stiflingly hot summer's day, in case her man legs it over the back wall.

'I'm going to be a bachelor girl,' says Sam, 'like Lucy.' As soon as the words leave Sam's mouth, her brain registers the improbability of this statement. She hesitates and then adds defiantly, 'I do have a good job; I'll buy a flat and I have my art classes.'

'How are the classes progressing, Sam?' asks Lucy. I barely contain my giggles. I think it is hilarious that Sam prefers to go to classes on a Saturday rather than the King's Road.

'Fine. Actually, very well,' says Sam with determination. 'It's great to be learning again.' I don't get it, the models aren't even men. 'In fact I saw something that might interest you, Con.' She hands me the summer timetable. 'Photography classes. You are always taking photos, it might be a good idea to take up a hobby.'

My first reaction is mortification. It is a distressing and dismal realization. Sam obviously believes I've joined the ranks of the truly single. Why else would I need a night class?

However, I am also grateful for her concern. Reluctantly I accept that she is right, learning something new would be good for me. I suddenly have so much time. Time I don't know how to fill. I do love taking photos, but my knowledge is slim.

'Thanks, Sam,' I say, as I put the timetable in my bag, 'I might just give it a go.' I try to ignore Lucy's amazed looks.

We only leave the bar when we are forcibly ejected. I can barely stand. But, somewhat illogically, I don't feel horrendous. I feel awash with possibility. Sam and Lucy make plans to meet up the next night but I decline.

'No, I've had enough alcohol units to last me until Christmas. I'm going to have a long bath and an early night tomorrow.'

'Good idea. Have a long hard think about things,' says Sam. I scowl at her.

'Yes, actually that is exactly what I planned,' I snipe defiantly. 'Because although none of you have actually said that I brought this on myself, *and* not a single soul has commented that if I'm looking for someone to blame, I need go no further than the mirror, *and* I have yet to hear the words "fucking selfish bitch", I do realize I am culpable, *and* what's more' – I'm yelling now, building to a crescendo with each 'and' – 'tonight is a big night. Tonight is the first night of the rest of my life. Tomorrow night I have a date with myself. Tomorrow night I am going to start *thinking*!' I stamp out a cigarette with unnecessary force.

'Err, great,' mutters Sam. 'Well, if you change your mind you know where to find us.' She scuttles away and I don't blame her. I am Beelzebub's spawn. Lucy raises her eyebrows.

I change the subject by asking her how she thinks Norway's oil-fuelled economy will deal with the falling crude oil prices. She is audibly impressed.

'Connie, you've been reading *The Economist*!'

'No, actually, I watch The News a lot,' I reply, a bit sulkily. I don't understand why she should be so surprised. It isn't fair to imply that I never think about anything other than myself. I fling myself into a cab. Lucy chooses not to notice my bad temper but waves and blows me a kiss. I sit alone with only my mortification for company. It is embarrassing that everyone's being so nice to me. So far all that has happened is that all my gorgeous friends have requested that I do a bit of soul-searching. They believe that basically I'm a decent enough person and if I do the soul-searching, I'll be OK. But fuck it, I'm not sure.

Still, I owe it to them to try.

And I owe it to myself.

I go to work to fill in some hours. I get home, make myself a cup of tea and put on the stereo. This isn't easy. What to listen to? Nearly every song can sway my mood and judgment. What sort of weak person am I, that a few tacky lyrics can send me into a carousel of confusion? Most of my usual favourites are too painful. The sloppy lines, which I normally delight in, seem to be cruelly teasing me. Ill-advisedly, I decide to try a live and vicious experiment; just how much misery can a human being inflict on herself? I select 'Love Is All Around'. Blatantly, the choice is a travesty with lyrics such as *I feel it in my fingers, I feel it in my toes, Love is all around me and so the feeling grows*. I begin to cry. *You know I love you, I always* will. *My mind's made up by the way that I feel. La la la la* fucking *laar.* Who writes this sentimental crap? How do they know, hey? How do they know they will *always* love someone? Luke said as much to me the night he walked out on me. I admit the walking out isn't that surprising, I suppose, under the circumstances. I sigh. I doubt that a song entitled *I'll conditionally love you, for a specific length of time, depending on the circumstances,* has what it takes to make it to number one.

Sobbing, I torture myself further with 'When I Fall In Love', *it will be for ever.* Which I warble into a packet of fags that is doubling up as a microphone, *Or I'll never fall in love. In a restless world like this is, Love is ended before it's begun and too many moonlight kisses, seem to cool in the warmth of the sun.*

It is true. It is a restless world. I had, do, can, should, do again, love Luke. But it hadn't been enough to occupy me. Large, fat tears drop on to the stereo. Then I go distinctly upbeat.

I consider calling the Samaritans but instead I manically boogie around the dining-room table. Flaying my arms and kicking my legs. I do this throughout 'When Will I See You Again', 'The Power Of Love', 'Don't Leave Me This Way', 'Stay, I Miss You'. Eventually I collapse on to a chair. Heaving breathlessly and sweating profusely. I am out of shape, gym visits were a lifetime ago. Sobbing, I admit, I am out of sorts too. Despite my virtuous intention of sitting down for a good old-fashioned think, for some reason or another, it hasn't happened. Suddenly it is midnight and I have worked my way through 'I Love You Always For Ever', 'Where Have All The Cowboys Gone' and 'Touch Me In The Morning'. I have abandoned the idea of tea, downed my third gin and tonic and I am booing hysterically.

I go to bed.

Ah well, all good intentions of mice and men.

Christ, I have turned into Sam.

The next day I sit down again, this time with renewed determination. I select Enya, make a cup of tea, I tuck my legs up underneath me and pick up a pen and paper. I chew the pen. I drain my tea. I get up to put the kettle on to make a second cup. Sit down again. Get up to turn the CD player down a bit. It is too noisy and distracting. Sit. I tap my pen on to the paper and start to think. The curtains are grubby, I certainly need to give them a wash. Goodness, what a lot of dust there is under the settee, I've never noticed that before. Just as I am noting that the third picture from the right on the bathroom wall is actually a bit wonky, the phone rings. I pounce on it, grateful for the distraction. All this intensive soul-searching is exhausting.

'It's me.'

'Hi, Tarn.'

'Darling, you're gushing. Does that mean you've just been laid or that you are very happy to talk to me?'

'I'm very happy to talk to you.'

'Pity. Look, I'm sorry to interrupt you, I understand that tonight is the night that you are deciding *what you want from life*.' Naturally my soul-searching is a matter of national debate. 'Well, in my experience darling, it is a couple of stiffies and one of them is a G&T.' I laugh. He continues, 'But I suppose you'll want something much more dramatic, more creative than that. Darling, my heart bleeds for you. How dreadful to have such a compulsive nature that you are forced to complicate everything. Now you are out in the cold, harsh light of singledom. It's a bitter climate. All men are bastards, women simply aren't fanciable, the human race is doomed. Well, toodle pip. I just thought I'd call to let you know you still have friends.'

'Yes, thanks for that, Tarn,' I stutter.

I put down the phone and turn back to my pen and paper. The only sound I can hear is the clock ticking and the irony isn't lost on me. Tarn is right. It is a bitter, bloody climate. What possessed me? How did I land here? It is John's fault, the bastard. The heartless bastard. And Luke's – he is being such a cold bugger. I have been tricked, seduced and unfairly abandoned by one man, while at the same time I have been neglected, taken for granted and fairly abandoned by another. Sam should have tried to stop me in Paris, I add self-righteously. Lucy has encouraged me all the way along. I am incensed. Daisy isn't exactly faultless. By having hot sex with Simon she made me feel dull and dissatisfied. I become irate. Rose should also accept responsibility for some of this. She was such a frump. No wonder marriage was a turn off when she was my real live role model. I blame my parents (although this is trickier, I am a little pushed to see exactly how they are accountable), my schoolteachers and my horse-riding instructor (for over-training me, which led to a big bum. They wouldn't have left me if I'd had a smaller bum). When I run out of people to blame I begin to blame inanimate objects. I blame faxes, conferences, telephones, e-mails. It is tiring all this blaming, so I go to bed.

I wake up and the first thing I see is the blasted pen and

paper. I shower and as I do so, I see a floating pen in front of me. I dress and prepare, but fail to eat breakfast. I read the back of all the cereal packs. What to do? What next? It is a Saturday. The whole day stretches out in front of me. A Saturday that leads to a Sunday and a Bank Holiday Monday. How cruel. The whole weekend is taunting me, 'You're on your own! You're on your own!' I've never before been on my own for such a prolonged period. I'm a busy person who is usually surrounded by other busy people. I did Girl Guides and Youth Clubs as a child and then replaced them with shopping and boyfriends as an adolescent. O and A levels and my degree were a distraction and then back to men and all the associated sideshows: diets, clothes, make-up, parties, clubs, dates. Then I'd met Luke. Before I knew it I was planning a wedding and choosing carpets and glassware. Now, here I am, in my lovely fully fitted house with crystal and colour coordinated bed linen but *sans* husband.

I have so much time on my hands.

I have no distractions, asides, diversions or entertainment. Maybe I should ring my mum? I haven't spoken to her for a while. But then what would I say? I have no amusements to talk about, no occupation, no adventures.

No goals.

No purpose. The fridge is humming. Lucky fridge.

Blinding light. Hallelujah. It comes to me. Ringing my mum, or anyone else for that matter, is an avoidance technique. By calling her for a chat I would avoid the date I've made with myself to think about my situation. Carefully, I write that first word on the naked page.

Avoidance.

Avoidance, ah ah. I've stumbled on to something. It dawns on me why my mates are constantly asking me to think about things, because actually, I am not terribly good at thinking. Err, it's not my forte. I am great at feeling, I excel on gut instincts, emotions, going with the flow, compulsive behaviour. And that is excellent. It's very passionate, exciting, dramatic. I guess I may have slightly neglected 'thinking it through', 'seeing the consequences', 'considering the impact'. Especially on other people. But to be frank those things don't exactly ring my bells. How many films are there named *Enduring Encounter*, *Safe Liaisons* or *A Peaceful Night's Sleep in Seattle*? I don't think so. The problem with the more humdrum aspects of life is that they *are* more humdrum.

Enduring.

Safe.

Peaceful.

I write the words on my notepad. It strikes me that these words define a good marriage. It strikes me that these are words that are different from anything I ever experienced before I married. I married Luke because he is my best friend. He is kind, considerate and loving. I love him but before I got married everything was immediate, risky, exciting.

I am not like Sam. My *raison d'être* had never been marrying. God, how shocking if it had. That is so pathetic. I was keen on the chase, yes. And I liked blokes falling in love with me, admittedly. But it wasn't my be-all-and-end-all.

Was it?

It was.

I hadn't been aware that I'd bought into the fairy-tales and the films and the pop songs, but I had done just that. Was it the case that when I was systematically working my way through the Kama Sutra and the eligible males of London, that subconsciously it was my ambition to meet, marry, live Happily Ever After? But the fairy-tale books close with the church doors and I know why. Because there's nothing exotic in a conversation regarding lagging lofts. John talked to me about flogging logs. It is so rude, and raw, and different.

And pointless.

I mean, in retrospect, was I really interested in knowing how often he wanked off? No. But at the time it was sexy and alive. It was just that I missed noticing if men were cute, and I missed them noticing I was. I missed deliberating over what to wear. I missed them discovering things about me, and gossiping and wondering.

I am tempted to leave it at that. Get up, make a cup of tea, have a walk, rearrange my video cupboard into alphabetical order. There I go. I have the answer. Luke is great, but marriage got too routine. I was bored, so I looked for adventure and John was the supplier of that adventure. Then I hear Lucy's voice in my head, what was it she said? . . . 'John did mean something.' I forget the video cupboard.

John is a bastard. Hmmm. And yet I did want John, very much. Why was that? I was sure that we were . . . what is the word? Meant? Linked? Attached? It felt right.

It felt familiar. It was familiar.

Flirting. Chasing. Seducing. It's what I do. Did. Did before I met Luke. Did to Luke. Could it be that the sense of destiny had been nothing more than my repeating a familiar pattern? Once I'd slept with him I was in too deep to admit to anyone, especially myself, that I'd made a mistake. Yet the more I got to know John the more I realized that there would be no delicacy, no intimacy, no trust, no flattery between us. How could there be? Old rules but a new game. I was married. He had slept with me because I was married. He didn't want familiarity, he didn't want it to *go* anywhere. He thought he was safe because I already had The One, or at least, Some One. He asked me only for what was wild, raunchy, sexy, dirty. I mistook his arrogance for passion. I confused the aching in my cunt for a longing in my heart. I fancied him *sooooooooooo* much. That is a cold hard fact. If I could have, I'd have strapped him to me, and even then that wouldn't have been close enough. I wanted him inside me. I'd wanted to chop John up into tiny consumable pieces. I understood, for the first time in life, the expression, carnal knowledge. For a while I existed on another dimension. And, let's face it, I liked it there.

It was exciting.

But it wasn't real.

It was about tight clothes, skinny limbs, hollowed stomach, pop music, smoking, drinking. As far as a supplier of drama and passion is concerned, John didn't disappoint. True to his word, he dished, ditched, distressed, depressed me. He is an irresponsible, disrespectful infidel.

So there wasn't just one reason for my infidelity: the fact that I was bored or felt neglected, or did it because of old patterns, or fancied him excessively. It was all of those factors coming together at once. Why hadn't alarm bells rung after that first meeting in Blackpool? I was nearly derailed. I should have gone home and battered that thought around.

If I could start all over again, I would still marry Luke.

It all adds up to something very uncomfortable. It adds up to the fact that 'nice' girls have affairs too. Especially nice girls who are vain and bored. In this situation nice girls can fall for stunning insincerity. What's more, if they are incurable romantics, who really want to believe in the thrusting-passion-thing equalling destiny, they can get everything confused. The only difference between nice girls and not very nice girls, is that nice girls are sorry.

Very, very sorry.

And they wish it had never happened.

It is four o'clock on Saturday afternoon. I am swamped by cigarette fumes. I force open a window, assuring my neighbour not to be alarmed, there is no need for the fire brigade. I hunt out some pot-pourri and put the kettle on for about the millionth time. OK, to recap. I've learnt, and can admit the following about myself: I love Luke, and by marrying him I achieved a life-long ambition. Realization of this ambition left me bored and without a goal. John was a horn. Seduction is habitual. I've hurt my husband, perhaps irreparably. I am a selfish, sorry, fuckwit, not very nice, nice girl. I realize I am losing my sense of clarity. But there is definitely a good thought in there somewhere.

10

I am so excited with my new understanding that I make the mistake of thinking Luke will be excited, too. After nearly a month of no communication I call him. He won't come to the phone so I call again and again – sober, drunk, hysterical, desperate, humiliated, oblivious. I leave pleading messages begging him to listen to me, to pick up the phone. On the occasions that he does, I'm met with, 'Connie. I can't imagine you have anything to say that I want to hear. I don't want explanations, thank you.' The days insist on thundering by; I'm paralysed with fear as I begin to understand that he really doesn't want to talk to me.

I write to him. Short notes imploring him to call. Funny, stylish and sentimental cards trying to explain. Long epistles detailing how sorry I am and screaming for forgiveness. I don't know if he even opens my letters. I realize that calling and writing are cowardly and so I go to see him at Simon's. Simon tells me he is away. I go to his football club, his office; I try to track him down on site. It seems that he has a sixth sense about when I'm going to turn up because he has always 'Just left'. His ability to walk away from me, without so much as a cursory glance over his shoulder, depresses me. Initially, I rail that it is typical, another example of his lack of passion, lack of feeling, but that doesn't stack up. Even to me. Have I wounded him so deeply that he is unable to act in any other way, than to walk away? I'm dripping in shame. I wonder if it would help if I explained that I wasn't seeing John when the fax came through? Would it help if I explained that I made a hideous mistake and I can see that now? I doubt it. Explaining it to myself has been an almost superhuman feat. Explaining it to anyone else – even if that 'anyone else' is that amazing someone else, Luke – will be impossible.

I miss Luke. I miss him every moment, of every minute, of every hour, of every day.

Well, that's not exactly true. That's a bit of an exaggeration but I do miss him. And I don't just miss him in a selfish, I-don't-know-how-to-fix-the-fuse-box, or whether-our-leaking-dishwasher-is-insured way. Although at first I missed him in this way. I spent weeks just getting to grips with the enormous number of tasks he did round the house. But I've managed. I sat in front of our big, mahogany desk and cried over deeds and Access bills. Not because the bills were high, but sitting there I remembered that Luke spent every Tuesday evening, as regular as clockwork, poring over bills, estimates and junk mail. Sorting our post into our life. Making sure that it all ticked over, ran seamlessly. Having done it for a number of weeks myself I realize just how time consuming and dull it is. My responsibility in the house had been limited to remembering everybody's birthdays. I bought the cards and the stamps, I posted them. God, I blush now when I remember how much I used to go on about that. To be honest, it's quite fun choosing cards, celebrating birthdays, buying cakes and presents. Much more interesting than direct debit and minimum payments, which is what I have to get my head round now. Of course I'd done these things for myself before I met Luke. I managed to pay bills on time (ish) and my landlords never had cause to change the locks on my door. But in those days the bills I used to pay were limited to Miss Selfridge accounts. My bills are so much more important now: mortgages, insurance, health care, pensions. It isn't as if the money is a problem. My wage allows me financial independence, and anyway, Luke, in his predictably decent way, hasn't stopped having his wage paid into our joint account. The cash flow is the same, it just seems such an enormous responsibility for one person.

For this person.

For me. But I've got to grips with it slowly, and after a couple of weeks I realize it isn't so hard, and I realize that I don't need Luke to explain council tax and rates. But this doesn't mean I miss him less. I miss him more. I realize I don't need him, I just want him. I want his smile, his mess, his sense, his advice. I want him around to see the new and improved me. The me that organizes her own MOT and returns library books on time. I want him to be proud of me. I want him to congratulate me. I even want him to shout at me for leaving soggy towels on the floor.

I miss Luke when I have a good day at work because he used to be so pleased with me when I'd managed a project well. I miss him when I've had a foul day at work; there is no one to rub my feet and tell me that they don't deserve me. I have no idea how the restaurant redesign is progressing. I miss his excited chatter about sourcing marble from Italy that is 'just perfect', or finding a clever, stylish solution to a stairway that has to accommodate fire regulations. I want to tell him about my photography classes. They are going surprisingly well. I'd been very nervous at first and probably would have ducked out of the first class, except that Lucy turned up unexpectedly. Apparently she was meeting someone in a bar right by the adult education centre so she gave me a lift there.

The centre smelt funny. A peculiar but distinct smell that is known only in places of education (read torture). A mix of chalk, floor polish, dust and nervous bodies. But it turned out that I had nothing to worry about, the other guys on the course are great. A mixed bunch; some fairly experienced, others unsure of the difference between a lens cap and a tripod. To my relief, there are very few beards or sandals, hardly anyone is a communist, or wishes to die for their art. I'm learning such a lot, so quickly. I know quite a bit about shutter speeds, composition, action pictures, flash photography. I'm learning a whole new vocabulary: bracketing exposure, pushing film, apertures, grain and depth of field. I spend every spare moment I can composing, taking and developing pictures. I've upgraded my retail therapy from clothes to cameras. I love it. I get a buzz from it. A number of my friends have been surprisingly impressed with my work. Lucy even suggested that I put a portfolio together.

'But what for? It isn't as though I am going to suddenly change career and become a photographer.'

'Why not? You stopped being a devoted wife and became an adulteress relatively easily. I think that shows your willingness to embrace change.'

What a sense of humour she has. I'd scowled, 'Yeah and look where that got me. Anyway, I need to get more formal qualifications. Taking a few snaps on a night course is hardly going to turn me into the next Robert Mapplethorpe.'

'Like what?'

'Well, maybe I'd have to go to art school or at least do a foundation course.'

'So what's stopping you? I think you've got something here.' Lucy was looking at a portrait of herself, which probably explains why she was being so free with her compliments, but I am aware that she never says things she doesn't mean. I don't really think that I have enough talent to get on one of those courses, but out of curiosity I might send away for one or two prospectuses. I am, for the first time in weeks, able to think about a future. But it doesn't make me miss Luke any less. I just want to talk to him. I want to know how he is. I want to see if he looks OK. I hope he does. I hope he is fine, and not suffering.

No, I don't. I hope he looks like hell and is so unhappy that it shows.

I wonder, I can't help it, if there is even the smallest chance that he is missing me. He's been so controlled. Packing in silence, leaving without a row. His subsequent visits to pick up his CDs and more clothes have always been while I'm at work. Occasionally, an admin necessity forces him to call me, but then he's succinct and businesslike.

Cold.

Apart.

I am leafing through my wedding photos, noting the smiles and the composition, when the phone rings.

'It's me, Luke.' I hate it that he adds 'Luke'. Of course I

recognize his voice even though he hasn't returned fifty-three of my fifty-nine calls over the last six weeks.

'I'm calling to say that I think you are right, we should talk.'

Thank you, God! Thank you!! *Thank you, God!*

'I've got a solicitor and I think it's time you got one, too.'

God? God? Luke? Solicitor? Shit!

'I'll be around at seven-thirty – OK?'

'OK,' I whisper.

He rings off.

OK? OK? No, it's not OK. It's very un-OK, actually. No. No. I will not let this happen. My stomach churns. I discover that it is true. When you are extremely scared, when the bottom drops out of your world, the world does drop out of your bottom. I run to the bathroom and sit on the loo. No. No. He is *my* husband. He is my *husband*. I am *not* going to lose him. My heart is beating so fast I can almost feel it pulse against my tongue. I think I might pass out, but this is no time for Victorian histrionics.

It is not over until it is over.

It is not over until the fat lady sings. I cannot hear any singing.

I have a husband to re-snare. And I have precisely, I look at my watch, five and a half hours to prepare for it. What to wear? What to wear? I fling open my wardrobe and almost climb inside. Frantically I search rail after rail. Nothing is suitable. I try on the usual black and white tops, the black, navy, brown, khaki and grey trousers. I pull garments off and then on again, with extreme irritation. Nothing is special enough. I grab my credit card and car keys.

I return home, four hours later, with an assortment of bags from posh shops. I'd hoped to purchase a bit of suitability, and perhaps some luck as well. In fact all the shops are out of both. Instead, I settle for a short, red, flirty dress, with a halter neck and some red-leather mules. Neither Luke nor I are particular fans of Chris De Burgh but no one in the Western world can fail to appreciate the 'lady in red' reference. I pray that the dress will send subliminal messages to him.

I bathe in Body Shop sensuous bath oil, shower, scrub, shower again and then rub on Clarins anti-cellulite cream. I apply a dozen moisturizers. I put on full make-up, take it off, decide to do without make-up, he's always liked me natural. This all reminds me of something, but I don't have time to think of what. I have to look perfect. I have to get him to fall in love with me again. I wonder if I should consider my underwear. It seems presumptuous, yet I don't want to risk white/grey M&S briefs. I spend some time trying on every set of underwear I own, then I decide that I won't wear any. It is a long time since I've done that for Luke, but if I remember correctly he used to love it. Finally, at twenty-past seven, I am ready.

As I'll ever be.

The house is ready, the food is ready. I stand in front of the mirror. My reflection surprises me. I look good. I look nervous. I see a woman. Not a girl. I have a bust and a couple of wrinkles. I'm not young. I look substantial but not old. I think that, maybe, I could be mistaken for someone I might have admired, many years ago, when I imagined what 'older women' look like. I wonder why I am wearing red! I look so garish. But before I have time to think of changing, the bell rings.

'Hi, come in.'

Luke looks tanned and splendid. I catch my breath and my belly does a flip. I look closer; he also seems tired and drawn. He is wearing jeans, a Ted Baker T-shirt and a lightweight Boss jacket. I notice his gaze rest on me and flick up and down. Is it appreciatively? He hesitates on the doorstep, his doorstep! If it was anyone other than Luke, I would have been convinced that a point was being made. A rather hurtful point, at that – 'I don't live here any more, I'm a guest.' My confidence is momentarily dented when he hangs around the hallway, rather than striding into the house as if he owns it. Still I'm not going to be intimidated that easily. I am going to change his mind. I am going to get him back. We can put this behind us.

'Let me take your jacket.'

'No.'

Still, I smile.

'Come in, come in. Glass of beer? Wine?' Tea, coffee, light refreshments? What the fuck is going on here? Who is this stranger? He looks like my husband. But he isn't acting like Luke. Where has my husband gone? The man who rubs my tummy when I have period pain, the man whose spots I'd squeeze, the man I force-feed vitamins, the man who taught me to play golf, the man I introduced to mashed-potato sandwiches? Where is he? I have to get us back on to our old footing. I have to.

Luke opens his Budvar and mooches round the house. As he passes me in the hall, I smell him. The smell is so familiar, and so him, I have to fight back tears that are using my eyes as pin cushions. It takes every bit of strength I have to resist flinging my arms around him. He picks up ornaments, as though he is trying to get reacquainted, and then he puts them down again. He leafs through the post, casually shoving the envelopes addressed to him into his breast pocket. He seems so manly, so in charge. How did I ever stop fancying this man? He wanders to the window and looks out at the garden. I wonder if he misses it. Any of it? The shed? The photo albums? Me?

'I am just making myself some pasta, there's enough for two. Will you join me?' This Oh-so-casual-I-am-just-making-supper thing is, of course, a lie. I've pre-planned every detail of this evening. The pasta just happens to be fuselli, his favourite, and I have a Caesar salad already prepared (not Tesco's pre-packed stuff, I've fried the croutons myself). I have a bottle of Robert Mondavi's Napa Valley Fume Blanc chilling in the fridge. I want the opportunity to remind him of our good times. I reckon that I've a chance, if I can get him to relax over a bottle of wine and some good food. In the absence of good food, my cooking will have to do.

'I'm not hungry,' he says without looking at me. Plan one out of the window, which is a bitter shame because I don't have a plan two. I'd considered laying a couple of poignant wedding photos around the sitting room. Or laying myself on our settee, with nothing but a rose between my teeth. I don't think so. Chocolates, diamonds and flowers all seemed inappropriate. There isn't an etiquette book to help out here. Unfaithful husbands have two thousand years of history setting precedents in every aspect of the reconciliation: the apology, the gift, dealing with the recriminations, the right tone to hit. I am without previous case histories.

'Can we talk, Luke?'

'I can't imagine you have anything to say that – '

'You want to hear,' I finish the sentence for him, nodding like one of those plastic poodles in the back of a car. 'Well, I'm asking you for the opportunity to talk,' I persist. His natural good manners and habit of compliance allow him to acquiesce. He falls into the settee and sighs. I notice the way his wrist joins his hand and arm, and it's the most beautiful wrist I've ever seen, strong and fine at the same time.

'What?' Well, now he asks, I'm not so sure what I want to say. I go for the big one.

Mistake.

'I love you.'

'Ha,' he nearly chokes. Which worries me. Who will believe me innocent when it comes to collecting the life insurance?

'I do,' I insist.

'You've been telling me you love me for over five years, but it turns out that you were screwing someone else, all the time.'

'Not all the time,' I correct, reasonably.

'Since when?' He asks the question from under his fringe. For a fleeting second his amazing green eyes meet mine. I knew that he would ask this type of question. It's only natural. I steel myself to answer them calmly and honestly. I think he does, at least, deserve my honesty now.

'September.'

'September.' He silently stares at the ceiling. I know what he is doing. He is rerunning our entire life since September.

He is rerunning the occasional, uncalled-for rows and thinking that for the first time he knows the reason for them. He is rerunning our good times and wondering if they meant anything. He is rerunning our sex life and asking himself if I've been faking it. Faking everything from the orgasms to ironing shirts. How can I explain it?

'You've often told me you loved me during that time. You were obviously lying. Why should I believe you now?'

'I've never stopped loving you. It is just for a time I stopped being *in* love with you.' Each word is painfully lodged in my throat. He makes a 'ha' sound, which communicates his utter disgust. Perturbed, I soldier on. 'And I think that you weren't in love with me, for a time, either. We were more like best friends, brother and sister.'

'You don't have a brother.' Is he deliberately missing the point? Normally he is such an intelligent man. 'You kept telling me you were happy.' He looks inextricably bewildered.

'I was happy.'

'So, tell me, when did "happy" go out of fashion? When did it become so redundant? Isn't "happy" enough?' Now he is becoming incensed. But I am relieved; it is better than the hushed, impenetrable Luke. I daren't answer the question, I don't have to. He answers it for me.

'No, apparently it wasn't enough for you, Connie. You wanted it all, didn't you?' I move my head up and down a fraction. Not quite a nod.

'But how, Connie? How? Tell me how you think you can reconcile being happily married and having extra-marital affairs?'

'I don't know. I hadn't worked out the detail,' I say callously.

I don't know why I do that. I want to be penitent not petulant. But nobody likes to be put on the spot. Luke decides to demonstrate the ludicrous nature of my argument logically. He is missing the point. This has nothing to do with logic.

'It's like saying you want a boy and a girl but you only want one child. It's impossible.'

'How *is* Tarn?' I ask. I don't know why I try to hide in humour. It is just that real life is turning into a bit of a tragedy and I've always preferred comedy or romance. Shabby move. Luke stands up and starts to walk towards the door.

'Don't go,' I wail. He stops walking, which is good. But doesn't turn back to me, which is bad.

'What did you mean when you said that I was not in love with you?' he asks.

'I think we'd started to take each other for granted,' I reply carefully. I don't want to sound as though I'm blaming him. Because I'm not. 'We worked long hours. We put our friends' needs before each other's. We stopped talking to each other. We stopped delighting in each other.'

'It's called being comfortable.'

'It's called being complacent.'

'So you had an affair to shake things up?'

'No. No. I didn't plan it.' Whoops, I am raising my voice. I try to suppress my anger. 'There was no passion. No danger. No drama.'

'You did all of this because you were bored? You risked our marriage, our home, our love, because you were bored?' Luke has taken my lead and is raising his voice too. I know he is exasperated, confused and vicious.

'And a bit lonely,' I add, shamefacedly.

'Couldn't you have said something? Did you have to whip your knickers off and wave them above your head to get my attention?' He is yelling now.

'Yes. I think I did,' I scream back.

'I thought you'd done your share of sleeping around before you met me.' I think that is a bit nasty, but accurate, so I let it go. We silently stand in the hall, listening to the washing machine whirling in the laundry room below us. Luke leans against the wall and then slides down it, landing with a thud on the floor.

'What has he got that I haven't?'

I look at Luke and the anguish on his face as he waits for an answer. He still looks golden. He's still caring, still remarkable, a bit short on understanding but that is to be expected. I think, bitterly, that Luke is worth ten of the dreadful man I slept with. Knowing that John is a dreadful man doesn't make my pain go away. I am simply left feeling stupid and sore. I slowly venture on.

'I think it was timing. He was exciting.'

'Really, I think that he seems a bloody idiot from his fax.'

'Yes, he is an idiot, too.'

'I just don't understand it.' Luke is genuinely bewildered.

'From time to time, every woman wants the same thing. A man that makes her feel she's worth a million dollars, but at the same time has his hand on her best friend's knee.'

'Christ. To think women say men are immature. I hope, Connie, that for the sake of the human race you are absolutely wrong. Every woman can't want that. Say this is just you.'

'It's just me,' I repeat tonelessly.

'Good, at least the tragedy is limited to our marriage.'

I don't find that comforting.

'He listened to me. He talked to me. He was fascinated by me.'

'But you always say that touchy feely things nauseate you.'

'I lied. To you and to myself.'

Silence again.

'So what did you talk about?'

'Dreams, thoughts, films, books.'

'But, Connie, I know that your favourite film is *Dangerous Liaisons*,' notes Luke.

I've never felt more ashamed.

'We can't recreate those first few months, Connie. We have,' he corrects himself, 'we *had* something much more solid.' He is right. We have mortgages, wedding vows, families, history. At one point we even had a future. Question is, do we still? I am a passion junkie. I needed a fix. Oh God. What a mistake. What a huge elephantine fuck-up.

'Maybe I just needed reminding.'

'Reminding of what?'

'That what we have is real. And that real is no bad thing.' He says nothing but just continues to glare at me. I will him to comment, or even move his head. Obviously, my telepathic skills aren't up to scratch. I hurry to fill the silence. 'You were never here, Luke. Do you know I never had to lie to you when I was seeing him? Because you were never here and you rarely asked me where I'd been.' Whoops, I'm dangerously close to blaming there. I pull it back. 'Unfortunately, whenever I was lonely I turned to my fantasy. And you, my husband, being real, never had a chance of living up to a fantasy.' I pause. 'I am sorry, Luke. I do love you. I know that for sure.'

He still says nothing. He stares blankly at me. I can't read his expression. I think he's found the valve that allows him to shut down his emotions – lucky sod. I feel like the cow that I am. I decide to cast myself on his mercy.

'Oh Luke, haven't you ever made a mistake?'

He still doesn't answer. We stay still. Motionless. Then Luke stands up. I scramble to my feet. Will he kiss me now? Will he forgive me? I close my eyes and wish very tightly. Then I hear the door close.

I think I can hear a fat lady singing.

11

'Are you ready?' Daisy shrieks down the telephone.

'Nearly,' I answer helpfully but untruthfully. My hair is still wet and I am dressed in a towel.

'GoodbecauseIneedyouhereNOW!' she garbles.

'What's the problem? Calm down, Daisy,' I say authoritatively, although my heart is sinking. What can possibly have gone wrong with the wedding now? Daisy is getting married on the last Saturday in July, our second wedding anniversary. On realizing this she had expressed concern.

'Should I change the date, Connie?'

Daisy turned her pretty but anxiety ridden face to me.

'I don't think it's possible at this late stage,' I'd said to her, touched by her concern for me. 'The invites have gone out. Really, it's very kind of you to be so thoughtful but Luke and I will be fine.'

Her face looked like a freshly ploughed field.

'But do you think it's an unlucky date, Con, do you? I couldn't bear it if anything went wrong with Simon and me.'

Charming! She gushed this out with her simple honesty and although I wanted to slap her, I resisted. Instead I answered her as positively as I was able.

'You make your own luck, Daisy. You and Simon will be fine.'

Fine, besides the fact that the Best Man and his wife have split up, making it impossible for the said wife to be a bridesmaid. Fine, except that we are a second bridesmaid down because she has run off with one of the ushers, who just happens to be the husband of the third bridesmaid. Luckily, Daisy's latest crisis is a very simple, natural, wedding-day crisis, as opposed to the life-changing crises of the last few months. The florist has called to say that she can't deliver the flowers to Daisy's house, she's burst a tyre.

'Don't worry, Daisy, I'll collect them, I'll set off in five minutes. Go and take a tranquillizer and drink more champagne.'

I had planned to dress with the same amount of care and attention for Daisy's wedding day, as I had for my own, because Luke will be there. Initially, I wanted to look drop-dead gorgeous, to show Luke that I am thriving. I rejected this on the grounds that it is extremely difficult to feel drop-dead gorgeous when you don't like yourself. Also I'm not thriving and it shows.

Without Luke's love, and more practically his cooking, I am wilting. I've reached that state which, until now, I didn't believe in. The one when people tell you that you look drawn and tired and that you looked better when you carried a bit more weight. I am skeletal. It isn't that I can't cook. I can't, but I could have relied on the freezer and M&S individual portions. Problem is eating without him is dull, I have no interest in food or nurturing myself. I do not deserve gourmet-lasagne-for-one, or the individual portions of summer pudding.

I then considered looking independent, confident and a

little bit revised. Unfortunately this look was hard to achieve, too, because when I described it to the woman in the hat section of John Lewis, she told me it wasn't this year's look. Bloody marvellous, I'm not even fashionable any more. The shop assistant suggested that I go for something with lots of roses in cerise pink. She assured me that the little-girl look was very in. I listened politely, then ignored her. I've been there. Done the Disney ride. I chose a beige trouser suit, accessorized with chocolate-brown shoes, hat and bag.

Now it's academic because my preparation time is brought to a rude and abrupt halt by Daisy's SOS. I don't have the chance to agonize over how I look. I pay no attention whatsoever to earrings or make-up. My hair is still damp and is drying into unruly frizzy ringlets; it looks as though I'm sporting a bowl of spaghetti on my head. Rather fetching, not. I manage to slap on lipstick and mascara but not perfume; I haven't tried on my hat and I've had no chance to select nice underwear. Not that anyone ever sees my underwear these days, but it's still pleasant to feel pretty. In the interest of time I fall back on my old favourites, white cotton briefs and pop socks. Never mind. It's not my day, it's Daisy's, and she needs her bouquet. So does Sam. Sam is depending on catching it.

Five minutes later, I jump into my Golf and swing out of the road. It's not sunny, but we're British and we weren't really expecting sun; it's dry and bright, which is enough. I am pleased to have this task, I feel more involved and purposeful. I understand why I can't be a bridesmaid; this way Luke's and my situation won't create any unnecessary tension, but it has left me feeling rather lonely. I've spent this morning thinking about the other weddings I've attended.

348

Particularly my own but also other friends'. Normally, I'm excited and nervous and expectant. Normally, Luke and Lucy are fighting for the bathroom and pouring champagne. Normally, the mood is buoyant and gleeful. It's just occurred to me why Lucy always insisted on dressing from our house, it's seriously depressing getting ready for a wedding on your own. She must have anticipated my mood, as she called me this morning.

'What are you wearing?' I filled in the details. I don't think she was too impressed. 'Slate is the new brown is the new black,' she chastised.

'Well, I can hardly turn up to a wedding in black, or even the modern equivalent, can I?'

'Why not? I think it would be appropriate.' But she's laughing and she doesn't mean it. She no longer loathes the idea of marriage because she and Peter are so deeply in love. Only last week, I caught her idly loitering outside the Amanda Wakely Wedding Shop.

'I wondered about sending a gift,' adds Lucy. She sounds shy and unsure.

'I advise against it.'

She immediately dashes toward her more confident self.

'You're right. Stupid idea. Fuck them. Look, Sweetie I have to dash, Pete and I are going to Brighton for the day.'

'Brighton?' I'm amazed. Lucy has never been a kiss-me-quick-hat and pink-rock sort of girl.

'We're aching for sand between our toes,' she giggles.

'We' meaning Lucy and Pete. I shuffle awkwardly, not knowing what to say. I don't point out that it's a pebble beach. I'm happy for Lucy but that emotion is inextricably linked with the sorrow I feel for Rose. So many emotions snarled and embroiled. Lucy and Pete, these three words have rapidly replaced Rose and Peter. The rapidity actually horrifies me. Connie and Luke are rarely said in the same sentence now.

Luke and I have been living apart for fourteen weeks. He has a solicitor. I do not. He wants to divorce. I do not. My attempt to win him back was disastrous. Never again will I rely on the absence of underwear and subliminal messages from mawky pop songs. I am left with no alternative but to rely on 'time being a great healer' (Sam's advice). I already know that this situation is so serious that I am likely to hear her say that 'there are plenty more fish in the sea/pebbles on the beach'. I know I've blown it with Luke for ever. I know it with cruel, permanent certainty, but I still want to see him. Just to rest my eyes on him. Just to have him in the same room as me will be thrilling.

I pick up the flowers and deliver them to Daisy's house. Bedlam. I take a few snaps of rows of ballet slippers and flowers. Then I retreat, rather hastily, leaving Sam and Rose to divide up the half-dozen small bridesmaids. They are trying, but failing, to pull them into some semblance of order. I wave cheerfully and suggest bribery.

I drive to the church, still feeling decidedly spare-partish. I kill forty minutes taking photos of the guests arriving.

'Tarn!' I yell across the crowds. He is skulking behind a gravestone, having a quick fag.

'Darling.' We air kiss. 'Dramatic stunt to avoid wearing a bridesmaid's dress,' he said, rolling his eyes. 'Connie, darling, I know that you take sartorial elegance seriously, but don't you think that your actions were a bit drastic? Even for you.'

'Go inside and save me a pew. Stop being irritating or I'll tell Daisy's mum that you have a crush on lesbian Liz. She can never understand why you are both single.'

Suitably scared, Tarn enters the church leaving me alone again. Hundreds of children from Daisy's school arrive. How cute. She'll regret it, of course. It looks sweet in *Brides and Setting Up Home*: photo after photo of smiley children. However, fact is, photos are silent, and children are not. Also none of them will bring a decent present. How many chocolate oranges does a girl need? The guests file past looking stunning; the women in hats and the men in tails. It is awesome that with all the general cynicism regarding marriage and the particular upheaval that our gang have gone through this year, that everyone still wants to celebrate with Daisy and Simon. Sam, Rose and the six mini she-devils arrive. Sam winks at me and Rose flashes a smile. I'm glad to see that she isn't wearing a pink tulle caftan, which has been a fleeting possibility now that she has become Renaissance Rose. The vicar tries to get me to go inside but I insist on waiting for Daisy.

It is worth it.

She steps out of the car, her petticoats and veil swaddling her.

'You look beautiful,' I mouth. Which she does. She looks elated, not in the slightest bit nervous. I start to madly click away, trying to capture this moment of intense possibility. I kiss her and then run inside the church. I'm violently happy, amazingly ecstatic for her. For them.

My high heels click loudly on the worn, enamelled tiles. Everyone in the church turns to watch my late arrival.

351

Everyone, that is, except for Luke. He is at the front with Simon. I see him and someone kicks me in the stomach. My feeling of exhilaration vanishes. Simon turns around and nods to me, he whispers something to Luke. I pause wondering if he'll turn round and acknowledge me. He doesn't. It is utter torment. He doesn't stir, but continues to resolutely stare at the altar. I slip into the pew, next to Tarn. Tarn smiles and whispers, 'Chin up, darling.'

I can't drag my eyes off Luke. Even if it is just the back of him. I burn up his big, strong frame. He looks sensational in tails, all men do, but he does particularly. His blond, sporty, handsome face and stature provides a nice contrast to the formal gear. Yet, even knowing that he always looks good in tails, I hadn't expected to be so affected by being near him. What had I expected? What had I imagined? That he'd turn round, see me, run down the aisle saying that he would forgive me? That it has all been a horrible mistake?

No, of course not.

Yes, of course.

In the deepest, darkest, recess of my mind I had held that glimmer of hope. The disappointment is ferocious. I feel a pulling and tingling in the roof of my mouth and in my nose. Tears threaten. I am so sorry. Luckily the organ music starts and everyone assumes that my misty eyes are due to the entrance of Daisy.

The ceremony is stunning. Daisy and Simon hit the correct note of austere respect and obvious jubilation. I want to roar, to bay. I do cry but not much, in case I'm removed from the church, like Henry. But then he is only nineteen months old,

352

he has an excuse. Everyone cries at weddings (I'd often heard Lucy argue that there is reason to) but for me it isn't just the emotion of the big day. It is only two years since I skipped down the aisle to 'The arrival of the Queen of Sheba'. I know I've lost him and it is the hardest lesson of my life.

Soon it's 'Joyful Trumpets'. I try to catch Luke's eye, as he leads Rose back down the aisle, but he studiously avoids mine. Rose gives me a sympathetic smile. This is kind of her but it's like placing a Band-Aid over an amputated limb. Sam is chatting animatedly with one of the ushers. I trail out behind them, holding Sebastian's sticky hand.

The reception is idyllic. We drink champagne on the lawn, basking in the now hot sun, shining down on our new hats, and listening to the string quartet. Jugglers and those awful people that paint caricatures for a living create some amusement. Daisy has thought of everything, even Sam is stuck for suggestions on how to improve the day, which is remarkable considering the man hours she's put into designing her wedding. I listen to the amiable chatter of the guests.

'Isn't she lovely?'

'Such a long day.'

'Poor her having to endure it.'

'Desperate for it for years.'

'Isn't it perfect?' asks Rose, who has sidled up to me. She is sipping champagne.

'Yes.' It is. But I've never felt worse. Inadvertently, I glance across the lawn to where Luke is standing having his photo taken.

'He looks well, doesn't he?' comments Rose.

I nod. Because it is true. He does look well. He looks

fabulous. I am depressed that it's so obvious that he isn't missing me.

'I was just thinking about when I met him. He was wearing tails then – '

'My wedding,' adds Rose.

'I'm sorry,' I stutter, blushing. But Rose hushes me with a big grin. I think she knows she'll be happier without Peter. She squeezes my arm; we both know I'd be happier with Luke. Sam suddenly explodes on to the scene interrupting my moody self-indulgence.

'Connie, can I have a quick word?' I nod, not moving. 'Urgently!' she squawks through gritted teeth, 'and privately.'

I excuse myself from the group.

'What is it? Problem with the caterers?'

Whatever it is, it is serious. Sam is breathing very shallowly, her chest moving up and down like a pantomime dame's.

'He's here,' she gasps.

'Jason, I know. I was talking to him earlier.'

Sam really is acting very peculiarly. Yes, it is unusual for her to bring a date to a wedding. Commitment-phobics don't usually hang out at weddings, but it isn't *so* remarkable.

'Not Jason.' She waves her hands dismissively. 'John.' My face asks who? 'John Harding!'

'You're mistaken.'

Sam looks at me pityingly.

'Do I make mistakes when it comes to spotting exes at inopportune moments?'

Good point. She is undisputed queen of that particularly embarrassing situation. There was that time when she spotted one of her exes as she was going into the sexually transmitted diseases clinic, and to make matters worse he was with his mother. On another occasion, she was shopping in Bond Street and she saw an ex of hers come out of a jeweller's. Wrongly assuming he was buying her a love token, she tongued him. At that point he introduced her to his fiancée. I suspect that this was the shortest engagement in history. Sam has a habit of bumping into her exes at drying-out clinics, funerals, their weddings, gay bars, monasteries.

'Where is he?'

'At the bar.'

Ah. Naturally.

'But I was taking photos of the guests when they arrived. How come I didn't see him?'

'He was late. His date came to the church alone.'

'Who is he here with?' Sam will have done all the essential enquiring.

'Apparently, he is going out with one of Simon's cousins. He's here with her.'

'Andrea is Simon's cousin?'

'No, that wasn't the name. Daisy said Bella, or Belinda, or something.'

We stare at one another. Sam is trying to gauge my reaction. So am I.

'Bloody hell,' I swear.

'Exactly,' agrees Sam. 'Look, Con, there's something else I'd better tell you. Luke heard me making investigations. He knows who John is.'

'Bloody hell.' I swear again. 'Bloody, bloody hell.'

'Stay calm,' instructs Sam. But she is as white as a sheet and says it in a manner not unlike Basil Fawlty's.

Daisy had wanted an intimate wedding for her close friends and family, all five million of them. I am now very grateful.

'Safety in numbers,' assures Sam. 'John probably has no idea that you are at the wedding. You can avoid him.'

So I do. I have no impulse at all to search him out. I do not want to see him. It strikes me that this is an astounding contrast to the months when I'd lived on a knife edge, hoping to catch a glimpse of him. Astoundingly quickly John has fallen from my mind. My mind is full of Luke.

After the beef, but before the speeches, I see Luke go to the loo and I decide to force an opportunity for us to 'bump' into each other. I make a fairly effective show of putting away my lipstick as I emerge from the powder room (on no other occasion than a wedding is this nomenclature acceptable). By burying my head in my handbag I contrive a literal bumping into him. As I touch him, my skin burns.

'Hello, Luke.' I force a nervous smile, which I'm pretty sure comes out looking like a painful grimace.

'Connie,' he replies formally. He does not try to kiss me, not even on the cheek. He doesn't hug me, or touch me at all. Instead he nods in a stilted, ceremonious way. He is close enough to touch. He has never been so far away. We stand for some seconds saying nothing. Tacit. Speechless, when I have so much to say! When at one time we'd told each other every single thought in our heads! But then, that was a life-time ago.

'She looks wonderful, doesn't she?' Luke smiles in the direction of Daisy. I'm grateful for the neutral territory.

'Doesn't she,' I agree enthusiastically. Then I'm beached for words again. It's too late. I just stay silent.

'You look good, too,' says Luke, hoarsely.

'Thank you.' I beam, indebted that he is filling in the conversational gaps. I tug at my frizzy hair. My head is devoid of small talk.

'Bye then.' He shrugs, then turns and starts to walk away. Damn. Damn. Shit. Fool, Fool. Stupid, damn, shit, fool. Why hadn't I been able to keep him talking? I so long for just a minute of him. Him, the way he was. Not this cold impenetrable Luke, but the warm, understanding, clever Luke. My husband Luke. I watch him melt his way through the pastel crowds. A woman in a large lemon hat stops him to talk. I watch her as she picks a (probably non-existent) hair from his suit breast. Bitch. I watch him laugh animatedly with her. He looks so like warm, understanding, clever Luke but he just doesn't look like mine any more.

'Luke!' I bark, slicing through the hullabaloo, nearly crushing the lemon-hatted vamp. Big shame. He turns startled.

'I've some news.' I try to catch my breath. I grin at him, helplessly and hopefully.

'What's your news, Connie?'

'I'm changing career,' I say. I sound pathetic to my ears. 'I've been doing some photography recently. Well, quite a lot, actually, and I put a portfolio together. Then I applied to do an art foundation course. I just thought that I'd give it a go. Didn't really think I'd get a place. Didn't think I had a chance, but I got an interview. And today I got a letter saying that they are offering me a place. I'll have to give up my job. Financially it won't be easy, but I know I'm doing the right thing.'

Oh great, so suddenly I have the verbal equivalent to irritable bowel syndrome. Luke grins. His face stretches into the amicable, unreserved, comfortable smile, which I remember belonging to my Luke.

'That is brilliant news, Connie.' He laughs and nods his head. 'Really excellent.'

'Really?' I glow under his praise, like a seven-year-old coming top of the class.

'I'm very pleased for you. And proud of you. It's a brave move.'

'You're proud of me?' I ask with delighted incredulity. He slowly nods again. I grin back. 'I haven't told anyone else yet. I wanted you to be the first to know.'

We stand there, nodding and beaming, me basking in his approval. I hadn't realized just how important that approval is to me, just how much I'm missing it. Will he lean in and hug me? Or even kiss me on the cheek? I hope so, I'm desperate to feel his skin on mine. Him deliberately placing his hands on my body again.

'Greenie,' John yells, and without pausing he plunges his lips down on mine. He is kissing me. I furiously push away but too late. I see Luke disappear into the throng. His disgust audible, above the animated chatter that swamps me.

'How the hell are you? I couldn't believe it when I saw you sitting at that table. Then I heard that you'd split up from your husband. That was always on the cards, wasn't it? I thought I'd come and say hello.'

I stare, murderously.

'Shit, Greenie. That wasn't him was it?' He looks momentarily embarrassed. 'Christ I don't want to be named in court or anything.'

Briefly I wonder whether I could plead diminished responsibility if I clobber him to death with a Prada handbag. John is beautiful. Even now in the midst of my unprecedented fury I can see that. His eyes are still exquisite, his grin seductive. I look at him. I feel the way I felt when I grew out of my crush on David Soul. Embarrassed, frankly. I look beyond John and see a pretty, nervous woman hovering in the background; Bella I presume. Poor Bella, she'd be wondering if I'm Andrea, or Carolyn, or Diane, or any number of women right up to Zoë. I push past John and run after Luke. I can't waste any more time.

'Luke,' I shout, but he ignores me and keeps walking. 'Luke!'

A number of heads and hats turn in my direction. But none of them are his. I begin to run. This time I have to explain. I can't allow him to think there is still something going on with John. I know I can't fix things, that he'll never forgive me but I don't want him to think that this is another assault on his dignity. I pull at his arm. He shakes me off. We are at the top table. I register that at least twenty pairs of eyes are glued to me. Everyone from the vicar to the she-devil bridesmaids. I don't care. I shove embarrassment to the side. I catapult dignity out to the horizon. He sits. I bend down, almost on my knees, so that my eyes are level with his and he can't push me from his consciousness.

'That wasn't what it seemed,' I say with determination.

'Oh no,' he snipes, 'so that isn't the man you had your adulterous affair with?'

Mrs Kirk nearly chokes on her profiterole.

'Yes it is,' I hiss. 'But I'm not with him now.'

'Dumped you has he? Never mind I'm sure you can pick up another dick as quickly as you can say "Let no man put asunder".' Luke spits bitterly.

'Luke, I'm sorry. I'm sorry he's here. I'm sorry he was ever anywhere near me.' I wail. Tears are welling into my eyes. 'I made a mistake. I'd do anything to undo it but I can't. All I can do is say *I am sorry*.'

I say the words slowly, deliberately.

'I really didn't mean to hurt you.'

It's infuriating that the most important phrases are already songs. He glowers, his green eyes are icy.

'I had no integrity. I know that I failed you. I let you down. I'm a disappointment. It was disloyal. What can I do, Luke? What can I say? I made a mistake, Luke. A big one.'

He isn't moved.

'A fucking mammoth one!' I yell.

This gets his attention. And everybody else's actually.

'If only there was a word that is bigger than "sorry", I'd say it. But there isn't.'

I lose my battle with my tears; they insist on spilling down my cheeks.

'I'm sorry. I'm sorry,' I mutter repeatedly and pointlessly, 'haven't you ever made a mistake?'

Totally impassive, he ignores me.

'Luke, I'm better now. I am what you always thought I could be. I don't need you any more but I want you more than ever.'

He still stares at his champagne glass and ignores me. That was my best shot. But it missed. I sigh defeated.

'All I can say, Luke, is that I hope you never make a mistake this big. And you never feel as sorry as I do now. I wouldn't wish this on anyone.'

I stumble to my feet and walk away. Blind with tears, snot and mascara, I trip on the lead to the microphone, the heel of my shoe comes right off and I limp back to my seat.

'Very stylish,' comments Tarn. I snarl at him. Fortunately Daisy's father stands up to make his speech, which moves the attention away from my undignified display. Then Simon makes his but I don't take in a word. An impenetrable black fudge sits on the back of my brain. If only John hadn't been here. If only John had never existed. But I can't blame John. This is down to me. Me alone. I love Luke so much it hurts. I know he's no longer mine and I have to brace myself for solicitors and dividing furniture but if I could have had the opportunity to express, really express how sorry I am and that I am trying to be . . . different these days. I snap out of my self-indulgent fog when the Master of Ceremonies announces ' . . . and now the Best Man.'

Luke, ever the professional, stands up. Has he always been that tall? He beams around the room. In contrast to my own dishevelled and dispirited stance, he looks calm, confident and assured. Very sexy. This is annoying. I know that every single woman in the room will be thinking the same. Best Men are notorious as targets for women hunting sex at weddings. He clears his throat.

'It is traditional for the Best Man to thank the bridesmaids for being beautiful. Often, the Best Man hardly knows the bridesmaids, and although he can usually be polite, even gallant, I am in the lucky position of knowing the bridesmaids very well, in fact, intimately.'

There is a laugh. Naturally. Luke raises an eyebrow. I love it when he does that, but it disturbs me that he is flirting with the room. He is being deliberately provocative. He does not know the bridesmaids intimately, well, not as intimately as everyone now thinks!

'To the bridesmaids.'

'Aghhhh,' say the women.

'The bridesmaids,' say the men. We raise our glasses and sip champagne. The room falls to a hush again and Luke recommences.

'I'm also supposed to ritually humiliate the groom. Again, I'm happy to oblige here, too.'

Luke then relays a few discreetly selected stories. Stories which demonstrate that Simon is definitely one of the boys, but nothing that makes Mr Kirk think he's made a heinous mistake by allowing Daisy to marry him. Even I chortle at Luke's well-delivered punch-lines. And I feel about as ready to laugh as your average agoraphobic feels about doing a charity parachute jump to save the dodo. But he is funny. I can't help myself.

'I've leant heavily on the *Oxford Book of Marriage* for my speech today. If any of you struggle with the long words, ask Daisy, she's a teacher.'

More smiles.

'I'm not sure how many of you are familiar with the *OBM*. It's a weighty tome with numerous literary extracts, from dozens of authors, who have taken it upon themselves to describe the many facets of marriage. It's split into lively and entertaining chapters like "Decisions", "Choices" and "Recognition", or is that "Resignation"?'

Luke pretends to squint at the paper where he's written his speech. The room laughs. I know the book he is talking about. Someone bought it for us when we got engaged. In those euphoric days we pored over it, reading one another our favourite bits. I still have our copy at home. Luke must have bought another one. Thinking about him reading the book alone is too horrible to imagine.

'It goes on to the chapter about proposals. Simon's legendary proposal hasn't been written up yet. It will be in the next edition.'

Guffaw.

'Can I just say, Simon' – Luke turns to him with a genuine smile – 'brilliant proposal, mate. But you've made it difficult for all the blokes that are going to follow you. I mean, how can Jason top that?'

Luke looks mischievously at Sam, who is beaming. Jason looks as though he's swallowed a chilli.

Luke carries on. 'However, Daisy and Mrs Kirk are very relieved that you decided to leave the Santa suit at home today.'

'Here, here.' More chortling.

'The book covers the wedding day, and "With my body I thee worship" – those are the naughty bits.'

There are a few catcalls.

'Then it gets very serious and it devotes no less than eight chapters to "From this day forward".' Luke takes a breath and looks at Simon again. 'If you thought all the planning and preparation were all-consuming, let me tell you, it's only just begun.'

Faces flushed with booze and happiness are turned towards Luke. Suddenly he puts down the paper with his speech written on it. He runs his fingers through his hair. For a moment he looks doubtful, defeated and then he seems to find his way again. His tone of voice has changed. He is uncertain, unsure.

'It's a big book, Simon, Daisy. I wanted to find a single passage that I could read out, that would sum up the institution of marriage. But I couldn't. So many great writers, all saying great things. Telling us how they felt when they were in love and what it meant to them. But for all the brilliant words of Chaucer, Shakespeare, John Donne and H. G. Wells, to name but a few, my conclusion is that the most . . .' he stumbles. The words are strangled. He picks up a glass of water and takes a sip. The room is with him. I am with him. We are hanging on Luke's every word. This isn't rehearsed. He isn't deliberately trying to tease us. He has something difficult to say. He puts down his paper. He is speaking from his soul now. So I, more than anyone, want to hear what he has to say. He looks up, and this time, I'm certain that he is looking just at me.

'My conclusion is that the most beautiful words ever written about marriage have already been read out today: *"Wilt thou have this woman to thy wedded wife? To live together, after God's ordinance, in the holy estate of Matrimony?"'*

He's definitely missed his vocation. He owes it to his public to get into a pulpit, now! Thinking about it, perhaps not, he

sounds far too sexy to be a vicar. Maybe an actor. The room
is silent, suddenly awash with reverence. He goes on.

' "*I take thee to my wedded wife, to have and to hold from this
day forward, for better for worse, for richer and poorer, in sickness
and in health, to love and to cherish, till death do us part, according
to God's holy ordinance: and thereto I plight thee my troth.*"'

This is too hard. Too painful. I gasp for breath. But I can't
breathe because somebody is ripping me apart. No one moves.
The room is frozen. Not a clink of cutlery, not a wailing
child.

'So I'd like to raise a toast to Daisy and Simon, together.'

I blindly stumble to my feet and through my tears I raise
my glass, mumbling, 'Daisy and Simon, together.' The room
oohs and *arghs*. We relax and sit down waiting for the tele-
grams. But Luke is still standing, not finished yet. He looks at
Daisy and Simon.

'I hope Daisy, Simon that you can forgive me for breaking
etiquette and continuing to talk even after we've toasted you.'

Daisy and Simon nod happily, too drunk on champagne
and love to really care what anyone does.

'It's just that I'd like to take this opportunity . . .'

Luke has fallen back on to the safety of formal words.

' . . . to stress that I really do believe those vows. I believed
them when I said them to my wife, two years ago and I
believe them now.'

The people who don't know us clap and cheer. The people
who do know us sit stone still. Not many people have a clue
what he is on about. Probably just Daisy, Simon, Rose, Sam
and Tarn. And me. I understand. Or at least, I think I do.
Hasn't my husband just said that he is giving me another

365

chance? Hasn't he said that it would be a mistake to separate, to become a him and me, instead of an us?

He has.

He threads his way through the crowds, politely accepting compliments on his speech but not allowing the well-wishers to derail him. Then he is in front of me. Right there with me, not because I've engineered a meeting outside the loo but because he wants to be with me. His eyes bore into me. Blistering my mind. He runs his hands through his hair and swallows.

'I'm still in love with you.'

'I love you,' I say but I'm not sure that he hears me because I can barely find my voice. Like iron filings on a magnet I'm all over him and he is all over me. It all comes back to me. The downright horniness of him. The sweet gentleness of him. The unquestionable rightness of him. I can smell his skin, his hair. He is kissing me. I can taste his champagne-soused tongue. I can feel him. His cold hands on my hot, tear-stained face. His hot lips on my equally hot lips. My cold hands on his hot body. All over it. Touching it, grabbing it, holding it, squeezing it. Again. My husband's body.

Thank you

Mum for teaching me about love, determination and dreams. Joanna James, Tracy Murray, Nic Williams, Peggy Dalton for being patient, faithful, tireless, funny, unshockable, shockable, and wise friends.

Acknowledgements

Extract from 'If' by Rudyard Kipling used by kind permission of A. P. Watt on behalf of The National Trust for Places of Historic Interest and Natural Beauty.

'When I Fall In Love'
Words and Music by Edward Heyman and Victor Young.
© 1952 Chappell & Co Inc, USA.
Warner/Chappell Music Ltd, London W6 8BS.
Reproduced by permission of International Music Publications Ltd.

Lyrics from 'Love Is All Around' (Presley) © 1967 by kind permission of Universal Music Publishing Ltd.

'Freak Me'
Words and Music by Keith Sweat, Roy Murray and Anthony Johnson.
© 1993 Keith Sweat Publishing Inc/EA Music Inc/Saints Alive Music/TH Music/EMI Blackwood Music Inc.
45% Warner/Chappell Music Ltd, London W6 8BS.
Reproduced by permission of IMP Ltd and EMI Music Publishing Ltd, London WC2H 0EA.